SELECTED STORIES

V.S. PRITCHETT

SELECTED STORIES

Vintage Books
A Division of Random House
New York

First Vintage Books Edition, June 1979

Copyright ©1959, 1960, 1961, 1962, 1966, 1968, 1969, 1973, 1974, 1978
by V.S. Pritchett
All rights reserved under International and Pan-American
Copyright Conventions. Published in the United States by
Random House, Inc., New York, and simultaneously in Canada
by Random House of Canada Limited, Toronto.
Originally published by Random House, Inc., in June 1978.

Selections of this book first appeared in *The New Yorker* and *Playboy*

Library of Congress Cataloging in Publication Data
Pritchett, Victor Sawden, Sir, 1900-
Selected stories.
PZ3.P9395Se 1979   [PR6031.R7]   823'.9'12   78-23587
ISBN 0-394-72859-9 pbk.

Manufactured in the United States of America

FOR DOROTHY

CONTENTS

ONE

The Diver

IN a side street on the Right Bank of the Seine where the river divides at the Ile de la Cité, there is a yellow and red brick building shared by a firm of leather merchants. When I was twenty I worked there. The hours were long, the pay was low, and the place smelled of cigarettes and boots. I hated it. I had come to Paris to be a writer but my money had run out, and in this office I had to stick. How often I looked across the river, envying the free lives of the artists and writers on the other bank. Being English, I was the joke of the office. The sight of my fat pink innocent face and fair hair made everyone laugh; my accent was bad, for I could not pronounce a full "o"; worst of all, like a fool, I not only admitted I hadn't got a mistress, but boasted about it. To the office boys this news was extravagant. It doubled them up. It was a favourite trick of theirs, and even of the salesman, a man called Claudel with whom I had to work, to call me to the street door at lunchtime and then, if any girl or woman passed, they would give me a punch and shout:

"How much to sleep with this one? Twenty? Forty? A hundred?" I put on a grin, but, to tell the truth, a sheet of glass seemed to come down between me and any female I saw.

About one woman the lads did not play this game. She was a woman between thirty and forty I suppose, Mme. Chamson, who kept the menders and cleaners down the street. You could hear her heels as she came, half-running, to see Claudel, with jackets and trousers of his on her arm. He had some arrangement with her for getting his suits cleaned and repaired on the cheap. In return—well, there was a lot of talk. She had sinfully tinted hair built up high over arching, exclaiming eyebrows, hard as varnish and when she got near our door there was always a joke coming out of the side of her mouth. She would bounce into the office in her tight navy blue skirt, call the boys and Claudel together, shake hands with them all, and tell them some tale which always ended, with a dirty glance around, in whispering. Then she stood back and shouted with laughter. I was never in this secret circle and if I happened to grin, she gave me a severe and offended look and marched out scowling. One day, when one of her tales was over, she called back from the door:

"Standing all day in that gallery with all those naked women, he comes home done for, finished."

The office boys squeezed each other with pleasure. She was talking about her husband who was an attendant at the Louvre, a small moist-looking fellow whom we some times saw with her, a man fond of fishing, whose breath smelled of white wine. Because of her arrangement with Claudel, and her stories, she was a very respected woman.

I did not like Mme. Chamson; she looked to me like some predatory bird; but I could not take my eyes off her pushing bosom and her crooked mouth. I was afraid of her tongue. She caught on quickly to the fact that I was the office joke, but when they told her on top of this I wanted to be a writer, any curiosity she had about me was finished. "I could tell him a tale," she said. For her I didn't exist. She didn't even bother to shake hands with me.

Streets and avenues in Paris are named after writers; there are statues to poets, novelists and dramatists, making gestures to the birds, nursemaids and children in the gardens. How was it these men had become famous? How had they begun? For myself, it was impossible to begin. I walked about packed with stories, but when I sat in cafés or in my room with a pen in my hand and a bare sheet of paper before me, I could not touch it. I seemed to swell in the head, the chest, the arms and legs, as if I was trying to heave an enormous load on to the page and could not move. The portentous moment had not yet come. And there was another reason. The longer I worked in the leather trade and talked to the office boys, the typists there and Claudel, the more I acquired a double personality; when I left the office and walked to the Metro, I practised French to myself. In this bizarre language the stories inside me flared up, I was acting and speaking them as I walked, often in the subjunctive: but when I sat before my paper, the English language closed its sullen mouth.

And what were these stories? Impossible to say. I would set off in the morning and see the grey, ill-painted buildings of the older quarters leaning together like people, their shutters thrown back, so that the open windows looked like black and empty eyes. In the mornings the bedding was thrown over the sills to air and hung out, wagging like tongues about what goes on in the night between men and women. The houses looked sunken-shouldered, exhausted, by what they told; and crowning the city, was the church of Sacré Coeur, very white, standing like some dry Byzantine bird, to my mind, hollow-eyed and without conscience, presiding over the habits of the flesh and—to judge by what I read in newspapers—its crimes also; its murders, rapes, its shootings for jealousy and robbery. As my French improved the secrets of Paris grew worse. It amazed me that the crowds I saw on the street had survived the night and many indeed looked as sleepless as the houses.

After I had been a little more than a year in Paris, fourteen months in fact, a drama broke the monotonous life of our office. A consignment of dressed skins had been sent to us from Rouen. It had been sent by barge—not the usual method in our business. The barge was an old one and was carrying a mixed cargo and, within a few hundred yards from our warehouse, it was rammed and sunk one misty morning, by a Dutch boat taking the wrong channel. The manager, the whole office, especially Claudel, who saw his commission go to the bottom, were outraged. Fortunately the barge had gone down slowly near the bank, close to us; the water was not too deep. A crane was brought down on another barge to the water's edge and soon, in an exciting week, a diver was let down to salvage what he could. Claudel and I had to go to the quay and, if a bale of our stuff came up, we had to get it to the warehouse and see what the damage was.

Anything to get out of the office. For me the diver was the hero of the week. He stood in his round helmet and suit on a wide tray of wood hanging from four chains and then, the motor spat, the chains rattled and down he went with great dignity under the water. While the diver was under the water, Claudel would be reckoning his commission over again—would it be calculated only on the sale price or on what was saved? "Five bales so far," he would mutter fanatically. "One and a half per cent." His teeth and his eyes were agitated with changing figures. I, in imagination, was groping in the gloom of the river bed with the hero. Then we'd step forward; the diver was coming up. Claudel would hold my arm as the man appeared with a tray of sodden bales and the brown water streaming off them. He would step off the plank on to the barge where the crane was installed and look like a swollen frog. A workman unscrewed his helmet, the vizor was raised and then we saw the young diver's rosy, cheerful face. A workman lit a cigarette and gave it to him and out of the helmet came a long surprising jet of smoke. There was always a crowd watching from the quay wall and when he did this, they all smiled and many laughed. "See that?" they would say. "He is having a puff," and the diver grinned and waved to the crowd.

Our job was to grab the bale. Claudel would check the numbers of the bales on his list. Then we saw them wheeled to our warehouse, dripping all the way, and there I had to hang up the skins on poles. It was like hanging up drowned animals—even, I thought, human beings.

On the Friday afternoon of that week, when everyone was tired and even the crowd looking down from the street wall had thinned to next to nothing, Claudel and I were still down on the quay waiting for the final load. The diver had come up. We were seeing him for the last time before the weekend. I was waiting to watch what I had not yet seen; how he got out of his suit. I walked down nearer at the quay's edge to get a good view. Claudel shouted to me to get on with the job and as he shouted I heard a whizzing noise above my head and then felt a large, heavy slopping lump hit me on the shoulders. I turned round and the next thing I was flying in the air, arms outspread with wonder. Paris turned upside down. A second later, I crashed into cold darkness, water was running up my legs swallowing me. I had fallen into the river.

The wall of the quay was not high. In a couple of strokes I came up spitting mud and caught an iron ring on the quay wall. Two men pulled my hands. Everyone was laughing as I climbed out.

I stood there drenched and mud-smeared, with straw in my hair, pouring water into a puddle that came from me, getting larger and larger.

"Didn't you hear me shout?" said Claudel.

Laughing and arguing, two or three men led me to the shelter of the wall where I began to wring out my jacket and shirt and squeeze the water out of my trousers. It was a warm day and I stood in the sun and saw my trousers steam and heard my shoes squelch.

"Give him a hot rum," someone said. Claudel was torn between looking after our few bales left on the quay and taking me across the street to a bar. But, checking the numbers and muttering a few more figures to himself, he decided to enjoy the drama and go with me. He called out that we'd be back in a minute.

We got to the bar and Claudel saw to it that my arrival was a sensation. Always nagging at me in the office, he was now proud of me.

"He fell into the river. He nearly drowned. I warned him. I shouted. Didn't I?"

The one or two customers admired me. The barman brought me the rum. I could not get my hand into my pocket because it was wet.

"You pay me tomorrow," said Claudel, putting a coin on the counter.

"Drink it quickly," said the barman.

I was laughing and explaining now.

"One moment he was on dry land, the next he was flying in the air, then plonk in the water. Three elements," said Claudel.

"Only fire is missing," said the barman.

They argued about how many elements there were. A whole history of swimming feats, drowning stories, bodies found, murders in the Seine, sprang up. Someone said the morgue used to be full of corpses. And then an argument started, as it sometimes did in this part of Paris, about the exact date at which the morgue was moved from the island. I joined in but my teeth had begun to chatter.

"Another rum," the barman said.

And then I felt a hand fingering my jacket and my trousers. It was the hand of Mme. Chamson. She had been down at the quay once or twice during the week to have a word with Claudel. She had seen what had happened.

"He ought to go home and change into dry things at once," she said in a firm voice. "You ought to take him home."

"I can't do that. We've left five bales on the quay," said Claudel.

"He can't go back," said Mme. Chamson. "He's shivering."

I sneezed.

"You'll catch pneumonia," she said. And to Claudel: "You ought to have kept an eye on him. He might have drowned."

She was very stern with him.

"Where do you live?" she said to me.

I told her.

"It will take you an hour," she said.

Everyone was silent before the decisive voice of Mme. Chamson.

"Come with me to the shop," she ordered and pulled me brusquely by the arm. She led me out of the bar and said, as we walked away, my shoes squeaking and squelching:

"That man thinks of nothing but money. Who'd pay for your funeral? Not he!"

Twice, as she got me, her prisoner, past the shops, she called out to people at their doors:

"They nearly let him drown."

Three girls used to sit mending in the window of her shop and behind them was usually a man pressing clothes. But it was half past six now and the shop was closed. Everyone had gone. I was relieved. This place had disturbed me. When I first went to work for our firm Claudel had told me he could fix me up with one of the mending girls; if we shared a room it would halve our expenses and she could cook and look after my clothes. That was what started the office joke about my not having a mistress. When we got to the shop Mme. Chamson led me down a passage inside which was muggy with the smell of dozens of dresses and suits hanging there, into a dim parlour beyond. It looked out on to the smeared grey wall of a courtyard.

"Stay here," said Mme. Chamson planting me by a sofa. "Don't sit on it in those wet things. Take them off."

I took off my jacket.

"No. Don't wring it. Give it to me. I'll get a towel."

I started drying my hair.

"All of them," she said.

Mme. Chamson looked shorter in her toom, her hair looked duller, her eyebrows less dramatic. I had never really seen her closely. She had become a plain, domestic woman; her mouth had straightened. There was not a joke in her. Her bosom swelled with management. The rumour that she was Claudel's mistress was obviously an office tale.

"I'll see what I can find for you. You can't wear these."

I waited for her to leave the room and then I took off my shirt and dried my chest, picking off the bits of straw from the river that had stuck to my skin. She came back.

"Off with your trousers, I said. Give them to me. What size are they?"

My head went into the towel. I pretended not to hear. I could not bring myself to undress before Mme. Chamson. But while I hesitated she bent down and her sharp fingernails were at my belt.

"I'll do it," I said anxiously.

Our hands touched and our fingers mixed as I unhitched my belt. Impatiently she began on my buttons, but I pushed her hands away.

She stood back, blank-faced and peremptory in her stare. It was the blankness of her face, her indifference to me, her ordinary womanliness, the touch of her practical fingers that left me without defence. She was not the ribald, coquettish, dangerous woman who came wagging her hips to our office, not one of my Paris fantasies of sex and danger. She was simply a woman. The realization of this was disastrous to me. An unbelievable change was throbbing in my body. It was uncontrollable. My eyes angrily, helplessly, asked her to go away. She stood there implacably. I half-turned, bending to conceal my enormity as I lowered my trousers, but as I lowered them inch by inch so the throbbing manifestation increased. I got my foot out of one leg but my shoe caught in the other. On one leg I tried to dance my other trouser leg off. The towel slipped and I glanced at her in red-faced angry appeal. My trouble was only too clear. I was stiff with terror. I was almost in tears.

The change in Mme. Chamson was quick. From busy indifference, she went to anger.

"Young man," she said. "Cover yourself. How dare you. What indecency. How dare you insult me!"

"I'm sorry. I couldn't help . . ." I said.

Mme. Chamson's bosom became a bellows puffing outrage.

"What manners," she said. "I am not one of your tarts. I am a respectable woman. This is what I get for helping you. What would your parents say? If my husband were here!"

She had got my trousers in her hand. The shoe that had betrayed me fell now out of the leg to the floor.

She bent down coolly and picked it up.

"In any case," she said and now I saw for the first time this afternoon the strange twist of her mouth return to her, as she nodded at my now concealing towel—"that is nothing to boast about."

My blush had gone. I was nearly fainting. I felt the curious, brainless stupidity that goes with the state nature had put me in. A miracle saved me. I sneezed and then sneezed again; the second time with force.

"What did I tell you!" said Mme. Chamson, passing now to

angry self-congratulation. She flounced out to the passage that led to the shop and coming back with a pair of trousers she threw them at me and, red in the face, said:

"Try those. If they don't fit I don't know what you'll do. I'll get a shirt," and she went past me to the door of the room beyond saying:

"You can thank your lucky stars my husband has gone fishing."

I heard her muttering as she opened drawers. She did not return. There was silence.

In the airless little salon, looking out (as if it were a cell in which I was caught), on the stained smudgy grey wall of the courtyard, the silence lengthened. It began to seem that Mme. Chamson had shut herself away in her disgust and was going to have no more to do with me. I saw a chance of getting out but she had taken away my wet clothes. I pulled on the pair of trousers she had thrown; they were too long but I could tuck them in. I should look an even bigger fool if I went out in the street dressed only in these. What was Mme. Chamson doing? Was she torturing me? Fortunately my impromptu disorder had passed. I stood listening. I studied the mantelpiece where I saw what I supposed was a photograph of Mme. Chamson as a girl in the veil of her first communion. Presently I heard her voice:

"Young man," she called harshly, "do you expect me to wait on you. Come and fetch your things."

Putting on a polite and apologetic look, I went to the inner door which led into a short passage only a yard long. She was not there.

"In here," she called curtly.

I pushed the next door open. This room was dim also and the first thing I saw was the end of a bed and in the corner a chair with a dark skirt on it and a stocking hanging from the arm, and on the floor a pair of shoes, one of them on its side. Then, suddenly, I saw at the end of the bed a pair of bare feet. I looked at the toes; how had they got there? And then I saw: without a stitch of clothing on her, Mme. Chamson—but could this naked body be she?—was lying on the bed, her chin propped on her hand, her lips parted as they always were when she came in on the point of laughing to the office, but now with no sound coming from them; her eyes, generally wide open, were now half-closed, watching me with the stillness of some large white cat. I looked away and then I saw two other large brown eyes gazing at me, two other faces: her breasts.

It was the first time in my life I had ever seen a naked woman, and it astonished me to see the rise of a haunch, the slope of her belly and the black hair like a moustache beneath it. Mme. Chamson's face was always strongly made up with some almost orange colour, and it astonished me to see how white her body was from the neck down, not the white of statues, but some sallow colour of white and shadow, marked at the waist by the tightness of the clothes she had taken off. I had thought of her as old, but she was not; her body was young and idle.

The sight of her transfixed me. It did not stir me. I simply stood there gaping. My heart seemed to have stopped. I wanted to rush from the room, but I could not. She was so very near. My horror must have been on my face but she seemed not to notice that, she simply stared at me. There was a small movement of her lips and I dreaded that she was going to laugh; but she did not; slowly she closed her lips and said at last between her teeth in a voice low and mocking:

"Is this the first time you have seen a woman?"

And after she said this, a sad look came into her face.

I could not answer.

She lay on her back and put out her hand and smiled fully.

"Well?" she said. And she moved her hips.

"I," I began, but I could not go on. All the fantasies of my walks about Paris as I practised French, rushed into my head. This was the secret of all those open windows of Paris, of the vulture-like head of Sacré Coeur looking down on it. In a room like this, with a wardrobe in the corner and with clothes thrown on a chair was enacted—what? Everything—but, above all, to my panicking mind, crimes I read about in the newspapers. I was desperate as her hand went out.

"You have never seen a woman before?" she said again.

I moved a little and out of reach of her hand I said fiercely:

"Yes, I have." I was amazed at myself.

"Ah!" she said and when I did not answer, she laughed: "Where was that? Who was she?"

It was her laughter, so dreaded by me, that released something in me. I said something terrible. The talk of the morgue at the bar, jumped into my head.

I said coldly: "She was dead. In London."

"Oh my God," said Mme. Chamson sitting up and pulling at

the coverlet, but it was caught and she could only cover her feet.

It was her turn to be frightened. Across my brain newspaper headlines were tapping out.

"She was murdered," I said. I hesitated. I was playing for time. Then it came out.

"She had been strangled."

"Oh no!" she said and she pulled the coverlet violently up with both hands, until she had got some of it to her breast.

"I saw her," I said. "On her bed."

"You *saw* her? *How* did you see her?" she said. "Where was this?"

Suddenly the story sprang out of me, it unrolled as I spoke.

"It was in London," I said. "In our street. The woman was a neighbour of ours, we knew her well. She used to pass our window every morning on her way up from the bank."

"She was robbed!" said Mme. Chamson. Her mouth buckled with horror.

I saw I had caught her.'

"Yes," I said. "She kept a shop."

"Oh my God, my God," said Mme. Chamson looking at the door behind me, then anxiously round the room.

"It was a sweet shop," I said, "where we bought our papers too."

"Killed in her shop," groaned Mme. Chamson. "Where was her husband?"

"No," I said, "in her bedroom at the back. Her husband was out at work all day and this man must have been watching for him to go. Well, we knew he did. He was the laundry man. He used to go in there twice a week. She'd been carrying on with him. She was lying there with her head on one side and a scarf twisted round her neck."

Mme. Chamson dropped the coverlet and hid her face in her hands; then she lowered them and said suspiciously:

"But how did *you* see her like this?"

"Well," I said, "it happened like this. My little sister had been whining after breakfast and wouldn't eat anything and Mother said, 'That kid will drive me out of my mind. Go up to Mrs Blake's' —that was her name—'and get her a bar of chocolate, milk chocolate, no nuts, she only spits them out.' And Mother said, 'You may as well tell her we don't want any papers after Friday because we're going to Brighton. Wait, I haven't finished yet—here take this money and pay the bill. Don't forget that, you forgot last year and the papers were littering up my hall. We owe for a month.' "

Mme. Chamson nodded at this detail. She had forgotten she was naked. She was the shopkeeper and she glanced again at the door as if listening for some customer to come in.

"I went up to the shop and there was no one there when I got in . . ."

"A woman alone!" said Mme. Chamson.

"So I called, 'Mrs. Blake,' but there was no answer. I went to the inner door and called up a small flight of stairs, 'Mrs. Blake'— Mother had been on at me as I said, about paying the bill. So I went up."

"You went up?" said Mme. Chamson, shocked.

"I'd often been up there with Mother, once when she was ill. We knew the family. Well—there she was. As I said, lying on the bed, naked, strangled, dead."

Mme. Chamson gazed at me. She looked me slowly up and down from my hair, then studied my face and then down my body to my feet. I had come barefooted into the room. And then she looked at my bare arms, until she came to my hands. She gazed at these as if she had never seen hands before. I rubbed them on my trousers, for she confused me.

"Is this true?" she accused me.

"Yes," I said, "I opened the door and there . . ."

"How old were you?"

I hadn't thought of that but I quickly decided.

"Twelve," I said.

Mme. Chamson gave a deep sigh. She had been sitting taut, holding her breath. It was a sigh in which I could detect just a twinge of disappointment. I felt my story had lost its hold.

"I ran home," I said quickly, "and said to my mother, 'Someone has killed Mrs. Blake.' Mother did not believe me. She couldn't realize it. I had to tell her again and again. 'Go and see for yourself,' I said."

"Naturally," said Mme. Chamson. "You were only a child."

"We rang the police," I said.

At the word "police" Mme. Chamson groaned peacefully.

"There is a woman at the laundry," she said, "who was in the hospital with eight stitches in her head. She had been struck with an iron. But that was her husband. The police did nothing. And what does my husband do? He stands in the Louvre all day. Then he goes fishing, like this evening. Anyone," she said vehemently to me, "could break in here."

She was looking through me into some imagined scene and it was a long time before she came out of it. Then she saw her own bare shoulder and pouting she said, slowly:

"Is it true you were only twelve?"

"Yes."

She studied me for a long time.

"You poor boy," she said. "Your poor mother."

And she put her hand to my arm and let her hand slide down it gently to my wrist; then she put out her other hand to my other arm and took that hand too, as the coverlet slipped a little from her. She looked at my hands and lowered her head. Then she looked up slyly at me.

"You didn't do it, did you?" she said.

"No," I said indignantly, pulling back my hands, but she held on to them. My story vanished from my head.

"It is a bad memory," she said. She looked to me, once more, as she had looked when I had first come with her into her salon soaking wet—a soft, ordinary, decent woman. My blood began to throb.

"You must forget about it," she said. And then, after a long pause, she pulled me to her. I was done for, lying on the bed.

"Ah," she laughed, pulling at my trousers. "The diver's come up again. Forget. Forget."

And then there was no more laughter. Once in the height of our struggle I caught sight of her eyes; the pupils had disappeared and there were only the blind whites and she cried out: "Kill me. Kill me," from her twisted mouth.

Afterwards we lay talking. She asked if it was true I was going to be a writer and when I said, "Yes," she said:

"You want talent for that. Stay where you are. It's a good firm. Claudel has been there for twelve years. And now, get up. My little husband will be back."

She got off the bed. Quickly she gave me a complete suit belonging to one of her customers, a grey one, the jacket rather tight.

"It suits you," she said. "Get a grey one next time."

I was looking at myself in a mirror when her husband came in, carrying his fishing rod and basket. He did not seem surprised. She picked up my sodden clothes and rushed angrily at him:

"Look at these. Soaked. That fool Claudel let this boy fall in the river. He brought him here."

Her husband simply stared.

"And where have you been? Leaving me alone like this," she carried on. "Anyone could break in. This boy saw a woman strangled in her bed in London. She had a shop. Isn't that it? A man came in and murdered her. What d'you say to that?"

Her husband stepped back and looked with appeal at me.

"Did you catch anything?" she said to him, still accusing.

"No," said her husband.

"Well, not like me," she said, mocking me. "I caught this one."

"Will you have a drop of something?" said her husband.

"No, he won't," said Mme. Chamson. "He'd better go straight home to bed."

So we shook hands. M. Chamson let me out through the shop door while Mme. Chamson called down the passage to me, "Bring the suit back tomorrow. It belongs to a customer."

Everything was changed for me after this. At the office I was a hero.

"Is it true that you saw a murder?" the office boys said.

And when Mme. Chamson came along and I gave her back the suit, she said: "Ah, here he is—my fish."

And then boldly: "When are you coming to collect your things?"

And then she went over to whisper to Claudel and ran out.

"You know what she said just now," said Claudel to me, looking very shrewd: She said 'I am afraid of that young Englishman. Have you seen his hands?' "

TWO

The Wheelbarrow

"ROBERT," Miss Freshwater's niece called down from the window of the dismantled bedroom, "when you have finished that, would you mind coming upstairs a minute? I want you to move a trunk."

And when Evans waved back from the far side of the rumpled lawn where he was standing by the bonfire, she closed the window to keep out the smoke of slow-burning rubbish—old carpeting, clothes, magazines, papers, boxes—which hung about the waists of the fir trees and blew towards the house. For three days the fire had been burning and Evans, red-armed in his shirt sleeves and sweating along the seams of his brow, was prodding it with a garden fork. A sudden silly tongue of yellow flame wagged out: some inflammable piece of family history—who knew what?— perhaps one of her Aunt's absurd summer hats or a shocking year of her father's day dream accountancy was having its last fling. She saw Evans pick up a bit of paper from the outskirts of the fire and read it. What was it? Miss Freshwater's niece drew back her lips and opened her mouth expectantly. At this stage all family privacy had gone. Thirty, forty, fifty, years of life were going up in smoke.

Evans took up the wheelbarrow and swaggered back with it across the lawn towards the house, sometimes tipping it a little to one side to see how the rubber-tyred wheel was running and to admire it. Miss Freshwater's niece smiled. With his curly black hair, his sun-reddened face and his vacant blue eyes, and the faint white scar or chip on the side of his nose, he looked like some hard-living, hard-bitten doll. "Burn this? This lot to go?" was his cry. He was an impassioned and natural destroyer. She could not have found a better man. "Without you, Robert," she said on the first day and with real feeling, "I could never have faced it."

It was pure luck getting him but, lazy, smiling and drifting, she always fell on her feet. She had stepped off the morning train from London at the beginning of the week and had stood on the kerb in the station yard, waiting for one of the two or three taxi drivers who were talking there to take notice of her. Suddenly, Evans drove in fast from the street outside, pulled up beside her, pushed her in and drove off. It was like an abduction. The other taxi drivers shouted at him in the bad language of law-abiding men, but Evans slowly moved his hand up and down, palm downwards, silently and insultingly telling them to shut up and keep their hair on. He looked very pious as he did this. It made her laugh out loud.

"They are manner-less," he said in a slow, rebuking voice, giving each syllable its clear value as if he were speaking the phrase of a poem. "I am sorry I did not ask you where you want to go."

They were going in the wrong direction and he had to swing round the street. She now saw him glance at her in the mirror and his doll's eyes quickly changed from shrewd pleasure to vacancy: she was a capture.

"This is not the first time you are here, I suppose?" he said.

"I was born here," she said. "I haven't been here for twenty-five years, well perhaps just for a day a few years ago. It has changed. All this building!"

She liked friendly conversations.

They were driving up the long hill out of the town towards her aunt's house. Once there had been woodland here but now, like a red hard sea flowing in to obliterate her memory, thousands of sharp villas replaced the trees in angular waves.

"Yes," he said simply. "There is money everywhere."

The car hummed up the long, concrete hill. The villas gave way to ribbons of shacks and bungalows. The gardens were buzzing with June flowers. He pointed out a bungalow which had a small grocery shop in the lean-to at the side, a yard where a couple of old cars stood, and a petrol pump. That was his place, he said. And then, beyond that, were the latest municipal housing estates built close to the Green which was only half a mile from her aunt's house. As they passed, she saw a white marquee on the Green and a big, sagging white banner with the words Gospel Mission daubed on it.

"I see the Gospellers still keep it up," she said. For it was all bad land outside the town, a place for squatters, poor craftsmen, small-holders, little men with little sheds, who in their flinty way had had for generations the habit of breaking out into little religious sects.

"Oh, yes," said Evans in a soft voice, shocked that she could doubt it. "There are great openings. There is a mighty coming to the Lord. I toil in the vineyard myself. You are Miss Freshwater's niece?" he said. "She was a toiler too. She was a giantess for the Lord."

She saw she had been reckless in laughing. She saw she was known. It was as if he had knowingly captured her.

"You don't come from these parts, do you?" she said.

"I am from Wales," he said. "I came here from the mines. I ob-ject-ed to the starvation."

They arrived at the ugly yellow house. It could hardly be seen through the overgrown laurels and fir trees which in some places fingered the dirty windows. He steadied her as she got out for she had put on weight in the last year or so and while she opened her bag to find some money, he walked to the gate and looked in.

"It was left to you in the will, I suppose?" he said.

"Yes," she said. She was a woman always glad to confide. "I've come down to clear up the rubbish before the sale. Do you know anyone here who would give me a hand?"

"There are many," he pronounced. "They are too handy." It was like a line from an anthem. He went ahead, opened the gate and led the way in and when she opened the front door, splitting it away from the cobwebs, he went in with her, walking into the stale, sun-yellowed rooms. He looked at the worn carpet of the stairs. He looked at the ceilings, measuring the size of everything.

"It will fetch a high price," he said in a sorrowful voice and then, looking over her figure like a farmer at the market, in case she might go with the property, he added enthusiasm to his sorrow.

"The highest!" he said. "Does this door go to the back?" She lost him for a while. When she found him he was outside, at the back of the house looking into sheds. He had opened the door of one that contained gardening tools and there he was, gazing. He was looking at a new green metal wheelbarrow with a red wheel and a rubber tyre and he had even pulled it out. He pushed it back, and when he saw her he said accusingly:

"This door has no lock. I do not like to see a door without a lock. I will bring one this afternoon."

It was how she knew he had appointed himself.

"But who will do your taxi work?"

"My son will do that," he said.

From that moment he owned her and the house.

"There will be a lot of toil in this vineyard," she said to him

maliciously and wished she had not said it; but Evans's eyes lost
their vacancy again. He gave a shout of laughter.

"Oh boy, there will!" he said admiring her. And he went off.
She walked from room to room, opening windows and from an
upper one she saw distantly the white sheet of the Gospel tent
through the fir trees. She could settle to nothing.

It was an ugly house of large mean rooms, the landings dark,
the stairs steep. The furniture might have come out of old-fashioned
hotels and had the helpless look of objects too large, ill-met com-
mercially and too gregarious. After her mother's death, her father
had moved his things into his sister's house. Taste had not been a
strong point in the family. The books, mainly sermons, were her
grandfather's; his son had lived on a hoard of engineering textbooks
and magazines. His sister read chiefly the Bible and the rest of her
time changed her clothes, having the notion that she might be
going out.

What paralysed Miss Freshwater's niece was the emptiness of the
place. She had expected to disturb ghosts if she opened a drawer.
She had expected to remember herself. Instead, as she waited for
Evans to come on the first day she had the sensation of being
ignored. Nothing watched in the shadows, nothing blinked in the
beams of sunlight slanting across the room. The room she had slept
in meant nothing. To fit memories into it was a task so awkward
and artificial that she gave up trying. Several times she went to the
window, waiting for Evans to walk in at the gate and for the
destruction to begin.

When he did come he seized the idea at once. All files marked
A.H.F.—that was her father—were "rubbish".

"Thorpe?" he said. "A.H.F. more A.H.F.! Burn it?" He was off
with his first load to lay the foundation to the fire.

"And get this carpet up. We shall trip on it, it is torn," she said.
He ripped the carpet off the stairs. He tossed the door mats, which
were worn into holes, outside. By the barrow load out went the
magazines. Every now and then some object took his eye—a leather
strap, a bowl, a pipe rack, which he put into a little heap of other
perquisites at the back door.

But to burn was his passion, to push the wheelbarrow his joy.
He swaggered with it. He unloaded it carefully at the fire, not
putting it down too near or roughly tipping it. He often tried one
or two different grips on the handles before he started off. Once,

she saw him stop in the middle of the lawn and turn it upside down and look it over carefully and make the wheel spin. Something wrong? No, he lovingly wiped the wheel with a handful of grass, got an oilcan from his pocket, and gave the wheel a squirt. Then he righted the wheelbarrow and came on with it round the house, singing in a low and satisfied voice. A hymn, it sounded like. And at the end of the day, when she took him a cup of tea and they stood chatting, his passion satisfied for the time being, he had a good look at her. His eye was on the brooch she was carelessly wearing to fasten her green overall. He came closer and put his hand to the brooch and lifted it.

"Those are pearls, I shouldn't wonder?" he said.

"Yes," she said. He stepped nimbly away, for he was as quick as a flea.

"It is beautiful," he said, considering the brooch and herself together. "You would not buy it for fifty pounds, nor even a hundred, I suppose. A present, I expect?" And before she could answer, he said gravely: "Half past five! I will lock the sheds. Are you sleeping here? My wife would go off her head, alone in the house. When I'm at the Mission, she's insane!"

Evans stared at Miss Freshwater's niece, waiting for a response to his drama. She did not know what to do, so she laughed. Evans gave a shout of laughter too. It shook the close black curls of his hair and the scar on the side of his nose went white.

"I have the key," he said seriously and went off.

The next day Miss Freshwater's niece opened the window and called "Can you come now? I can't get on."

Evans was on his way back to the house. He stamped quickly up the bare stairs.

"I'm in here," she called. "If you can get in!"

There was a heap of old brown paper knee high at the door. Some of the drawers of a chest had been taken out, others were half open; a wardrobe's doors were open wide. There were shoes, boxes and clothes piled on the bed which was stripped. She had a green scarf in a turban round her head, and none of her fair hair could be seen. Her face, with its strong bones and pale skin marked by dirty fingers, looked hard, humorous and naked. Her strong lips were dry and pale with dust.

They understood each other. At first he had bossed her but she had fought back on this second day and they were equals now. She spoke to him as if they were in a conspiracy together, deciding what should be "saved" and what should be "cast into the flames". She used those words purposely, as a dig of malice at him. She was taller than he. She couldn't get over the fact that he preached every night at the Mission and she had fallen into the habit of tempting him by some movement of arm or body, when she caught him looking at her. Her Aunt had used the word "inconvenient", when her niece was young, to describe the girl's weakness for dawdling about with gardeners, chauffeurs, errand boys. Miss Freshwater's niece had lost the sense of the "convenient" very early in life.

"I've started upstairs now," she said to Evans. "It's worse than downstairs. Look at it."

Evans came a step further into the room and slowly looked round, nodding his head.

She leaned a little forward, her hands together, eagerly awaiting for him to laugh so that they could laugh together.

"She never threw away a scrap of paper. Not even paper bags. Look at this," she said.

He waded into the heap and peeped into a brown paper bag. It contained a bun, as hard as stone.

"Biscuits too," she said. "Wrapped up! Like a larder. They must have been here for years. In the top drawer."

Evans did not laugh.

"She feared starvation," he said, "old people are hungry. They are greedy. My grandmother nibbled like a little rat, all day. And in the night too. They wake up in the night and they are afraid. They eat for comfort. The mice did not get in, I hope," he said, going to look in the drawer.

"She was eighty-four," she said.

"My grandmother was ninety," he said. "My father's mother. She liked to hear a mouse. It was company, she said."

"I think my aunt must have been fond of moths," she said. "They came out in clouds from that wardrobe. Look at all those dresses. I can hardly bear to touch them."

She shook a couple of dresses in the wardrobe and then took them out. "There you are, did you see it? There goes one."

She held up an old-fashioned silk dress.

"Not worn for twenty years, you can see by the fashion. There!"

She gave the dress a pull. "Did you hear? Perished. Rotten. They are all like that. You can't give them away. They'd fall off you."

She threw the dresses on the floor and he picked up one and he saw where moths had eaten it.

"It is wicked," he said. "All that money has gone to waste."

"Where moth and dust doth corrupt," she mocked him, and took an armful of the clothes and threw them on the floor. "Why did she buy them if she did not want them? And all those hats we had to burn? You haven't seen anything yet. Look at this."

On the bed was lying a pile of enormous lace-up corsets. Evans considered them.

"The men had patience," he said.

"Oh, she was not married," she said.

He nodded.

"That is how all the property comes to you, I suppose." he said. There was a shrewd flash in his blue eyes and she knew he had been gazing at her all this time and not at the clothes; but even as she caught his look the dissembling, still, vacant light slid back into it.

"Shoes!" she said, with excitement. "Do you want any shoes?" A large number of shoes of all kinds, little worn or not worn at all, were rowed in pairs on the bed and some had been thrown into a box as well.

"Fifty-one pairs I counted," she said. "She never went out but she went on ordering them. There's a piece of paper in each pair. Have a look. Read it. What does it say?"

He took a piece of paper out of a shoe.

" 'Comfortable for the evening'," he read out. He took another. " 'For wet weather'. Did it rain indoors?"

She took one and read out:

" 'With my blue dress'! Can you imagine? 'Sound walking pair'," she laughed but he interrupted her.

"In Wales they lacked them," he said. "In the bad times they were going barefoot. My sisters shared a pair for dances."

"What shall I do with them?" she asked. "Someone could wear them."

"There are good times now. They have the money," he said, snubbing her. "They buy new."

"I mean—anyone," she said. "They are too big for me. I'll show you."

She sat down on a packing case and slipped her foot into a silver evening shoe.

"You can see, my feet are lost in them," she said.

"You have small feet," he said. "In Wales the men would be chasing you."

"After chapel, I've no doubt," she said. "Up the mountain—what was the name of it? You told me."

"It has the best view in Wales. But those who go up it never see it," he laughed. "Try this pair," he said, kneeling down and lifting her foot. "Ah no, I see. But look at those legs, boy!"

Miss Freshwater's niece got up.

"What size does your wife take?" she asked.

"I don't know," he said, very pleased with himself. "Where is this trunk you said we had to move?"

"Out in the landing cupboard. I'll show you. I can't move it.'

She led the way to the landing and bent down to tug at it.

"You must not do that," he said, putting his hands on her waist and moving her out of the way. He heaved at the trunk and tipped it on end. She wanted it, she said, in the light, where she could see.

"Here on the chest," she said.

He lifted it up and planked it down on the chest.

"Phew!" he said. "You have a small waist for a married woman. Soft. My wife is a giantess, she weighs thirteen stone. And yet, you're big, too, oh yes, you are. But you have light bones. With her, now, it is the bones that weigh. Shall we open it?"

She sat down on a chair and felt in her pocket for a mirror.

"Why didn't you tell me I looked such a sight?" she said, wiping her face. "Yes, open it."

The trunk was made of black leather, it was cracked, peeling, stained and squashed by use. Dimly printed on it was her father's fading name in white large letters. The trunk had been pitched and bumped and slithered out of ships' holds and trains, all over the world. Its lid, now out of the true, no longer met the lock and it was closed by a strap. It had lain ripening and decaying in attics and lofts for half a lifetime.

"What is in it?" she called, without looking from her mirror.

"Clothes," he said. "Books. A pair of skates. Did the old lady go skating?"

He pulled out a Chinese hat. There was a pigtail attached to it and he held it up.

"Ah," he called. "This is the job." He put the hat on his head and pulled out a mandarin coat.

Miss Freshwater's niece stared and then she flushed.

"Where did you get that?" she cried jumping up, taking the hat from his head and snatching the coat. "They're mine! Where were they?"

She pushed him aside and pulled one or two things from the trunk.

"They're mine!" she accused him. "All mine."

She aged as she looked at him. A photograph fell to the floor as she lifted up a book. "To darling Laura," she read out. "Tennyson."

"Who is this?" he said, picking up the photograph.

She did not hear. She was pulling out a cold, sequined evening dress that shrank almost to nothing as she picked it up.

"Good God," she said and dropped it with horror. For under the dress was an album. "Where," she said, sharply possessive, "did you put the skates?" She opened the album. She looked at a road deep in snow leading to an hotel with eaves a yard wide. She had spent her honeymoon there.

"Kitzbühel," she said. "Oh, no!"

She looked fiercely at him to drive him away. The house, so anonymous, so absurd, so meaningless and ghostless, had suddenly got her. There was a choke of cold wonder in her throat.

She turned on him: "Can't you clear up all that paper in the room?" She did not want to be seen by him.

Evans went to the door of the bedroom and, after a glance inside, came back. He was not going to leave her. He picked up the book of poems, glanced at a page or two and then dropped it back in the trunk.

"Everyone knows," he said scornfully, "that the Welsh are the founders of all the poetry of Europe."

She did not hear him. Her face had drained of waking light. She had entered blindly into a dream in which she could hardly drag herself along. She was looking painfully through the album, rocking her head slowly from side to side, her mouth opening a little and closing on the point of speech, a shoulder rising as if she had been hurt, and her back moving and swaying as she felt the clasp of the past like hands on her. She was looking at ten forgotten years of her life, her own life, not her family's, and she did not laugh when she saw the skirts too long, the top-heavy hats hiding the eyes, her face too full and fat, her plainness so sullen, her prettiness too open-mouthed and loud, her look too grossly sly. In this one, sitting at the café table by the lake when she was nineteen, she looked master-ful and at least forty. In this garden picture she was theatrically fancying herself as an ancient Greek in what looked like a night-gown! One of her big toes, she noticed, turned up comically in the sandal she was wearing. Here on a rock by the sea, in a bathing dress, she had got thin again—that was her marriage—and look at her hair! This picture of the girl on skis, sharp-faced, the eyes narrowed —who was that? Herself—yet how could she have looked like that! But she smiled a little at last at the people she had forgotten. This man with the crinkled fair hair, a German—how mad she had been about him. But what pierced her was that in each picture of herself she was just out of reach, flashing and yet dead; and that really it was the *things* that burned in the light of permanence—the chairs, the tables, the trees, the car outside the café, the motor launch on the lake. These blinked and glittered. They had lasted and were ageless, untouched by time, and she was not. She put the album back into the trunk and pulled out an old tweed coat and skirt. Under it was an exercise book with the word 'Diary' written on it in a hand more weakly rounded than the hand she wrote today. Part of a letter fell out of the diary, the second page it seemed, of a letter of her own. She read it.

". . . the job at any rate," she read. "For a whole week he's forgotten his chest, his foot, his stomach. He's not dying any more!!! He conde (crossed out) congratulates himself and says it just shows how doctors are all fools. Inner self-confidence is what I need, he tells me!! It means giving up the flat and that's what I keep thinking—Oxford will be much more difficult for you and me. Women, he says, aren't happy unless they're sacrificing them-selves. Darling, he doesn't know; it's the thought of You that keeps . . ."

She turned over the page. Nothing. She looked through the diary. Nothing. She felt sick and then saw Evans had not gone and was watching her. She quickly put the letter back into the diary.

"Ah," she said nervously. "I didn't know you were here. I'll show you something." She laughed unnaturally and opened the album until she found the most ludicrous and abashing picture in the book, one that would humiliate her entirely. "Here, look at this."

There was a see-saw in the foreground surrounded by raucously laughing people wearing paper hats and looking as though they had been dipped in glycerine: she was astride at the higher end of the see-saw, kicking her legs and on the lower end was a fat young man in a pierrot costume. On her short, fuzzy fair hair was a paper hat. She showed the picture to Evans and picked out the terrible sequin dress from the trunk.

"That's the dress!" she said, pointing to the picture. "I was engaged to him. Isn't it terrible?" And she dropped the dress back again. It felt cold and slippery, almost wet. "I didn't marry him."

Evans scowled.

"You were naked," he said with disgust.

"I remember now. I left it all here. I kept that dress for years. I'll have to go through it all." And she pulled down the lid.

"This photograph fell out," he said.

It was the picture of another young man.

"Is this your husband?" Evans asked, studying the man.

"My husband is dead," she said sharply. "That is a friend." And she threw the picture back into the trunk. She realized now that Evans had been holding her arm a long time. She stepped away from him abruptly. The careless friendliness, the sense of conspiracy she had felt while they worked together, had all gone. She drew away and said, in the hostile voice of unnecessary explanation:

"I mean," she said, "my husband died a few years ago. We were divorced. I mustn't waste any more time."

"My wife would not condescend to that," he said.

"She has no reason, I am sure," said Miss Freshwater's niece, severely, and returned to the bedroom.

"Now! We can't waste time like this. You'd better begin with what is on the bed. And when you've cleared it you can put the kettle on."

When Evans had gone downstairs with his load, she went to the landing and glared at the trunk. Her fists were clenched; she wished it was alive and that she could hit it. Glancing over the banisters to be sure she was alone, she opened it again, took out the photograph and the letter from her diary and put them in her handbag. She thought she was going to be sick or faint for the past was drumming, like a train coming nearer and nearer, in her head.

"My God!" she said. And when she saw her head in its turban and her face hardened by shock and grief in her absurd aunt's dressing-table mirror, she exclaimed with real horror. She was crying. "What a mess," she said and pulled the scarf off her head. Her fair, thick hair hung round her face untidily. Not once, in all those photographs, had a face so wolfish with bitterness and without laughter looked back at her.

"I'm taking the tea out," Evans called from below.

"I'm just coming," she called back and hurriedly tried to arrange her hair and then, because she had cried a little, she put on her glasses. Evans gave a keen look at the change in her when she got downstairs and walked through the hall to the door.

He had put the tray on the grass near a yew hedge in the hot corner at the side of the house and was standing a few yards away drinking his tea. In the last two days he had never drunk his tea near her but had chatted from a distance.

In her glasses and with her hair girlishly brushed back, Miss Freshwater's niece looked cold, tall and grand, like a headmistress.

"I hope we shan't get any more smoke here," she said. "Sit down. You look too restless."

She was very firm, nodding to the exact place on the lawn on which she required him to sit. Taken aback, Evans sat precisely in that place. She sat on the grass and poured herself a cup of tea.

"How many souls came to Jesus last night?" she asked in her ladylike voice. Evans got up and squatted cheerfully, but watchfully, on his heels.

"Seventeen," he said.

"That's not very good," she said. "Do you think you could save mine?"

"Oh, yes," he said keenly.

"You look like a frog," she said mocking. He had told her miners always squat in this way after work. "It's too late," she went on. "Twenty years too late. Have you always been with the Mission?"

"No," he said.

"What was it? Were you converted, did you see the light?" she mocked, like a teacher.

"I had a vision," he said seriously.

"A vision!" she laughed. She waved her hand. "What do you mean—you mean, you—well, where? Up in the sky or something?"

"No," he said. "It was down the mine."

"What happened?"

He put down his cup and he moved it away to give himself more room. He squatted there, she thought, not like a frog at all, but like an imp or a devil, very grave and carven-faced. She noticed now how wide his mouth was and how widely it opened and how far the lips drew back when he spoke in his declamatory voice. He stared a long time waiting for her to stop fidgeting. Then he began:

"I was a drunkard," he declaimed, relishing each syllable separately. "I was a liar. I was a hypocrite. I went with women. And married women too!" His voice rose. "I was a fornicator. I was an adulterer. Always at the races, too, gambling, it was senseless. There was no sin the Devil did not lead me into, I was like a fool. I was the most noteworthy sinner in the valley, everyone spoke of it. But I did not know the Lord was lying in wait for me."

"Yes, but what happened?" she said.

He got to his feet and gazed down at her and she was compelled to look up at him.

"I will tell you," he said. "It was a miracle." He changed his manner and after looking round the garden, he said in a hushing and secretive voice:

"There was a disaster in the mine," he said. "It was in June. I was twenty-three and I was down working and I was thinking of the sunlight and the hills and the evening. There was a young girl called Alys Davies, you know, two or three had been after her and I was thinking I would take her up the rock, that is a quiet place, only an old mountain ram would see you . . ."

"You were in the mine," she said. "You are getting too excited about this Alys Jones . . ."

"Davies," he said with a quick grin. "Don't worry about her. She is married now." He went back to his solemn voice.

"And suddenly," he said, "there was a fall, a terrible fall of rock like thunder and all the men shouting. It was at eleven in the morning when we stopped work for our tea. There were three men in the working with me and they had just gone off. I was trapped alone."

"Were you hurt?" she said anxiously.

"It was a miracle, not a stone touched me. I was in a little black cave. It was like a tomb. I was in that place alone for twelve hours. I could hear them working to get at me but after the first fall there was a second and then I thought I was finished. I could hear nothing."

"What did you do? I would have gone out of my mind," she said. "Is that how you got the scar on your nose?"

"That was in a fight," he said, offhand. "Madness is a terrible thing. I stared into the blackness and I tried to think of one thing to stop my mind wandering but I could not at first for the fear, it was chasing and jumping like a mad dog in my head. I prayed and the more I prayed the more it chased and jumped. And then, suddenly, it stopped. I saw in my mind a picture. I saw the mantelpiece at home and on it a photograph of our family—my father and mother, my four sisters and my brother. And we had an aunt and uncle just married, it was a wedding photograph. I could see it clearly as if I had been in my home. They were standing there looking at me and I kept looking at them and thinking about them. I held on to them. I kept everything else out of my mind; wherever I looked that picture was before my eyes. It was like a vision. It saved me."

"I have heard people say they hear voices," said Miss Freshwater's niece, kindly now.

"Oh, no! They were speechless," said Evans. "Not a word! I spoke to them," he said. "Out loud. I promised God in front of all my family that I would cleanse my soul when I got out."

Evans stood blazing in his trance and then he picked up his cup from the grass and took it to her.

"May I please have some more tea?" he said.

"Of course," she said. "Sit down."

He considered where he should sit and then put himself beside her.

"When I saw you looking at your photographs," he said, "I thought, 'She is down the mine'."

"I have never been down a mine in my life. I don't know why. We lived near one once when I was in the north," she evaded.

"The mine of the past," he said. "The dark mine of the past."

"I can see why you are a preacher, Robert," she smiled. "It's funny how one cannot get one's family out of one's head. I could feel mine inside me for years—but not now."

She had entirely stopped mocking him.

"I can't say they ever saved me," she said. "I think they nearly ruined me. Look at that ugly house and all that rubbish. Did you ever see anything like their furniture? When I was a girl I used to

think, Suppose I got to look like that sideboard! And then money
was all they ever talked about—and good and nice people, and nice
people always had money. It was like that in those days, thank God
that has gone. Perhaps it hasn't. I decided to get away from it and
I got married. They ought to have stopped me—all I wanted was
to get away—but they thought my husband had money, too. He
just had debts and a bad stomach. When he had spent all my money,
he just got ill to punish me . . . You don't know anything about life
when you're young and when you are old it's too late . . ."

"That's a commonplace remark," she went on, putting her cup
on the tray and reaching for his. "My mother used to make it."
She picked up her scarf and began to tie it on her head, but as she
was tying it Evans quickly reached for it and pulled it off. His hand
held the nape of her neck gently.

"You are not old," he shouted, laughing and sparkling. "Your
hair is golden, not a grey one in it, boy."

"Robert, give me that scarf. It is to keep out the dust," she said,
blushing. She reached for the scarf and he caught her wrist.

"When I saw you standing at the station on Monday, I said,
Now, there is a woman! Look at the way she stands, a golden
woman, that is the first I have seen in this town, she must be a
stranger," he said.

"You know all the others, I expect," she said with amusement.

"Oh, indeed, yes I do! All of them!" he said. "I would not look
at them twice."

His other hand slipped from her neck to her waist.

"I can trust myself with them, but not with you," he said,
lowering his voice and speaking down to her neck. "In an empty
house," he whispered, nodding to the house, letting go of her hand
and stroking her knee.

"I am far past that sort of thing," said Miss Freshwater's niece,
choosing a lugubrious tone. She removed his arm from her waist.
And she stood up, adroitly picking up the tray and from behind
that defence, looked round the garden. Evans sprang up but instead
of coming near her, he jumped a few yards away and squatted on
his heels, grinning at her confidently.

"You look like the devil," she said.

He had placed himself between her and the way to the house.

"It is quiet in the garden, too," he said with a wink. And then
she saw the wheelbarrow which he had left near the fire.

"That barrow ought to go well in the sale," she said. "It is almost new. How much do you think it will fetch?"

Evans stood up at once and his grin went. An evasive light, almost the light of tears, came into his hot blue eyes and he stared at her with an alarm that drove everything else out of his head.

"They'll put it with the tools, you will not get much for it."

"I think every man in the town will be after it," she said, with malice.

"What price did you want for it?" he said, uncertain of her.

"I don't know what they cost," she said carelessly and walked past him very slowly back to the house, maddening him by her walk. He followed her quickly and when she turned, still carrying the tray, to face him in the doorway, she caught his agitation.

"I will take the tray to the kitchen," he said politely.

"No," she said, "I will do that. I want you to go upstairs and fetch down all those shoes. And the trunk. It can all go."

And she turned and walked through the house to the kitchen. He hesitated for a long time; at last she heard him go upstairs and she pottered in the kitchen where the china and pans were stacked on the table, waiting for him to come down. He was a very long time. He came down with the empty trunk.

"It can all go. Burn it all. It's no good to anyone, damp and rotten. I've put aside what I want," she said.

He looked at her sullenly. He was startled by her manner and by the vehemence of her face, for she had put on the scarf and her face looked strong-boned, naked and ruthless. She was startled herself.

His sullenness went; he returned to his old excitement and hurried the barrow to the fire and she stood at the door impatiently waiting for the blaze. When he saw her waiting he came back.

"There it goes," he said with admiration.

The reflection of the flame danced in points of light in her eyes, her mouth was set, hard and bitter. Presently the flame dropped and greenish smoke came out thickly.

"Ah!" she gasped. Her body relaxed and she smiled at Evans, tempting him again.

"I've been thinking about the barrow," she said. "When we've finished up here, I'll make you a present of it. I would like to give it to you, if you have a use for it?"

She could see the struggle going on inside him as he boldly

looked at her; and she saw his boldness pass into a small shrug of independent pride and the pride into pretence and dissembling.

"I don't know," he said, "that I have a use—well, I'll take it off you. I'll put the shoes in it, it will save bringing the car." He could not repress his eagerness any longer. "I'll put the shoes into it this evening. Thank you." He paused. "Thank you, ma'am," he said.

It was the first time he had called her ma'am. The word was like a blow. The affair was over. It was, she realized, a dismissal.

An hour later she heard him rumbling the barrow down the path to the gate. The next day he did not come. He had finished with her. He sent his son up for his money.

It took Miss Freshwater's niece two more days to finish her work at the house. The heavy jobs had been done, except for putting the drawers back into the chests. She could have done with Evans's help there, and for the sweeping which made her hot but she was glad to be alone because she got on more quickly with the work. She hummed and even sang as she worked, feeling light and astonishingly happy. Once or twice, when she saw the white sheet of the Mission tent distantly through the trees, she laughed:

"He got what he wanted! And I'm evidently not as old as I look."

The last hours buzzed by and she spun out the time, reluctant to go. She dawdled, locking the sheds, the windows and doors, until there was nothing more to keep her. She brought down a light suitcase in which she had put the few things she wanted to take away and she sat in the dining-room, now as bare as an office, to go through her money. After the destruction she was having a fit of economy and it had occurred to her that instead of taking a taxi to the station, she could walk down to the bus stop on the Green. She knew that the happiness she felt was not ebbing, but had changed to a feeling she had not had for many years: the feeling of expectancy, and as this settled in her she put her money and papers back into her bag. There was a last grain of rubbish here: with scarcely a glance at them, she tore up the photograph and the unfinished letter she had found in the trunk.

"I owe Evans a lot," she thought.

Nothing retained her now.

She picked up her case. She left the house and walked down the road in the strong shade of the firs and the broad shade of the oak trees, whose leaves hardened with populous contentment in the long evening light. When she got to the open Green children were playing round the Gospel Tent and, in twos and threes, people were walking from the houses across the grass towards it. She had twenty minutes to wait until her bus arrived. She heard the sound of singing coming from the tent. She wondered if Evans would be there.

"I might give him the pleasure of seeing what he missed," she thought.

She strolled across to the tent.

A youth who had watered his hair and given it a twirl with a comb was standing in his best clothes at the entrance to the tent.

"Come to Jesu! Come to Jesu!" he said to her as she peeped inside.

"I'm just looking for someone," she said politely.

The singing had stopped when she looked in but the worshippers were still standing. They were packed in the white light of the tent and the hot smell of grass and somewhere at the far end, invisible, a man was shouting like a cheapjack selling something at an auction. He stopped suddenly and a high, powerful country voice whined out alone: "Ow in the vale . . ." and the congregation joined in for another long verse.

"Is Mr. Evans here tonight?" she asked the youth.

"Yes," he said. "He's witnessing every night."

"Where is he? I don't see him."

The verse came to an end and once more a voice began talking at the other end of the tent. It was a woman's voice, high and incomprehensible and sharp. The hymn began again and then spluttered into an explosive roar that swept across the Green.

"They've fixed it. The loudspeaker!" the youth exclaimed. Miss Freshwater's niece stepped back. The noises thumped. Sadly, she looked at her watch and began to walk back to the bus stop. When she was about ten yards from the tent, the loudspeaker gave a loud whistle and then, as if God had cleared his throat, spoke out with a gross and miraculous clearness.

"Friends," it said, sweeping right across the Green until it struck the furthest houses and the trees. "My friends . . ."

The word seemed to grind her and everyone else to nothing, to mill them all into the common dust.

"When I came to this place," it bellowed, "the serpent . . ." (An explosion of noise followed but the voice cleared again) ". . . heart. No bigger than a speck it was at first, as tiny as a speck of coal grit in your eye . . ."

Miss Freshwater's niece stopped. Was it Evans's voice? A motor coach went by on the road and drowned the next words, and then she heard, spreading into an absurd public roar:

"I was a liar. I was an adulterer. Oh my friends, I was a slave of the strange woman the Bible tells about, the whore of Babylon, in her palace where moth and dust . . ." Detonations again.

But it was Evans's voice. She waited and the enormously magnified voice burst through:

"And then by the great mercy of the Lord I heard a voice cry out, 'Robert Evans, what are you doing, boy? Come out of it' . . ." But the voice exploded into meaningless concussions, suddenly resuming:

". . . and burned the adulteress in the everlasting fire, my friends —and all her property."

The hymn started up again.

"Well not quite all, Robert," said Miss Freshwater's niece pleasantly aloud, and a child eating an ice-cream near her watched her walk across the grass to the bus stop.

THREE

Blind Love

"I'm beginning to be worried about Mr. 'Wolverhampton' Smith," said Mr. Armitage to Mrs. Johnson who was sitting in his study with her notebook on her knee and glancing from time to time at the window. She was watching the gardener's dog rooting in a flower-bed. "Would you read his letter again; the second paragraph about the question of a partnership."

Since Mr. Armitage was blind it was one of Mrs. Johnson's duties to read his correspondence.

"He had the money—that is certain; but I can't make out on what conditions," he said.

"I'd say he helped himself. He didn't put it into the business at Ealing—he used it to pay off the arrears on the place at Wolverhampton," she said in her cheerful manner.

"I'm afraid you're right. It's his character I'm worried about," said Mr. Armitage.

"There isn't a single full stop in his letter—a full page on both sides. None. And all his words are joined together. It's like one word two pages long," said Mrs. Johnson.

"Is that so?" said Mr. Armitage. "I'm afraid he has an unpunctuated moral sense."

Coming from a blind man whose open eyes and face had the fixed gleam of expression you might have seen a piece of rock, the word "unpunctuated" had a sarcasm unlike an ordinary sarcasm. It seemed, quite delusively, to come from a clearer knowledge than any available to the sighted.

"I think I'll go and smell out what he's like. Where is Leverton Grove? Isn't it on the way to the station? I'll drop in when I go up to London tomorrow morning," said Mr. Armitage.

The next morning he was driven in his Rolls-Royce to Mr. Smith's house, one of two or three little villas that were part of a building speculation that had come to nothing fifty years before. The yellow brick place was darkened by the firs that were thick in this district. Mrs. Johnson who had been brought up in London

places like these, winced at the sight of them. (Afterwards she said
to Mr. Armitage, "It brings it back." They were talking about her
early life.) The chauffeur opened the car door, Mrs. Johnson got out
saying, "No kerb", but Armitage waving her aside, stepped out
unhelped and stood stiff with the sainted upward gaze of the blind;
then, like an army detail, the party made a sharp right turn, walked
two paces, then a sharp left to the wooden gate which the chauffeur
opened, and went forward in step.

"Daffodils," said Mrs. Johnson noting a flower-bed. She was
wearing blue to match her bold, practical eyes, and led the way up
the short path to the door. It was opened before she rang by an
elderly, sick-looking woman with swollen knuckles who half-hid
behind the door as she held it, to expose Smith standing with his
grey jacket open, his hands in his pockets—the whole man an
arrangement of soft smiles from his snowball head to his waistcoat,
from his flies to his knees, sixteen stone of modest welcome with
nothing to hide.

"It is good of you to come," he said. He had a reverent voice.

"On my way to the station," said Armitage.

Smith was not quite so welcoming to Mrs. Johnson. He gave her
a dismissive frown and glanced peremptorily at his wife.

"In here?" said Mrs. Johnson briskly taking Armitage's arm in
the narrow hall.

"Yes," he said.

They all stood just inside the doorway of the front room. A fir
tree darkened it. It had, Mrs. Johnson recorded at once, two fenders
in the fireplace, and two sets of fire-irons; then she saw two of
everything—two clocks on the mantelpiece, two small sofas, a
dining-table, a small table folded up, even two carpets on the floor,
for underneath the red one, there was the fringe of a worn yellow
one. Mr. Smith saw that she noted this and raising a grand chin and
now unsmiling, said, "We're sharing the 'ouse, the house, until we
get into something bigger."

And at this, Mrs. Smith looked with the searching look of an
agony in her eyes, begging Mrs. Johnson for a word.

"Bigger," echoed Mrs. Smith and watched to see the word sink
in. And then, putting her fingers over her face, she said: "Much
bigger," and laughed.

"Perhaps," said Mr. Smith, who did not care for his wife's
laugh, "while we talk—er . . ."

"I'll wait outside in the car," said the decisive Mrs. Johnson and when she was in the car she saw Mrs. Smith's gaze of appeal from the step.

Half an hour later, the door opened and Mrs. Johnson went to fetch Mr. Armitage.

"At this time of the year the daffodils are wonderful round here," said Armitage as he shook hands with Smith, to show that if he could not see there were a lot of things he knew. Mr. Smith took the point and replaced his smiling voice with one of sportive yet friendly rebuke, putting Mr. Armitage in his place.

"There is only one eye," he stated as if reading aloud. "The eye of God."

Softly the Rolls drove off, with Mrs. Smith looking at it fearfully from the edge of the window curtain.

"Very rum fellow," said Armitage in the car. "I'm afraid he's in a mess. The Inland Revenue are after him as well. He's quite happy because there's nothing to be got out of him. Remarkable. I'm afraid his friends have lost their money."

Mrs. Johnson was indignant.

"What's he going to do down here? He can't open up again."

"He's come here," Armitage said, "because of the chalk in London water. The chalk, he says, gets into the system with the result that the whole of London is riddled with arthritis and nervous diseases. Or rather the whole of London is riddled with arthritis and nervous diseases because it believes in the reality of chalk. Now chalk has no reality. We are not living on chalk nor even on gravel: we dwell in God. Mr. Smith explains that God led him to manage a chemist's shop in Wolverhampton, but to open one of his own in Ealing without capital, was a mistake. He now realizes that he was following his own will not the will of God. He is now doing God's work. Yesterday he had a cable from California. He showed it to me. 'Mary's cancer cured gratitude cheque follows.' He's a faith-healer."

"He ought to be in gaol," said Mrs. Johnson.

"Oh no. He's in heaven," said Armitage. "I'm glad I went to see him. I didn't know about his religion, but it's perfect: you get witnesses like him in court every day, always moving on to higher things."

The Rolls arrived at the station and Mr. Armitage picked up his white stick.

"Cancer today. Why not blindness tomorrow? Eh?" he said. Armitage gave one low laugh from a wide mouth. And though she enjoyed his dryness, his rare laugh gave a dangerous, animal expression to a face that was usually closed. He got out of the car and she watched him walk into the booking-hall and saw knots of people divide to make way for him on the platform.

In the damp town at the bottom of the hills, in the shops, at the railway station where twice a week the Rolls waited for him to come back from London, it was agreed that Armitage was a wonder. A gentleman, of course, they said; he's well-off, that helps. And there is that secretary-housekeeper, Mrs. Johnson. That's how he can keep up his legal business. He takes his stick to London, but down here he never uses it. In London he has his lunch in his office or in his club, and can manage the club stairs which worry some of the members when they come out of the bar. He knows what's in the papers—ever had an argument with him?—of course Mrs. Johnson reads them to him.

All true. His house stood, with a sudden flash of Edwardian prosperity between two larch coppices on a hill five miles out and he could walk out on to the brick terrace and smell the lavender in its season, and the grass of the lawns that went steeply down to his rose garden and the blue tiles of his swimming-pool boxed in by yew.

"Fabian Tudor. Bernard Shaw used to come here—before our time, of course," he would say, disparaging the high, panelled hall. He was really referring to his wife who had left him when he was going blind twenty-two years ago. She had chosen and furnished the house. She liked leaded windows, brass, plain velvet curtains, Persian carpets, brick fireplaces and the expensive smell of wood smoke.

"All fake," he would say, "like me."

You could see that pride made him like to embarrass. He seemed to know the effect of jokes from a dead face. But, in fact, if he had no animation—Mrs. Johnson had soon perceived in her common-sensical way—this was because he was not affected, as people are, by the movements on other faces. Our faces, she had learned from Armitage, threw their lives away every minute. He stored his. She knew this because she stored hers. She did not put it like this, in fact what she said appeared to contradict it. She liked a joke.

"It's no good brooding. As mother used to say, as long as you've got your legs you can give yourself an airing."

Mrs. Johnson had done this. She had fair hair, a good figure and active legs, but usually turned her head aside when she was talking as if to an imaginary friend. Mrs. Johnson had needed an airing very badly when she came to work for Mr. Armitage.

At their first interview—he met her in the panelled hall.

"You do realize, don't you, that I am totally blind? I have been blind for more than twenty years," he said.

"Yes," she said. "I was told by Dr. James." She had been working for a doctor in London.

He held out his hand and she did not take it at once. It was not her habit to shake hands with people; now, as always, when she gave in she turned her head away. He held her hand for a long time and she knew he was feeling the bones. She had heard that the blind do this and she took a breath as if to prevent her bones or her skin passing any knowledge of herself to him. But she could feel her dry hand coming to life and she drew it away. She was surprised that, at the touch, her nervousness had gone.

To her, Armitage's house was a wonderful place. The space, the light made friendly by the small panes of the tall leaded windows, charmed her.

"Not a bit like Peckham," she said cheerfully.

Mr. Armitage took her through the long sitting-room where there were yellow roses in a bowl, into his study. He had been playing a record and took it off.

"Do you like music?" he said. "That was Mozart."

"I like a bit of a sing-song," she said. "I can't honestly say I like the classical stuff."

He took her round the house, stopped to point to a picture or two and, once more down in the long room, took her to a window and said,

"This is a bad day for it. The haze hasn't lifted. On a clear day you can see Sevenham Cathedral. It's twelve miles away. Do you like the country?"

"Frankly I've never tried it."

"Are you a widow, Mrs. Johnson?"

"No. I changed my name from Thompson to Johnson and not for the better. I divorced my husband," said Mrs. Johnson crisply.

"Will you read something to me—out of the paper," he said. "A court case."

She read and read.

"Go on," he said. "Pick out something livelier."

"Lonely monkeys at the zoo?"

"That will do."

She read again and she laughed.

"Good," he said.

"As father used to say 'Speak up . . .' " she began, but stopped. Mr. Armitage did not want to hear what father said.

"Will you allow me," Armitage said, getting up from his desk. "Would you allow me to touch your face?"

Mrs. Johnson had forgotten that the blind sometimes asked this.

She did not answer at once. She had been piqued from the beginning because he could not see her. She had been to the hair-dresser's. She had bought a blouse with a high frilled neck which was meant to set off the look of boyish impudence and frankness of her face. She had forgotten about touch. She feared he would have a pleading look, but she saw that the wish was part of an exercise for him. He clearly expected her to make no difficulty about it.

"All right," she said, but she meant him to notice the pause, "if you want to."

She faced him and did not flinch as his hand lightly touched her brow and cheek and chin. He was, she thought, "after her bones" not her skin and that, though she stiffened with resistance, was "O.K. by her". When, for a second, the hand seemed to rest on her jaw, she turned her head.

"I weigh eight stone," she said in her bright way.

"I would have thought less," he said. That was the nearest he came to a compliment. "It was the first time," she said afterwards to her friend Marge in the town, "that I ever heard of a secretary being bought by weight."

She had been his secretary and housekeeper for a long time now. She had understood him at once. The saintly look was nonsense. He was neither a saint nor a martyr. He was very vain; especially he was vain of never being deceived, though in fact his earlier secretaries had not been a success. There had been three or four before her. One of them—the cook told her—imagined him to be a martyr because she had a taste for martyrdom and drank to gratify it; another yearned to offer the compassion he hated, and muddled everything. One reckoning widow lasted only a month. Blatantly she had added up his property and wanted to marry him. The last, a "lady", helped herself to the household money, behind a screen of wheezing grandeur and name-dropping.

Remembering the widow, the people who came to visit Mr. Armitage when he gave a party were relieved after their meeting with Mrs. Johnson.

"A good honest to God Cockney" or "Such a cheery soul". "Down to earth," they said. She said she had "knocked about a bit." "Yes, sounds as if she had": they supposed they were denigrating. She was obviously not the kind of woman who would have any dangerous appeal to an injured man. And she, for her part, would go to the pictures when she had time off or simply flop down in a chair at the house of her friend, Marge, and say:

"Whew, Marge. His nibs has gone to London. Give me a strong cuppa. Let's relax."

"You're too conscientious."

"Oh, I don't mind the work. I like it. It occupies your mind. He has interesting cases. But sometimes I get keyed up."

Mrs. Johnson could not herself describe what keyed her up; perhaps, being on the watch? Her mind was stretched. She found herself translating the world to him and it took her time to realize that it did not matter that she was not "educated up to it". He obviously liked her version of the world, but it was a strain having versions. In the mornings she had to read his letters. This bothered her. She was very moral about privacy. She had to invent an impersonal, uninterested voice. His lack of privacy irked her; she liked gossip and news as much as any woman, but here it lacked the salt of the secret, the whispered, the found out. It was all information and statement. Armitage's life was an abstraction for him. He had to know what he could not see. What she liked best was reading legal documents to him.

He dressed very well and it was her duty to see that his clothes were right. For an orderly practical mind like hers, the order in which he lived was a new pleasure. They lived under fixed laws: no chair or table, even no ashtray must be moved. Everything must be in its place. There must be no hazards. This was understandable: the ease with which he moved without accident in the house or garden depended on it. She did not believe when he said "I can hear things before I get to them. A wall can shout, you know." When visitors came she noticed he stood in a fixed spot: he did not turn his head when people spoke to him and among all the head-turning and gesturing he was the still figure, the law-giver. But he was very cunning. If someone described a film they had seen, he was soon talking as if he had been there. Mrs. Johnson who had duties when he had visitors, would smile to herself, at the surprise on the faces of people who had not noticed the quickness with which he collected every image or scene or character described. Sometimes, a lady would say to her: "I do think he's absolutely marvellous", and, if he overheard this—and his hearing was acute—Mrs. Johnson would notice a look of ugly boredom on his face. He was, she noted, particularly vain of his care of money and accounts. This pleased Mrs. Johnson because she was quick to understand that here a blind man who had servants might be swindled. She was indignant about the delinquency of her predecessor. He must have known he was being swindled.

Once a month Mrs. Johnson would go through the accounts with him. She would make out the cheques and take them to his study and put them on his desk.

The scene that followed always impressed her. She really admired him for this. How efficient and devious he was! He placed the cheque at a known point on his blotter. The blunt fingers of his hairless hands had the art of gliding and never groping, knowing the inches of distance; and then as accurately as a geometrician, he signed. There might be a pause as the fingers secretly measured, a pause alarming to her in the early days, but now no longer alarming; sometimes she detected a shade of cruelty in this pause. He was listening for a small gasp of anxiety as she watched.

There was one experience which was decisive for her. It occurred in the first month of her employment and had the lasting stamp of a revelation. (Later on, she thought he had staged the incident in order to show her what his life was like and to fix in her mind the nature of his peculiar authority.) She came into the sitting-room one evening in the winter to find a newspaper and heard sharp, unbelievable sounds coming from his study. The door was open and the room was in darkness. She went to it, switched on the light, and saw he was sitting there typing in the darkness. Well, she could have done that if she had been put to it—but now she *saw* that for him there was no difference between darkness and light.

"Overtime, I see," she said, carefully not to show surprise.

This was when she saw that his mind was a store of maps and measured things; a store of sounds and touches and smells that became an enormous translated paraphernalia.

"You'd feel sorry for a man like that," her friend Marge said.

"He'd half kill you if you showed you were sorry," Mrs. Johnson said. "I don't feel sorry. I really don't."

"Does he ever talk about his wife?"

"No."

"A terrible thing to do to leave a man because he's blind."

"She had a right to her life, hadn't she?" said Mrs. Johnson flatly. "Who would want to marry a blind man?"

"You are hard," Marge said.

"It's not my business," said Mrs. Johnson. "If you start pitying people you end up by hating them. I've seen it. I've been married, don't forget."

"I just wish you had a more normal life, dear."

"It suits me," said Mrs. Johnson.

"He ought to be very grateful to you."

"Why should he be? I do my job. Gratitude doesn't come into it. Let's go and play tennis."

The two women went out and played tennis in the park and Mrs. Johnson kept her friend running all over the court.

"I smell tennis balls and grass," said Mr. Armitage when she returned.

In the March of her third year a bad thing happened. The winter was late. There was a long spell of hard frost and you could see the cathedral tower clearly over the low-lying woods on most days. The frost coppered the lawns and scarcely faded in the middle of the day. The hedges were spiked and white. She had moved her typing table into the sitting-room close to the window to be near a radiator and when she changed a page she would glance out at the garden. Mr. Armitage was out there somewhere and she had got into the habit of being on the watch. Now she saw him walk down the three lawns and find the brick steps that led to the swimming-pool. It was enclosed by a yew hedge and was frozen over. She could see Armitage at the far side of it pulling at a small fallen branch that had been caught by the ice. His foot had struck it. On the other side of the hedge, the gardener was cutting cabbage in the kitchen garden and his dog was snuffling about. Suddenly a rabbit ran out, ears down, and the dog was yelping after it. The rabbit ran through the hedge and almost over Armitage's feet with the dog nearly on it. The gardener shouted. The next moment Armitage who was squatting had the dog under his legs, lost his balance and fell full length through the ice into the pool. Mrs. Johnson saw this. She saw the gardener drop his knife and run to the gap in the hedge to help Armitage out. He was clambering over the side. She saw him wave the gardener's hand away and shout at him and the gardener step away as Armitage got out. He stood clawing weed off his face, out of his hair, wringing his sleeves and brushing ice off his shirt as he marched back fast up the garden. He banged the garden door in a rage as he came in.

"That bloody man. I'll have that dog shot," shouted Armitage. She hurried to meet him. He had pulled off his jacket and thrown it on a chair. Water ran off his trousers and sucked in his shoes. Mrs. Johnson was appalled.

"Go and change your things quickly," she said. And she easily raced him to the stairs to the landing and to his room. By the time he got there she had opened several drawers, looking for underclothes and had pulled out a suit from his cupboard. Which suit? She pulled out another. He came squelching after her into the room.

"Towel," she cried. "Get it all off. You'll get pneumonia."

"Get out. Leave me alone," shouted Armitage who had been tugging his shirt over his head as he came upstairs.

She saw, then, that she had done a terrible thing. By opening drawers and putting clothes on the bed, she had destroyed one of his systems. She saw him grope. She had never seen him do this before. His bare white arms stretched out in a helpless way and his brown hands pitiably closed on air. The action was slow and his fingers frightened her.

"I told you to leave me alone," he shouted.

She saw she had humiliated him. She had broken one of the laws. For the first time she had been incompetent.

Mrs. Johnson went out and quietly shut the door. She walked across the landing to the passage in the wing where her own room was, looking at the wet marks of his muddy shoes on the carpet, each one accusing her. She sat down on the edge of her bed. How could she have been such a fool! How could she have forgotten his rule? Half-naked to the waist, hairy on the chest and arms, he shocked because the rage seemed to be not in his mind but in his body like an animal's. The rage had the pathos of an animal's. Perhaps when he was alone he often groped; perhaps the drilled man she was used to, who came out of his bedroom or his study, was the expert survivor of a dozen concealed disasters?

Mrs. Johnson sat on her bed listening. She had never known Armitage to be angry; he was a monotonously considerate man. The shout abashed her and there was a strange pleasure in being abashed; but her mistake was not a mere mistake. She saw that it struck at the foundation of his life and was so gross that the surface of her own confidence was cracked. She was a woman who could reckon on herself, but now her mind was scattered. Useless to say to herself "What a fuss about nothing," or "Keep calm." Or, about him, "Nasty temper." His shout: "Get out. I told you to leave me alone" had, without reason (except that a trivial shame is a spark that sets fire to a long string of greater shames), burned out all the security of her present life.

She had heard those words, almost exactly those words, before. Her husband had said them. A week after their wedding.

Well, *he* had had something to shout about, poor devil.

She admitted it. Something a lot more serious than falling into a pond and having someone commit the crime of being kind to you and hurting your silly little pride.

She got up from the bed and turned on the tap of the wash-basin to cool down her hot face and wash her hands of the dirt off the jacket she had brought upstairs. She took off her blouse and as she sluiced her face she looked through the water at herself in the mirror. There was a small birth mark, the size of a red leaf which many people noticed and which, as it showed over the neck of the high blouses she usually wore, had the enticement of some signal or fancy of the blood; but, under it, and invisible to them, were two smaller ones and then a great spreading ragged liver-coloured island of skin which spread under the tape of her slip and crossed her breast and seemed to end in a curdle of skin below it. She was stamped with an ineradicable bloody insult. It might have been an attempt to impose another woman on her. She was used to seeing it, but she carried it about with her under her clothes, hiding it and yet vaunting.

Now she was reaching for a towel and inside the towel, as she dried herself, she was talking to Armitage.

"If you want to know what shame and pride are, what about marrying a man who goes plain sick at the sight of your body and who says 'You deceived me. You didn't tell me'."

She finished drying her face and put the towel on the warm rail and went to her dressing-table. The hairbrush she picked up had been a wedding present and at each hard stroke of the brush on her lively fair hair, her face put up a fight, but it exhausted her. She brushed the image of Armitage away and she was left staring at the half-forgotten but never forgotten self she had been.

How could she have been such a fool as to deceive her husband? It was not through wickedness. She had been blinded too—blinded by love; in a way, love had made her so full of herself that, perhaps, she had never seen *him*. And her deceptions: she could not stop herself smiling at them, but they were really pitiable because she was so afraid of losing him and to lose him would be to lose this new beautifully deluded self. She ought to have told him. There were chances. For example, in his flat with the grey sofa with the spring that bit your bottom going clang, clang at every kiss, when he used to carry on about her wearing dresses that a man couldn't get a hand into. He knew very well she had had affairs with men, but why, when they were both "worked up", wouldn't she undress and go to the bedroom? The sofa was too short. She remembered how shocked his face looked when she pulled up her skirts and lay on the floor. She said she believed in sex before marriage, but she thought some things ought to wait: it would be wrong for him to see her naked before their wedding day. And to show him she was no prude—there was that time they pretended to be looking out of the window at a cricket match; or Fridays in his office when the staff was gone and the cleaners were only at the end of the passage.

"You've got a mole on your neck," he said one day.

"Mother went mad with wanting plums when she was carrying me. It's a birthmark."

"It's pretty," he said and kissed it.

He kissed it. He kissed it. She clung to that when after the wedding they got to the hotel and she hid her face in his shoulder and let him pull down the zip of her dress. She stepped away and pretending to be shy, she undressed under her slip. At last the slip came off over her head. They both looked at each other, she with brazen fear and he—she couldn't forget the shocked blank disgust on his face. From the neck over the left shoulder down to the breast and below, and spreading like a red tongue to the back was this ugly blob—dark as blood, like a ragged liver on a butcher's window, or some obscene island with ragged edges. It was as if a bucket of paint had been thrown over her.

"You didn't tell me," he said. If only she had told him, but how could she have done! She knew she had been cursed.

"That's why you wouldn't undress, you little hypocrite."

He himself was in his underpants with his trousers on the bed and with his cuff-links in his hand which made his words absurd and awful. His ridiculous look made him tragic and his hatred frightening. It was terrible that for two hours while they talked he did not undress and worse that he gave her a dressing-gown to cover herself. She heard him going through the catalogue of her tricks.

"When . . ." he began in a pathetic voice. And then she screamed at him.

"What do you think? Do you think I got it done, that I got myself tattooed in the Waterloo Road? I was born like it."

"Ssh," he said, "you'll wake the people in the next room."

"Let them hear. I'll go and show them," she screamed. It was kind of him to put his arm around her. When she had recovered, she put on her fatal, sporty manner.

"Some men like it," she said.

He hit her across the face. It was not then but in the following weeks when pity followed and pity turned to cruelty he had said:

"Get out. Leave me alone."

Mrs. Johnson went to her drawer and got out a clean blouse.

Her bedroom in Armitage's house was a pretty one, far prettier than any she had ever had. Up till now she had been used to bed-sitters since her marriage. But was it really the luxury of the house and the power she would have in it that had weighed with her when she had decided to take on this strange job? She understood now something else had moved her in the low state she had been in when she came. As a punished and self-hating person she was drawn to work with a punished man. It was a return to her girlhood: injury had led her to injury.

She looked out of the window at the garden. The diamond

panes chopped up the sight of the frozen lawns and the firs that were frost-whiskered. She was used to the view. It was a view of the real world; that, after all, was her world, not his. She saw that gradually in three years she had drifted out of it and had taken to living in Armitage's filed memory. If he said, for example, "That rambler is getting wild. It must be cut back," because a thorn caught his jacket, or if he made his famous remark about seeing the cathedral on a clear day, the landscape limited itself to these things and, in general, reduced itself to the imposed topographical sketch in his mind. She had allowed him, as a matter of abnegation and duty to impose his world on hers. Now this shock brought back a lost sense of the right to her own landscape; and then to the protest, that this country was not hers at all. The country bored her. The fir trees bored her. The lanes bored her. The view from this window or the tame protected view of the country from the Rolls-Royce window bored her. She wanted to go back to London, to the streets, the buses and the crowds, to crowds of people with eyes in their heads. And—her spirits rising— "to hell with it, I want people who can *see* me".

She went downstairs to give orders for the carpet to be brushed. In the sitting-room she saw the top of Armitage's dark head. She had not heard him go down. He was sitting in what she called the cathedral chair facing the window and she was forced to smile when she saw a bit of green weed sticking to his hair. She also saw a heavy glass ashtray had fallen off the table beside him. "Clumsy," she said. She picked it up and lightly pulled off the piece of weed from his hair. He did not notice this.

"Mr. Armitage," she said in her decisive manner. "I lost my head. I'm sorry."

He was silent.

"I understand how you feel," she said. For this (she had decided in her room) was the time for honesty and for having things out. The impersonality could not go on, as it had done for three years.

"I want to go back to London," she said.

"Don't be a damn fool," he said.

Well, she was not going to be sworn at.

"I'm not a damn fool," she said. "I understand your situation." And then, before she could stop herself, her voice shaking and loud, she broke out with: "I know what humiliation is."

"Who is humiliated?" said Armitage. "Sit down."

"I am not speaking about you," she said stiffly.

That surprised him, she saw, for he turned his head.

"I'm sorry. I lost my temper," he said. "But that stupid fellow and his dog . . ."

"I am speaking about myself," she said. "We have our pride, too."

"Who is we?" he said, without curiosity.

"Women," she said.

He got up from his chair, and she stepped back. He did not move and she saw that he really had not recovered from the fall in the pool, for he was uncertain. He was not sure where the table was.

"Here," he said roughly, putting out a hand. "Give me a hand out of this."

She obediently took him by the arm and stood him clear of the table.

"Listen to me. You couldn't help what happened and neither could I. There's nothing to apologize for. You're not leaving. We get on very well. Take my advice. Don't be hard on yourself."

"It is better to be hard," she said. "Where would you have been if you had not been hard? I'm not a girl. I'm thirty-nine." He moved towards her and he put his hand on her right shoulder and she quickly turned her head. He laughed and said, "You've brushed your hair back."

He knew. He always knew.

She watched him make for his study and saw him take the wrong course, brush against the sofa by the fireplace, and then a yard or two farther, he shouldered the wall.

"Damn," he said.

At dinner conversation was difficult. He offered her a glass of wine which she refused. He poured himself a second glass and as he sat down he grimaced with pain.

"Did you hurt your back this afternoon?" she asked.

"No," he said. "I was thinking about my wife."

Mrs. Johnson blushed. He had scarcely ever mentioned his wife. She knew only what Marge Brook had told her of the town gossip: how his wife could not stand his blindness and had gone off with someone and that he had given her a lot of money. Someone said, ten thousand pounds. What madness! In the dining-room Mrs. Johnson often thought of all those notes flying about over the table and out of the window. He was too rich. Ten thousand pounds of hatred and rage, or love, or madness. In the first place, she wouldn't have touched it.

"She made me build the pool," he said.

"A good idea," she said.

"I don't know why. I never thought of throwing her into it," he said.

Mrs. Johnson said: "Shall I read the paper?"

She did not want to hear more about his wife.

Mrs. Johnson went off to bed early. Switching on the radio in her room and then switching it off because it was playing classical music, she said to herself: "Well, funny things bring things back. What a day!" and stepped yawning out of her skirt. Soon she was in bed and asleep.

An hour later, she woke up, hearing her name.

"Mrs. Johnson. The water got into my watch, would you set it for me." He was standing there in his dressing-gown.

"Yes," she said. She was a woman who woke up alert and clear-headed.

"I'm sorry. I thought you were listening to a programme. I didn't know you were in bed," he said. He was holding the watch to his ear.

"Would you set it for me and put my alarm right?" He had the habit of giving orders. They were orders spoken into space —and she was the space, non-existent. He gave her the watch and went off. She put on her dressing-gown and followed him to his room. He had switched on the light for her. She went to the bedside table and bent down to wind the clock. Suddenly she felt his arms round her, pulling her upright, and he was kissing her head. The alarm went off suddenly and she dropped the clock. It went on screeching on the floor at her feet.

"Mr. Armitage," she said in a low angry voice, but not struggling. He turned her round and he was trying to kiss her on the lips. At this she did struggle. She twisted her head this way and that to stop him, so that it was her head rather than her body that was resisting him. Her blue eyes fought with all their light, but his eyes were dead as stone.

"Really, Mr. Armitage. Stop it," she managed to mutter. "The door is open. Cook will hear."

She was angry at being kissed by a man who could not see her face, but she felt the shamed insulted woman in her, that blotched inhabitant, blaze up in her skin.

The bell of the alarm clock was weakening and then choked to a stop and in her pettish struggle she stepped on it; her slipper had come off.

"I've hurt my foot." Distracted by the pain she stopped struggling and Armitage took his opportunity and kissed her on the lips. She looked with pain into his sightless eyes. There was no help there. She was terrified of being drawn into the dark where he lived. And then the kiss seemed to go down her throat and spread into her shoulders, into her breasts and branch into all the veins and arteries of her body and it was the tongue of the shamed woman who had sprung up in her that touched his.

"What are you doing?" she was trying to say, but could only groan the words. When he touched the stained breast she struck back violently saying: "No, no."

"Come to bed with me," he said.

"Please let me go. I've hurt my foot."

The surprising thing was that he did let her go and as she sat panting and white in the face on the bed to look at her foot, she looked mockingly at him. She forgot that he could not see her mockery. He sat beside her but did not touch her and he was silent. There was no scratch on her foot. She picked up the clock and put it back on the table.

Mrs. Johnson was proud of the adroitness with which she had kept men away from her since her marriage. It was a war with the inhabitant of the ragged island on her body. That creature craved for the furtive, for the hand that slipped under a skirt, for the scuffle in the back seat of a car, for a five-minute disappearance into a locked office.

But the other Mrs. Johnson, the cheerful one, was virtuous. She took advantage of his silence and got quickly up to get away; she dodged past him, but he was quick too. He was at the closed door. For a moment she was wily. It would be easy for her to dodge him in the room. And, then, she saw once more the sight she could not bear that melted her more certainly than the kisses which had filled her mouth and throat: she saw his hands begin to open and search and grope in the air as he came towards the sound of her breathing. She could not move. His hand caught her. The woman inside her seemed to shout "Why not? You're all right. He cannot see." In her struggle she had not thought of that. In three years he had made her forget that blindness meant not seeing.

"All right," she said and the virtue in Mrs. Johnson pouted. She gently tapped his chest with her fingers and said with the sullenness of desire, "I'll be back in a minute."

It was a revenge: that was the pleasure.

"Dick," she called to her husband. "Look at this," when the man was on top of her. Revenge was the only pleasure and his excitement was soon over. To please him she patted him on the head as he lay beside her and said, "You've got long legs." And she nearly said, "You are a naughty boy" and "Do you feel better?" but she stopped herself and her mind went off on to what she had to do in the morning; she listened and wondered how long it would be before he would fall asleep and she could stealthily get away. Revenge astonished by its quickness.

She slyly moved. He knew at once and held her. She waited. She wondered where Dick was now. She wished she could tell him. But presently this blind man in the bed leaned up and put both his hands on her face and head and carefully followed the round of her forehead, the line of her brow, her nose and lips and chin, to the line of her throat and then to her nape and shoulders. She trembled, for after his hands had passed, what had been touched seemed to be new. She winced as his hand passed over the stained shoulder and breast and he paused, knowing that she winced, and she gave a groan of pleasure to deceive him; but he went on, as if he were modelling her, feeling the pit under the arms, the space of ribs and belly and the waist of which she was proud, measuring them, feeling their depth, the roundness of her legs, the bone in her knees until, throwing all clothes back he was holding her ankle, the arch of her foot and her toes. Her skin and her bones became alive. His hands knew her body as she had never known it. In her brief love affairs which had excited her because of the risk of being caught, the first touch of a man stirred her at once, and afterwards left her looking demurely at him; but she had let no one know her with a pedantry like his. She suddenly sat up and put her arms round him and now she went wild. It was not a revenge now; it was a triumph. She lifted the sad breast to his lips. And, when they lay back she kissed his chest and then—with daring—she kissed his eyes.

It was six o'clock before she left him and when she got to her room the stained woman seemed to bloom like a flower. It was only after she had slept and saw her room in daylight again that she realized that once more she had deceived a man.

It was late. She looked out of the window and saw Armitage in his city clothes talking to the chauffeur in the garden. She watched them walk to the garage.

"O.K.," she said dryly to defend herself. "It was a rape." During the day there would be moments when she could feel his hands moving over her skin. Her legs tingled. She posed as if she were a new-made statue. But as the day went on she hardened and instead of waiting for him to return she went into the town to see Marge.

"You've put your hair up," said Marge.

"Do you like it?"

"I don't know. It's different. It makes you look severe. No, not severe. Something. Restless."

"I am not going back to dinner this evening," she said. "I want a change. Leonard's gone to London."

"Leonard!" said Marge.

Mrs. Johnson wanted to confide in Marge, but Marge bored her. They ate a meal together and she ate fast. To Marge's astonishment she said, "I must fly."

"You *are* in a mood," Marge said.

Mrs. Johnson was unable to control a longing to see Armitage. When she got back to the house and saw him sitting by the fire she wanted him to get up and at least put his arms round her; but he did not move, he was listening to music. It was always the signal that he wanted to be alone.

"It is just ending," said Armitage.

The music ended in a roll of drums.

"Do you want something, Helen?" he said.

She tried to be mocking, but her voice could not mock and she said seriously: "About last night. It must not happen again. I don't want to be in a false position. I could not go on living in the house."

She did not intend to say this; her voice, between rebuke and tenderness, betrayed this.

"Sit down."

She did not move.

"I have been very happy here," she said. "I don't want to spoil it."

"You are angry," he said.

"No, I'm not," she said.

"Yes you are; that is why you were not here when I got back," he said.

"You did not wait for me this morning," she said. "I was glad you didn't. I don't want it to go on."

He came nearer to her and put his hand on her hair.

"I like the way your hair shows your ears," he said. And he kissed them.

"Now, please," she said.

"I love you," he said and kissed her on the forehead and she did not turn her head.

"Do you? I'm glad you said that. I don't think you do. When something has been good, don't spoil it. I don't like love affairs," she said.

And then she changed. "It was a party. Good night."

"You made me happy," he said, holding on to her hand.

"Were you thinking about it a long time?" she said in another voice, lingering for one more word.

"Yes," he said.

"It is very nice of you to say that. It is what you ought to say. But I mean what I said. Now, really, good night. And," giving a pat to his arm, she said: "Keep your watch wound up."

Two nights later he called to her loudly and curtly from the stairs: "Mrs. Johnson, where are you?" and when she came into the hall he said quietly, "Helen."

She liked that. They slept together again. They did not talk.

Their life went on as if nothing had happened. She began to be vain of the stain on her body and could not resist silently displaying, almost taunting him, when she undressed, with what he could not see. She liked the play of deceiving him like this; she was paying him out for not being able to see her; and when she was ashamed of doing this the shame itself would rouse her desire: two women uniting in her. And fear roused her too; she was afraid of his blindness. Sometimes the fear was that the blind can see into the mind. It often terrified her at the height of her pleasure that she was being carried into the dark where he lived. She knew she was not but she could not resist the excitement of imagining it. Afterwards she would turn her back to him, ashamed of her fancies, and as his finger followed the bow of her spine she would drive away the cynical thought that he was just filing this affair away in one of the systems of his memory.

Yet she liked these doubts. How dead her life had been in its practical certainties. She liked the tenderness and violence of sexual love, the simple kindness of the skin. She once said to him, "My skin is your skin." But she stuck to it that she did not love him and that he did not love her. She wanted to be simply a body: a woman like Marge who was always talking about love seemed to her a fool. She liked it that she and Armitage were linked to each other only by signs. And she became vain of her disfigurement and, looking at it, even thought of it as the lure.

"I know what would happen to me if I got drunk," she thought at one of Armitage's cocktail parties, "I'm the sort of woman who would start taking her clothes off." When she was a young woman she had once started doing so and someone, thank God, stopped her.

But these fancies were bravado.

They were intended to stop her from telling him.

On Sundays Mrs. Johnson went to church in the village near the house. She had made a habit of it from the beginning, because she thought it the proper thing to do: to go to church had made her feel she need not reproach herself for impropriety in living in the same house as a man. It was a practical matter: before her love affair the tragic words of the service had spoken to her evil. If God had done this to her, He must put up with the sight of her in His house. She was not a religious woman; going to church was an assertion that she had as much right to fair play as anyone else. It also stopped her from being "such a fool" as to fall to the temptation of destroying her new wholeness by telling him. It was "normal" to go to church and normality had been her craving ever since her girlhood. She had always taken her body not her mind to church.

Armitage teased her about her church-going when she first came to work for him; but lately his teasing became sharper.

"Going to listen to Dearly Beloved Brethren?" he would say.

"Oh leave him alone," she said.

He had made up a tale about her being in love with the vicar; at first it was a joke, but now there was a sharp edge to it.

"A very respectable man," he said.

When the church bells rang on Sunday evening he said: "He's calling to you." She began to see that this joke had the grit of jealousy in it; not of the vicar, of course, but a jealousy of many things in her life.

"Why do you go there? I'd like to understand, seriously," he said.

"I like to get out," she said.

She saw pain on his face. There was never much movement in it beyond the deepening of two lines at the corners of his mouth: but when his face went really dead, it was as sullen as earth in the garden. In her sense, she knew, he never went out. He lived in a system of tunnels. She had to admit that when she saw the grey church she was glad, because it was not his house. She knew from gossip that neither he nor his wife had ever been to it.

There was something else in this new life; now he had freed her they were both more watchful of each other. One Sunday in April she saw his jealousy in the open. She had come in from church and she was telling him about the people who were there. She was sitting on the sofa beside him.

"How many lovers have you had?" he said. "That doctor you worked for, now?"

"Indeed not," she said. "I was married."

"I know you were married. But when you were working for those people in Manchester and in Canada after the war?"

"No one else. That was just a trip."

"I don't believe you."

"Honestly, it's true."

"In Court I never believe a witness who says 'Honestly'."

She blushed for she had had three or four lovers, but she was defending herself. They were no business of his.

The subject became darker.

"Your husband," he said. "He saw you. They all saw you."

She knew what he meant, and this scared her.

"My husband. Of course he saw me. Only my husband."

"Ah, so there were others."

"Only my husband saw me," she said. "I told you about it. How he walked out of the hotel after a week."

This was a moment when she could have told him, but to see his jealousy destroy the happiness he had restored to her, made her indignant.

"He couldn't bear the sight of me. He had wanted," she invented, "to marry another woman. He told me on the first night of our marriage. In the hotel. Please don't talk about it."

"Which hotel was this?" he said.

The triviality of the question confused her.

"In Kensington."

"What was the name?"

"Oh, I forget, the something Royal . . ."

"You don't forget."

"I do honestly . . ."

"Honestly!" he said.

He was in a rage of jealousy. He kept questioning her about the hotel, the length of their marriage. He pestered for addresses, for dates and tried to confuse her by putting his questions again and again.

"So he didn't leave you at the hotel!" he said.

"Look," she said. "I can't stand jealous men and I'm not going to be questioned like one of your clients."

He did not move or shout. Her husband had shouted and paced up and down, waving his arms. This man sat bolt upright and still, and spoke in a dry exacting voice.

"I'm sorry," he said.

She took his hand, the hand that groped like a helpless tentacle and that had modelled her; it was the most disturbing and living thing about him.

"Are you still in love with your husband?"

"Certainly not."

"He saw you and I have never seen you." He circled again to his obsession.

"It is just as well. I'm not a beautiful woman," she laughed. "My legs are too short, my bottom is too big. You be grateful—my husband couldn't stand the sight of me."

"You have a skin like an apple," he said.

She pushed his hand away and said, "Your hands know too much."

"*He* had hands. And he had eyes," he said in a voice grinding with violence.

"I'm very tired. I am going to bed," she said. "Good night."

"You see," he said. "There is no answer."

He picked up a Braille book and his hand moved fast over the sheets.

She went to her room and kicked off her shoes and stepped out of her dress.

"I've been living in a dream," she thought. "Just like Marge, who always thinks her husband's coming back every time the gate goes."

"It is a mistake," she thought, "living in the same house."

The jealous fit seemed to pass. It was a fire, she understood, that flared up just as her shame used to flare, but two Sundays later the fit came on again. "He must hate God," she thought and pitied him. Perhaps the music that usually consoled him had tormented him. At any rate, he stopped it when she came in and put her prayer book on the table. There was a red begonia which came from the greenhouse on the table beside the sofa where he was sitting very upright, as if he had been waiting impatiently for her to come back.

"Come and sit down," he said and began kindly enough. "What was Church like? Did they tell you what to do?"

"I was nearly asleep," she said. "After last night. Do you know what time it was?" She took his hand and laughed.

He thought about this for a while. Then he said. "Give me your hands. No. Both of them. That's right. Now spit on them."

"Spit!"

"Yes, that is what the Church tells you."

"What *are* you talking about?" she said trying to get her hands away.

"Spit on them." And he forced her hands, though not roughly, to her lips.

"What are you doing?" She laughed nervously and spat on her fingers.

"Now—rub the spittle on my eyes."

"Oh no," she said.

He let go of her wrist.

"Do as I tell you. It's what your Jesus Christ did when he cured the blind man."

He sat there waiting and she waited.

"He put dust or earth or something on them," he said. "Get some."

"No," she said.

"There's some here. Put your fingers in it," he said shortly. She was frightened of him.

"In the pot," he insisted as he held one of her wrists so that she could not get away. She dabbed her wet fingers in the earth of the begonia pot.

"Put in on my eyes."

"I can't do that. I really can't," she said.

"Put it on my eyes," he said.

"It will hurt them."

"They are hurt already," he said. "Do as I tell you." She bent to him and, with disgust, she put her dirty fingers on the wet eyeballs. The sensation was horrible and when she saw the dirty patches on his eyes, like two filthy smudges, she thought he looked like an ape.

"That is what you are supposed to do," he said.

Jealousy had made him mad.

"I can't stay with a madman," she thought. "He's malicious." She did not know what to do, but he solved that for her. He reached for his Braille book. She got up and left him there.

The next day he went to London.

His habits changed. He went several times into the nearby town on his own and she was relieved that he came back in a silent mood which seemed happy. The horrible scene went out of her mind. She had gone so far as to lock her bedroom door for several nights after that scene, but now she unlocked it. He had bought her a bracelet from London; she drifted into unguarded happiness. She knew so well how torment comes and goes.

It was full undreaming June, the leaves in the garden still undarkened, and for several days people were surprised when day after day the sun was up and hot and unclouded. Mrs. Johnson went down to the pool. Armitage and his guests often tried to persuade her to go in; she always refused.

"They once tried to get me to go down to Peckham Baths when I was a kid, but I screamed," she said.

The guests left her alone. They were snobbish about Peckham Baths.

But Mrs. Johnson decided to become a secret bather. One afternoon when Armitage was in London and the cook and gardener had their day off, she went down with the gardener's dog. She wore a black bathing-suit that covered her body and lowered herself by the steps into the water. Then she splashed at the shallow end of the pool and hung on to the rail while the dog barked at her. He stopped barking when she got out and sniffed round the hedge, when she pulled down her bathing-dress to her waist and lay down to get sun-drunk on her towel.

She was displaying herself to the sun, the sky and the trees. The air was like hands that played on her as Armitage did and she lay listening to the snuffles of the dog and the humming of the bees in the yew hedge. She had been there an hour when the dog barked at the hedge. She quickly picked up a towel and covered herself and called to the dog: "What is it?"

He went on barking and then gave up and came to her. She sat down. Suddenly the dog barked again. Mrs. Johnson stood up and tried to look through one of the thinner places in the hedge. A man who must have been close to the pool and who must have passed along the footpath from the lane, a path used only by the gardener, was walking up the lawns towards the house carrying a trilby hat in his hand. He was not the gardener. He stopped twice to get his breath and turned to look at the view. She recognized the smiling grey suit, the wide figure and snowball head: it was "Wolverhampton" Smith. She waited and saw him go on to the house and ring a bell. Then he disappeared round the corner and went to the front of the house. Mrs. Johnson quickly dressed. Presently he came back to look into the windows of the sitting-room. He found the door and for a minute or two went into the house and then came out.

"The cheek," she said. She finished dressing and went up the lawn to him.

"Ah, there you are," he said. "What a sweet place this is. I was looking for Mr. Armitage."

"He's in London."

"I thought he might be in the pool," he said. Mr. Smith looked rich with arch, smiling insinuation.

"When will he be back?"

"About six. Is there anything I can do?"

"No, no, no," said Mr. Smith in a variety of genial notes, waving a hand. "I was out for a walk."

"A long walk—seven miles."

"I came," said Mr. Smith modestly lowering his eyes in financial confession, "by bus."

"The best way. Can I give you a drink?"

"I never touch it," Mr. Smith said putting up an austere hand. "Well, a glass of water perhaps. As the Americans say 'I'm mighty thirsty'. My wife and I came down here for the water, you know. London water is chalky. It was very bad for my wife's arthritis. It's bad for everyone really. There's a significant increase in neuralgia, neuritis, arthritis in a city like London. The chalky water does it. People don't realize it," and here Mr. Smith stopped smiling and put on a stern excommunicating air.

"If you believe that man's life is ruled by water, I personally don't," he said.

"Not by water only, anyway," said Mrs. Johnson.

"I mean," said Mr. Smith gravely, "if you believe that the material body exists." And when he said this, the whole sixteen stone of him looked scornfully at the landscape which no doubt, concealed thousands of people who believed they had bodies. He expanded: he seemed to threaten to vanish.

Mrs. Johnson fetched a glass of water. "I'm glad to see you're still here," she laughed when she came back. Mr. Smith was resting on the garden seat.

"I was just thinking—thank you—there's a lot of upkeep in a place like this," he said.

"There is."

"And yet—what is upkeep? Money—so it seems. And if we believe in the body, we believe in money, we believe in upkeep and so it goes on," said Mr. Smith sunnily, waving his glass at the garden. And then sharply and loftily, free of this evil: "It gives employment." Firmly telling her she was employed. "But," he added, in warm contemplation, putting down his glass and opening his arms, gathering in the landscape, "but there is only one employer."

"There are a hell of a lot of employers."

Mr. Smith raised an eyebrow at the word "hell" and said: "Let me correct you there. I happen to believe that God is the only employer."

"I'm employed by Mr. Armitage," she said. "Mr. Armitage loves this place. You don't have to see to love a garden."

"It's a sweet place," said Mr. Smith. He got up and took a deep

breath. "Pine trees. Wonderful. The smell! My wife doesn't
like pine trees. She is depressed by them. It's all in the mind," said
Mr. Smith. "As Shakespeare says. By the way, I suppose the water's
warming up in the pool? June—it would be. That's what I should
like—a swim."

"He *did* see me!" thought Mrs. Johnson.

"You should ask Mr. Armitage," she said coldly.

"Oh no, no," said Mr. Smith. "I just *feel* that to swim and have
a sun-bathe would be the right idea. I should like a place with a
swimming-pool. And a view like this. I feel it would suit me. And,
by the way," he became stern again, "don't let me hear you say
again that Mr. Armitage enjoys this place although he doesn't
see it. Don't tie his blindness on him. You'll hold him back. He
does see it. He reflects all-seeing God. I told him so on Wednesday."

"On Wednesday?"

"Yes," he said. "When he came for treatment. I managed to
fit him in. Good godfathers, look at the time! I've got to get the
bus back. I'm sorry to miss Mr. Armitage. Just tell him I called.
I just had a thought to give him, that's all. He'll appreciate it."

"And now," Mr. Smith said sportively, "I must try and avoid
taking a dive into that pool as I go by, mustn't I?"

She watched his stout marching figure go off down the path.

For treatment! What on earth did Mr. Smith mean? She knew
the rest when Armitage came home.

"He came for his cheque," he said. "Would you make out a
cheque for a hundred and twenty pounds . . ."

"A hundred and twenty pounds!" she exclaimed.

"For Mr. Smith," he repeated. "He is treating my eyes."

"Your eyes! He's not an ophthalmic surgeon."

"No," said Armitage coldly. "I have tried those."

"You're not going to a faith-healer!"

"I am."

And so they moved into their second quarrel. It was baffling
to quarrel with Armitage. He could hear the firm ring of your
voice but he could not see your eyes blooming wider and bluer with
obstinacy; for her, her eyes were herself. It was like quarrelling
with a man who had no self or, perhaps, with one that was always
hidden.

"Your Church goes in for it," he said.

"Proper faith-healing," she said.

"What is proper?" he said.

She had a strong belief in propriety.

"A hundred and twenty pounds! You told me yourself Smith is a fraud. I mean, you refused his case. How can you go to a fraud?"

"I don't think I said fraud," he said.

"You didn't like the way he got five thousand pounds out of that silly young man."

"Two thousand," he said.

"He's after your money," she said. "He's a swindler."

In her heart having been brought up poor, she thought it was a scandal that Armitage was well off; it was even more scandalous to throw money away.

"Probably. At the end of his tether," he said. He was conveying, she knew, that he was at the end of his tether too.

"And you fall for that? You can't possibly believe the nonsense he talks."

"Don't you think God was a crook? When you think of what He's done?"

"No, I don't." (But in fact, the stained woman thought He was.)

"What did Smith talk about?"

"I was in the pool. I think he was spying on me. I forget what he was talking about—water, chalky water, was it?"

"He's odd about chalk!" Armitage laughed. Then he became grim again: "You see—even Smith can see *you*. You see people, you see Smith, everyone sees everything and so they can afford to throw away what they see and forget. But I have to remember everything. You know what it is like trying to remember a dream. Smith is right, I'm dreaming a dream," Armitage added sardonically. "He says that I'm only dreaming I cannot see."

She could not make out whether Armitage was serious.

"All right. I don't understand, but all right. What happens next?"

"You can wake up." Mr. Armitage gave one of his cruel smiles. "I told you. When I used to go to the Courts I often listened to witnesses like Smith. They were always bringing 'God is my witness' into it. I never knew a more religious lot of men than dishonest witnesses. Perhaps they were in contact with God."

"You don't mean that. You are making fun of me," she said. And then vehemently: "I hate to see you going to an ignorant man like that. I thought you were too proud. What has happened to you?"

She had never spoken her mind so forcibly to him before.

"If a man can't see," he said, "if you couldn't see, humiliation is what you'd fear most. I thought I ought to accept it."

He had never been so open with her.

"You couldn't go lower than Mr. Smith," she said.

"We're proud. That is our vice," he said. "Proud in the dark. Everyone else has to put up with humiliation. You said you knew what it was—I always remember that. Millions of people are humiliated: perhaps it makes them stronger because they forget it. I want to join them."

"No you don't," she said.

They were lying in bed and leaning over him she put her breast to his lips, but he lay lifeless. She could not bear it that he had changed her and that she had stirred this profound wretchedness in him. She hated confession; to her it was the male weakness—self-love. She got out of bed.

"Come to that," she said. "It's you who are humiliating me. You are going to this quack man because we've slept together. I don't like the compliment."

"And you say you don't love me," he said.

"I admire you," she said. She dreaded the word "love". She picked up her clothes and left the room. She hadn't the courage to say she hadn't the courage. She stuck to what she had felt since she was a child: that she was a body. He had healed it with his body.

Once more she thought, "I shall have to go. I ought to have stuck to it and gone before. If I'd been living in the town and just been coming up for the day it would have been O.K. Living in the house was your mistake, my girl. You'll have to go and get another job." But, of course, when she calmed down, she realized that all this was self-deception: she was afraid to tell him. She brusquely drove off the thought and her mind went to the practical.

That hundred and twenty pounds! She was determined not to see him swindled. She went with him to Mr. Smith's next time. The roof of the Rolls-Royce gleamed over the shrubbery of the uncut hedge of Mr. Smith's house. A cat was sitting on the window-sill. Waiting on the doorstep was the fat little man, wide-waisted and with his hands in his optimistic pockets, and changing his smile of welcome to a reminder of secret knowledge when he saw her. Behind the undressing smile of Mr. Smith stood the kind, cringing figure of his wife, looking as they all walked into the narrow hall.

"Straight through?" said Mrs. Johnson in her managing voice. "And leave them to themselves, I suppose?"

"The back gets the sun. At the front it's all these trees," said Mrs. Smith encouraged by Mrs. Johnson's presence to speak out in a weak voice, as if it was all she did get. "I was a London girl."

"So am I," said Mrs. Johnson.

"But you've got a beautiful place up there. Have you got these pine trees too?"

"A few."

"They give me the pip," said Mrs. Smith. "Coffee? Shall I take your coat? My husband said you'd got pines."

"No thank you, I'll keep it," said Mrs. Johnson. "Yes, we've got pines. I can't say they're my favourite trees. I like to see leaves come off. And I like a bit of traffic myself. I like to see a shop."

"Oh you would," said Mrs. Smith.

The two women looked with the shrewd London look at each other.

"I'm so busy up there I couldn't come before. I don't like Mr. Armitage coming alone. I like to keep an eye on him," said Mrs. Johnson set for attack.

"Oh yes, an eye."

"Frankly, I didn't know he was coming to see Mr. Smith."

But Mrs. Johnson got nothing out of Mrs. Smith. They were both half listening to the rumble of men's voices next door. Then the meeting was over and they went out to meet the men. In his jolly way Mr. Smith said to Mrs. Johnson as they left: "Don't forget about that swim!"

Ostentatiously to show her command and to annoy Armitage, she armed him down the path.

"I hope you haven't invited that man to swim in the pool," said Mrs. Johnson to Mr. Armitage on the way home.

"You've made an impression on Smith," said Armitage. "No, I haven't."

"Poor Mrs. Smith," said Mrs. Johnson.
Otherwise they were silent.

She went a second then a third time to the Smiths' house. She sat each time in the kitchen talking and listening to the men's voices in the next room. Sometimes there were long silences.

"Is Mr. Smith praying?" Mrs. Johnson asked.

"I expect so," said Mrs. Smith. "Or reading."

"Because it *is* prayer, isn't it?" said Mrs. Johnson.

Mrs. Smith was afraid of this healthy downright woman and it was an effort for her to make a stand on what evidently for most of her married life had been poor ground.

"I suppose it is. Prayer, yes, that is what it would be. Dad"— she changed her mind—"my husband has always had faith." And with this, Mrs. Smith looked nervously at being able loyally to put forward the incomprehensible.

"But what does he actually *do*? I thought he had a chemist's shop," pursued Mrs. Johnson.

Mrs. Smith was a timid woman who wavered between the relics of dignity and a secretive craving to impart.

"He has retired," said Mrs. Smith. "When we closed the shop he took this up."

She said this hoping to clutch a certainty.

Mrs. Johnson gave a bustling laugh.

"No, you misunderstand me. What I mean is, what does he actually *do*? What is the treatment?"

Mrs. Smith was lost. She nodded as it were to nothingness several times.

"Yes," she said. "I suppose you'd call it prayer. I don't really understand it."

"Nor do I," said Mrs. Johnson. "I expect you've got enough to do keeping house. I have my work cut out too."

They still heard the men talking. Mrs. Johnson nodded to the wall.

"Still at it," said Mrs. Johnson. "I'll be frank with you Mrs. Smith. I am sure your husband does whatever he does do for the best . . ."

"Oh yes, for the best," nodded Mrs. Smith. "It's saved us. He had a writ out against him when Mr. Armitage's cheque came in. I know he's grateful."

"But I believe in being open . . ."

"Open," nodded Mrs. Smith.

"I've told him and I've told Mr. Armitage that I just don't believe a man who has been blind for twenty-two years . . ."

"Terrible," said Mrs. Smith.

". . . can be cured. Certainly not by—whatever this is. Do you believe it, Mrs. Smith?"

Mrs. Smith was cornered.

"Our Lord did it," she said desperately. "That is what my husband says . . ."

"I was a nurse during the war and I have worked for doctors," said Mrs. Johnson. "I am sure it is impossible. I've knocked about a lot. You're a sensible woman, Mrs. Smith. I don't want to offend you, but you don't believe it yourself, do you?"

Mrs. Johnson's eyes grew larger and Mrs. Smith's older eyes were helpless and small. She longed for a friend. She was hypnotized by Mrs. Johnson whose face and pretty neck grew firmly out of her frilled and high-necked blouse.

"I try to have faith . . ." said Mrs. Smith rallying to her husband. "He says I hold him back. I don't know."

"Some men need to be held back," said Mrs. Johnson and she gave a fighting shake to her healthy head. All Mrs. Smith could do in her panic was to watch every move of Mrs. Johnson's, study her expensive shoes and stockings, her capable skirt, her painted nails. Now, at the shake of Mrs. Johnson's head, she saw on the right side of the neck the small petal of the birth-mark just above the frill of the collar.

"None of us are perfect," said Mrs. Smith slyly.

"I have been with Mr. Armitage four years," Mrs. Johnson said.

"It is a lovely place up there," said Mrs. Smith, eager to change the subject. "It must be terrible to live in such a lovely place and never see it . . ."

"Don't you believe it," said Mrs. Johnson. "He knows that place better than any of us, better than me."

"No," groaned Mrs. Smith. "We had a blind dog when I was a girl. It used to nip hold of my dress to hold me back if it heard a car coming when I was going to cross the road. It belonged to my aunt and she said, 'that dog can see. It's a miracle'."

"He heard the car coming," said Mrs. Johnson. "It's common sense."

The words struck Mrs. Smith.

"Yes, it is really," she said. "If you come to think of it."

She got up and went to the gas-stove to make more coffee and new courage came to her. "We know why she doesn't want Mr. Armitage to see again!" she was thinking: the frightening Mrs. Johnson was really weak. "Housekeeper and secretary to a rich man, sitting very pretty up there, the best of everything. Plenty of money, staff, cook, gardener, chauffeur, Rolls-Royce—if he was cured where would her job be? Oh, she looks full of herself now, but she is afraid. I expect she's got round him to leave her a bit."

The coffee began to bubble up in the pot and that urgent noise put excitement into her and her old skin blushed.

"Up there with a man alone. As I said to Dad, a woman can tell! Where would she get another man with that spot spreading all over. She's artful. She's picked the right one." She was telling the tale to herself.

The coffee boiled over and hissed on the stove and a sudden, forgotten jealousy hissed up in Mrs. Smith's uncertain mind. She took the pot to the table and poured out a boiling hot cup and as the steam clouded up from it, screening her daring stare at the figure of Mrs. Johnson, Mrs. Smith wanted to say: "Lying there stark naked by that swimming-pool right in the face of my husband. What was he doing up there anyway?"

She could not say it. There was not much pleasure in Mrs. Smith's life; jealousy was the only one that enlivened her years with Mr. Smith. She had flown at him when he came home and had told her that God had guided him, that prayer always uncovered evil and brought it to the surface; it had revealed to him that the Devil had put his mark on Mrs. Johnson, and that he wouldn't be surprised if that was what was holding up the healing of Mr. Armitage.

"What were you doing," she screamed at him, "looking at a woman?"

The steam cleared and Mrs. Smith's nervousness returned as she saw that composed face. She was frightened now of her own imagination and of her husband's. She knew him. He was always up to something.

"Don't you dare say anything to Mr. Armitage about this," she had shouted at him.

But now she fell back on admiring Mrs. Johnson again.

"Settled for life," she sighed. "She's young. She is only fighting for her own. She's a woman."

And Mrs. Smith's pride was stirred. Her courage was fitful and weakened by what she had lived through. She had heard Mrs. Johnson was divorced and it gave Mrs. Smith strength as a woman who had "stuck to her husband". She had not gone round taking up with men as she guessed Mrs. Johnson might have done. She was a respectable married woman.

Her voice trembled at first but became stronger.

"Dad wanted to be a doctor when he was a boy," Mrs. Smith was saying, "but there wasn't the money so he worked in a chemist's, but it was always Church on Sundays. I wasn't much of a one for Church myself. But you must have capital and being just behind the counter doesn't lead anywhere. Of course I tried to egg him on to get his diploma and he got the papers—but I used to watch him. He'd start his studying and then he'd get impatient. He's a very impatient man and he'd say 'Amy, I'll try the Ministry'—he's got a good voice—'Church people have money'."

"And did he?"

"No, he always wanted to, but he couldn't seem to settle to a Church—I mean a religion. I'll say this for him he's a fighter. Nixon, his first guv'nor, thought the world of him: quick with the sales. Nixon's Cough Mixture—well, he didn't invent it, but he changed the bottles and the labels, made it look—fashionable, dear—you know? A lot of Wesleyans took it."

Mrs. Smith spread her hands over her face and laughed through her fingers.

"When Nixon died someone in the Church put up some money, a very religious, good man. One day Dad said to me—I always remember it—'It's not medicine. It's faith does it.' He's got faith, Faith is—well, Faith."

"In himself?" suggested Mrs. Johnson.

"That's it! That's it!" cried Mrs. Smith with excitement. Then she quietened and dabbed a tear from her cheek. "I begged him not to come down here. But this Mrs. Rogers, the lady who owns the house, she's deaf and on her own, he knew her. She believes in him. She calls him Daniel. He's treating her for deafness, she can't hear a word, so we brought our things down after we closed up in Ealing, that's why it's so crowded, two of everything, I have to laugh."

"So you don't own the house?"

"Oh no, dear—oh no," Mrs. Smith said, frightened of the idea. "He wants something bigger. He wants space for his work."

Mrs. Smith hesitated and looked at the wall through which the sound of Mr. Smith's voice was coming. And then, fearing she had been disloyal, she said: "She's much better. She's very funny. She came down yesterday calling him. 'Daniel, Daniel. I hear the cuckoo'. Of course I didn't say anything: it was the man calling out 'Coal'. But she is better. She wouldn't have heard him at all when we came here."

They were both silent.

"You can't live your life from A to Z," Mrs. Smith said, waking up. "We all make mistakes. We've been married for forty-two years. I expect you have your troubles too, even in that lovely place."

After the hour Mr. Smith came into the kitchen to get her.

"What a chatter!" he said to her. "I never heard such a tittle-tattle in my life."

"Yes, we had a fine chat, didn't we?"

"Oh yes," said Mrs. Smith boldly.

"How is it going on?" said Mrs. Johnson.

"Now, now," Mr. Smith corrected her. "These cases seemingly take time. You have to get to the bottom of it. We don't intend to, but we keep people back by the thoughts we hold over them."

And then, in direct attack on her. "I don't want you to hold no wrong thoughts over me. You have no power over Divine Love."

And he turned to his wife to silence her.

"And how would I do that?" said Mrs. Johnson.

"Cast the mote out of thine own eye," said Smith. "Heal yourself. We all have to." He smiled broadly at her.

"I don't know what all this talk about Divine Love is," said Mrs. Johnson. "But I love Mr. Armitage as he is."

Smith did not answer.

Armitage had found his way to the door of the kitchen. He listened and said: "Good-bye, Mrs. Smith."

And to Mr. Smith: "Send me your bill. I'm having the footpath closed."

They drove away.

"I love Mr. Armitage as he is". The words had been forced out of her by the detestable man. She hated that she had said to him what she could not say to Armitage. They surprised her. She hoped Armitage had not heard them.

He was silent in the car. He did not answer any of her questions.

"I'm having that path closed," he repeated.

"I know!" she thought. "Smith has said something about me. Surely not about 'it'!"

When they got out of the car at the house he said to the chauffeur: "Did you see Mr. Smith when he came up here three weeks ago? It was a Thursday. Were you down at the pool?"

"It's my afternoon off, sir."

"I know that. I asked whether you were anywhere near the pool. Or in the garden?"

"No, sir."

"Oh God," Mrs. Johnson groaned. "Now he's turned on Jim."

"Jim went off on his motor-bike. I saw him," said Mrs. Johnson. They went into the house.

"You don't know who you can trust," Armitage said and went across to the stairs and started up. But instead of putting his hand to the rail which was on the right, he put it out to the left and not finding it, stood bewildered. Mrs. Johnson went to that side of him and nudged him in the right direction.

When he came down to lunch he sat in silence before the cutlets on his plate.

"After all these years! I know the rail is on the right and I put out my left hand."

"You just forgot," she said. "Why don't you try forgetting a few more things?"

She was cross about the questioning of the chauffeur.

"Say, one thing a day," she said.

He listened and this was one of those days when he cruelly paused a long time before replying. A minute went by and she started to eat.

"Like this?" he said, and he deliberately knocked his glass of water over. The water spread over the cloth towards her plate.

"What's this silly temper?" she said and lifting her plate away, she lifted the cloth and started mopping with her table napkin and picked up the glass.

"I'm fed up with you blind people," she said angrily. "All jealousy and malice, just childish. You're so clever, aren't you? What happened? Didn't that good Mr. Smith do the magic trick? I don't wonder your wife walked out on you. Pity the poor blind! What about other people? I've had enough. You have an easy life; you sail down in your Rolls and think you can buy God from Mr. Smith just because—I don't know why—but if he's a fraud you're a fraud." Suddenly the wronged inhabitant inside her started to shout: "I'll tell you something about that Peeping Jesus: he saw the lot. Oh yes, I hadn't a stitch on. The lot!" she was shouting. And then she started to unzip her dress and pull it down over her shoulder and drag her arm out of it. "You can't see it, you silly fool. The whole bloody Hebrides, the whole plate of liver."

And she went to his place, got him by the shoulder and rubbed her stained shoulder and breast against his face.

"Do you want to see more?" she shouted. "It made my husband sick. That's what you've been sleeping with. And," she got away as he tried to grip her and laughed; "you didn't know! *He* did."

She sat down and cried hysterically with her head and arms on the table.

Armitage stumbled in the direction of her crying and put his hand on her bare shoulder.

"Don't touch me! I hate your hands."

And she got up, dodged round him to the door and ran out sobbing: slower than she was, he was too late to hear her steps. He found his way back to the serving hatch and called to the cook.

"Go up to Mrs. Johnson. She's in her room. She's ill," he said.

He stood in the hall waiting; the cook came downstairs and went into the sitting-room.

"She's not there. She must have gone into the garden." And then she said at the window: "She's down by the pool."

"Go and talk to her," he said.

The cook went out of the garden door and on to the terrace. She was a thin round-shouldered woman. She saw Mrs. Johnson move back to the near side of the pool; she seemed to be staring at something in the water. Then the cook stopped and came shouting back to the house.

"She's fallen in. With all her clothes on. She can't swim. I know she can't swim."

And then the cook called out "Jim. Jim," and ran down the lawns.

Armitage stood helpless.

"Where's the door?" he called. There was no one there.

Armitage made an effort to recover his system, but it was lost. He found himself blocked by a chair, but he had forgotten which chair. He waited to sense the movement of air in order to detect where the door was, but a window was half open and he found himself against glass. He made his way feeling along the wall, but he was travelling away from the door. He stood still again and smelling a kitchen smell he made his way back across the centre of the long room and at last found the first door and then the door to the garden. He stepped out, but he was exhausted and his will had gone. He could only stand in the breeze, the disorderly scent of the flowers and the grass mocking him. A jeering bird flew up. He heard the gardener's dog barking below and a voice, the gardener's voice, shouting "Quiet!" Then he heard voices coming slowly nearer up the lawn.

"Helen," called Armitage, but they pushed past him. He felt her wet dress brush his hand and her foot struck his leg; the gardener was carrying her.

"Marge," Armitage heard her voice as she choked and was sick.

"Upstairs. I'll get her clothes off," said the cook.

"No," said Armitage.

"Be quiet," said the cook.

"In my room," said Armitage.

"What an idea!" said the cook. "Stay where you are. Mind you don't slip on all this wet."

He stood, left behind in the hall, listening, helpless. Only when the doctor came did he go up.

She was sitting up in bed and Armitage held her hand.

"I'm sorry," she said. "You'd better fill that pool up. It hasn't brought you any luck."

Armitage and Mrs. Johnson are in Italy now; for how long it is hard to say. They themselves don't know. Some people call her Mrs. Armitage, some call her Mrs. Johnson; this uncertainty pleases her. She has always had a secret and she is too old, she says, to give up the habit now. It still pleases Armitage to baffle people. It is impossible for her to deny that she loves Armitage, because he heard what she said to Smith; she has had to give in about that. And she does love him because his system has broken down completely in Italy.

"You are my eyes," he says. "Everything sounds different here."

"I like a bit of noise," she says.

Pictures in churches and galleries he is mad about and he likes listening to her descriptions of them and often laughs at some of her remarks, and she is beginning, she says, to get "a kick out of the classical stuff" herself.

There was an awkward moment before they set off for Italy when he made her write out a cheque for Smith and she tried to stop him.

"No," he said. "He got it out of you. I owe you to him."

She was fighting the humiliating suspicion that in his nasty prying way Smith had told Armitage about her before *she* had told him. But Armitage said, "I knew all the time. From the beginning. I knew everything about you."

She still does not know whether to believe him or not. When she does believe, she is more awed than shamed; when she does not believe she feels carelessly happy. He depends on her entirely here. One afternoon, standing at the window of their room and looking at the people walking in the lemonish light across the square, she suddenly said: "I love you. I feel gaudy!" She notices that the only thing he doesn't like is to hear a man talk to her.

FOUR

The Fall

IT was the evening of the Annual Dinner. More than two hundred accountants were at that hour changing into evening clothes, in the flats, villas and hotel rooms of a large, wet, Midland city. At the Royal was Charles Peacock, slender in his shirt, balancing on one leg and gazing with frowns of affection in the wardrobe mirror at the other leg as he pulled his trouser on; and then with a smile of farewell as the second went in. Buttoned up, relieved of nakedness, he visited other mirrors—the one at the dressing table, the two in the bathroom, assembling the scattered aspects of the unsettled being called Peacock "doing"—as he was apt to say—"no so badly" in this city which smelled of coal and where thirty-eight years ago he had been born. When he left his room there were mirrors in the hotel lift and down below in the foyer and outside in the street. Certain shop windows were favourable and assuring. The love affair was taken up again at the Assembly Rooms by the mirrors in the tiled corridor leading towards the bullocky noise of two hundred-odd chartered accountants in black ties, taking their drinks under the chandeliers that seemed to weep above their heads.

Crowds or occasions frightened Peacock. They engaged him, at first sight, in the fundamental battle of his life: the struggle against nakedness, the panic of grabbing for clothes and becoming someone. An acquaintance in a Scottish firm was standing near the door of the packed room as Peacock went in.

"Hullo, laddie," Peacock said, fitting himself out with a Scottish accent, as he went into the crowded, chocolate coloured buffet.

"What's to do?" he said, passing on to a Yorkshireman.

"Are you well now?" he said, in his Irish voice. And, gaining confidence, "Whatcha cock!" to a man up from London, until he was shaking hands in the crowd with the President himself, who was leaning on a stick and had his foot in plaster.

"I hope this is not serious, sir," said Peacock in his best southern English, nodding at the foot.

"Bloody serious," said the President sticking out his peppery beard. "I caught my foot in a grating. Some damn fools here think I've got gout."

No one who saw Peacock in his office, in Board Rooms, on committees, at meetings, knew the exhausting number of rough sketches that had to be made before the naked Peacock could become Peacock dressed for his part. Now, having spoken to several human beings, the fragments called Peacock closed up. And he had one more trick up his sleeve if he panicked again: he could drop into music hall Negro.

Peacock got a drink at the buffet table and pushed his way to a solitary island of carpet two feet square, in the guffawing corral. He was looking at the back of the President's neck. Almost at once the President, on the crest of a successful joke he had told, turned round with appetite.

"Hah!" he shouted. "Hah! Here's friend Peacock again." "Why 'again'?" thought Peacock.

The President looked Peacock over.

"I saw your brother this afternoon," shouted the President. The President's injured foot could be said to have made his voice sound like a hilarious smash. Peacock's drink jumped and splashed his hand. The President winked at his friends.

"Hah!" said the President. "That gave our friend Peacock a scare!"

"At the Odeon," explained a kinder man.

"Is Shelmerdine Peacock your brother? The actor?" another said, astonished, looking at Peacock from head to foot.

"Shelmerdine Peacock was born and bred in this city," said the President fervently.

"I saw him in *Waste*," someone said. And others recalled him in *The Gun Runner and Doctor Zut*.

Four or five men stood gazing at Peacock with admiration, waiting for him to speak.

"Where is he now?" said the President, stepping forward, beard first. "In Hollywood? Have you seen him lately?"

They all moved forward to hear about the famous man.

Peacock looked to the right—he wanted to do this properly—but there was no mirror in that direction; he looked to the left, but there was no mirror there. He lowered his head gravely and then looked up shaking his head sorrowfully. He brought out the old reliable Negro voice:

"The last time I saw l'il ole brudder Shel," he said, "he was being thrown out of the Orchid Room. He was calling the waiters goatherds."

Peacock looked up at them all and stood, collected, assembled, whole at last, among their shouts of laughter. One man who did not laugh and who asked what the Orchid Room was, was put in his place. And in a moment, a voice bawled from the door, "Gentlemen. Dinner is served". The crowd moved through two anterooms into the Great Hall where, from their portraits on the wall, Mayors, Presidents and Justices looked down with the complacent rosiness of those who have dined and died. It was gratifying to Peacock that the President rested his arm on his shoulder for a few steps as they went into the hall.

Shel often cropped up in Peacock's life, especially in clubs and at dinners. It was pleasing. There was always praise; there were always questions. He had seen the posters about Shel's film during the week on his way to his office. They pleased, but they also troubled. Peacock stood at his place at table in the Great Hall and paused to look around, in case there was one more glance of vicarious fame to be collected. He was enjoying one of those pauses of self-possession in which, for a few seconds, he could feel the sensations Shel must feel when he stepped before the curtain to receive the applause of some great audience in London or New York. Then Peacock sat down. More than two hundred soup spoons scraped.

"Sherry, sir?" said the waiter.

Peacock sipped.

He meant no harm to Shel, of course. But in a city like this, with Shel appearing in a big picture, with his name fifteen feet long on the hoardings, talked about by girls in offices, the universal instinct of family disparagement was naturally tickled into life. The President might laugh and the crowd admire, but it was not always agreeable for the family to have Shel roaming loose—and often very loose—in the world. One had to assert the modesty, the anonymity of the ordinary assiduous Peacocks. One way of doing this was to add a touch or two to famous scandals: to enlarge the drunken scrimmages and add to the divorces and the breaches of contract, increase the over-doses taken by flighty girls. One was entitled to a little rake off—an accountant's charges—from the fame that so often annoyed. One was entitled, above all, because one loved Shel.

"Hock, sir?" said the waiter.

Peacock drank. Yes, he loved Shel. Peacock put down his glass and the man opposite to him spoke across the table, a man with an amused mouth, who turned his sallow face sideways so that one had the impression of being inquired into under a loose lock of black hair by one sharp, serious eye only.

"An actor's life is a struggle," the man said. Peacock recognized him: it was the man who had not laughed at his story and who had asked what the Orchid Room was, in a voice that had a sad and puncturing feeling for information sought for its own sake.

Peacock knew this kind of admirer of Shel's and feared him. They were not content to admire, they wanted to advance into intimacy, and collect facts on behalf of some general view of life's mysteriousness. As an accountant Peacock rejected mystery.

"I don't think l'il ole brudder Shel has struggled much," said Peacock, wagging his head from side to side carelessly.

"I mean he has to dedicate himself," said the man.

Peacock looked back mistrustfully.

"I remember some interview he gave about his schooldays—in this city," said the man. "It interested me. I do the books for the Hippodrome."

Peacock stopped wagging his head from side to side. He was alert. What Shel had said about his early life had been damned tactless.

"Shel had a good time," said Peacock sharply. "He always got his own way."

Peacock put on his face of stone. He dared the man to say out loud, in that company, three simple English words. He dared him. The man smiled and did not say them.

"Volnay, sir?" said the waiter as the pheasant was brought. Peacock drank.

Fried Fish Shop, Peacock said to himself as he drank. Those were the words. Shel could have kept his mouth shut about that. I'm not a snob, but why mention it? Why, after they were all doing well, bring ridicule upon the family? Why not say, simply, "Shop". Why not say, if he had to, "Fishmonger?" Why mention "Frying?" Why add "*Bankrupt* Fried Fish Shop?"

It was swinish, disloyal, ungrateful. Bankrupt—all right; but some of that money (Peacock said, hectoring the pheasant on his plate), paid for Shel's years at the Dramatic School. It was unforgiveable.

Peacock looked across at the man opposite, but the man had turned to talk to a neighbour. Peacock finished his glass and chatted with the man sitting to his right, but he felt like telling the whole table a few facts about dedication.

Dedication—he would have said. Let us take a look at the figures. An example of Shel's dedication in those Fried Fish Shop days he is so fond of remembering to make fools of us. Saturday afternoon. Father asleep in the back room. Shel says "Come down the High Street with me, Tom. I want to get a record." Classical, of course. Usual swindle. If we get into the shop he won't have the money and will try and borrow from me. "No," I say. "I haven't got any money." "Well, let's get out of this stink of lard and fish." He wears me down. He wore us all down, the whole family. He would be sixteen, two years older than me. And so we go out and at once I know there is going to be trouble. "I saw the Devil in Cramers," he says. We go down the High Street to Cramers, it's a music shop, and he goes up to the girl to ask if they sell bicycle pumps or rubber heels. When the girl says "No", he makes a terrible face at her and shouts out "Bah". At Hooks, the stationers, he stands at the door, and calls to the girl at the cash desk: "You've got the Devil in here. I've reported it," and slams the door. We go on to Bonds, the grocers, and he pretends to be sick when he sees the bacon. Goes out. "Rehearsing", he says. The Bonds are friends of Father's. There is a row. Shel swears he was never anywhere near the place and goes back the following Saturday and falls flat on the floor in front of the Bond daughter groaning, "I've been poisoned. I'm dying. Water! Water!" Falls flat on his back . . .

"Caught his foot in a grating, he told me, and fell," the man opposite was saying. "Isn't that what he told you, Peacock?"

Peacock's imaginary speech came suddenly to an end. The man was smiling as if he had heard every word.

"Who?" said Peacock.

"The President," said the man. "My friend, Mr. McAlister is asking me what happened to the President. Did he fall in the street?"

Peacock collected himself quickly and to hide his nakedness became Scottish.

"Ay, mon," he nodded across the table. "A wee bit of a tumble in the street."

Peacock took up his glass and drank.

"He's a heavy man to fall," said the man called McAlister.

"He carries a lot of weight," said his neighbour. Peacock eyed him. The impression was growing that this man knew too much, too quietly. It struck him that the man was one of those who ask what they know already, a deeply unbelieving man. They have to be crushed.

"Weight makes no difference," said Peacock firmly.

"It's weight and distance," said the Scotsman. "Look at children."

Peacock felt a smile coming over his body from the feet upwards.

"Weight and distance make no difference," Peacock repeated.

"How can you say that?"

An enormous voice, hanging brutally on the air like a sergeant's, suddenly shouted in the hall. It was odd to see the men in the portraits on the wall still sitting down after the voice sounded. It was the voice of the toastmaster.

"Gen—tle—men," it shouted. "I ask you. To rise to. The Toast of Her. Maj—es—ty. The Queen."

Two hundred or more accountants pushed back their chairs and stood up.

"The Queen," they growled. And one or two, Peacock among them, fervently added, "God bless her," and drained his glass.

Two hundred or more accountants sat down. It was the moment Peacock loved. And he loved the Queen.

"Port or brandy, sir?" the waiter asked.

"Brandy," said Peacock.

"You were saying that weight and distance make no difference. How do you make that out?" the sidelong man opposite said in a sympathetic and curious voice that came softly and lazily out.

Peacock felt the brandy burn. The question floated by, answerable if seized as it went and yet, suddenly, unanswerable for the moment. Peacock stared at the question keenly as if it were a fly that he was waiting to swat when it came round again. Ah, there it came. Now! But no, it had gone by once more. It was answerable. He knew the answer. Peacock smiled loosely biding his time. He felt the flame of authority, of absolute knowledge burn in him.

There was a hammering at the President's table, there was hand-clapping. The President was on his feet and his beard had begun to move up and down.

"I'll tell you later," said Peacock curtly across the table. The interest went out of the man's eye.

"Once more," (the President's beard was saying and it seemed sometimes that he had two beards), "Honour," said one beard. "Privilege," said the other. "Old friends," said both beards together. "Speeches . . . brief . . . reminded of story . . . shortest marriage service in the world . . . Tennessee . . ."

"Hah! Hah! Hah!" shouted a pack of wolves, hyenas, hounds in dinner jackets.

Peacock looked across at the unbeliever who sat opposite. The interest in weight and distance had died away in his face.

"Englishman . . . Irishman . . . Scotsman . . . train . . . Englishman said . . . Scotsman said . . . Och, says Paddy . . ."

"Hah! Hah! Hah!" from the pack.

Over the carnations in the silver plated vases on the table, over the heads of the diners, the cigar smoke was rising sweetly and the first level indigo shafts of it were tipping across the middle air and turning the portraits of the Past Masters into day dreams. Peacock gazed at it. Then a bell rang in his ear, so loudly that he looked shyly to see if anyone else had heard it. The voice of Shel was on some line of his memory, a voice richer, more insinuating than the toastmaster's or the President's, a voice utterly flooring.

"Abel?" Shel was saying. "Is that you Abel? This is Cain speaking. How's the smoke? Is it still going up straight to heaven? Not blowing about all over the place . . ."

The man opposite caught Peacock's eye for a second, as if he too had heard the voice and then turned his head away. And, just at the very moment, when once more Peacock could have answered that question about the effect of weight and distance, the man opposite stood up, all the accountants stood up. Peacock was the last. There was another toast to drink. And immediately there was more hammering and another speaker. Peacock's opportunity was lost. The man who sat opposite had moved his chair back from the table and was sitting sideways to it listening, his interest in Peacock gone for good.

Peacock became lonely. Sulkily he played with matchsticks and arranged them in patterns on the tablecloth. There was a point at Annual Dinners when he always did this. It was at that point when

one saw the function had become fixed by a flash photograph in
the gloss of celebration and when everyone looked sickly and old.
Eyes became hollow, temples sank, teeth loosened. Shortly the
diners would be carried out in coffins. One waited restlessly for
the thing to be over. Ten years of life went by and then, it seemed,
there were no more speeches. There was some business talk in
groups; then twos and threes left the table. Others filed off into a
large chamber next door. Peacock's neighbours got up. He, who
feared occasions, feared even more their dissolution. It was like
that frightening ten minutes in a theatre when the audience slowly
moves out, leaving a hollow stage and row after row, always
increasing, of empty seats behind them. In a panic Peacock got up.
He was losing all acquaintance. He had even let the man opposite
slip away, for that man was walking down the hall with some
friends. Peacock hurried down his side of the long table to meet
them at the bottom and when he got there he turned and barred
their way.

"What we were talking about," he said. "It's an art. Simply a
matter of letting the breath go, relaxing the muscles. Any actor
can do it. It's the first thing they learn."

"I'm out of my depth," said the Scotsman.

"Falling," said Peacock. "The stage fall." He looked at them with
dignity, then he let the expression die on his face. He fell quietly
full length to the floor. Before they could speak he was up on his
feet.

"My brother weighs two hundred and twenty pounds," he said
with condescension to the man opposite. "The ordinary person falls
and breaks an arm or a foot, because he doesn't know. It's an art."

His eyes conveyed that if the Peacocks had kept a fried fish shop
years ago, they had an art.

"Simple," said Peacock.

And down he went, thump, on the carpet again and lying at
their feet he said:

"Painless. Nothing broken. Not a bruise. I said 'an art'. Really
one might call it a science. Do you see how I'm lying?"

"What's happened to Peacock?" said two or three men joining
the group.

"He's showing us the stage fall."

"Nothing," said Peacock, getting up and brushing his coat sleeve
and smoothing back his hair. "It is just a stage trick."

"I wouldn't do it," said a large man, patting his stomach.

"I've just been telling them—weight is nothing. Look." Peacock fell down and got up at once.

"You turn. You crumple. You can go flat on your back. I mean, that is what it looks like," he said.

And Peacock fell.

"Shel and I used to practise it in the bedroom. Father thought the ceiling was coming down," he said.

"Good God, has Peacock passed out?" A group standing by the fireplace in the hall called across. Peacock got up and brushing his jacket again walked up to them. The group he had left watched him. There was a thump.

"He's done it again," the man opposite said.

"Once more. There he goes. Look, he's going to show the President. He's going after him. No, he's missed him. The old boy has slipped out of the door."

Peacock was staring with annoyance at the door. He looked at other groups of two and threes.

"Who was the casualty over there?" someone said to him as he walked past.

Peacock went over to them and explained.

"Like judo," said a man.

"No!" said Peacock indignantly, even grandly. And in Shel's manner. Anyone who had seen Shelmerdine Peacock affronted knew what he looked like. That large white face trod on you. "Nothing to do with judo. This is the theatre . . ."

"Shelmerdine Peacock's brother," a man whispered to a friend.

"Is that so?"

"It's in the blood," someone said.

To the man who had said "Judo", Peacock said, "No throwing, no wrestling, no somersaulting or fancy tricks. That is not theatre. Just . . . simply . . ." said Peacock. And crumpling, as Shel might have done in *Macbeth* or *Hamlet*, or like some gangster shot in the stomach, Peacock once more let his body go down with the cynicism of the skilful corpse. This time he did not get up at once. He looked up at their knees, their waists, at their goggling faces, saw under their double chins and under their hairy eyebrows. He grinned at their absurdity. He saw that he held them. They were obliged to look at him. Shel must always have had this sensation of hundreds of astonished eyes watching him lie, waiting for him to move. Their gaze would never leave him. Peacock never felt less at a loss, never felt more completely himself. Even the air was better at carpet level; it was certainly cooler and he was glad of that. Then he saw two pairs of feet advancing from another group. He saw two faces peep over the shoulders of the others, and heard one of them say:

"It's Peacock—still at it."

He saw the two pairs of boots and trousers go off. Peacock got to his feet at once and resentfully stared after them. He knew something, as they went, that Shel must have known: the desperation, the contempt for the audience that is thinning out. He was still brushing his sleeve and trousers legs when he saw everyone moving away out of the hall. Peacock moved after them into the chamber.

A voice spoke behind him. It was the quiet, intimate voice of the man with the loose lock of black hair who had sat opposite to him.

"You need a drink," the man said.

They were standing in the chamber where the buffet table was. The man had gone into the chamber and, clearly, he had waited for Peacock. A question was going round as fast as a catherine wheel in Peacock's head and there was no need to ask it: it must be so blindingly obvious. He looked for someone to put it to, on the quiet, but there were only three men at the buffet table with their backs turned to him. Why (the question ran) at the end of a bloody good dinner is one always left with some awful drunk, a man you've never liked—an unbeliever?

Peacock mopped his face. The unbeliever was having a short disgusting laugh with the men at the bar and now was coming back with a glass of whisky.

"Sit down. You must be tired," said the unbeliever.

They sat down. The man spoke of the dinner and the speeches. Peacock did not listen. He had just noticed a door leading into a small ante-room and he was wondering how he could get into it.

"There was one thing I don't quite get," the man said. "Perhaps it was the quickness of the hand deceiving the eye. I should say feet. What I mean is—do you first take a step, I mean like in dancing: I mean is the art of falling really a paradox—I mean the art of keeping your balance all the time?"

The word "paradox" sounded offensive to Peacock.

The man looked too damn clever, in Peacock's opinion and didn't sit still. Wearily Peacock got up.

"Hold my drink," he said. "You are standing like this, or facing sideways—on a level floor, of course. On a slope like this . . ."

The man nodded.

"I mean—well, now, watch carefully. Are you watching?"

"Yes," said the man.

"Look at my feet," said Peacock.

"No," said the man, hastily, putting out a free hand and catching Peacock by the arm. "I see what you mean. I was just interested in the theory."

Peacock halted. He was offended. He shook the man's arm off.

"Nothing theoretical about it," he said, and shaking his sleeves added, "No paradox."

"No," said the man standing up and grabbing Peacock so that he could not fall. "I've got the idea." He looked at his watch. "Which way are you going? Can I give you a lift?"

Peacock was greatly offended. To be turned down! He nodded to the door of the ante-room: "Thanks," he said. "The President's waiting for me."

"The President's gone," said the man. "Oh well, good night." And he went away. Peacock watched him go. Even the men at the bar had gone. He was alone.

"But thanks," he called after him. "Thanks."

Cautiously Peacock sketched a course into the ante-room. It was a small, high room, quite empty and yet (one would have said), packed with voices, chattering, laughing and mixed with music along the panelled walls, but chiefly coming from behind the heavy green velvet curtains that were drawn across the window at one end. There were no mirrors, but Peacock had no need of them. The effect was ornate—gilded pillars at the corners, a small chandelier rising and falling gracefully from a carven ceiling. On the wall hung what, at first sight, seemed to be two large oil paintings of Queens of England but, on going closer, Peacock saw there was only one oil painting—of Queen Victoria. Peacock considered it. The opportunity was enormous. Loyally, his face went blank. He swayed, loyally fell, and loyally got to his feet. The Queen might or might not have clapped her little hands. So encouraged, he fell again and got up. She was still sitting there.

Shel, said Peacock aloud to the Queen, has often acted before royalty. He's in Hollywood now, having left me to settle all his tax affairs. Hundreds of documents. All lies, of course. And there is this case for alimony going on. He's had four wives, he said to Queen Victoria. That's the side of theatre life I couldn't stand, even when we were boys. I could see it coming. But—watch me, he said.

And delightfully he crumpled, the perfect backwards spin. Leaning up on his elbow from where he was lying he waited for her to speak.

She did not speak, but two or three other queens joined her, all crowding and gossiping together, as Peacock got up. The Royal Box! It was full. Cars hooting outside the window behind the velvet curtains had the effect of an orchestra and then, inevitably, those heavy green curtains were drawn up. A dark, packed and restless auditorium opened itself to him. There was dense applause.

Peacock stepped forward in awe and wholeness. Not to fall, not to fall, this time, he murmured. To bow. One must bow and bow and bow and not fall, to the applause. He set out. It was a strangely long up-hill journey towards the footlights and not until he got there did it occur to him that he did not know how to bow. Shel had never taught him. Indeed, at the first attempt the floor came up and hit him in the face.

FIVE

The Skeleton

Awful things happen to one every day: they come without warning and—this is the trouble, for who knows?—the next one may be the Great Awful Thing. Whatever that is.

At half past seven, just as the new day came aching into the London sky, the waiter-valet went up in the old-fashioned lift of the service flats with a tray of tea to Mr. Clark's flat on the top floor. He let himself in and walked down the long, tiled hallway, through part of Mr. Clark's picture collection, into the large sitting-room and putting the tray down on the desk, drew back the curtains and looked down on the roofs. Arrows of fine snow had shot along the slate, a short sight of the Thames between the buildings was as black as iron, the trees stuck out their branches like sticks of charcoal and a cutting wind was rumbling and occasionally squealing against the large windows. The man wiped his nose and then went off to switch on one bar of the electric fire—he was forbidden to put on two—and moved the tray to a table by the fire. He had often been scolded for putting the tray upon Clark's valuable Chippendale desk, and he looked around to see if anything else was out of place in this gentlemanly room where every flash of polish or glass was as unnerving to him as the flash of old George Clark's glasses.

With its fine mahogany, its glazed bookcases which contained a crack regiment of books on art in dress uniform, its Persian rugs, its bronzes, figurines and silken-seated chairs and deep sofa that appeared never to have been sat on, and on the walls some twenty-five oil-paintings, the room had the air of a private museum. The valet respected the glass. He had often sat for a while at Mr. Clark's desk gossiping with one of the maids while he saw to it that she did not touch the bronze and the Chinese figures—"He won't allow anyone to touch them. They're worth hundreds—thousands," —and making guesses at what the lot would fetch when the old man died. He made these guesses about the property of all the rich old people who lived in the flats.

The girls, an ignorant lot, Irish mainly these days, gaped at the pictures.

"He's left them all to the nation," the valet would say importantly. He could not disguise his feeling that the poor old nation had a lot to put up with from the rich. He could always get in a sexy word to the maids when they looked at the cylindrical nude with a guitar lying across her canister-like knees. But the other pictures of vegetation—huge fruits, enormous flowers that looked tropical with gross veins and pores on stalk and leaves—looked humanly physical and made him feel sick. The flowers had large evil sucking mouths; there were veined intestinal marrows; there was a cauliflower like a gigantic brain that seemed to swell as you looked at it. Nature, to this painter, was a collection of clinical bodies and looked, as Seymour said, "Nood." The only living creature represented—apart from the cylindrical lady—was a fish, but it, too, was over-sized and gorged. Its scales, minutely enumerated, gave Seymour "the pip". It was hung over the central bookcase.

"It doesn't go with the furniture," Seymour had often said. The comforting thing to him was that, at any rate, the collection could not move and get at him. Like the books, the pictures, too, were cased behind glass.

"All by the same man. Come into the bedroom. Come on. And don't touch anything there because he'll notice. He sees everything," he'd say.

In the bedroom he would show the girls the small oil-painting of the head of a young man with almost white hair standing on end, and large blue eyes.

"That's the bloke," the valet would say. "He did it himself. Self-portrait. John Flitestone—see, the name's at the bottom—cut his throat. You watch—his eyes follow you," he would say, steering the girl. "He used to come here with the old man."

"Oh," the girls were apt to gasp.

"Stop it, Mr. Seymour," they added, taken off their guard.

"Years ago," Seymour said, looking pious after the pinch he'd given them.

The valet left the room and went down the passage to George Clark's bedroom. Carpet stopped at the door of the room. Inside the room the curtains were blowing, the two sparse rugs lifting in the draught on the polished floor and snow spitting on the table beside the bed. He caught the curtains and drew them back and tried to shut the heavy window. The room contained a cheap yellow wardrobe and chest of drawers which old George Clark had had since he was a boy. The sitting-room was luxurious but his bedroom was as bleak as a Victorian servant's. On a very narrow iron bedstead he lay stiff as a frozen monk and still as a corpse, so paper thin as to look bodiless, his wiry black hair, his wiry black moustache and his greenish face and cold red nose showing like a pug's over the sheet. It sneered in sleep.

"Seven-thirty, sir. Terrible morning," he said. There was no answer. "By God," the valet said after a pause, "the old man's dead." In death—if that was what it was—the face on the pillow looked as if it could bite. Then the old man gave a snuffle.

The old man opened a wicked eye.

"The old bastard," murmured the valet. Often the old boy had terrified and tricked him with his corpse-like look. It was Clark's opening victory in a day, indeed a life, devoted to victory. Then he woke up fully, frightened, reaching for his glasses, to see Seymour's blood-coloured face looking down at him.

"What?" George Clark said. And then the valet heard him groan. These groans were awful.

"Oh my God!" George Clark groaned, but spoke the words in a whisper.

"It's a terrible morning. Shall I put on the fire?"

"No." The old man sat up.

The valet sighed. He went and fetched a cup of tea.

"You'll need this," he put on his bullying voice. "Better drink it hot in here. You'd better have your lunch here today. Don't you go to the club. It's snowing, the wind's terrible."

George Clark got out of bed in his flannel pyjamas. He stepped barefooted to the window, studying the driving grey sky, the slant of snow and the drift of chimney smoke.

"Who closed the window?" he said.

"Oh dear," said the valet to himself, "now he's going to begin. The snow was coming in, Mr. Clark. You'll get pneumonia. Please, sir."

Clark was upright and tall. His small head jerked when he talked, on a long, wrinkled neck. His voice was naturally drawling but shortness of breath was in conflict with the drawl and the sounds that came out were jerky, military and cockerel-like. At eighty-two he looked about sixty, there was hardly any grey in his moustache, the bridge of his gold-framed glasses cut into his red nose. Seymour who was fifty was humped and lame and looked seventy. In a fight old George would win and he gave a sniff that showed he knew it. In fact, he got up every day to win; Seymour knew that and accepted it.

What reduced him to misery was that the old man would *explain* his victories. He was off on one now.

"No, I won't get pneumonia," old George snapped. "You see, Seymour, it's a north wind. The north wind doesn't touch me. There's no fat on me, I'm all bones. I'm a skeleton, there's nothing for it to bite on."

"No, sir," said Seymour wretchedly. Ten to one George Clark would now mention his family. He did.

"My father was thin, so was my grandfather, we're a thin family. My youngest sister—she's seventy-eight—she's all bones like me."

Oh God (Seymour used to moan to himself), I forgot—he's got sisters! Two of them! He moved to get out of the room, but the old man followed him closely, talking fast.

"One day last week I thought we were going to catch it, oh yes. Now we're going to get it, I said! Awful thing! That clean white light in the sky, stars every night, everything clear, everything sparkling. I saw it and said, Oh no! No, no. I don't like this, oh no."

He had now got Seymour in the doorway.

"You see—I know what *that* means."

"Yes, sir."

"East wind," said George victoriously.

"That's it, sir."

"Ah, then you've got to look out, Seymour. Oh yes. Awful business. That's what finishes old people. Awful thing." He drove Seymour forward into the sitting-room and went to this window, studying the sky and sniffed two or three times at it.

"We're all right, Seymour. You see, I was right. It's in the north. I shall have lunch at the club. Bring my cup in here. Why did you take it to the bedroom?"

It was a cold flat. George Clark took a cold bath, as he had done ever since his schooldays. Then he ate a piece of toast and drank a second cup of tea and looked eagerly to see what was annoying in the papers—some new annoyance to add to a lifetime's accumulation of annoyances. It was one of the calamities of old age that one's memory went and one forgot a quite considerable number of exasperations and awful things in which, contrary to general expectation, one had been startlingly right. This forgetting was bad—as if one were the Duke of Wellington and sometimes forgot one had won the Battle of Waterloo.

In fact, George sat in comfort in a flat packed with past rows, annoyances and awful things, half-forgotten. It was an enormous satisfaction that many of his pictures annoyed the few people who came to see him nowadays. The Flitestones annoyed violently. They had annoyed the nation to such an extent, in the person of a "nasty little man" called Gaiterswell, that the nation had refused them. (Seymour was wrong there.) George was very proud of this: his denunciation of Gaiterswell was one of the major victories of his life. George had been the first to buy Flitestones and even Flitestone himself, and had warned the vain and swollen-headed young man against Gaiterswell, years and years ago.

"Modish, Jack, he's merely modish. He'll drop you when it suits him."

At twelve o'clock George walked across the Park to one of his Clubs. He belonged to three. The Park was empty. He blew across it like a solitary, late leaf. The light snow was turning Whitehall black, and spat on his gold glasses; he arrived, a little breathless, but ready to deal with that bugbear of old men: protective sympathy.

"George! You ought not to be out on a day like this!" several said. One put his arm round his shoulder. They were a sneezing and coughing lot with slack affectionate faces, and friendly over-burdened bellies, talking of snowed-up roads, late trains and scrambles for taxis.

"You *walked* through this! Why didn't you make your chauffeur bring you?"

"No car."

"Or a cab?"

"Fares have gone up. I'm too mean."

"Or a bus?"

"Oh no, no, you see," said George glittering at them. "I don't know if I told you"—he had told them innumerable times—"when you're brought up by a rich brute of a father, as I was—oh yes, he was very rich—you get stingy. I'm very stingy. I must have told you about my father. Oh well, now, there's a story," he began eagerly. But the bar was crowded; slow to move, George Clark found his listener had been pushed away and had vanished. He stood suddenly isolated in his autobiography.

"Oh God," he groaned loudly, but in a manner so sepulchral and private, that people moved respectfully away. It was a groan that seemed to come up from the earth, up from his feet, a groan of loneliness that was raging and frightening to the men around him. He had one of those moments which, he had to admit, were much commoner than they used to be, when he felt dizzy, when he felt he was lost among unrecognizable faces, without names, alone, in the wrong club, at the wrong address even, with the tottering story of his life, a story which he was offering or, rather, throwing out as a life-line, for help. His hand shook as he finished his glass of sherry. The moment passed and, recovering and trembling, he aged as he left the bar and crossed the hall to the dining-room, saying aloud to himself, in his fighting drawl: "Now, now, now, we must be careful."

The side tables were already taken but there were gaps at the two long tables. George stood blinking at the battlefield. He had in the last years resigned from several clubs. Sometimes it was because of bridge, central heating, ventilation, smoking, about house committees, food and servants, usually over someone who, unknowingly, had become for a period uncommonly like the Arch Enemy, but who turned out to be no more than an understudy for the part. After a year or so George would rejoin the club. For him the dining-room was one more aspect of the general battlefield.

Where should he place his guns? Next to Doyle? No, he was "a Roman". George hated "Romans". He hated "Protestants" too. He was an atheist who never found anyone sufficiently atheistical. George was tired of telling Doyle how he had happened to be in Rome in '05 staying with one of the great families ("she was a cousin of the Queen's") and had, for a year, an unparalleled inside view of what was going on in the Vatican. "Oh yes, you see, a Jesuit, one of their relations, became a great friend and exposed the whole hocus-pocus to me. You see, I have often been in a position to know more of what is going on than most people. I was close to Haig in the war." There was Gregg, the painter; but it was intolerable to listen to Academicians; there was Foster who had been opposed to Munich and George could not stand that. There was Macdonald—but Scots climb. Look at Lang! There was Jefferies, such a bore about divorce reform: the bishops want it but daren't say so. "I told the Archbishop in this club that the moment you drag in God you lose your reason. My mother ought to have got a divorce. You should have seen his face. Oh no, he didn't like it. Not a bit."

George looked at the tops of heads and the table-loads of discarded enemies, casualties of his battles, with a grin. At last, glancing around him, he chose a seat beside a successful, smirking pink man of fifty whose name he had forgotten. "Pretty harmless," muttered George. "He thinks Goya a great painter when we all know he is just a good painter of the second rank. Ah, he's eating oysters." This stirred a memory. The man was talking to a deaf editor but on the other side there were empty chairs. It was against George's military sense to leave an exposed flank but the chance of attacking the club oysters was too good to miss.

"I see you've risked the oysters. I never eat oysters in this club," said George, sitting down. "Poisonous. Oh yes, yes—didn't I tell you? Oh you see, it was an awful thing, last year . . ."

"Now George," said the man. "You told me that story before."

"Did I? Nothing in that," sniffed George. "I always repeat myself, you see I make a point of telling my stories several times. I woke up in the night . . ."

"Please George," said the man more sternly. "I want to enjoy my lunch."

"Oh ah, ah, ah," said George sniffing away. "I'll watch your plate. I'll warn you if I see a bad one."

"Oh, really George!" said the young man.

"You're interrupting our conversation, George," the editor called across. "I was telling Trevor something very interesting about my trip to Russia."

"I doubt if it is interesting," said George in a loudish whisper to the other man. "Interesting! I never found a Whig interesting."

"Dear George is old. He talks too much," said the deaf editor speaking louder than he knew.

"Not a lot of rot," said George in a loud mutter.

"What's he say?" said the deaf editor.

"You see," George continued to interrupt. "I talk a lot because I live alone. I probably talk more than anyone in this club and I am more interesting than most people. You see, I've often been in a position to know more than most people here. I was in Rome in '05 . . ."

But George looked restlessly at the vacant chair beside him. "I hope," he said, suddenly nervous, "some awful bore is not going to sit here. You never know who, who—oh no, oh no, no . . ."

It happened as simply as that, when one was clean off one's guard. Not a single awful thing: but the Great Awful Thing. He saw a pair of small, polished, sunburned hands with soft black hair on them pull back the chair and then a monkeyish man of seventy with wretched eyes and an academic heaving up of the right shoulder, sat beside him.

"Good morning, George," uttering the name George as if it contained a lifetime's innuendo.

"Oh God," George said.

The man was the Arch Enemy and in a form he had never expected. Out of the future he should have come, a shape at a slowly opening door, pausing there, blocking it, so that one could not get out. Who he would be, what he would be, was unknown: he was hidden in next week, next year, as yet unborn.

But this man was known. He had sneaked in not from the future, but from the past. It was Gaiterswell.

"Just the man I want to speak to," said Gaiterswell, picking up the menu in hands that George could only think of as thieving.

"I didn't know you were a member," George choked out in words like lead shot.

"Just elected."

George gave a loud sniff.

"Monstrous," said George, but, holding on to manners, said it under his breath. He grasped his table napkin, ready to fly off and at once, resign. It was unbelievable that the Committee, knowing his feelings as they must do, had allowed this man in. Gaiterswell who had stolen Flitestone from him: who had turned down Flitestone; who had said in *The Times*—in a letter above all—that George's eccentric tastes had necessarily taught him nothing about the chemical composition of oil-paint; Gaiterswell of the scandalous official appointment!

George had forgotten these Waterloos; but now the roar of them woke up in his brain. The fusillades he had let off in committees were heard again. The letters to *The Times* were shot off once more. Gaiterswell had said there were too many "gentlemen" in the art world. It was a pity (he was known to have said), it was a pity that the Empire had gone and there were no more natives for them to pester. George had replied, around the clubs, that the "nasty little man" suffered glaringly from merit and the path of the meritorious was strewn with the bodies they had kicked down the ladder as they climbed.

After he had said things like this, George considered that Gaiterswell was dead. The body could no doubt be found still lying after twenty-five years, in that awful office of his with the fake Manet—of course it was a fake—on the wall.

"Just the man I want to speak to," Gaiterswell said to the menu. (You noticed he never looked you in the face.)

"Wants to speak to me. For no good reason," George murmured loudly to the man sitting on the other side of him.

"I bet you won't guess who came to see me the other day," Gaiterswell said. "Gloria Archer, Stokes that was. She's married to a Frenchman called Duprey. You remember her? What are you eating? The pie! Is it any good? She's got a lot of poor Jack Flitestone's letters. She's short of money. You wrote the *Memoir*, didn't you, George? Charming little book, charming. I told her to drop in on you. I said you'd be delighted to see her."

George was about to put a piece of pie into his mouth. He put his fork down. He was shaking. He was choking.

"Drop in!" he said, astounded. "Drop in?"

"Look here," he called out, pushing his chair from the table. "Oh, this is monstrous." And he called to one of the waiters who rushed past and ignored him. "Look here, I say, why do we have to have meat like this in this club . . . It's uneatable . . . I shall find the Secretary . . ."

And getting up, with his table napkin waving from his hand, he hurried to the end of the room, the light tossing in his glasses, and then after wild indecision, left the room.

"Where has George Clark gone," said an old gentleman who had been sitting opposite. "He never finishes a meal."

"It's his teeth", the deaf editor said.

George had made for the morning-room of the Club where he circled like a dog.

"What manners!" he said to the portraits of dead members on the wall. Happier than he, they were together, he was alone. He was older than most of them had been and, with a flick of ironic pride which never quite left him in any distress, he could not but notice that he was rather better connected and had more inside knowledge than most of them had had. He addressed them again: "Drop in! What manners! I shall resign."

The Arch Enemy had appeared in a fashion unpredictable: from the past—and now he saw—not as a male but as a female. Gloria Archer—as he had always said: "What a name!" It recalled (as he firmly pronounced it), the "Kinema", striking a blow for classical scholarship. Her portrait, if one could call it that, was in his sitting-room, cylindrical and naked. It had been there for over twenty-five years, with the other Flitestones and he had long ago stopped remembering her or even Flitestone himself as human beings he had known. They were not life; they were art—not even art now, but furniture of his self-esteem. He had long ago closed his mind to them as persons. They had become fossilizations of mere anecdote. Now that damn little shot-up official, Gaiterswell who had been polished off long ago, had brought first Gloria back to life, and the name of Gloria had brought Flitestone back. The seals of anecdote were broken; one of the deepest wounds of George's existence was open and raw again. A woman's work; it was Gloria who had shown how dangerous Flitestone was to him: it was Gloria who had shown him the chaos of his heart.

He left the morning-room, got his hat and coat, buttoned himself up to the neck, and walked out into the street where the snow was coming in larger shots. At once he felt something like a film of ice form between his shirt and his bony chest and he stepped back afraid.

"No, no," he said very loudly and passers-by raised their ducked heads thinking he was talking to them. But he was speaking to the wind: it had gone round to the east.

Seymour met him in the lift at the flat. He smelled of beer.

"You shouldn't have gone out, sir," said Seymour.

Seymour looked murderous with self-righteousness.

George sat down on his sofa, frightened and exhausted. He was assaulted by real memories and was too weak to fend them off: he had felt frightened to death—he now admitted—in that so enjoyable 1914 war. Flitestone's pictures took on life. Flitestone, too. The cliché vanished—"Not a bad minor painter, like a good many others ruined by the school of Paris"—the dangerous Flitestone appeared. He saw again the poor boy from a Scottish mill town, with gaunt cheeks, light blue eyes and almost white hair that stood up like a dandelion clock—("took hours brushing it, always going to expensive hairdressers"). A pedant, too, with morbid and fanatical patience: it took him longer to paint a picture than anyone George Clark had ever known; the young man was rather deaf which made him seem to be an unworldly, deeply innocent listener, but there was—as George Clark saw—nothing innocent about him, there was a mean calculating streak—("After all he realized I was a rich man", George swaggered) and he was soon taken up by wealthy people. He was clever and made them laugh. He was in trouble all the time with women, chasing them like a maniac and painting them with little heads and large bottoms, like pairs of enormous pink poppies.

("Now, there's a bloody fine bottom, George.")

Very annoying he was, too, especially when he got into Society. That was one thing George Clark knew all about and to be told about Lord This or That or a lot of duchesses, by a crude young genius from the slums, was infuriating.

"He's got five bloody great castles . . ."

"Only one. Forstairs and Aldbaron belong to his half-brother who married Glasnevin's sister. Jack, I wish you wouldn't pick your teeth at meals. I can't bear it. It's such frightful manners."

"Lord Falconer does. He's got a gold toothpick."

But these squabbles were merely annoying. Flitestone was the only human being George ever loved. Jealously loved. He was his prize and his possession. And the boy liked him. Here was the danger. George had dreaded to be liked. You lose something when people like you. You are in danger of being stripped naked and of losing a skin. With Flitestone he felt—ah there was the danger: he did not know what he felt except that it was passion. He could listen to him for hours. For eleven years, George had the sensation that he had married late in life someone who, fortunately, did not exist, and that Flitestone was their fantastic, blindly-invented son. Like a son he clawed at George's bowels.

His love affairs? Well, one had to avert the eye. They were nevertheless, an insurance against George's instant jealous fear: that Flitestone would marry. The thought of that made George shrink. "Marriage will ruin you"—he nagged at it. And that was where Gloria came in.

When Gaiterswell spoke of Gloria, a shot of jealous terror and satisfaction had gone through George. She bored him, of course. Yet in the last years of their friendship, Flitestone's insane love for this girl who would have nothing to do with him, was the real guarantee. George even admired the young girl for the cruelty of her behaviour, for being so complete an example of everything that made women impossible. He was so absorbed in this insurance that he forgot the obvious: that Gloria might marry. She did. In a month on the rebound, Flitestone had married some milky, student girl whose first act was to push her husband into the influence of Gaiterswell. For Gaiterswell was the nation. A breach with George was inevitable.

He went to his desk and started writing to Gaiterswell.

I shall be obliged if you will inform Miss Stokes, Mrs Archer or whatever her name is, that I have no desire to meet her or enter into correspondence . . . His hand shook. He could not continue.

"Awful business" was all he could say. The Arch Enemy had deprived him even of the power to talk to himself.

The east wind. Impossible to go out to any of his clubs that night. After dinner, he poured himself a very large whisky and left the bottle, uncorked, on his desk—a sinister breach of habit, for he always locked up his drink.

"I always reckon to be rather drunk every evening," George used to say. It was a gesture to the dignity of gentlemanly befuddle-ment. But now, he felt his legs go; he was rapidly very drunk. He tottered to his bedroom, dropped his clothes on the floor and got into bed with his shirt, collar and tie on and was asleep at once. Often at night he had enjoyable dreams of social life at Staff H.Q. in the 1914 war. Haig, Ronnie Blackwater and others would turn up. A bit of gunfire added an interest: but this night he had a frightful dream. He dreamed that at the club, before all the mem-bers, he had kissed the teeth of George the Fifth.

This woke him up and he saw that it was daylight. His heart was racing. He could not find his glasses. He got out of bed. The room was getting light; he wondered if he were dead and he pulled back the curtain and what he saw convinced him that he was. The snow had stopped, the sky was hard and clear, and the sun was coming up in a gap between two high buildings. It was still low and this made it an enormous raw yellow football that someone had kicked there, without heat or radiance yet. It looked like a joke or some aimless idea; one more day (George realized as he became more conscious), had begun its unsolicited course over the blind slates of the city. "Old men are lonely," he often said but now he saw a greater loneliness than his own.

"I want those letters." The desire came out before he could stop it. "I must see Gloria. I must get Gaiterswell's dirty little hands off them." He was longing for the past. Then he saw he was wearing his day shirt, his collar and tie.

"Oh God," he said. And he got into his pyjamas and back into bed before Seymour should catch him.

At half past seven Seymour let himself into the flat. His demeanour was of one whose expectations were at last being fulfilled. He had warned several of the old people in the flats about the weather; he had seen Mr. Clark come back yesterday exhausted when, against all advice, he had gone to the club. Reaching the sitting-room, Seymour saw the bottle of whisky standing on the table. This was a sight that he had thirsted for for years and he gazed at it entranced, unbelieving and with suspicion. He listened. There was no sound. Seymour made a grab at the bottle and took a long swig, letting a drop rest on his chin while he replaced what he had drunk with water from the hot-water pot on the tea-tray. He stood still trying to lick the drip off his chin but, failing, he wiped it off with his sleeve and after looking at the letters on Mr. Clark's desk, walked confidently to Mr. Clark's bedroom.

"Good morning, Seymour. Half past seven," said George. He was sitting up in bed. Seymour heard this reversal of their usual greeting with alarm. He stood well away and slopped the tea in its saucer. He was even more alarmed to see Mr. Clark had switched on his own fire and that his clothes were dropped in a muddle on the floor. George caught his glance and got out of bed to show that he was properly dressed and stood with one foot on his rumpled jacket. Panic and the whisky brought guilt into Seymour's face: he suddenly remembered he had made a disastrous mistake. He had forgotten to give Mr. Clark a message.

"A lady rang last night, sir, when you were at dinner."

"A lady—why didn't you tell me?"

"The head waiter took the call. He said you were out. She didn't leave a name."

To distract an angry question, Seymour looked at the clothes on the floor.

"Dear, dear, dear, what a way to leave a suit." He pulled the trouser leg from under George's foot and held the trousers up. "Look at it."

"What lady?" said George.

"She didn't leave a name. She said she'd drop in."

"Drop in!" The horrible phrase.

"That's what she said, she'd drop in."

"Who was it?"

"I don't know, sir. I never took the message. I told you—it was the new head waiter."

"Don't stand there waving my trousers about like a fool, Seymour. It's your business to know."

"They're all foreigners downstairs."

George had his glasses on now and Seymour stepped away. In his panic he took a gamble.

"Might have been Miss Stokes," he said. He had read the name on George's unfinished letter. The gamble was a mistake.

"Archer!" cried George. "Where is the head waiter?" And hurrying to the sitting-room, he started banging the telephone. There was no answer.

"What time do the servants come on?" he called to Seymour. Seymour came in and listened to George banging away. He was very scared now. He dreaded that the head waiter would answer.

"They come when it suits them, now. They suit themselves," said Seymour putting on a miserable manner. And then he got in his blow, the sentence he often used to the old people in the flats when they got difficult. It always silenced them.

"Might just as well sell the place," he said.

"Sell!" George was silenced, too. He stared at Seymour who straightened himself and said, accusingly:

"Where's the jacket of this? Dear, dear, I suppose that's on the floor too." And walked out, leaving George shivering where he stood.

"Sell?" said George.

On a long ledge of the stained building opposite, thirty or forty dirty pigeons were huddled, motionless, with puffed out feathers, too cold to fly.

"Out on the street! Homeless." Like Stebbing-Walker crippled and deaf who had married Kempton's half-sister—she was a

Doplestone—and now lay in his nursing home, or Ronnie Black-water who sat paralysed in the army infirmary. Sell—it was the awful word anxiously whispered in the lift by the old ladies, as they went up and down to their meals. Was the place being sold? Were the rents going up? Were they going to pull the whole place down? For months there would be silence; everyone breathed again; then once more, mostly from Seymour, the rumours began. Fear made them sly and they believed Seymour rather than the management. He moved among them like a torment.

George Clark went down early to luncheon, to get in before the restaurant vanished; rushed upstairs afterwards to barricade himself, so to speak, in his flat. There were few pigeons on the ledge now. What? Had tenancy gone out of Nature too? At seven o'clock he went to dinner. Instead of the two or three tables of old doll-like couples in the middle of the room, there was large table at which ten large young men, loud and commercial, were laughing together. One or two had brief-cases with them. Obviously this was the group who were going to pull down the flats. George raced through the meal, feeling that, possibly, even before the apples and custard, he might be sitting out alone on a vacant site. George's fighting spirit revived over his wine. "Ha," he sneered at them as he left the table and went to the lift, "I'll be dead before you can turn me out."

The lift wheezed and wobbled upwards, making the sound of all the elderly throats in the building. He was startled to see the door of his flat open and, for a moment, thought the men had broken in already; but Seymour was standing in the cold hall. His heavy face looked criminal. In an insinuating, lugubrious voice he said:

"The lady's waiting to see you, sir."

"Seymour, I've told you, never . . ." George hurried to his sitting-room. Gloria was standing by his desk reading the letter he had begun so often.

Dear Gaiterswell, I would have thought that common decency . . .

"Oh, oh, no, no, I say," said George greeting her, but was stopped.

A fur coat and a close fitting black hat like a faded turban with brass colour hair sticking out of it, rushed at him, a hot powdery face kissed him with a force that made him crack in his joints like a stick.

"Oh George, darling, I dropped in," Gloria shouted at him through large stained teeth and laughed.

All he could see was these teeth and lipstick and blue eyes and she was laughing and laughing as she wiped the lipstick off his face.

"Oh well," he said, "they're selling the place . . ." Then she stood back in a pair of cracking shoes.

"George," she said in a Cockney voice. "It's marvellous. You haven't changed at all. You're not a day older."

And she let her fur coat fall open and slip back on her shoulders and he saw the cigarette ash and one or two marks on the bosom of her black dress. She was a big woman.

"Oh," George recovered and gave a victorious sniff. "I'm eighty-two."

"You're a boy," she cried.

"Oh no, don't think I'm deceived by that sort of talk—er, well, you see I mean . . ." George nearly smiled. By his reckoning she was in her fifties and he could see what she wanted, what all women wanted, compliments. He was not, at his age, going to fall for that old game. She sat down on the sofa so as to show off her fine legs.

"Did you recognize me?" she asked.

"Oh well, you know . . ."

"Oh come on, George."

"I dare say I—er—might have done. You see, I forget names and faces, it's an awful business . . . old people . . . they're selling this place . . ."

"Oh you crusty old thing. What do you mean—selling?" she said. "You always were crusty. I knew you'd be at dinner, so I I got that man to bring me up. What is his name? Is he all right? I didn't feel very confortable with him in the lift."

She moved her body and pouted.

"When your lady friends call you ought to tell them to keep an eye—well, George, how are you? How many years is it? It must be twenty-five. You weren't living here then."

"It was the beginning of the war," said George, but he could not remember. He had discarded memory as useless a long time back. He had seen her a lot, yet one of his few clear recollections was of sitting with Flitestone in the old Café Royal waiting for her to come in and arguing with him that she was not a woman who would stick to any man: he remembered her really as an absence.

"You've put on weight," he said. But she hadn't changed much.

"Yes," she said. "I like it, don't you?"

The Cockney voice came warm and harsh out of the wide mouth. Her skin was rougher and was now looser on her bones but still had a wide-pored texture and the colourlessness which Flitestone used to say was like linen. One spot of colour in her cheeks and Flitestone would probably never have fallen for her. "She's like a canvas. I'd like to paint *on* her," Flitestone used to say to George. He did remember. The bare maleness of face on a girlish body was still there on the body of the full woman.

George stood, shaking at the sight of her.

"You're still an old bachelor, George?" she said. "You didn't marry?"

"No," said George with a grin of victory. "You see, in my day, one never met any girls, everyone was chaperoned, you couldn't speak and we had no one to the house, oh no, my father wouldn't allow anyone and then the war, and all that. I told you about my father, oh, now, there's a story . . ."

"Oh, I've been. Three times," she cut in, parading herself.

"Oh three! Well, that's interesting. Or I suppose it is. It doesn't surprise me. Please sit down. Let me get you a drink. Now let me see, keys. I have to keep it locked, well with the servants it isn't fair to leave drink about. Ah, in this pocket. I keep them here."

He fussed at the cupboard and brought out a bottle of whisky and a bottle of sherry.

"Oh gin please," she said. "Can I help?"

"No, no, it's here. I keep it at the back. I'll put this bottle down here, yes, that's the way . . ." he chattered to himself.

Gloria walked across the room to look at the pictures, but stopped instead to look at her reflection in the glass of the bookcases and to rearrange the frilled neck of her dress. Then she looked up at the large picture of the fish.

"George! You've got my fish."

"Ah yes, the fish. He painted four fish pictures. One is in the Tate, one is . . . now where is it?"

"*My* fish, I mean", she said. "Don't you remember, it's the one I made you carry to Jack's place and the paper came off . . ."

"No, no," said George.

"Yes, you must remember. You're not still cross, are you? You looked so funny."

She took a deep breath in front of the picture, inhaling it.

"I don't know why we didn't eat it."

"Ah yes. Awful business. Café Royal," said George, a memory coming back.

She turned to the cylindrical woman in a shift, with enormous column-like legs, who was playing the guitar, and looked with flirtatious annoyance at it, paying off an old score.

"That's me," she said.

"Oh no," said George sarcastically. He was beginning to enjoy himself. "It was done in Paris."

"It's me," said Gloria. "But they're Violet's legs." Gloria turned abruptly away, insulted, and taking her drink from George went back to the sofa. Once more she gave a large sigh and gazed with admiring calculation at the room. She leaned her head to one side and smiled at George.

"You are a dear, George. How cosy you are. It's wonderful to see old friends," said Gloria sweetly. "It brings it all back."

She got up and put more gin in her drink and then leaned over his chair as she passed him and kissed the top of his head.

"Dear George," she said and sat down. "And you live here, all alone! Well, George, I've brought the letters, all Jack's letters to me. I didn't know I had them. It's a funny thing: François found them, my husband, he's French. We live in France and he has an antique business. He said 'They ought to fetch a bit,' you know what the French are about money, so I remembered Monkey . . ."

"Monkey?"

"Monkey Gaiterswell, I always used to call him Monkey. We used," said Gloria very archly, "to be friends and he said 'Sell them to America'. Do you think he's right—I mean Monkey said you'd written a book about Jack and you'd know? He said I'd get five hundred pounds for them. I mean they're all about painting, famous people, the whole circle . . ."

Ah, it was a plot!

"Five hundred," said George. "You won't get five pounds. No one has ever heard of Flitestone in America. None of his pictures went there."

"But the letters are very *personal*, George. Naturally you're in them."

"I doubt it."

"Oh you are. I remember. I know you are. You were his best friend. And you wrote so beautifully about him. Monkey says so."

Obviously there was a plot between Monkey and Gloria.

"I've no doubt they are full of slanders. I should tear them up," said George shortly.

"George," she appealed. "I need the money. François has gone off with some woman and I'm broke. Look."

She opened her black shopping bag and took out a parcel of crumpled brown paper and put it on George's desk.

"Open it. I'll leave them with you to look at. You'll see."

"Oh no. I can't do that," said George. "I don't care to be responsible. It leads to all sorts of awful business."

"Read them. Open it. Here."

She put down her empty glass and untied the string. A pile of letters of all sizes in Flitestone's large hand, each word formed carefully like the words of a medieval manuscript, slid on to George's desk.

George was sitting there and he withdrew his hand so as not to touch the letters. They brought Jack Flitestone into the room. George wanted them. He knew now what was meant when she said *he* was in them. It was not what *she* meant. The letters contained the, to him, afflicting fact that he had not after all succeeded in owning his own life and closing it to others; that he existed in other people's minds and that all people dissolved in this way, becoming fragments of one another, and nothing in themselves. He had known that once, when Jack Flitestone had brought him to life. He knew, too, that he had once lived or nearly lived. Flitestone, in his dangerous way, had lived for him. One letter had fallen to the floor and Gloria read aloud:

. . . . *Archie's car broke down outside Medley and we didn't get to Gorse until the middle of dinner. La Tarantula was furious and I offered to eat in the kitchen and the Prime Minister who was already squiffy . . .*

"There you are, George. The Prime Minister," cried Gloria.

George took the letter in the tips of his fingers and Gloria helped herself to another drink.

"Jack was an awful snob," said George, but admiringly, putting the letter back. "No manners, writing about people when he was a guest."

"Oh come off it, George," said Gloria, picking out one or two more. "You know, I haven't read them for years. Actually Jack frightened me. So morbid. Here's one. Oh, this is good. It's about the time you and Jack went to Chartres. The tie drawer, George!"

The new blow from the past struck him. He remembered it: the extraordinary thing about small French hotels: they never gave you a drawer for your ties. He took the letter and read:

. . . . *George surpassed himself this morning* . . . .

He had walked down the corridor to Flitestone's room and knocked.

"Here. I say, Jack. I want to speak to you."

"What is it?" Flitestone called. Ordinary manners, one would have thought, would at least have led Flitestone to open the door, Jack was so *thoughtless*.

"Jack, Jack, I've no tie drawer in my room."

Flitestone came to the door naked and pushed a drawer from his wardrobe into George's hand.

"Take mine."

"Jack, here I say, dear fellow. Chambermaid."

"Umph," said George to Gloria. "Inaccurate."

He reached out for the next letter she offered to him. He looked at it distantly, read a few lines and stopped.

"Here, I say, I can't read this. It is to you," he sneered a little.

"They're all to me."

"Yes, but this is—er—private, personal."

George looked quizzically and sternly at her; it was "not done" to look into another's moral privacy. It was also shameless and woman-like to show letters like these to him. But the phrases he had run into head-on had frightened him, they brought back to him the danger he had once lived in: his heart had been invaded, he had been exposed once to a situation in which the question of a victory or a defeat vanished.

"You see," he said turning his head away nervously from her as he handed back the letter to her.

Gloria took it. She put on her glasses and read. Immediately she smiled. The smile became wider and she gave pleased giggles. She was blushing.

"Jack ought to have been a writer," she said. "I hated his paintings. It's quite true what he says, George. I was very attractive. I had marvellous legs."

She turned to look at her reflection in the glass of the bookcase and took her fur coat off and posed. Gradually she lifted her skirt above her knees and pleased by what she saw, she lifted her skirt higher, putting one leg forward, then the other.

"Look, George," she said. "Look. They're still good. There aren't many women of my age with legs like these. They're damn fine, George. You've never seen a pair like that." She turned sideways and pranced with pleasure.

"Gloria, please," said George sharply.

But she marched over to the picture of the woman with cylindrical legs and said:

"I could have killed him for that. What's the matter with painters? Didn't he have enough to eat when he was a boy? He was always carrying on about his hard times."

She lowered her dress and sat down to go on reading the letter.

"The pink peony, did you get to that?" she said. "Really, Jack's ideas! Not very nice, is it? I mean, not in a letter. He wasn't very . . ." she stopped and was sad. "No," she checked herself. "I'll tell you, something, George: we only went to bed together once . . ."

"Gloria," said George in agitation. "Give me the letter. I'll put it with the others . . ."

She was making Flitestone far too alive.

"It was your fault, George. It was the dinner you gave us that night, the night I bought the fish. You say you don't remember? At the Café Royal. I made you go off to the Café Royal kitchen and get the largest fish they had. I don't know why. I wanted to get rid of you and I thought it would annoy you. I was getting plastered. Don't you remember? I said: 'Tell them we want it for our cat. Our cat is enormous. It eats a salmon a day.' And Jack kept on saying—we were both drunk—'I want to paint a large salmon. You're bloody stingy, George, you won't buy me a salmon.'"

"Awful business," snapped George. "Jack never understood money."

"You remember! Isn't that wonderful?" cried Gloria pulling off her hat and looking into her empty glass.

"You followed us out of the restaurant, all up Shaftesbury Avenue and he was going to show me his new pictures. You had no tact, George. He was carrying the fish and he suddenly gave it to you and made you carry it and the paper blew off. George," she said, "do you mind if I have just a teeny-weeny one? There's a letter about it."

And she pushed him aside and got at the parcel on his desk.

"I think you've had enough, Gloria."

"For old times' sake," said Gloria, filling her glass. She unfolded the parcel again and scattered the letters. George looked at the clock.

"I can't find it," she said. "It's here somewhere."

"Gloria, I don't want drink spilled on my desk. I've forbidden Seymour . . ."

Gloria stopped and, now red in the face, smiled amorously.

"That man?" she said. "Is he here?"

"Gloria," said George. "I'll have to—er—I'll have to—It's eleven o'clock, I . . ."

Gloria replied with dignity.

"Jack had no sense of behaviour. I could see it was spoiling your suit. I begged him, begged him," she said grandly, "to carry it himself. I was furious with him. He could see you had an umbrella as well, you always carried one and wore a bowler hat. He said 'Stick it on the umbrella.' I was terribly upset when he slammed the door in your face when we got to the studio. We had a terrible row and I made him swear to go round to your flat and apologize. It was awful, George. What did you do?"

"I took a cab, of course," said George.

"Well, I mean, you couldn't leave a salmon in the street," said Gloria. "It was a suit like the one you are wearing now, dark grey. That isn't the one, is it? It can't be."

"Gloria, I am sorry, but . . ."

Gloria frowned.

"I am sure it's there," she said and went to the letters on the desk again. "No, not that. Not that," she began throwing the letters on the floor. "Ah, here."

She waved the letter and looked through it in silence until she read aloud:

. . . I apologized to George and he said he had left the fish with the hall porter, so I went down there. We had a bit of a row about my low class manners. I said I thought half the salmon in England had been to Eton. He told me to ask Seymour, the hall porter for it . . ."

"Inaccurate," interrupted George. "Seymour was never hall porter."

*". . . I said I have called for the specimen I loaned to Sir George Clark,
the marine biologist, who is doing research on spawn . . .*

"You see, George," she said. She went back to the sofa. "Come
and sit here, George, don't be so stuffy. We can talk, can't we, after
all these years? We are friends. That is what we all need, George,
friends. I'm serious, George." She had tears in her eyes.

"It was wicked of Jack to call you stingy. You gave him money.
You bought his pictures."

"But I *am* stingy," said George. "You see, rich people never give
their children a penny. We never had anyone to the house at
Maddings . . ."

"It was his jealousy," said Gloria darkly. "He was jealous of
you."

"Oh well, class envy . . ." George began.

"No, of you and me," she said. "Oh yes, George, he really was.
That's why he tried to shake you off, that night, that's why we
had such terrible scenes . . . You were rich . . ."

"Don't be ludicrous, Gloria."

"Letters by every post, pursuing, bombarding me, I couldn't
stand it."

"Nonsense."

"It isn't nonsense. You were very blind, George. And so you
live in this place, alone. Jealous men are so *boring*, George. I've had
four. I said 'Oh to hell' and I went off to France. Vive de Gaulle!
You know?" she said, raising her glass.

"To *les feuilles mortes d'automne*," she said. "That's what my
husband says."

He bent to take her glass to prevent her drinking more and she
stroked his spiky hair. He put the glass away out of reach.

"That is why Jack married that stupid student girl," she said in a
suddenly sharp calculating voice. "That broke up you and Jack,
didn't it?"

"I don't wish to talk about it," said George. "It ruined him.
Marriage is the ruin of painters."

"George, come clean. After all, we all know it. You were in love
with him, weren't you?"

There was a silence.

"Weren't you?" she persisted.

He recovered and achieved his worldly drawl.

"Oh I know there's a lot of that sort of thing about, was in my time, too. I paid no attention to it . . . Women don't understand talent. I understood Jack's talent. Women ruined it."

"Jack said you'd never been to bed with a woman in your life," she said.

"It wasn't possible, it wasn't possible," said George angrily. "Not in my day. Not for a gentleman." And he turned on her. "I won't be questioned. I should burn those letters. You treated him badly. You killed his imagination. It's obvious in his work."

He looked at the clock.

"George," she said. "You don't mean that. You don't know what you are saying. You were always so sweet to me."

"I do mean what I said. Read your letters," said George. And briskly he collected them off the floor and packed them up and tied the parcel. He was going to turn her out now.

She was staring stupidly.

"You don't want them?" she said. "Monkey said you'd jump at them."

"You've got one in your hands," he said. "No, I won't give a penny for them. I won't be blackmailed."

Gloria got up to give the letter to him. She could not walk and put her hand on the table beside the sofa. It fell over, carrying her glass with it.

"What's that man Seymour doing in here? Tell him to get out. Out with Seymour," she suddenly shouted. "Out. Out. What d'you mean? Stop playing the innocent. You've never lived. That's you, George, that fish?" And she tried to point at the picture.

"Gloria, I won't have this," shouted George. "You're drunk."

"You won't have it? You've never had it. My coat, who's taken that?"

But when she turned she fell heavily on to the sofa, twisted her body, with her skirt above her knees and one majestic leg trailing on the floor.

"Gloria. How dare you! In my house!"

"Darling," she smiled and fell asleep instantly.

"Women," George always said, glittering dryly, "they contribute nothing." She was contributing a stentorian snore.

He had couples up after dinner sometimes, elderly friends and you could see how it was: they either couldn't let their husbands

speak—poor Caldicott, for instance—or they sat as stupid as pud-
dings. The men aged as they sat: rather them than me. Eighty-two
and not a day's illness.

Gloria was contributing more than a snore. She was contributing
an enormous haunch, an indecent white thigh—"Really". He would
have to cover it. Couldn't she pull her skirt down. Couldn't she be
drunk like a—like a lady! She contributed brutality, an awful
animality to the room.

He went over and tried to pull her skirt down.

"Gloria," he shouted.

He couldn't move the skirt. He have her a shake. It stirred an
enormous snore and a voluptuous groan and it seemed that she
was going to roll off the sofa on to the floor. He couldn't have
women lying on the floor on his flat. He could never get her up.
He moved a chair against the sofa.

He sat down and waited. Gaiterswell was responsible for this. In
the promiscuous Bohemian set he had lived in, the dirty little man
would be used to it.

George could not ring for Seymour. Think of the scandal. She
had trapped him. He hated her for what she had done to Jack,
driving him out of his mind with jealousy of other men, encourag-
ing him, evading him, never letting go. She, more than Jack's
expensive wife, was responsible for his suicide. Gloria had paralysed
him. You could see it in his paintings, after they had broken up:
the paintings had become automatic, academic, dead, without air,
without life. There were ten drawings of that fish. He had become
obsessed with it.

It was a death of the heart; of George's heart as well. This body
lying in the room, was like the brutal body of his father. The old
brute with his rages and his passions, his disgraceful affairs with
governesses and maids in the very room next to where he slept as
a boy—awful business—he would never forget that—the manners!
—the shouts, his terrible behaviour to his wife: it had paralysed the
whole family. They all hated him so violently, with a violence that
so magnetized them all, that none of them had heart for others.
He had killed their hearts; not one of them had been able to love.
For a moment, George left these exact memories and went off into
anecdotes about how he fought back against his father, sniffing
triumphantly, as he did at the club. But the sight of Gloria there
smashed the anecdotal in him. He recognized that he had *not* fought

back and had not been victorious. He had risked nothing. He had been whipped into the life of a timid, self-absorbed scholar.

It was past midnight. He poured himself a large whisky. Perhaps by the time he checked up on the windows in the flat and saw all the doors were closed, she would wake up. He carried his glass to his bedroom and put it by the bedside; and there exhaustion drove him to his habits. He took off his watch and put it on the table. He forgot why he had come into the room. It was not what he intended to do but he was tired, murmuring to himself "Coat, hanger, shirt, trousers, shoes, socks," he undressed and shivering he got into bed. He finished his whisky, turned out the light and—Gloria forgotten—he was soon asleep and later dreaming he was back in the sitting-room, parcelling the letters, watching her. He dreamed that he called Seymour who got a taxi and they hauled her into it. But as fast as they got her into the cab she was back upstairs on the sofa and his father and Jack were there too, but ignoring him, standing a yard or two away, though he shouted at them to help. And then the awful thing happened. He picked her up himself. He was at a railway station: he could go no farther: he dropped her. With an appalling noise, the enormous body fell just as a train came, steaming, blasting, wheels grinding, a massive black engine, advancing upon him. He gave a shout. It had hit him and crushed him. He was dying. He had had a heart attack. He screamed and he woke shouting, sitting up in bed.

In the bedroom Gloria was standing in her stockinged feet and her petticoat, holding her skirt in her hand, her hair in disorder.

"What's the matter, George?" she said thickly. George could not speak.

"What is it? I woke up. I heard you shout." Her breathing was heavy, it was the sound of the engine he had heard. George gaped at her.

"Are you ill?" she said. "I passed out."

"I, I, I . . .," he could say nothing more. He got out of bed. George was shuddering. "What's the time?"

"Get into bed. You're freezing. You're ill." She came over and took him by the arm and he allowed himself to be put back to bed.

"What an ice-box," she said. She shut the window, switched on the fire.

"I'd better get a doctor," she said.

"No," said George. "I'm all right." He was panting. She felt his head.

"Where's my watch?"

"It's half past three nearly. George, for God's sake don't do that again. Have you got any aspirins? What happens when you're alone and there is no one here?"

"Ah, you see, I have an arrangement with the . . ."

"What? The doctor?"

"The telephone," said George.

"The telephone? What the hell's the good of that? You might die, George. Where are those aspirins, be a dear and tell me. I'm sorry, George. You screamed. God, I hadn't time to put a skirt on," she said archly.

"Oh well, so I see," said George sarcastically.

"Ah, thank God," said Gloria sighing. "Now you sound more like yourself. You gave me a turn. I would have fallen on the floor if you hadn't put the chair there. I'll make you a cup of tea. Can you make tea in this awful museum?"

"No," said George victoriously. "You can't. I never keep tea here. Tea, I never drink it. Seymour brings it."

"Well, my God, how you live, George, in this expensive barn," she said, sitting on the bed.

"Awful business. Awful dream," said George, coming round. "I had an awful dream the other night, oh yes . . ."

"You look green, George. I'll get you a drink."

She brought it to him and watched him drink it.

"I've been round your flat. There are no beds. If you don't mind I'll go back to the sofa. Now, stop talking."

For George was off on some tale of a night in the war.

"This is the only bed," he said. "I used to keep a spare bed but I stopped that. People exploit you. Want to stay the night. It upsets the servants here."

"There's not room for two in it, George," she said. George stopped his drink.

"Gloria," he stammered in terror of her large eyes. She came closer and sat on the bed. She took his free hand.

"You're cold," she said.

"No," he said. "I'm not. All bone, you see, skeleton. My sister . . ."

She stood up and then bent over him and kissed him.

"I'll find a blanket," she said. "I'll go back to the sofa. I'm terribly sorry, George. George, I really am."

"Well," said George.

"George, forgive me," she said and suddenly kneeled at the bed and put her arms round him. "Let me warm you."

"Oh no, no. No. Awful business," said George.

She went away. George heard her opening cupboards, looking for blankets. He listened to every movement. He thought, Seymour will find her in the morning. Where could he hide her? Could he make her go to the bathroom and stay there till Seymour left? No, Seymour always ran his bath. He was trapped. He heard her go to the sitting-room. It was six before he fell asleep again.

At half past seven she came to his room with Seymour.

"My brother was taken very ill in the night," she was saying to Seymour. "I cannot find out who his doctor is? He oughtn't to be alone like this. At his age."

"No ma'am," said Seymour, looking guilty.

"Bring me his tea. Where does he keep his thermometer? Get me one."

"I told him not to go out ma'am," said Seymour.

"Thank heaven I came in."

When Seymour left she said to George:

"Don't talk. It's tiring. A little scandal would have done you good, George, but not at your age."

"Umph," said George. "That man knows my sister. She's as thin as a pole. She's meaner than me," he cackled. "She never tips anyone."

"I told him I was the fat one," she said. "You stay there. I'm calling a doctor."

Waiting for him to come was a nuisance. "Awful business" having a woman in the house. They spend half their lives in the bathroom. You can't get into it. When George did get to it he was so weak he had to call for her. She was sitting in a chair reading Flitestone's letters and smiling. She had—George had to admit—made herself presentable.

"You're right, George," she said. "I'm going to keep them. He was so full of news. They're too," she said demurely, ". . . personal."

And then the doctor came.

At the Club George was sitting at luncheon.

"You're looking well, George," said the academician who had just passed him the decanter.

"I never drink until the evening. I always reckon to drink a bottle of wine at dinner, a couple of glasses of port. I usually have a whisky here and one more back at the flat when I get home. I walk home, taxis are expensive and oh, oh, oh, I don't like the underground. Oh no, I don't like that."

"You're looking fine."

"I have been very ill. I had pneumonia. I was taken very ill a month ago, in the night. Luckily my sister has been looking after me. That is the trouble with old people who live alone, no one knows. They can't reach the bell. I told you about that awful night when I ate the oysters . . ."

"George, not now, please. I didn't know you had a sister?"

"Oh yes, oh yes. Two," said George sharply. "One is very thin, all bones like me, the other very fat."

"But you're better? You look fine. I hear, by the way, that Sanders is getting married."

"Oh, I knew about that. I advised him to, at his age. I warned him about the loneliness of bachelors in old age. I'm used to it. Keep occupied. See people. That's the secret. Oh yes, I worked it out. My father lived till he was ninety. You see, when I was young one never met any women. Just girls at deb parties, but speak to them, oh dear no. Not done. That's a big change. The bishops don't like sex, though Canterbury is beginning to come round. The Pope will have to make a move, he's been the stumbling block. A scandal. Oh yes, I happened to be in Rome in '05, staying with a Papal Count and, well, I was able to tell him the whole inside story at the Vatican, you see I knew a very able Jesuit who was very frank about it privately . . ."

"What happened about Gloria?" said a voice. It was the Arch Enemy, sitting opposite.

"Hah," said George. "I recommended her not to sell. She offered to give me the letters, but I didn't care to take them. They were very intimate, personal."

"I thought her husband had left her and she was short of money?"

"That's not the worst thing to be short of," sniffed George.

"The trouble with Gloria was that she was also so sentimental," said the Arch Enemy. "The moment she sees a man her mind simply goes. Still does, and she must be sixty if she's a day," he said, looking at George.

By God, George thought, the Arch Enemy is a fool.

SIX

When My Girl Comes Home

S HE was kissing them all, hugging them, her arms bare in her
summer dress, laughing and taking in a big draught of breath
after every kiss, nearly knocking old Mrs. Draper off her feet,
almost wrestling with Mrs. Fulmino, who was large and tall.
Then Hilda broke off to give another foreign-sounding laugh
and plunged at Jack Draper ("the baby") and his wife, at Mr.
Fulmino, who cried out "What again?" and at Constance who
did not like emotion; and after every kiss, Hilda drew back,
getting her breath and making this sound like "Hah!"

"Who is this?" she said, looking at me.

"Harry Fraser," Mr. Fulmino said. "You remember Harry?"

"You worked at the grocer's," she said. "I remember you."

"No," I said, "that was my brother."

"This is the little one," said Mrs. Fulmino.

"Who won the scholarship," said Constance.

"We couldn't have done anything without him," said Mr.
Fulmino, expanding with extravagance as he always did about
everything. "He wrote to the War Office, the Red Cross, the
Prisoners of War, the American Government, all the letters. He's
going to be our Head Librarian."

Mr. Fulmino loved whatever had not happened yet. His forecasts
were always wrong. I left the library years ago and never fulfilled
the future he had planned for me. Obviously Hilda did not remember me. Thirteen years before, when she married Mr. Singh
and left home, I was no more than a boy.

"Well, I'll kiss him too," she said. "And another for your
brother."

That was the first thing to happen, the first of many signs of
how her life had had no contact with ourselves.

"He was killed in the war, dear," said Mrs. Fulmino.

"She couldn't know," said Constance.

"I'm sorry," said Hilda.

We all stood silent, and Hilda turned to hold on to her mother little Mrs. Johnson, whose face was coquettish with tears and who came only up to Hilda's shoulder. The old lady was bewildered. She was trembling as though she were going to shake to pieces like a tree in the autumn. Hilda stood still, touching her tinted brown hair which was done in a tight high style and still unloosened, despite all the hugs and kissings. Her arms looked as dry as sand, her breasts were full in her green, flowered dress and she was gazing over our heads now from large yellow eyes which had almost closed into two blind, blissful curving lines. Her eyebrows seemed to be lacquered. How Oriental she looked on that first day! She was looking above our heads at old Mrs. Draper's shabby room and going over the odd things she remembered, and while she stood like that, the women were studying her clothes. A boy's memory is all wrong. Naturally, when I was a boy I had thought of her as tall. She was really short. But I did remember her bold nose—it was like her mother's and old Mrs. Draper's; those two were sisters. Otherwise I wouldn't have known her. And that is what Mr. Fulmino said when we were all silent and incredulous again. We had Hilda back. Not just "back" either, but "back from the dead", reborn.

"She was in the last coach of the train, wasn't she, Mother?" Mr. Fulmino said to Mrs. Johnson. He called her "mother" for the occasion, celebrating her joy.

"Yes," said Mrs. Johnson. "Yes." Her voice scraped and trembled.

"In the last coach, next the van. We went right up the platform, we thought we'd missed her, didn't we? She was," he exclaimed with acquisitive pride, "in the First Class."

"Like you missed me coming from Penzance," said Mrs. Fulmino swelling powerfully and going that thundery violet colour which old wrongs gave her.

"Posh!" said Hilda. And we all smiled in a sickly way.

"Don't you ever do it again, my girl! Don't you ever do it again," said her mother, old Mrs. Johnson, clinging to her daughter's arm and shaking it as if it were a bell-rope.

"I was keeping an eye on my luggage," Hilda laughed.

Ah! That was a point! There was not only Hilda, there was her luggage. Some of it was in the room, but the bigger things were outside on the landing, piled up, looking very new, with the fantastic labels of hotels in Tokyo, San Francisco, and New York

WHEN MY GIRL COMES HOME   125

on it, and a beautiful jewel box in white leather on top like a crown.
Old Mrs. Draper did not like the luggage being outside the room
in case it was in the way of the people upstairs. Constance went out
and fetched the jewel box in. We had all seen it. We were as
astonished by all these cases as we were by Hilda herself. After
thirteen years, six of them war, we recognized that the poor
ruined woman we had prepared for, had not arrived. She shone
with money. Later on, one after the other of us, except old Mrs.
Draper who could not walk far, went out and looked at the
luggage and came back to study Hilda in a new way.

We had all had a shock. She had been nearly two years coming
home from Tokyo. Before that there was the occupation, before
that the war itself. Before that there were the years in Bombay and
Singapore, when she was married to an Indian they always called
Mr. Singh. All those years were lost to us. None of us had been
to India. What happened there to Mr. Singh? We knew he had
died—but how? Even if we had known, we couldn't have
imagined it. None of us had been to Singapore, none of us to
Japan. People from streets like Hincham Street do go to such
places—it is not past belief. Knock on the doors of half the houses
in London and you will find people with relations all over the
world—but none of us had. Mention these places to us, we look
at our grey skies and see boiling sun. Our one certainty about
Hilda was what, in fact, the newspaper said the next day, with her
photograph and the headline: *A Mother's Faith. Four Years in
Japanese Torture Camp. London Girl's Ordeal.* Hilda was a terrible
item of news, a gash in our lives, and we looked for the signs of
it on her body, in the way she stood, in the lines on her face, as
if we were expecting a scream from her mouth like the screams
we were told Bill Williams gave out at night in his sleep, after
he had been flown back home when the war ended. We had had
to wait and wait for Hilda. At one time—there was a postcard
from Hawaii—she was pinned like a butterfly in the middle of
the Pacific Ocean; soon after there was a letter from Tokyo saying
she couldn't get a passage. Confusing. She was travelling backwards. Letters from Tokyo were still coming after her letters from
San Francisco.

We were still standing, waiting for Constance to bring in the
teapot for the tea was already laid. The trolley buses go down
Hincham Street. It is a mere one hundred and fifty yards of a

few little houses and a few little shops, which has a sudden charmed importance because the main road has petered out at our end by the Lord Nelson and an enormous public lavatory, and the trolley buses have to run down Hincham Street before picking up the main road again, after a sharp turn at the convent. Hincham Street is less a street than an interval, a disheartened connection. While we stood in one of those silences that follow excitement, a trolley bus came by and Hilda exclaimed:

"You've still got the old trams. Bump! Bump! Bump!" Hilda was ecstatic about the sound. "Do you remember I used to be frightened the spark from the pole would set the lace curtains on fire when I was little?"

For, as the buses turned, the trolley arms would come swooping with two or three loud bumps and a spit of blue electricity, almost hitting Mrs. Draper's sitting-room window which was on the first floor.

"It's trolleys now, my girl," said old Mrs. Draper, whose voice was like the voice of time itself chewing away at life. "The trams went years ago, before the war."

Old Mrs. Draper had sat down in her chair again by the fire which always burned winter and summer in this room; she could not stand for long. Hers was the first remark that had given us any sense of what was bewildering all of us, the passing of time, the growing of a soft girl into a grown, hard-hipped woman. For old Mrs. Draper's mind was detached from events around her and moved only among the signal facts and conclusions of history.

Presently we were, as the saying is, "at our teas". Mr. Fulmino, less puzzled than the rest of us, expanded in his chair with the contentment of one who had personally operated a deeply British miracle. It was he who had got Hilda home.

"We've got all the correspondence, haven't we, Harry?" he said. "We kept it—the War Office, Red Cross, Prisoner of War Commission, everything, Hilda. I'll show it to you."

His task had transformed him and his language. Identification, registration, accommodation, communication, rehabilitation, hospitalization, administration, investigation, transportation—well we had all dreamed of Hilda in our different ways.

"They always said the same thing," Mrs. Fulmino said reproachfully. "No one of the name of Mrs. Singh on the lists."

"I wrote to Bombay," said Mr. Fulmino.

"He wrote to Singapore," said Mrs. Fulmino.

Mr. Fulmino drank some tea, wiped his lips and became geography.

"All British subjects were rounded up, they said," Mrs. Fulmino said.

We nodded. We had made our stand, of course, on the law. Mrs. Fulmino was authority.

"But Hilda was married to an Indian," said Constance.

We glanced with a tolerance we did not usually feel for Constance. She was always trying to drag politics in.

"She's a British subject by birth," said Mrs. Fulmino firmly.

"Mum," Hilda whispered, squeezing her mother's arm hard, and then looked up to listen, as if she were listening to talk about a faraway stranger.

"I was in Tokyo when the war started," she said. "Not Singapore."

"Oh Tokyo!" exclaimed Mr. Fulmino, feeling in his waistcoat for a pencil to make a note of it and, suddenly, realizing that his note-taking days were over.

"Whatever the girl has done she has been punished for it," came old Mrs. Draper's mournful voice from the chair by the fire, but in the clatter no one heard her, except old Mrs. Johnson, who squeezed her daughter's arm and said:

"My girl is a jewel."

Still, Hilda's words surprised us. We had worked it out that after she and Mr. Singh were married and went to Bombay he had heard of a better job in the state railway medical service and had gone to Singapore where the war had caught her. Mrs. Fulmino looked annoyed. If Mr. Fulmino expanded into geography and the language of state—he worked for the Borough Council—Mrs. Fulmino liked a fact to be a fact.

"We got the postcards," said Mrs. Fulmino sticking to chronology.

"Hawaii," Mr. Fulmino said. "How'd you get there? Swim, I suppose." He added, "A sweet spot, it looks, suit us for a holiday—palms."

"Coconuts," said young Jack Draper, who worked in a pipe factory, speaking for the first time.

"Be quiet," said his wife.

"It's an America base now," said Constance with her politically sugared smile.

We hesitated but let her observation pass. It was simple to ignore her. We were happy.

"I suppose they paid your fare," said Jack Draper's wife, a North-country woman.

"Accommodation, transportation," said Mr. Fulmino. "Food, clothing. Everything. Financed by the international commission."

This remark made old Mrs. Johnson cry a little. In those years none of us had deeply believed that Hilda was alive. The silence was too long; too much time had gone by. Others had come home by the thousand with stories of thousands who had died. Only old Mrs. Johnson had been convinced that Hilda was safe. The land-lord at the Lord Nelson, the butcher, anyone who met old Mrs. Johnson as she walked by like a poor, decent ghost with her sewing bundles, in those last two years, all said in war-staled voices:

"It's a mother's faith, that's what it is. A mother's faith's a funny thing."

She would walk along, with a cough like someone driving tacks. Her chest had sunk and under her brown coat her shoulder blades seemed to have sharpened into a single hump. Her faith gave her a bright, yet also a sly, dishonest look.

"I'm taking this sewing up to Mrs. Tracy's. She wants it in a hurry," she might say.

"You ought to rest, Mrs. Johnson, like the doctor said."

"I want a bit of money for when my girl comes home," she said. "She'll want feeding up."

And she would look around perhaps, for a clock, in case she ought, by this time, to have put a pot on the stove.

She had been too ill, in hospital, during the war, to speak about what might have happened to Hilda. Her own pain and fear of dying deafened her to what could be guessed. Mrs. Johnson's faith had been born out of pain, out of the inability—within her prison of aching bones and crushed breathing—to identify herself with her daughter. Her faith grew out of her very self-centredness. And when she came out from the post office every week, where she put her savings, she looked demure, holy and secretive. If people were too kind and too sympathetic with her, she shuffled and looked mockingly. Seven hospitals, she said, had not killed *her*.

Now, when she heard Mr. Fulmino's words about the fare, the

clothes, the food, the expense of it all, she was troubled. What had she worked for—even at one time scrubbing in a canteen—but to save Hilda from a charity so vast in its humiliation, from so blank a herding mercy. Hilda was hers, not theirs. Hilda kept her arm on her mother's waist and while Mr. Fulmino carried on with the marvels of international organization (which moved Mrs. Fulmino to say hungrily, "It takes a war to bring it out"), Hilda ignored them and whispered to comfort her mother. At last the old lady dried her eyes and smiled at her daughter. The smile grew to a small laugh, she gave a proud jerk to her head, conveying that she and her Hil were not going to kowtow in gratitude to anyone, and Hilda, at last, said out loud to her mother what, no doubt, she had been whispering:

"He wouldn't let me pay anything, Mum. Faulkner his name was. Very highly educated. He came from California. We had a fancy dress dance on the ship and he made me go as a geisha . . . He gave me these . . ." And she raised her hand to show her mother the bracelets on it.

Mrs. Johnson laughed wickedly.

"Did he . . .? Was he . . .?" said Mrs. Johnson.

"No. Well, I don't know," said Hilda. "But I kept his address."

Mrs. Johnson smiled round at all of us, to show that in spite of all, being the poorest in the family and the ones that had suffered most, she and Hilda knew how to look after themselves.

This was the moment when there was that knock on the door. Everyone was startled and looked at it.

"A knock!" said Mr. Fulmino.

"A knock, Constance," said young Mrs. Draper who had busy North-country ears.

"A knock," several said.

Old Mrs. Draper made one of her fundamental utterances again, one of her growls from the belly of the history of human indignation.

"We are," she said, "in the middle of our teas. Constance go and see and tell them."

But before Constance got to the door, two young men, one with a camera, came right into the room, without asking. Some of us lowered our heads and then, just as one young man said, "I'm from the *News*," the other clicked his camera.

Jack Draper said, nearly choking:

"He's taken a snap of us eating."

While we were all staring at them, old Mrs. Draper chewed out grandly:

"Who may they be?"

But Hilda stood up and got her mother to her feet, too.

"Stand up all of us," she said eagerly. "It's for the papers."

It was the Press. We were in confusion. Mrs. Fulmino pushed Mr. Fulmino forward towards the reporter and then pulled him back. The reporter stood asking questions and everyone answered at once. The photographer kept on taking photographs and, when he was not doing that, started picking up vases and putting them down and one moment was trying the drawer of a little table by the window. They pushed Hilda and her mother into a corner and took a picture of them. Hilda calling to us all to "come in" and Mr. Fulmino explaining to the reporters. Then they went, leaving a cigarette burning on one of old Mrs. Draper's lace doyleys under the fern and two more butts on the floor. "What did they say? What did they say?" we all asked one another, but no one could remember. We were all talking at once, arguing about who had heard the knock first. Young Mrs. Draper said her tea was spoiled and Constance opened the window to let the cigarette smoke out and then got the kettle. Mr. Fulmino put his hand on his wife's knee because she was upset and she shook it off. When we had calmed down Hilda said:

"The young one was a nice-looking boy, wasn't he, Mum?" and Mr. Fulmino, who almost never voiced the common opinion about anything but who had perhaps noticed how the eyes of all the women went larger at this remark, laughed loudly and said:

"We've got the old Hilda back!"

I mention this because of the item in the papers next day: A Mother's Faith. Four Years in a Japanese Torture Camp. London Girl's Ordeal.

Wonderful, as Mr. Fulmino said.

To be truthful, I felt uncomfortable at old Mrs. Draper's. They were not my family. I had been dragged there by Mr. Fulmino, and by a look now and then from young Mrs. Draper and from Constance I had the feeling that they thought it was indecent for me to be there when I had only been going with Iris, Mr. Fulmino's daughter, for two or three months. I had to be tolerated as one more example of Mr. Fulmino's uncontrollable gifts—the gift for colonizing.

Mr. Fulmino had shot up from nothing during the war. It had given him personality. He was a short, talkative, heavy man of forty-five with a wet gold tooth and glossy black hair that stream-lined back across his head from an arrow point, getting thin in front. His eyes were anxious, overworked and puddled, indeed if you had not known him you would have thought he had had a couple of black eyes that had never got right. He bowled along as he walked like someone absorbed by fondness for his own body. He had been in many things before he got to work for the Council —the Army (but not a fighting soldier) in the war, in auctions and the bar of a club. He was very active, confiding and inquiring.

When I first met him I was working at the counter of the Public Library, during the war, and one day he came over from the Council Offices and said, importantly:

"Friend, we've got a bit of a headache. We've got an inquiry from the War Office. Have you got anything about Malaya—with maps."

In the next breath he was deflating himself:

"It's a personal thing. They never tell you anything. I've got a niece out there."

Honesty made him sound underhand. His manner suggested that his niece was a secret fortification somewhere east of Suez. Soon he was showing me the questionnaire from the Red Cross. Then he was telling me that his wife, like the rest of the Drapers, was very handsome—"A lovely woman" in more ways, his manner suggested, than one—but that since Hilda had gone, she had become a different woman. The transition from handsome to different was, he suggested, a catastrophe which he was obliged to share with the public. He would come in from Fire Watching (he said) and find her demented. In bed, he would add. He and I found ourselves Fire Watching together and from that time he started facetiously calling me "My secretary".

"I asked my secretary to get the sand and shovel out," he would say about our correspondence. "And he wrote the letter."

So I was half a stranger at Hilda's homecoming. I looked round the room or out at the shops opposite and, when I looked back at the family several times, I caught Hilda's eyes wandering too. She also was out of it. I studied her. I hadn't expected her to come back in rags, as old Mrs. Draper had, but it was a surprise to see she was the best dressed woman in the room and the only one who looked as if she had ever been to a hairdresser. And there was another way in which I could not match her with the person Mr. Fulmino and I had conjured. When we thought of everything that must have happened to her it was strange to see that her strong face was smooth and blank. Except for the few minutes of arrival and the time the reporters came, her face was vacant and plain. It was as vacant as a stone that has been smoothed for centuries in the sand of some hot country. It was the face of someone to whom nothing had happened; or, perhaps, so much had happened to her that each event wiped out what had happened before. I was disturbed by something in her—the lack of history, I think. We were worm-eaten by it. And that suddenly brought her back to me as she had been when she was a schoolgirl and when my older brother got into trouble for chasing after her. She was now sharper in the shoulders and elbows, no longer the swollen schoolgirl but, even as a girl, her face had the same quality of having been fixed and unchangeable between its high cheek bones. It was disturbing, in a face so anonymous, to see the eyes move, especially since she blinked very little; and if she smiled it was less a smile than an alteration of the two lines at the corners of her lips.

The party did not settle down quite in the same way after the reporters had been and there was talk of not tiring Hilda after her long journey. The family would all be meeting tomorrow, the Sunday, as they always did, when young Mrs. Jack Draper brought her children. Jack Draper was thinking of the pub which was open now and asking if anyone was going over. And then, something happened. Hilda walked over to the window to Mr. Fulmino and said, just as if she had not been there at the time.

"Ted—what did that man from the *News* ask you—about the food?"

"No," said Mr. Fulmino widening to a splendid chance of not giving the facts. "No—he said something about starving the prisoners. I was telling him that in my opinion the deterioration in conditions was inevitable after the disorganization in the camps resulting from air operations . . ."

"Oh, I thought you said we starved. We had enough."

"What?" said Mr. Fulmino.

"Bill Williams was a skeleton when he came back. Nothing

but a bowl of rice a day. Rice!" said Mrs. Fulmino. "And torture."

"Bill Williams must have been in one of those labour camps," said Hilda. "Being Japanese I was all right."

"Japanese!" said Mr. Fulmino. "You?"

"Shinji was a Japanese," said Hilda. "He was in the army."

"Your married a Japanese!" said Mrs. Fulmino, marching forward.

"That's why I was put in the American camp, when they came. They questioned every one, not only me. That's what I said to the reporter. It wasn't the food, it was the questions. What was his regiment? When did you hear from him? What was his number? They kept on. Didn't they, Mum?"

She turned to her mother who had taken the chance to cut herself another piece of cake and was about to slip it into her handkerchief, I think, to carry to her own room. We were all flabbergasted. A trolley bus went by and took a swipe at the wall. Young Mrs. Draper murmured something and her young husband Jack said loudly, hearing his wife:

"Hilda married a Nip!"

And he looked at Hilda with astonishment. He had very blue eyes.

"You weren't a prisoner!" said Mrs. Fulmino.

"Not of the Japanese," said Hilda. "They couldn't touch me. My husband was Japanese."

"I'm not stupid. I can hear," said young Mrs. Draper to her husband. She was a plain-spoken woman from the Yorkshire coalfields, one of a family of twelve.

"I've nowt to say about who you married, but where is he? Haven't you brought him?" she said.

"You were married to Mr. Singh," said Mrs. Fulmino.

"They're both dead," said Hilda, her vacant yellow eyes becoming suddenly brilliant like a cat's at night. An animal sound, like the noise of an old dog at a bone, came out of old Mrs. Draper by the fire.

"Two," she moaned.

No more than that. Simply, again: "Two."

Hilda was holding her handbag and she lifted it in both hands and covered her bosom with it. Perhaps she thought we were going to hit her. Perhaps she was going to open the bag and get out something extraordinary—documents, letters, or a handkerchief to weep into. But no—she held it there very tight. It was an American handbag—we hadn't seen one like that before, cream-coloured, like the luggage. Old Mrs. Johnson hesitated at the table, tipped the piece of cake back out of her handkerchief on to a plate, and stepped to Hilda's side and stood, very straight for once, beside her, the old blue lips very still.

"Ted," accused Hilda. "Didn't you get my letters? Mother," she stepped away from her mother, "didn't you tell them?"

"What, dear?" said old Mrs. Johnson.

"About Shinji. I wrote you. Did Mum tell you?" Hilda appealed to us and now looked fiercely at her mother.

Mrs. Johnson smiled and retired into her look of faith and modesty. She feigned deafness.

"I put it all in the post office," she said. "Every week," she said. "Until my girl comes home, I said. She'll need it."

"Mother!" said Hilda giving the old lady a small shake. "I wrote to you. I told you. Didn't you tell them?"

"What did Hilda say?" said Mr. Fulmino gently, bending down to the old lady.

"Sh! Don't worry her. She's had enough for today. What did you tell the papers, Ted?" said Mrs. Fulmino, turning on her husband. "You can't ever keep your big mouth shut, can you? You never let me see the correspondence."

"I married Shinji when the war came up," Hilda said.

And then old Mrs. Draper spoke from her armchair by the fire. She had her bad leg propped up on a hassock.

"Two," said Mrs. Draper savagely again.

Mr. Fulmino, in his defeat, lost his nerve and let slip a remark quite casually, as he thought, under his voice, but everyone heard it—a remark that Mrs. Fulmino was to remind him of in months to come.

"She strikes like a clock," he said.

We were stupefied by Mr. Fulmino's remark. Perhaps it was a relief.

"Mr. Fraser!" Hilda said to me. And now her vacant face had become dramatic and she stepped towards me, appealing outside the family. "You knew, you and Ted knew. You've got all the letters . . ."

If ever a man looked like the Captain going down with his ship and suddenly conscious, at the last heroic moment, that he is not on a ship at all, but standing on nothing and had hopelessly blundered, it was Mr. Fulmino. But we didn't go down, either of us. For suddenly old Mrs. Johnson couldn't stand straight any longer, her head wagged and drooped forward and, but for a chair, she would have fallen to the ground.

"Quick! Constance! Open the window," Mrs. Fulmino said. Hilda was on her knees by her mother.

"Are you there, Hilly?" said her mother.

"Yes, I'm here, Mum," said Hilda. "Get some water—some brandy." They took the old lady next door to the little room Hilda was sharing with her that night.

"What I can't fathom is your aunt not telling me, keeping it to herself," said Mr. Fulmino to his wife as we walked home that evening from Mrs. Draper's, and we had said "Good-bye" to Jack Draper and his wife.

He was not hurt by Mrs. Johnson's secretiveness but by an extraordinary failure of co-operation.

It was unwise of him to criticize Mrs. Fulmino's family.

"Don't be so smug," said Mrs. Fulmino. "What's it got to do with you. She was keeping it from Gran, you know Gran's tongue. She's her sister." They called old Mrs. Draper Gran or Grandma sometimes.

But when Mr. Fulmino got home he asked me in so that we could search the correspondence together. Almost at once we discovered his blunder. There it was in the letter saying a Mrs. Singh or Shinji Kobayashi had been identified.

"Shinji!" exclaimed Mrs. Fulmino, putting her big index finger on the page. "There you are, plain as dirt."

"Singh," said Mr. Fulmino. "Singh, Shinji, the same name. Some Indians write Singh, some Shinji."

"And what is Kobayashi? Indian too? Don't be a fool."

"It's the family name or Christian name of Singh," said Mr. Fulmino, doing the best he could.

Singh, Shinji, Shinji, Singh, he murmured to himself and he walked about trying to convince himself by incantation and hypnosis. He lashed himself with Kobayashi. He remembered the names of other Indians, Indian cities, mentioned the Ganges and the Himalayas; had a brief, brilliant couple of minutes when he argued that Shinji was Hindi for Singh. Mrs. Fulmino watched him with the detachment of one waiting for a bluebottle to settle so that she could swat it.

"*You* thought Kobayashi was Indian, didn't you, Harry?" he appealed to me. I did my best.

"I thought," I said weakly, "it was the address."

"Ah, the address!" Mr. Fulmino clutched at this, but he knew he was done for. Mrs. Fulmino struck.

"And what about the Sunday papers, the man from the *News*?" she said. "You open your big mouth too soon."

"Christ!" said Mr. Fulmino. It was the sound of a man who has gone to the floor.

I will come to that matter of the papers later on. It is not very important.

When we went to bed that night we must all have known in our different ways that we had been disturbed in a very long dream. We had been living on inner visions for years. It was an effect of the long war. England had been a prison. Even the sky was closed and, like convicts, we had been driven to dwelling on fancies in our dreary minds. In the cinema the camera sucks some person forward into an enormous close-up and holds a face there yards wide, filling the whole screen, all holes and pores, like some sucking octopus that might eat up an audience many rows at a time. I don't say these pictures aren't beautiful sometimes, but afterwards I get the horrors. Hilda had been a close-up like this for us when she was lost and far away. For myself, I could hardly remember Hilda. She was a collection of fragments of my childhood and I suppose I had expected a girl to return.

My father and mother looked down on the Drapers and the Johnsons. Hincham Street was "dirty" and my mother once whispered that Mr. Johnson had worked "on the line", as if that were a smell. I remember the old man's huge crinkled white beard when I was a child. It was horribly soft and like pubic hair. So I had always thought of Hilda as a railway girl, in and out of tunnels, signal boxes and main line stations, and when my older brother was "chasing" her as they said, I admired him. I listened to the quarrels that went on in our family—how she had gone to the convent school and the nuns had complained about her; and was it she or some other girl who went for car rides with a married man who waited round the corner of Hincham Street for her? The sinister phrase "The nuns have been to see her mother", stuck in my memory. It astonished me to see Hilda alive, calm, fat and walking after that, as composed as a railway engine. When I grew up and Mr. Fulmino came to the library, I was drawn into his search because she brought back those days with my brother, those clouts on the head from some friend of his, saying, "Buzz off. Little pigs have big ears," when my brother and he were whispering about her.

To Mrs. Fulmino, a woman whose feelings were in her rolling arms, flying out from one extreme to another as she talked, as if she were doing exercises, Hilda appeared in her wedding clothes and all the sexuality of an open flower, standing beside her young Indian husband who was about to become a doctor. There was trouble about the wedding, for Mr. Singh spoke a glittering and palatial English—the beautiful English a snake might speak, it seemed to the family—that made a few pock marks on his face somehow more noticeable. Old Mrs. Draper alone, against all evidence—Mr. Singh had had a red racing car—stuck to it that he was "a common lascar off a ship". Mrs. Fulmino had been terrified of Mr. Singh—she often conveyed—and had "refused to be in a room alone with him". Or "How can she let him touch her?" she would murmur, thinking about that, above all. Then whatever vision was in her mind would jump forward to Hilda, captured, raped, tortured, murdered in front of her eyes. Mrs. Fulmino's mind was voluptuous. When I first went to Mr. Fulmino's house and met Iris and we talked about Hilda, Mrs. Fulmino once or twice left the room and he lowered his voice. "The wife's upset," he said. "She's easily upset."

We had not all been under a spell. Not young Jack Draper nor his wife, for example. Jack Draper had fought in the war and where we thought of the war as something done to us and our side, Jack thought of it as something done to everybody. I remember what he said to his wife before the Fulminos and I said "Good night" to them on the Saturday Hilda came home.

"It's a shame," said Jack, "she couldn't bring the Nip with her."

"He was killed," said his wife.

"That's what I mean," said Jack. "It's a bleeding shame she couldn't."

We walked on and then young Mrs. Draper said, in her flat, northern laconic voice:

"Well, Jack, for all the to-do, you might just as well have gone to your fishing."

For Jack had made a sacrifice in coming to welcome Hilda. He went fishing up the Thames on Saturdays. The war for him was something that spoiled fishing. In the Normandy landing he had thought mostly of that. He dreamed of the time when his two boys would be old enough to fish. It was what he had had children for.

"There's always Sunday," said his wife, tempting him. Jack nodded. She knew he would not fall. He was the youngest of old Mrs. Draper's family, the baby, as they said. He never missed old Mrs. Draper's Sundays.

It was a good thing he did not, a good thing for all of us that we didn't miss, for we would have missed Hilda's second announcement.

Young Mrs. Draper provoked it. These Sunday visits to Hincham Street were a ritual in the family. It was a duty to old Mrs. Draper. We went there for our tea. She provided, though Constance prepared for it as if we were a school, for she kept house there. We recognized our obligation by paying sixpence into the green pot on the chiffonier when we left. The custom had started in the bad times when money was short; but now the money was regarded as capital and Jack Draper used to joke and say, "Who are you going to leave the green pot to, Mum?" Some of Hilda's luggage had been moved by the afternoon into her mother's little room at the back and how those two could sleep in a bed so small was a question raised by Mrs. Fulmino whose night with Mr. Fulmino required room for struggle, as I know, for this colonizing man often dropped hints about how she swung her legs over in the night.

"Have you unpacked yet, Hilda?" Mrs. Fulmino was asking.

"Unpacked!" said Constance. "Where would she put all that?"

"I've been lazy," said Hilda. "I've just hung up a few things because of the creases."

"Things do crease," said Mrs. Fulmino.

"Bill Williams said he would drop in later," said Constance.

"That man suffered," said Mrs. Fulmino, with meaning.

"He heard you were back," said Constance.

Hilda had told us about Shinji. Jack Draper listened with wonder. Shinji had been in the jute business and when the war

came he was called up to the army. He was in "Stores". Jack
scratched with delight when he heard this. "Same as I tried to
work it," Jack said. Shinji had been killed in an air raid. Jack's
wife said, to change the subject, she liked that idea, the idea of
Jack "working" anything, he always let everyone climb up on
his shoulders, "First man to get wounded. I knew he would be,"
she said. "He never looks where he's going."

"Is that the Bill Williams who worked for Ryan, the builder?"
said Hilda.

"He lives in the Culverwell Road," young Mrs. Draper said.

Old Mrs. Draper speaking from the bowels of history, said:
"He got that Sellers girl into trouble."

"Yes," exclaimed Hilda. "I remember."

"It was proved in court that he didn't," said Constance briskly
to Hilda. "You weren't here."

We were all silent. One could hear only the sounds of our cups
on the saucers and Mrs. Fulmino's murmur, "More bread and
butter?" Constance's face had its neat, pink, enamelled smile and
one saw the truthful blue of her small eyes become purer in colour.
Iris was next to me and she said afterwards something I hadn't
noticed, that Constance hated Hilda. It is one of the difficulties I
have in writing, that, all along, I was slow to see what was really
happening, not having a woman's eye or ear. And being young.
Old Mrs. Draper spoke again, her mind moving from the past
to the present with that suddenness old people have.

"If Bill Williams is coming, he knows the way," she said.

Hilda understood that remark for she smiled and Constance
flushed. (Of course, I see it now: two women in a house! Constance
had ruled old Mrs. Draper and Mrs. Johnson for years and her
money had made a big difference.) They knew that one could, as
the saying is, "trust Gran to put her oar in".

Again young Mrs. Draper changed the subject. She was a
nimble, tarry-haired woman, impatient of fancies, excitements and
disasters. She liked things flat and factual. While the family gaped
at Hilda's clothes and luggage, young Mrs. Draper had reckoned
up the cost of them. She was not avaricious or mean, but she
knew that money is money. You know that if you have done
without. So she went straight into the important question being
(as she would say), not like people in the South, double-faced
Wesleyans, but honest, plain and straight out with it, what are

they ashamed of? Jack, her husband, was frightened by her blunt-ness, and had the nervous habit of folding his arms across his chest and scratching fast under his armpits when his wife spoke out about money; some view of the river, with his bait and line and the evening flies came into his panicking mind. Mr. Fulmino once said that Jack scratched because the happiest moments of his life, the moments of escape, had been passed in clouds of gnats.

"I suppose, Hilda, you'll be thinking of what you're going to do?" young Mrs. Draper said. "Did they give you a pension?"

I was stroking Iris's knee but she stopped me, alerted like the rest of them. The word "pension'. is a very powerful word. In this neighbourhood one could divide the world into those who had pensions and those who hadn't. The phrase "the old pensioner" was one of envy, abuse and admiration. My father, for example, spoke contemptuously of pensioners. Old Mrs. Draper's husband had had a pension, but my father would never have one. As a librarian (Mr. Fulmino pointed out), I would have a pension and thereby I had overcome the first obstacle in being allowed to go out with his daughter.

"No," said Hilda. "Nothing."

"But he was your husband, you said," said Constance.

"He was in the army, you say," said young Mrs. Draper.

"Inflation," said Mr. Fulmino grandly. "The financial situation." He was stopped.

"Then," said young Mrs. Draper, "you'll have to go to work."

"My girl won't want for money," said old Mrs. Johnson sitting beside her daughter as she had done the day before.

"No," said young Mrs. Draper. "That she won't while you're alive, Mrs. Johnson. We all know that, and the way you slaved for her. But Hilda wants to look after you, I'm sure."

It was, of course, the question in everyone's mind. Did all those clothes and cases mean money or was it all show? That is what we all wanted to know. We would not have raised it at that time and in that way. It wasn't our way—we would have drifted into finding out—Hilda was scarcely home. But young Mrs. Draper had been brought up hard, as she said, twelve mouths to feed.

"*I'm* looking after *you*, Mum," said Hilda smiling at her mother.

Mrs. Johnson was like a wizened little girl gazing up at a taller sister.

"I'll take you to Monte Carlo, Mum," Hilda said.

The old lady tittered. We all laughed loudly. Hilda laughed with us.

"That gambling place!" the old lady giggled.

"That's it," laughed Hilda. "Break the bank."

"Is it across water?" said the old lady, playing up. "I couldn't go on a boat. I was so sick at Southend when I was a girl."

"Then we'll fly."

"Oh!" the old lady cried. "Don't, Hil—I'll have a fit."

"The Man Who Broke the Bank at Monte Carlo", Mr. Fulmino sang. "You might find a boy friend, Mrs. Johnson."

Young Mrs. Draper did not laugh at this game; she still wanted to know; but she did smile. She was worried by laughter. Constance did not laugh but she showed her pretty white teeth.

"Oh, she's got one for me," said Mrs. Johnson. "So she says."

"Of course I have. Haven't I, Harry?" said Hilda, talking across the table to me.

"Me? What?" I said completely startled.

"You can't take Harry," said Iris, half frightened.

"Did you post the letter?" said Hilda to me.

"What letter?" said Iris to me. "Did she give you a letter?"

Now there is a thing I ought to have mentioned! I had forgotten all about the letter. When we were leaving the evening before, Hilda had called me quietly to the door and said:

"Please post this for me. Tonight."

"Hilda gave me a letter to post," I said.

"You did post it?" Hilda said.

"Yes," I said.

She looked contentedly round at everyone.

"I wrote to Mr. Gloster, the gentleman I told you about, on the boat. He's in Paris. He's coming over at the end of the week to get a car. He's taking Mother and me to France. Mr. Gloster, Mum, I told you. No, not Mr. Faulkner. That was the other boat. He was in San Francisco."

"Oh," said Mrs. Johnson, a very long "oh" and wriggling like a child listening to a story. She was beginning to look pale, as she had the evening before when she had the turn.

"France!" said Constance in a peremptory voice.

"Who is Mr. Gloster—you never said anything," said Mrs. Fulmino.

"What about the currency regulations?" said Mr. Fulmino.

Young Mrs. Draper said, "France! He must have money."

"Dollars," said Hilda to Mr. Fulmino.

Dollars! There was a word!

"The almighty dollar," said Constance, in the cleansed and uncorrupted voice of one who has mentioned one of the commandments. Constance had principles; we had the confusion of our passions.

And from sixteen years or more back in time or perhaps it was from some point in history hundreds of years back and forgotten, old Mrs. Draper said: "And is this Indian married?"

Hilda—to whom no events, I believe, had ever happened—replied: "Mr. Gloster's an American, Gran."

"He wants to marry her," said old Mrs. Johnson proudly.

"If I'll have him!" said Hilda.

"Well, he can't if you won't have him, can he, Hilda?" said Mrs. Fulmino.

"Gloster. G-L-O-S-T-E-R?" asked Mr. Fulmino.

"Is he in a good job?" asked young Mrs. Draper.

Hilda pointed to a brooch on her blouse.

"He gave me this," she said.

She spoke in her harsh voice and with a movement of her face that in anyone else one would have called excited, but in her it had a disturbing lack of meaning. It was as if Hilda had been hooked into the air by invisible wires and was then swept out into the air and back to Japan, thousands of miles away again, and while she was on her way, she turned and knocked us flat with the next item.

"He's a writer," she said. "He's going to write a book about me. He's very interested in me . . ."

Mrs. Johnson nodded.

"He's coming to fetch us, Mum and me, and take us to France to write this book. He's going to write my life."

Her life! Here was a woman who had, on top of everything else, a life.

"Coming *here*?" said Mrs. Fulmino with a grinding look at old Mrs. Draper and then at Constance, trying to catch their eyes and failing; in despair she looked at the shabby room, to see what must be put straight, or needed cleaning or painting. Nothing had been done to it for years for Constance, teaching at her school all day, and very clean in her person, let things go in the house and young Mrs. Draper said old Mrs. Draper smelled. All the command in Mrs. Fulmino's face collapsed as rapidly, on her own, she looked at the carpets, the lino, the curtains.

"What's he putting in this book?" said young Mrs. Draper cannily.

"Yes," said Jack Draper, backing up his wife.

"What I tell him," Hilda said.

"What she tells him," said old Mrs. Johnson sparkling. Constance looked thoughtfully at Hilda.

"Is it a biography?" Constance asked coldly. There were times when we respected Constance and forgot to murmur "Go back to Russia" every time she spoke. I knew what a biography was and so did Mr. Fulmino, but no one else did.

"It's going to be made into a film," Hilda replied.

"A film," cried Iris.

Constance gleamed.

"You watch for American propaganda," said Constance. There you are, you see: Constance was back on it!

"Oh, it's about me," said Hilda. "My experience."

"Very interesting," said Mr. Fulmino, preparing to take over. "A Hollywood production, I expect. Publication first and then they go into production."

He spread his legs.

None of us had believed, or even understood what we heard, but we looked with gratitude to Mr. Fulmino for making the world steady again.

Jack Draper's eyes filled with tears because a question was working in him but he could not get it out.

"Will you be in this film?" asked Iris.

"I'll wait till he's written it," said Hilda with that lack of interest we had often noticed in her, after she had made some dramatic statement.

Mrs. Fulmino breathed out heavily with relief and after that her body seemed to become larger. She touched her hair at the back and straightened her dress, as if preparing to offer herself for the part. She said indeed:

"I used to act at school."

"She's still good at it," said Mr. Fulmino with daring to Jack Draper who always appreciated Mr. Fulmino, but seeing the danger of the moment hugged himself and scratched excitedly under both armpits, laughing.

"You shouldn't have let this Mr. Gloster go," said Constance.

Hilda was startled by this remark and looked lost. Then she shrugged her shoulders and gave a low laugh, as if to herself.

Mr. Fulmino's joke had eased our bewilderment. Hilda had been our dream but now she was home she changed as fast as dreams change. She was now, as we looked at her, far more remote to us than she had been all the years when she was away. The idea was so far beyond us. It was like some story of a bomb explosion or an elopement or a picture of bathing girls one sees in the newspapers—unreal and, in a way, insulting to being alive in the ordinary daily sense of the word. Or, she was like a picture that one sees in an art gallery, that makes you feel sad because it is painted.

After tea when Hilda took her mother to the lavatory, Constance beckoned to Iris and let her peep into the room Hilda was sharing, and young Mrs. Draper, not to be kept out of things, followed. They were back in half a minute:

"Six evening dresses," Iris said to me.

"She said it was Mr. Faulkner who gave her the luggage, not this one who was going to get her into pictures," said Mrs. Fulmino.

"Mr. Gloster, you mean," said Constance.

Young Mrs. Draper was watching the door, listening for Hilda's return.

"Ssh," she said, at the sound of footsteps on the stairs and, to look at us, the men on one side of the room and the women on the other, silent, standing at attention, facing each other, we looked like soldiers.

"Oh," said Constance. The steps we had heard were not Hilda's. It was Bill Williams who came in.

"Good afternoon one and all," he said. The words came from the corner of a mouth that had slipped down at one side. Constance drew herself up, her eyes softened. She had exact, small, round breasts. Looking around, he said to Constance: "Where is she?"

Constance lowered her head when she spoke to him, though she held it up shining, admiring him, when he spoke to us, as if she were displaying him to us.

"She'll be here in a minute," she said. "She's going into films."

"I'll take a seat in the two and fourpennies," said Bill Williams and he sat down at his ease and lit a cigarette.

Bill Williams was a very tall, sick-faced man who stooped his shoulders as if he were used to ducking under doors. His dry black hair, not oiled like Mr. Fulmino's, bushed over his forehead and he had the shoulders, arms and hands of a lorry driver. In fact, he drove a light van for a textile firm. His hazel eyes were always watching and wandering and we used to say he looked as though he was going to snaffle something but that may simply have been due to the restlessness of a man with a poor stomach. Laziness, cunning and aches and pains were suggested by him. He was a man taking his time. His eyebrows grew thick and the way one brow was raised, combined with the side-slip of his mouth, made him look like some shrewd man about to pick up a faulty rifle, hit the bull's eye five times running at a fair and moan afterwards. He glanced a good deal at Constance. He was afraid of his manners before her, we thought, because he was a rough type.

"Put it here," said Constance, bringing him an ashtray. That was what he was waiting for, for he did not look at her again.

Bill Williams brought discomfort with him whenever he came on Sundays and we were always happier when he failed to come. If there was anything private to say we tried to get it over before he came. How a woman like Constance, a true, clean, settled schoolteacher who even spoke in the clear, practical and superior manner of someone used to the voice of reason, who kept her nails so beautifully, could have taken up with him, baffled us. He was very often at Mrs. Draper's in the week, eating with them and Constance, who was thirty-five, quarrelled like a girl when she was getting things ready for him. Mrs. Fulmino could not bear the way he ate, with his elbows out and his face close to the plate. The only good thing about the affair was that, for once, Constance was overruled.

"Listen to her," Bill Williams would say with a nod of his head. "A rank red Communist. Tell us about Holy Russia, Connie."

"Constance is my correct name, not Connie," she said.

Their bickering made us die. But we respected Constance even when she was a trial. She had been twice to Russia before the war and though we argued violently with her, especially Mr. Fulmino who tried to take over Russia, and populate it with explanations, we always boasted to other people that she'd been there.

"On delegations," Mr. Fulmino would say.

But we could *not* boast that she had taken up with Bill Williams. He had been a hero when he came back from Japan, but he had never kept a job since, he was rough and his lazy zigzagging habits in his work, made even Constance impatient. He had for her the fascination a teacher feels for a bad pupil. Lately their love affair had been going better because he was working outside London and sometimes he worked at week-ends; this added to the sense of something vague and secretive in his life that had attracted Constance. For there was much that was secret in her or so she liked to hint—it was political. Again, it was the secretiveness of those who like power; she was the schoolmistress who has the threat of inside knowledge locked up in the cupboard. Once Mrs. Fulmino went purple and said to her husband—who told me, he always told me such things—that she believed Constance had lately started sleeping with Bill Williams. That was because Constance had once said to her:

"Bill and I are individuals."

Mrs. Fulmino had a row with Iris after this and stopped me seeing her for a month.

Hilda came back into the room alone. Bill Williams let his mouth slip sideways and spoke a strange word to her, saying jauntily to us: "That's Japanese."

Hilda wasn't surprised. She replied with a whole sentence in Japanese.

"That means"—but Bill Williams was beaten, and he passed it off. "Well, I'd best not tell them what it means," he said.

"East meets East," Mr. Fulmino said.

"It means," said Hilda, "you were on the other side of the fence but now the gate is open."

Bill Williams studied her inch by inch. He scratched his head.

"Straight?" he said.

"Yes," she said.

"Stone me, it was bloody closed when we were there," said Bill Williams offensively, but then said: "They fed her well, didn't they, Constance? Sit down." Hilda sat down beside him.

"Connie!" he called. "Seen these? Just the job, eh?" He was nodding at Hilda's stockings. Nylons. "Now," he said to Hilda, looking closely at her. "Where were you? It got a bit rough at the finish, didn't it?"

Jack Draper came close to them to hear, hoping that Hilda would say something about what moved him the most: the enemy. Bill Williams gave him a wink and Hilda saw it. She looked placidly at Bill Williams, considering his face, his neck, his shoulders and his hands that were resting on his knees.

"I was okey doke," she said.

Bill Williams dropped his mouth open and waggled the top of his tongue in a back tooth in his knowing manner. To our astonishment Hilda opened her mouth and gave a neat twist to her tongue in her cheek in the same way.

Bill Williams slapped his knee and to cover his defeat in this little duel, said to all of us:

"This little girl's got yellow eyes."

All the colour had gone from Connie's face as she watched the meeting.

"They say you're going to be in pictures," said Bill Williams.

And then we had Hilda's story over again. Constance asked what papers Mr. Gloster wrote for.

"I don't know. A big paper," said Hilda.

"You ought to find out," Constance said. "I'll find out."

"Um," said Hilda with a nod of not being interested.

"I could give him some of my experience," said Bill Williams. "Couldn't I, Connie? Things I've told you—you could write a ruddy book."

He looked with challenge at Hilda. He was a rival.

"Gawd!" he exclaimed. "The things."

We heard it again, how he was captured, where his battery was, the long march, Sergeant Harris who was hanged, Corporal Rowley bayoneted and left to die in the sun, the starvation, the work on the road that killed half of them. But there was one difference between this story and the ones he had told before. The sight of Hilda altered it.

"You had to get round the guards," he said with a wink. "If you used your loaf a bit, eh? Scrounge around, do a bit of trade. One or two had Japanese girls. Corporal Jones went back afterwards trying to trace his, wanted to marry her."

Hilda listened and talked about places she had lived in, how she had worked in a factory.

"That's it," said Bill Williams, "you had to know your way around and talk a bit of the lingo."

Jack Draper looked with affection and wonder at the talk, lowering his eyes if her eyes caught his. Every word entered him. The heat! she said. The rain. The flowers. The telegraph poles! Jack nodded.

"They got telegraph poles," he nodded to us.

You sleep on the floor. Shinji's mother, she mentioned. She could have skinned her. Jack, brought up among so many women, lost interest, but it revived when she talked of Shinji. You could see him mouthing his early marvelling sentence: "She married a Nip," but not saying it. She was confirming something he had often thought of in Normandy; the men on the other side were married too. A bloody marvel. Why hadn't she brought him home? He would have had a friend.

"Who looked after the garden when Shinji was called up?" he asked. "Were they goldfish, ordinary goldfish, in the pond?"

Young Mrs. Draper shook her head.

"Eh," she said. "If he'd a known he'd have come over to change the water. Next time we have a war you just let him know."

Mrs. Fulmino who was throbbing like a volcano said:

"We better all go next time by the sound of it." At the end, Bill Williams said:

"I suppose you're going to be staying here."

"No," said Constance quickly, "she isn't. She's going to France. When is it, Hilda? When is Mr. Gloster coming?"

"Next week, I don't know," said Hilda.

"You shouldn't have let him go!" laughed Bill Williams. "Those French girls will get him in Paree."

"That is what I have been saying," said Constance. "He gave her that brooch."

"Oh ah! It's the stockings I'm looking at," said Bill Williams. "How did you get all that stuff through the customs? Twenty cases, Connie told me."

"Twelve," said Hilda.

Bill Williams did not move her at all. Presently she got up and started clearing away the tea things. I will say this for her, she didn't let herself be waited on.

Iris, Mr. and Mrs. Fulmino and the young Drapers and their children and myself, left Hincham Street together.

"You walk in front with the children, Iris," said Mrs. Fulmino. Then they turned on me. What was this letter, they wanted to know. Anyone would have thought by their questions that I ought to have opened it and read it.

"I just posted it at the corner." I pointed to the pillar box. Mrs. Fulmino stopped to look at the pillar box and I believe was turning over in her mind the possibility of getting inside it. Then she turned on her husband and said with contemptuous suspicion: "Monte Carlo!" As if he had worked the whole thing in order to go there himself.

"Two dead," she added in her mother's voice, the voice of one who would have been more than satisfied with the death of one.

"Not having a pension hasn't hurt her," said Mrs. Draper.

"Not a tear," said Mrs. Fulmino.

Jack and Mr. Fulmino glanced at each other. It was a glance of surreptitious gratitude: tears—they had escaped that.

Mr. Fulmino said: "The Japanese don't cry."

Mrs. Fulmino stepped out, a bad sign; her temper was rising.

"Who was the letter to?" she asked me. "Was the name Gloster."

"I didn't look," I said.

Mrs. Fulmino looked at her husband and me and rolled her eyes. Another of our blunders!

"I don't believe it," she said.

But Mrs. Fulmino *did* believe it. We all believed and disbelieved everything at once.

I said I would come to the report in the *News*. It was in thick lettering like mourning, with Hilda's picture: A Mother's Faith. Four Years in Jap Torture Camp. London Girl's Ordeal. And then an account of how Hilda had starved and suffered and been brain-washed by questioners. Even Hilda was awed when she read it, feeling herself drain away, perhaps, and being replaced by this fantasy; and for the rest of us, we had become used to living in a period when events reduced us to beings so trivial that we had no strong feeling of our own existence in relation to the world around us. We had been bashed first one way, then the other, by propaganda, until we were indifferent. At one time people like my parents or old Mrs. Draper could at least trust the sky and feel that it was certain and before it they could have at least the importance of being something in the eye of heaven.

Constance read the newspaper report and it fulfilled her.

"Propaganda," she said. "Press lies."

"All lies," Mr. Fulmino agreed with wonder. The notion that the untrue was as effective as the true opened to him vast areas to his powers. It was like a temptation.

It did not occur to us that we might be in a difficult situation in the neighbourhood when the truth came out, until we heard Constance and Bill Williams had gone over to the Lord Nelson with the paper and Constance had said, "You can't believe a word you read in the capitalist Press."

Alfred Levy, the proprietor and a strong Tory, agreed with her. But was Hilda criticized for marrying an enemy? The hatred of the Japanese was strong at this time. She was not. Constance may not have had the best motives for spreading the news, we said, but it did no harm at all. That habit of double vision affected every one publicly. We lived in the true and the untrue, comfortably and without trouble. People picked up the paper, looked at her picture and said, "That's a shocking thing. A British subject," and even when they knew, even from Hilda's own lips the true story, they said, congratulating themselves on their cunning, "The papers make it all up."

Of course, we were all in that stage where the forces of life, the desire to live, were coming back, and although it was not yet openly expressed, we felt that curiosity about the enemy that ex-soldiers like Jack Draper felt when he wondered if some Japanese or some Germans were as fed up as he was on Saturdays by missing a day's fishing. When people shook Hilda's hand they felt they gave her life. I do not say there were not one or two mutterings afterwards, for people always went off from the Lord Nelson when it closed in a state of moralization: beer must talk; the louts singing and the couples saying this or that "wasn't right". But this gossip came to nothing because, sooner or later, it came to a closed door in everybody's conscience. There were the men who had shot off trigger fingers, who had got false medical certificates, deserters, ration frauds, black marketeers, the pilferers of army stores. And the women said a woman is right to stand by her husband and, looking at Hilda's fine clothes, pointed out to their husbands that that kind of loyalty was sometimes rewarded; indeed, Mrs. Fulmino asserted, by law.

We had been waiting for Hilda; now, by a strange turn, we were waiting for Hilda's Mr. Gloster. We waited for a fortnight and it ran on into three weeks. George Hartman Gloster. I looked up the name on our cards at the library, but we had no books of his. I looked up one or two catalogues. Still nothing. It was not surprising. He was an American who was not published in this country. Constance came in and looked too.

"It is one of those names the Americans don't list," she said. Constance smiled with the cool air of keeping a world of meaningful secrets on ice.

"They don't list everything," she said.

She brought Bill Williams with her. I don't think he had ever been in a public library before, because his knowing manner went and he was overawed. He said to me:

"Have you read all these books? Do you buy them secondhand? What's this lot worth?"

He was a man always on the look-out for a deal; it was typical of him that he had come with Constance in his firm's light-green van. It was not like Constance to travel in that way. "Come on," he said roughly.

The weather was hot; we had the sun blinds down in the Library. We were in the middle of one of those brassy fortnights of the London summer when English life, as we usually know it, is at a standstill, and everyone changes. A new grinning healthy race with long red necks sticking out of open shirts and blouses appears, and the sun brings out the variety of faces and bodies. Constance might have been some trim nurse marching at the head of an official procession. People looked calm, happy and open. There was hardly ever a cloud in the sky, the slate roofs looked like steel with the sun's rays hitting them, and the side streets were cool in sharp shadow. It was a pleasant time for walking, especially when the sky went whitish in the distances of the city in the evening and when the streets had a dry pleasant smell and the glass of millions of windows had a motionless but not excluding stare. Even a tailor working late above a closed shop looked pleased to be going on working, while everyone else was out, wearing out their clothes.

Iris and I used to go to the park on some evenings and there every blade of grass had been wire-brushed by sunlight; the trees were heavy with still leaves and when darkness came they gathered into soft black walls and their edges were cut out against the nail varnish of the city's night. During the day the park was crowded.

All over the long sweeps of grass the couples were lying, their legs at careless angles, their bottoms restless as they turned to the horseplay of love in the open. Girls were leaning over the men rumpling their hair, men were tickling the girls' chins with stalks of grass. Occasionally they would knock the wind out of each other with plunging kisses; and every now and then a girl would sit up and straighten her skirt at the waist, narrowing her eyes in a pretence of looking at some refining sight in the distance, until she was pulled down again and, keeping her knees together, was caught again. Lying down you smelt the grass and listened to the pleasant rumble of the distant traffic going round like a wheel that never stopped.

I was glad to know the Fulminos and to go out with Iris. We had both been gayer before we met each other, but seriousness, glumness, a sadness came over us when we became friends—that eager sadness that begins with thoughts of love. We encouraged and discouraged these thoughts in each other yet were always hinting and the sight of so much love around us turned us naturally away from it to think about it privately the more. She was a beautifully-formed girl as her mother must have once been, but slender. She had a wide laugh that shook the curls of her thick black hair. She was being trained at a typing school.

One day when I was sitting in the park and Iris was lying beside me, we had a quarrel. I asked her if there was any news of Mr. Gloster—for she heard everything. She had said there was none and I said, sucking a piece of grass:

"That's what I would like to do. Go round the world. Anywhere. America, Africa, China."

"A chance is a fine thing," said Iris, day dreaming.

"I could get a job," I said.

Iris sat up.

"Leave the Library?" she said.

"Yes," I said. "If I stay there I won't see anything." I saw Iris's face change and become very like her mother's. Mrs. Fulmino could make her face go larger and her mouth go very small. Iris did not answer. I went on talking. I asked her what she thought. She still did not answer.

"Anything the matter?" She was sulking. Then she said, flashing at me:

"You're potty on that woman too. You all are. Dad is, Jack is;

and look at Bill Williams. Round at Hincham Street every day. He'll be having his breakfast there soon. Fascinated."

"He goes to see Constance."

"Have you seen Constance's face," she jeered. "Constance could kill her."

"She came to the Library."

"Ah," she turned to me. "You didn't tell me that."

"She came in for a book, I told you. For Mr. Gloster's books. Bill Williams came with her."

Iris's sulk changed into satisfaction at this piece of news.

"Mother says if Constance's going to marry a man like Mr. Williams," she said, "she'll be a fool to let him out of her sight."

'I'll believe in Mr. Gloster when I see him," Iris said. It was, of course, what we were all thinking. We made up our quarrel and I took Iris home. Mrs. Fulmino was dressed up, just putting the key in the door of her house. Iris was astonished to see her mother had been out and asked where she had been.

"Out," said Mrs. Fulmino. "Have I got to stay in and cook and clean for you all day?"

Mrs. Fulmino was even wearing gloves, as if she had been to church. And she was wearing a new pair of shoes. Iris went pale at the sight of them. Mrs. Fulmino put her gloves down on the sitting-room table and said:

"I've got a right to live, I suppose?"

We were silenced.

One thing we all agreed on while we waited for Mr. Gloster was that Hilda had the money and knew how to spend it. The first time she asked the Fulminos and young Drapers to the cinema, Mrs. Fulmino said to her husband:

"You go. I've got one of my heads."

"Take Jack," young Mrs. Draper said. "I've got the children."

They were daring their husbands to go with her. But the second time, there was a party, Hilda took some of them down to Kew. She took old Mrs. Johnson down to Southend—and who should they meet there but Bill Williams who was delivering some goods there, spoiling their day because old Mrs. Johnson did not like his ways. And Hilda had given them all presents. And two or three nights a week she was out at the Lord Nelson.

It was a good time. If anyone asked, "Have you heard from Mr.

Gloster yet?" Hilda answered that it was not time yet and, as a dig at Constance that we all admired, she said once: "He has business at the American Embassy." And old Mrs. Johnson held her head high and nodded.

At the end of three weeks we became restless. We noticed old Mrs. Johnson looked poorly. She said she was tired. Old Mrs. Draper became morose. She had been taught to call Mr. Gloster by his correct name, but now she relapsed.

"Where is this Indian?" she uttered.

And another day, she said, without explanation:

"Three."

"Three what, Gran?"

"There've been two, that's enough."

No one liked this, but Mrs. Johnson understood.

"Mr. Gloster's very well, isn't he, Hil? You heard from him yesterday?" she said.

"I wasn't shown the letter," said old Mrs. Draper. "We don't want a third."

"We don't," said Mrs. Fulmino. With her joining in "on Gran's side", the situation changed. Mrs. Fulmino had a low voice and the sound of it often sank to the floor of any room she was in, travelling under chairs and tables, curling round your feet and filling the place from the bottom as if it were a cistern. Even when the trolley bus went by Mrs. Fulmino's low voice prevailed. It was an undermining voice, breaking up one's uppermost thoughts and stirring up what was underneath them. It stirred us all now. Yes, we wanted to say, indeed, we wanted to shout, where is this Mr. Gloster, why hasn't he come, did you invent him? He's alive, we hope? Or is he also—as Gran suggests—dead?

Even Mr. Fulmino was worried.

"Have you got his address?" he asked.

"Yes, Uncle dear," said Hilda. "He'll be staying at the Savoy. He always does."

Mr. Fulmino had not taken out his notebook for a long time but he did so now. He wrote down the name.

"Has he made a reservation?" said Mr. Fulmino. "I'll find out if he's booked."

"He hasn't," said Bill Williams. "I had a job down there and I asked. Didn't I, Connie?"

Mrs. Fulmino went a very dark colour. She wished she had

thought of doing this. Hilda was not offended, but a small smile clipped her lips as she glanced at Connie:

"I asked Bill to do it," she said.

And then Hilda in that harsh lazy voice which she had always used for announcements: "If he doesn't come by Wednesday you'll have to speak for me at your factory, Mr. Williams. I don't know why he hasn't come, but I can't wait any more."

"Bill can't get you a job. You have to register," said Constance.

"Yes, she'll have to do that," said Mr. Fulmino.

"I'll fix it. Leave it to me," said Bill Williams.

"I expect," said young Mrs. Draper, "his business has kept him." She was sorry for Hilda.

"Perhaps he's gone fishing," said Jack Draper, laughing loudly in a kind way. No one joined in.

"Fishing for orders," said Bill Williams.

Hilda shrugged her shoulders and then she made one of those remarks that Grandma Draper usually made—I suppose the gift really ran through the family.

"Perhaps it was a case," she said, "of ships that pass in the night."

"Oh no, dear," said Mrs. Johnson trembling, "not ships." We went to the bus stop afterwards with the Fulminos and the young Drapers. Mrs. Fulmino's calm had gone. She marched out first, her temper rising.

"Ships!" she said. "When you think of what we went through during the war. Did you hear her? Straight out?"

"My brother Herbert's wife was like that. She's a widow. Take away the pension and they'll work like the rest of us. I had to."

"Job! Work! I know what sort of work she's been doing. Frank, walk ahead with Iris."

"Well," said young Mrs. Draper, "she won't be able to go to work in those clothes and that's a fact."

"All show," said Mrs. Fulmino triumphantly. "And I'll tell you something else—she hasn't a penny. She's run through her poor mother's money."

"Ay, I don't doubt," said young Mrs. Draper, who had often worked out how much the old lady had saved.

Mr. Gloster did not come on Wednesday or on any other day, but Hilda did not get a job either, not at once. And old Mrs.

Johnson did not go to Monte Carlo. She died. This was the third, we understood, that old Mrs. Draper had foreseen.

Mrs. Johnson died at half past eight in the morning just after Constance had gone off to school, the last day of the term, and before old Mrs. Draper had got up. Hilda was in the kitchen wearing her blue Japanese wrap when she heard her mother's loud shout, like a man selling papers, she said, and when Hilda rushed in her mother was sitting up in bed. She gripped Hilda with the ferocity of the dying, as if all the strength of her whole life had come back and she was going to throw her daughter to the ground. Then she died. In an hour she looked like a white leaf that has been found after a lifetime pressed between the pages of a book and as delicate as a saint. The death was not only a shock; from the grief that spread from it staining all of us, I trace the ugly events that followed. Only the frail figure of old Mrs. Johnson, with her faith and her sly smile, had protected us from them until then, and when she went, all defence went with her.

I need not describe her funeral—it was done by Bickersons: Mr. Fulmino arranged it. But one thing astonished us: not only our families but the whole neighbourhood was affected by the death of this woman who, in our carelessness, we thought could hardly be known to anyone. She had lived there all her life, of course, but people come and go in London, only a sluggish residue stay still: and I believe it was just because a large number of passing people knew just a little about her, because she was a fragment in their minds, that her death affected them. They recognized that they themselves were not people but fragments. People remembered her going into shops now and then, or going down to the bus stop, passing down a street. They remembered the bag of American cloth she used to carry containing her sewing—they spoke for a long time afterwards about this bag, more about it, indeed, than about herself.

Bickersons is a few doors from the Lord Nelson, so that when the hearse stood there covered with flowers everyone noticed it, and although the old lady had not been in that public house for years since the death of her husband, all the customers came out to look. And they looked at Hilda sitting in her black in the car when the hearse moved slowly off and all who knew her story must have felt that the dream was burying the dreamer. Hilda's face was dirty with grief and she did not turn her head to right or left as they drove off. I remember a small thing that happened when we were all together at old Mrs. Draper's, after we had got her back with difficulty up the stairs.

"Bickersons did it very well," said Mr. Fulmino, seeking to distract the old lady who, swollen with sadness, was uncomfortable in her best clothes. "They organize everything so well. They gave me this."

He held up a small brass disc on a little chain. It was one of those identity discs people used to wear on their wrists in the war.

"She had never taken it off," he said. It swung feebly on its chain. Suddenly, with a sound like a shout Mr. Fulmino broke into tears. His face caved in and he apologized: "It's the feeling," he said. "You have the feeling. You feel." And he looked at us with panic, astonished by this discovery of an unknown self, spongy with tears, that had burst out and against whom he was helpless.

Mrs. Fulmino said gently:

"I expect Hilda would like to have it."

"Yes, yes. It's for her," he said, drying his eyes and Hilda took it from him and carried it to her room. While she was there (and perhaps she was weeping too), Mr. Fulmino looked out from his handkerchief and said, still sobbing:

"I see that the luggage has gone."

None of us had noticed this and we looked at Constance who said in a whisper: "She is leaving us. She has found a room of her own." That knocked us back. "Leaving!" we exclaimed. It told against Hilda for, although we talked of death being a release for the dead person we did not like to think of it as a release for the living; grief ought to hold people together and it seemed too brisk to have started a new life so soon. Constance alone looked pleased by this. We were whispering but stopped when we heard Hilda coming back.

Black had changed her. It set off her figure and although crying had hardened her, the skin of her neck and her arms and the swell of her breasts seemed more living than they had before. She looked stronger in body perhaps because she was shaken in mind. She looked very real, very present, more alive than ourselves. She had not heard us whispering, but she said, to all of us, but particularly to Mr. Fulmino:

"I have found a room for myself. Constance spoke to Bill

Williams for me, he's good at getting things. He found me a place
and he took the luggage round yesterday. I couldn't sleep in that
bed alone any more."

Her voice was shaky.

"She didn't take up much room. She was tiny and we managed.
It was like sleeping with a little child."

Hilda smiled and laughed a little.

"She even used to kick like a kid."

Ten minutes on the bus from Hincham Street and close to the
centre of London is a dance hall called "The Temple Rooms".
It has two bands, a low gallery where you can sit and a soft drink
bar. Quite a few West Indians go there, mainly students. It is a
respectable place; it closes at eleven and there is never any trouble.
Iris and I went there once or twice. One evening we were surprised
to see Constance and Bill Williams dancing there. Iris pointed to
them. The rest of the people were jiving, but Bill Williams and
Constance were dancing in the old-fashioned way.

"Look at his feet!" Iris laughed.

Bill Williams was paying no attention to Constance, but looking
around the room over her head as he stumbled along. He was tall.

"Fancy Auntie Constance!" said Iris. "She's getting fed up
because he won't listen."

Constance Draper dancing! At her age! Thirty-eight!

"It's since the funeral," said Mr. Fulmino over our usual cup of
tea. "She was fond of the old lady. It's upset her."

Even I knew Mr. Fulmino was wrong about this. The madness
of Constance dated from the time Bill Williams had taken Hilda's
luggage round to her room and got her a job at the reception desk
in the factory at Laxton. It dated from the time, a week later, when
standing at old Mrs. Draper's early one evening, Constance had
seen Hilda get out of Bill Williams's van. He had given her a lift
home. It dated from words that passed between Hilda and Constance
soon afterwards. Hilda said Williams hung around for her at the
factory and wanted her to go to a dance. She did not want to go,
she said—and here came the fatal sentences—both of her husbands
had been educated men. Constance kept her temper but said
coldly:

"Bill Williams is politically educated."

Hilda had her vacant look.

"Not his hands aren't," she said.

The next thing, Constance—who hardly went into a pub in her life—was in the Lord Nelson night after night, playing bar billiards with Bill Williams. She never let him out of her sight. She came out of school and instead of going home, marking papers and getting a meal for herself and old Mrs. Draper, she took the bus out to the factory and waited for him to come out. Sometimes he had left on some job by the time she got there and she came home, beside herself, questioning everybody. It had been her habit to come twice a week to change her library books. Now she did not come. She stopped reading. At The Temple Rooms, when Iris and I saw her, she sat out holding hands with Bill Williams and rubbing her head into his shoulder, her eyes watching him the whole time. We went to speak to them and Constance asked:

"Is Hilda here tonight?"

"I haven't seen her."

"She's a whore," said Constance in a loud voice. We thought she was drunk.

It was a funny thing, Mr. Fulmino said to me, to call a woman a whore. He spoke as one opposed to funny things.

"If they'd listened to me," he said, "I could have stopped all this trouble. I offered to get her a job in the council office but," he rolled his eyes, "Mrs. F. wouldn't have it and while we were arguing about it, Bill Williams acts double quick. It's all because this Mr. Gloster didn't turn up."

Mr. Fulmino spoke wistfully. He was, he conveyed, in the middle of a family battle; indeed, he had a genuine black eye the day we talked about this. Mrs. Fulmino's emotions were in her arms.

This was a bad period for Mr. Fulmino because he had committed a folly. He had chosen this moment to make a personal triumph. He had got himself promoted to a much better job at the Council Offices and one entitling him to a pension. He had become a genuine official. To have promoted a man who had the folly to bring home a rich whore with two names, so causing the robbery and death of her mother, and to have let her break Constance's heart, was, in Mrs. Fulmino's words, a crime. Naturally, Mr. Fulmino regarded his mistakes as mere errors of routine and even part of his training for his new position.

"Oh well," he said when we finished our tea and got up to pay the bill, "it's the British taxpayer that pays." He was heading for politics. I have heard it said, years later, that if he had had a better start in life he would have gone to the top of the administration. It is a tragic calling.

If Hilda was sinister to Constance and Mrs. Fulmino, she made a different impression on young Mrs. Draper. To call a woman a whore was neither here nor there to her. Up north where she came from people were saying that sort of thing all day long as they scrubbed floors or cleaned windows or did the washing. The word gave them energy and made things come up cleaner and whiter. Good money was earned hard; easy money went easy. To young Mrs. Draper Hilda seemed "a bit simple", but she had gone to work, she earned her living. Cut off from the rest of the Draper family, Hilda made friends with this couple. Hilda went with them on Saturday to the Zoo with the children. They were looking at a pair of monkeys. One of them was dozing and its companion was awake, pestering and annoying it. The children laughed. But when they moved on to another cage, Hilda said, sulkily:

"That's one thing. Bill Williams won't be here. He pesters me all the time."

"He won't if you don't let him," said young Mrs. Draper.

"I'm going to give my notice if he doesn't stop," said Hilda. She hunched a shoulder and looked around at the animals.

"I can't understand a girl like Constance taking up with him. He's not on her level. And he's mean. He doesn't give her anything. I asked if he gave her that clip, but she said it was Gran's. Well, if a man doesn't give you anything he doesn't value you. I mean she's a well-read girl."

"There's more ways than one of being stupid," said young Mrs. Draper.

"I wonder she doesn't see," said Hilda. "He's not delivering for the firm. When he's got the van out, he's doing something on the side. When I came home with him there was stuff at the back. And he keeps on asking how much things cost. He offered to sell my bracelet."

"You'd get a better price in a shop if you're in need," said young Mrs. Draper.

"She'd better not be with him if he gets stopped on the road," said Jack joining in. "You wouldn't sell that. Your husband gave it you."

"No. Mr. Faulkner," said Hilda, pulling out her arm and admiring it.

Jack was silent and disappointed; then he cheered up.

"You ought to have married that earl you were always talking about when you were a girl. Do you remember?" he said.

"Earls—they're a lazy lot," said young Mrs. Draper.

"I did, Jack," said Hilda. "They were as good as earls, both of them."

And to young Mrs. Draper she said: "They wouldn't let another man look at me. I felt like a woman with both of them."

"I've nowt against that if you've got the time," said young Mrs. Draper. She saw that Hilda was glum.

"Let's go back and look at the giraffes. Perhaps Mr. Faulkner will come for you now Mr. Gloster hasn't," young Mrs. Draper said.

"They were friends," said Hilda.

"Oh, they knew each other!" said young Mrs. Draper. "I thought you just . . . met them . . ."

"No, I didn't meet them together, but they were friends."

"Yes. Jack had a friend, didn't you?" said Mrs. Draper, remembering.

"That's right," said Jack. He winked at Hilda. "Neck and neck, it was." And then he laughed outright.

"I remember something about Bill Williams. He came out with us one Saturday and you should have seen his face when we threw the fish back in the water."

"We always throw them back," said young Mrs. Draper taking her husband's arm, proudly.

"Wanted to sell them or something. Black market perch!"

"He thinks I've got dollars," said Hilda.

"No, fancy that, Jack—Mr. Gloster and Mr. Faulkner being friends. Well, that's nice." And she looked sentimentally at Hilda.

"She's brooding," young Mrs. Draper said to Mrs. Fulmino after this visit to the Zoo. "She won't say anything." Mrs. Fulmino said she had better not or *she* might say something. "She knows what I think. I never thought much of Bill Williams, but he served his country. She didn't."

"She earns her living," said Mrs. Draper.

"Like we all do," said Mrs. Fulmino. "And it's not men, men, men all day long with you and me."

"One's enough," said young Mrs. Draper, "with two children round your feet."

"She doesn't come near me," said Mrs. Fulmino.

"No," Mr. Fulmino said sadly, "after all we've done."

They used to laugh at me when I went dancing with Iris at The Temple Rooms. We had not been there for more than a month and Iris said: "He can't stop staring at the band."

She was right. The beams of the spotlights put red, green, violet and orange tents on the hundreds of dancers. It was like the Arabian Nights. When we got there, Ted Coster's band was already at it like cats on dustbins and tearing their guts out. The pianist had a very thin neck and kept wagging his head as if he were ga-ga; if his head had fallen off he would have caught it in one of his crazy hands and popped it on again without losing a note; the trumpet player had thick eyebrows that went higher and higher as he tried and failed to burst; the drummers looked doped; the saxophone went at it like a man in bed with a girl who had purposely left the door open. I remember them all, especially the thin-lipped man, very white-faced with the double bass drawing his bow at knee level, to and fro, slowly, sinful. They all whispered, nodded and rocked together, telling dirty stories until bang, bang, bang, the dancers went faster and faster, the row hit the ceiling or died out with the wheeze of a balloon. I was entranced.

"Don't look as though you're going to kill someone," Iris said.

That shows how wrong people are. I was full of love and wanted to cry.

After four dances I went off to the soft drink bar and there the first person I saw was Bill Williams. He was wearing a plum-coloured suit and a red and silver tie and he stood, with his dark hair dusty-looking and sprouting forward as if he had just got out of bed and was ducking his head on the way to the bathroom.

"All the family here?" he asked, looking all round.

"No," I said. "Just Iris and me."

He went on looking around him.

"I thought you only came Saturdays," he said suspiciously. He had a couple of friends with him, two men who became restless on their feet, as if they were dancing, when I came up.

"Oh," said Bill Williams. Then he said, "Nicky pokey doda—that's Japanese, pal, for keep your mouth shut. Anyone say anything, you never see me. I'm at Laxton, get me? Bill Williams? He's on night shift. You must be barmy. Okay? Seeing you," he said. "No sign of Constance."

And he walked off. His new friends went a step or two after him, dancing on their pointed shoes and then stopped. They twizzled round, tapping their feet, looking all round the room until he had got to the carpeted stairs at the end of the hall. I got my squash and when I turned round, the two men had gone too.

But before Bill Williams had got to the top of the stairs he turned round to look at the dancers in one corner. There was Hilda. She was dancing with a young West Indian. When I got back to our table she was very near.

I have said that Hilda's face was eventless. It was now in a tranced state, looking from side to side, to the floor, in the quick turns of the dance, swinging round, stepping back, stepping forward. The West Indian had a long jacket on. His knees were often nearly bent double as though he were going to do some trick of crawling towards her, then he recovered himself and turned his back as if he had never met her and was dancing with someone else. If Hilda's face was eventless, it was the event itself, it was the dance.

She saw us when the dance was over and came to our table breathlessly. She was astonished to see us. To me she said, "And fancy you!" She did not laugh or even smile when she looked at me. I don't know how to describe her look. It was dead. It had no expression. It had nothing. Or rather, by the smallest twitch of a muscle, it became nothing. Her face had the nakedness of a body. She saw that I was deaf to what Iris was saying. Then she smiled and in doing that, she covered herself.

"I am with friends over there"—we could not tell who the friends were—then she leaned to us and whispered:

"Bill Williams is here too."

Iris exclaimed.

"He's watching me," Hilda said.

"I saw him," I said. "He's gone."

Hilda stood up frowning.

"Are you sure? Did you see him? How long ago?"

I said it was about five minutes before.

She stood as I remember her standing in Mrs. Draper's room on the first day when she arrived and was kissing everyone. It was a peculiar stance because she usually stood so passively; a stance of action and, I now saw, a stance of plain fright. One leg was planted forward and bent at the knee like a runner at the start and one arm was raised and bent at the elbow, the elbow pushed out beyond her body. Her mouth was open and her deep-set yellow eyes seemed to darken and look tired.

"He was with some friends," I said and, looking back at the bar, "They've gone now."

"Hah!" It was the sound of a gasp of breath. Then suddenly the fright went and she shrugged her shoulders and talked and laughed to all of us. Soon she went over to her friends, the coloured man and a white couple; she must have got some money or the ticket for her handbag from one of them, for presently we saw her walking quickly to the cloakroom.

Iris went on dancing. We must have stayed another half an hour and when we were leaving we were surprised to see Hilda waiting in the foyer. She said to me:

"His car has gone."

"Whose?"

"Bill Williams's car."

"Has he got a car?" Iris said.

"Oh, it's not his," said Hilda. "It's gone. That's something. Will you take me home? I don't want to go alone. They followed me here."

She looked at all of us. She was frightened.

I said, "Iris and I will take you on our way."

"Don't make me late," said Iris crossly. "You know what Mum is." I promised. "Did you come with him?"

"No, with someone else," Hilda said, looking nervously at the glass swing door. "Are you sure his friends went too? What did they look like?"

I tried to describe them.

"I've seen the short one," she said, frowning, "somewhere."

It was only a quarter of an hour's ride at that hour of the night. We walked out of The Temple Rooms and across the main road to the bus stop and waited under the lights that made our faces corpse-like. I have always liked the hard and sequinned sheen of London streets at night, their empty dockyard look. The cars come down them like rats. The red trolley bus came up at last and when we got in Hilda sat between us. The bus-load of people stared at her and I am not surprised. I have said what she looked like—the hair built up high, her bright green wrap and red dress. I don't know how you would describe such clothes. But the people were not staring at her clothes. They were staring at her eyebrows. I said before that her face was an extension of her nudity and I say it again. Those eyebrows of hers were painted and looked like the only things she had on—they were like a pair of beetles with turned up tails that had settled on her forehead. People laughed under their hands and two or three youths at the front of the bus turned round and guffawed and jostled and whistled; but Hilda, remember, was not a girl of sixteen gone silly, but a woman, hard rather than soft in the face, and the effect was one of exposure, just as a mask has the effect of exposing.

We did not talk but when the trolley arm thumped two or three times at a street junction, Hilda said with a sigh, "Bump! Bump! Bump!" She was thinking of her childhood in old Mrs. Draper's room at Hincham Street. We got off the bus a quarter of a mile further on and, as she was stepping off, Hilda said, speaking of what was in her mind, I suppose, during the ride:

"Shinji had a gold wrist-watch with a gold strap and a golden pen. They had gone when he was killed. They must have cost him a hundred pounds. Someone must have stolen them and sold them."

"I reported it," Hilda said. "I needed the money. That is what you had to do—sell something. I had to eat."

And the stare from her mask of a face stated something of her life that her strangeness had concealed from us. We walked up the street.

She went on talking about that watch and how particular Shinji was about his clothes, especially his shirts. All his collars had to be starched, she said. Those had gone too, she said. And his glasses. And his two gold rings. She walked very quickly between us. We got to the corner of her street. She stopped and looked down it.

"Bill Williams's van!" she said.

About thirty houses down the street we could indeed see a small van standing.

"He's waiting for me," she said.

It was hard to know whether she was frightened or whether she was reckoning, but my heart jumped. She made us stand still and watch. "My room's in the front," she said. I crossed over to the other side of the street and then came back.

"The light is on," I said.

"He's inside," she said.

"Shall I go and see?" I said.

"Go," said Iris to me.

Hilda held my wrist.

"No," she said.

"There are two people, I think, in the front garden," I said.

"I'm going home with you," Hilda said to Iris decisively. She rushed off and we had to race after her. We crossed two or three streets to the Fulminos' house. Mrs. Fulmino let us in.

"Now, now, Hilda, keep your hair on. Kill you? Why should he? This is England, this isn't China . . ."

Mr. Fulmino's face showed his agony. His mouth collapsed, his eyes went hard. He looked frantic with appeal. Then he turned his back on us, marched into the parlour and shouted as if he were calling across four lines of traffic:

"Turn the wireless off."

We followed him into the room. Mrs. Fulimo, in the suddenly silent room, looked like a fortress waiting for a flag to fall.

We all started talking at once.

"Can I stay with you tonight?" she said. "Bill Williams has broken into my house. I can't go there. He'll kill me." The flag fell.

"Japan," said Mrs. Fulmino disposing of her husband with her first shot. Then she turned to Hilda; her voice was coldly rich and rumbling. "You've always a home here, as you well know, Hilda," she went on, giving a very unhomely sound to the word. "And," she said, glancing at her neat curtains to anyone who might be in ambush outside the window, "if anyone tries to kill you, they will have to kill," she nodded to her husband, "Ted and me first. What have you been doing?"

"I was down at The Temple. Not with Bill Williams," said Hilda. "He was watching me. He's always watching me."

"Now look here, Hilda, why should Bill Williams want to kill you? Have you encouraged him?"

"Don't be a fool!" shouted Mrs. Fulmino.

"She knows what I mean. Listen to me, Hilda. What's going on between you and Bill Williams? Constance is upset, we all know."

"Oh keep your big mouth shut," said Mrs. Fulmino. "Of

course she's encouraged him. Hilda's a woman, isn't she? I encouraged you, didn't I?"

"I know how to look after myself," said Hilda, "but I don't like that van outside the house at this hour of night, I didn't speak to him at the dance."

"Hilda's thinking of the police," ventured Mr. Fulmino.

"Police!" said Mrs. Fulmino. "Do you know what's in the van?"

"No," said Hilda. "And that's what I don't want to know. I don't want him on my doorstep. Or his friends. He had two with him. Harry saw them."

Mrs. Fulmino considered.

"I'm glad you've come to us. I wish you'd come to us in the first place," she said. Then she commanded Mr. Fulmino: "You go up there at once with Harry," she said to him, "and tell that man to leave Hilda alone. Go on, now. I can't understand you"—she indicated me—"running off like that, leaving a van there. If you don't go I'll go myself. I'm not afraid of a paltry . . . a paltry . . . what does he call himself? You go up."

Mrs. Fulmino was as good a judge of the possibilities of an emotional situation as any woman on earth: this was her moment. She wanted us out of the house and Hilda to herself.

We obeyed.

Mr. Fulmino and I left the house. He looked tired. He was too tired to put on his jacket. He went out in his shirt sleeves.

"Up and down we go, in and out, up and down," said Mr. Fulmino. "First it's Constance, now it's Hilda. And the pubs are closed."

"There you are, what did I tell you?" said Mr. Fulmino when we got to Hilda's street. "No van, no sign of it, is there? You're a witness. We'll go up and see all the same."

Mr. Fulmino had been alarmed but now his confidence came back. He gave me a wink and a nod when we got to the house.

"Leave it to me," he said. "You wait here."

I heard him knock at the door and after a time knock again. Then I heard a woman's voice. He was talking a long time. He came away.

He was silent for a long time as we walked. At last he said:

"That beats all. I didn't say anything. I didn't say who I was. I didn't let on. I just asked to see Hilda. 'Oh,' says the landlady,

'she's out.' 'Oh,' I said, 'that's a surprise.' I didn't give a name—
'Out you say? When will she be back?' 'I don't know,' said the
landlady, and this is it, Harry—'she's paid her rent and given her
notice. She's leaving first thing in the morning,' the landlady said.
'They came for the luggage this evening,' Harry," said Mr.
Fulmino, "did Hilda say anything about leaving?"

"No."

"Bill Williams came for her luggage."

We marched on. Or rather we went stealthily along like two
men walking a steel wire of suspicion. We almost lost our balance
when two cats ran across the street and set up howls in a garden,
as if they were howling us down. Mr. Fulmino stopped.

"Harry!" he said. "She's playing us up. She's going off with
Bill Williams."

"But she's frightened of him. She said he was going to kill
her."

"I'm not surprised," said Mr. Fulmino. "She's been playing
him up. Who was she with at the dance hall? She's played everyone
up. Of course she's frightened of him. You bet. I'm sorry for anyone getting mixed up with Bill Williams—he'll knock some sense
into her. He's rough. So was her father."

"Bill Williams might have just dropped by to have a word,"
I said.

"Funny word at half past eleven at night," said Mr. Fulmino.
"When I think of all that correspondence, all those forms—War
Office, State Department, United Nations—we did, it's been a
poor turn-out. You might say," he paused for an image sufficiently
devastating, "a waste of paper, a ruddy wanton waste of precious
paper."

We got back to his house. I have never mentioned I believe
that it had an iron gate that howled, a noise that always brought
Mrs. Fulmino to her curtains, and a clipped privet hedge, like a
moustache, to the tiny garden.

We opened the gate, the gate howled, Mrs. Fulmino's nose
appeared at the curtains.

"Don't say a word," said Mr. Fulmino.

Tea—the room smelled of that, of course. Mrs. Fulmino had
made some while we were out. She looked as though she had
eaten something too. A titbit. They all looked sorry for Mr.
Fulmino and me. And Mrs. Fulmino *had* had a titbit! In fact I

know from Iris that the only thing Mrs. Fulmino had got out of
Hilda was the news that she had had a postcard from Mr. Faulkner
from Chicago. He was on the move.

"Well?" said Mrs. Fulmino.

"It's all right, Hilda," said Mr. Fulmino coldly. "They've
gone."

"There," said Mrs. Fulmino patting Hilda's hand.

"Hilda," said Mr. Fulmino, "I've been straight with you. I want
you to be straight with me. What's going on between you and Bill
Williams . . .?"

"Hilda's told me . . ." Mrs. Fulmino said.

"I asked Hilda, not you," said Mr. Fulmino to his wife who
was so surprised that she went very white instead of her usual
purple.

"Hilda, come on. You come round here saying he's going to
kill you. Then they tell me you've given your notice up there."

"She told me that. I think she's done the right thing."

"And did you tell her why you gave your notice?" asked Mr.
Fulmino.

"She's given her notice at the factory too," said Mrs. Fulmino.

"Why?" said Mr. Fulmino.

Hilda did not answer.

"You are going off with Bill Williams, aren't you?"

"Ted!" Hilda gave one of her rare laughs.

"What's this?" cried Mrs. Fulmino. "Have you been deceiving
me? Deceit I can't stand, Hilda."

"Of course she is," said Mr. Fulmino. "She's paid her rent.
He's collected her luggage this evening—where is it to be? Monte
Carlo? Oh, it's all right, sit down," Mr. Fulmino waved Mrs.
Fulmino back. "They had a row at the dance this evening."

But Hilda was on her feet.

"My luggage," she cried, holding her bag with both hands
to her bosom as we had seen her do once before when she was
cornered. "Who has touched my luggage?"

I thought she was going to strike Mr. Fulmino.

"The dirty thief. Who let him in? Who let him take it? Where's
he gone?"

She was moving to the door. We were stupefied.

"Bill Williams!" she shouted. Her rage made those artificial
eyebrows look comical and I expected her to pick them off and

throw them at us. "Bill Williams I'm talking about. Who let that bloody war hero in? That bitch up there . . ."

"Hilda," said Mr. Fulmino. "We don't want language."

"You fool," said Mrs. Fulmino in her lowest, most floor pervading voice to her husband. "What have you been and done? You've let Bill Williams get away with all those cases, all her clothes, everything. You let that spiv strip her."

"Go off with Bill Williams!" Hilda laughed. "My husband was an officer."

"I knew he was after something. I thought it was dollars," she said suddenly.

She came back from the door and sat down at the table and sobbed.

"Two hundred and fifty pounds, he's got," she sobbed. It was a sight to see Hilda weeping. We could not speak.

"It's all I had," she said.

We watched Hilda. The painted eyebrows made the grimace of her weeping horrible. There was not one of us who was not shocked. There was in all of us a sympathy we knew how to express but which was halted—as by a fascination—with the sight of her ruin. We could not help contrasting her triumphant arrival with her state at this moment. It was as if we had at last got her with us as we had, months before, expected her to be. Perhaps she read our thoughts. She looked up at us and she had the expression of a person seeing us for the first time. It was like an inspection.

"You're a mean lot, a mean respectable lot," she said. "I remember you. I remember when I was a girl. What was it Mr. Singh said, I can't remember—he was clever—oh well, leave it, leave it. When I saw that little room they put my poor mother in, I could have cried. No sun. No warmth in it. You just wanted someone to pity. I remember it. And your faces. The only thing that was nice was," she sobbed and laughed for a moment, "was bump, bump, bump, the trolley." She said loudly: "There's only one human being in the whole crew—Jack Draper. I don't wonder he sees more in fish."

She looked at me scornfully. "Your brother—he was nice," she said. "Round the park at night! That was love."

"Hilda," said Mrs. Fulmino without anger. "We've done our best for you. If we've made mistakes I hope you haven't. We haven't had your life. You talk about ships that pass in the night,

I don't know what you mean, but I can tell you there are no ships in this house. Only Ted."

"That's right," said Mr. Fulmino quietly too. "You're over-wrought."

"Father," said Mrs. Fulmino, "hadn't you better tell the police?"

"Yes, yes, dear," agreed Mr. Fulmino. "We'd better get in touch with the authorities."

"Police," said Hilda laughing in their faces. "Oh God! Don't worry about that. You've got one in every house in this country." She picked up her bag, still laughing and went to the door.

"Police," she was saying, "that's ripe."

"Hilda, you're not to go out in the street looking like that," said Mrs. Fulmino.

"I'd better go with her," said Mr. Fulmino.

"I'll go," I said. They were glad to let me.

It is ten years since I walked with Hilda to her lodgings. I shall not forget it, and the warm, dead, rubbery city night. It is frightening to walk with a woman who has been robbed and wronged. Her eyes were half-closed as though she was reckoning as she walked. I had to pull her back on to the pavement or she would have gone flat into a passing car. The only thing she said to me was:

"They took Shinji's rings as well."

Her room was on the ground floor. It had a divan and a not very clean dark green cover on it. A pair of shoes were sticking out from under it. There was a plain deal cupboard and she went straight to it. Two dresses were left. The rest had gone. She went to a table and opened the drawer. It was empty except for some letters.

I stood not knowing what to say. She seemed surprised to see me there still.

"He's cleared the lot," she said vacantly. Then she seemed to realize that she was staring at me without seeing me for she lowered her angry shoulders.

"We'll get them back," I said.

"How?" she said, mocking me, but not unkindly.

"I will," I said. "Don't be upset."

"You!" she said.

"Yes, I will," I said.

I wanted to say more. I wanted to touch her. But I couldn't. The ruin had made her untouchable.

"What are you going to do?" I said.

"Don't worry about me," she said. "I'm okey doke. You're different from your brother. You don't remember those days. I told Mr. Gloster about him. Come to that, Mr. Faulkner too. They took it naturally. That was a fault of Mr. Singh"—she never called him by his Christian name—"jealousy."

She kicked off her shoes and sat down on the cheap divan and frowned at the noise it made and she laughed.

"One day in Bombay I got homesick and he asked me what I was thinking about and I was green, I just said 'Sid Fraser's neck. It had a mole on it'—you should have seen his face. He wouldn't talk to me for a week. It's a funny thing about those countries. Some people might rave about them, I didn't see anything to them."

She got up.

"You go now," she said laughing. "I must have been in love."

I dreamed about Hilda's face all night and in the morning I wouldn't have been surprised to see London had been burned out to a cinder. But the next night her face did not come and I had to think about it. Further and further it went, a little less every day and night and I did not seem to notice when someone said Bill Williams had been picked up by the police, or when Constance had been found half dead with aspirins, and when, in both cases, Mr. Fulmino told me he had to "give assistance in the identification", for Hilda had gone. She left the day after I took her to her room. Where she went no one knew. We guessed. We imagined. Across water, I thought, getting further and further away, in very fine clothes and very beautiful. France, Mr. Fulmino thought, or possibly Italy. Africa, even. New York, San Francisco, Tokyo, Bombay, Singapore. Where? Even one day six months after she had left when he came to the library and showed me a postcard he had had from her, the first message, it did not say where she was and someone in the post office had pulled off the stamp. It was a picture of Hilda herself on a seat in a park, sitting with Mr. Faulkner and Mr. Gloster. You wouldn't recognize her.

But Mr. Gloster's book came out. Oh yes, It wasn't about Japan or India or anything like that. It was about us.

SEVEN

The Key to My Heart

WHEN Father dropped dead and Mother and I were left to run the business on our own, I was twenty-four years old. It was the principal bakery in our town, a good little business, and Father had built it up from nothing. Father used to wink at me when Mother talked about their "first wedding". "How many times have you been married? Who was it that time?" he used to say to her. She was speaking of the time they first ventured out of the bakery into catering for weddings and local dances. For a long time, when I was a child, we lived over the shop; then Mother made Father take a house down the street. Later still, we opened a café next door but two to the shop, and our idea was to buy up the two little places in between. But something went wrong in the last years of Father's life. Working at night in the heat and getting up at the wrong time of day disorganized him. And then the weddings were his downfall. There is always champagne left over at weddings, and Father got to like it and live on it. And then brandy followed. When Mr. Pickering, the solicitor, went into the will and the accounts, there was muddle everywhere, and bills we had never heard of came in.

"Father kept it all in his head," Mother said, very proud of him for that. Mr. Pickering and I had to sort it all out, and one of the things we discovered was that what we owed was nothing to what people owed us. Mother used to serve in the shop and do the books. She did it, we used to say, for the sake of the gossip—to daydream about why the schoolmistress ordered crumpets only on Thursdays, or guessing, if someone ordered more of this kind of cake or that, who was going to eat it with them. She was generally right, and she knew more about what was going on in the town than anyone else. As long as the daily and weekly customers paid their books, she didn't bother; she hated sending bills, and she was more pleased than upset when Mr. Pickering told her there was a good six hundred pounds owing by people who either hadn't been asked to pay or who were simply not troubling themselves. In a small business, this was a lot of money. It was the rich and the big pots

in the county who were the worst of these debtors. Dad and
Mother never minded being owed by the rich. They had both
grown up in the days when you were afraid of offending people,
and to hear my mother talk you would have thought that by
asking the well-off to fork out you were going to kill the goose
that lays the golden egg, knock the bottom out of society, and let
a Labour government in.

"Think of what they have to pay in taxes," she would say,
pitying them. "And the death duties!" And when I did what Mr.
Pickering said, and sent out accounts to these people, saying politely
that it had no doubt been overlooked, Mother looked mournful
and said getting a commission in the Army had turned my head.
The money came in, of course. When Colonel Williams paid up
and didn't dispute it, Mother looked at his cheque as if it were an
insult from the old gentleman and, in fact, "lost" it in her apron
pocket for a week. Lady Littlebank complained, but she paid all
the same. A few did not answer, but when I called at their houses
they paid at once. Though the look on Mother's face was as much
as to say I was a son ruining her lifework and destroying her chances
of holding her head up in society. At the end of two or three months
there was only one large account outstanding—a Mrs. Brackett's.
Mrs. Brackett did not answer, and you can guess Mother made the
most of this. Mother spoke highly of Mrs. Brackett, said she was
"such a lady", "came of a wonderful family", and once even
praised her clothes. She was the richest woman in the county, and
young. She became my mother's ideal.

Mrs. Brackett was married to a pilot and racing motorist known
in the town as Noisy Brackett; it was she, as my mother said,
nodding her head up and down, who "had the money". Noisy
was given a couple of cars and his pocket money, but, having done
that, Mrs. Brackett paid as little as she could, as slowly as she could,
to everyone else. When I talked about her account to other shopkeepers in the town, they put on their glasses, had a look at their
books, sniffed, and said nothing. Every shopkeeper, my father used
to say, woke up in the early hours of the morning thinking of how
much she owed him, and dreaming of her fortune. You can work
out how long her bill with us had run on when I say it was nearly
two hundred and thirty pounds. The exact sum was two hundred
and twenty-eight pounds fourteen and fourpence. I shall always
remember it.

The first time I made out Mrs. Brackett's bill, I gave it to Noisy. He often came into the café to flirt with the girls, or to our shop to see Mother and get her to cash cheques for him. He was a thin little man, straight as a stick and looked as brittle, and covered (they said) with scars and wounds from his crashes. He had the curly shining black hair of a sick gypsy, and the lines of a charmer all over his face. His smiles quickly ended in a sudden, stern twitching of his left cheek and eye, like the crack of a whip, which delighted the women. He was a dandy, and from Mother he had the highest praise she could give to any man. He was, she said, "snobby".

When I gave Noisy our bill, he handed it back to me at once. "Be a sweetie-pie," he said, "and keep it under your hat until the day after tomorrow. Tomorrow's my payday, and I don't want the Fairy Queen to get her mind taken off it—d'you follow? Good! Fine! Splendid fellow! Bang on!" And, with a twitch, he was back in his long white Bentley. "Bring it yourself," he said, looking me up and down. I am a very tall man, and little Noisy had a long way to look. "It'll do the trick."

Noisy did not hide his dependence on his wife. Everyone except the local gentry liked him.

So on the Thursday, when the shop was closed and I could leave the café to the waitresses—a good pair of girls, and Rosie, the dark one, very pretty—I took the station wagon and drove up to Heading Mount, four miles out of the town. It was June; they were getting the hay in. The land in the valley fetches its price—you wouldn't believe it if I told you what a farm fetches there. Higher up, the land is poor, where the oak woods begin, and all that stretch that belonged to old Mr. Lucas, Mrs. Brackett's father, who had made a fortune out of machine tools. The estate was broken up when he died. I came out of the oak woods and turned into the drive, which winds between low stone walls and tall rhododendron bushes, so that it is like a damp, dark sunken lane, and very narrow. Couples often walked up on Sundays in June to see the show of rhododendrons on the slopes at Heading; the bushes were in flower as I drove by. I was speeding to the sharp turn at the end of the drive, before you come to the house, when I had to brake suddenly. Mrs. Brackett's grey Bentley was drawn broadside across it, blocking the drive completely. I ought to have seen this was a bad omen.

To leave a car like that, anywhere, was typical of Mrs. Brackett. If there was a traffic jam in the town, or if someone couldn't get into the market, nine times out of ten Mrs. Brackett's car was the cause. She just stepped out of it wherever it was, as if she were dropping her coat off for someone else to pick up. The police did nothing. As she got back in, she would smile at them, raise one eyebrow, wag her hips, and let them see as much of her legs as she thought fit for the hour of the day, and drive off with a small wave of her hand that made them swell with apologies and blow up someone else. Sometimes she went green with a rage that was terrifying coming from so small a person.

As I walked across the lawn, I realized I had missed the back lane to the house, and that I ought to have driven along a wire-fenced road across the fields to the farm and the kitchen, where the house-keeper lived. But I had not been up there for several years, and had forgotten it. As I walked towards the white front door, I kicked a woman's shoe—a shoe for a very small foot. I picked it up. I was a few yards from the door when Mrs. Brackett marched out, stopped on the steps, and then, as sharp as a sergeant, shouted, "Jimmy!" She was looking up at the sky, as though she expected to bring her husband down out of it.

She was barefooted, wearing a blue-and-white checked shirt and dusty jeans, and her short fair hair untidy, and she was making an ugly mouth, like a boy's, on her pretty face. I was holding out the shoe as I went forward. There was no answer to her shout. Then she saw me and stared at the shoe.

"Who are you? What are you doing with that?" she asked. "Put it down."

But before I could answer, from the other side of the buildings there was the sound of a car starting and driving off on the back road. Mrs. Brackett heard this. She turned and marched into the house again, but in a few seconds she returned, running past me across the lawn. She jumped into her car, backed—and then she saw mine blocking the drive. She sounded her horn, again and again. A dog barked, and she jumped out and bawled at me. "You bloody fool!" she shouted. "Get that van of yours out of the way!"

The language that came out of her small mouth was like what you hear in the cattle market on Fridays. I slowly went up and got into my van. I could hear her swearing and the other car tearing off; already it must have turned into the main road. I got into mine, and there we sat, face to face, scowling at each other through our windscreens. I reversed down the long, winding drive, very fast, keeping one eye on her all the time, and turned sharply off the road at the entrance. I don't mind saying I was showing off. I can reverse a car at speed and put it anywhere to within an inch of where I want to. I saw her face change as she came on, for in her temper she was coming fast down the drive straight at me, radiator to radiator. At the end, she gave one glance of surprise at me, and I think held back a word she had ready as she drove past. At any rate, her mouth was open. Half a dozen cows started from under the trees and went trotting round the field in panic as she went, and the rooks came out of the elms like bits of black paper.

By bad luck, you see, I had arrived in the middle of one of the regular Brackett rows. They were famous in the neighbourhood. The Bracketts chased each other round the house, things came out of windows—clothes, boots, anything. Our roundsman said he had once seen a portable radio, playing full on, come flying out, and that it had fallen, still playing, in the roses. Servants came down to the town and said they had had enough of it. Money was usually at the bottom of the trouble. There was a tale going round that when a village girl who worked there got married, Mrs. Brackett gave her a three-shilling alarm clock for a wedding present.

The rows always went the same way. A car would race out of the drive with Noisy in it, and five minutes later Mrs. Brackett would be in her car chasing him, and no one was safe on the roads for twenty miles around. Sometimes it might end quietly in a country pub, with Mrs. Brackett in one bar and Noisy in the other, white-faced and playing hymns on the piano to mock her until she gave in. Other times, it might go on through the night. Noisy, who raced cars, was the better driver, but she was wilder. She would do anything—she once cut through the footpath of the cemetery to catch him on the other side. She sometimes caught him, but more than once her meanness about money would leave her standing. There would be a telephone call to Brigg's garage: Mrs. Brackett had run out of petrol. She was too mean ever to have much more than a gallon in the tank.

"Bless her," Noisy used to say if anyone mentioned these chases to him. "I always rely on the Fairy Queen to run out of gas."

Noisy was a woman-hater. His trouble was his habit of saying "Bless you" to the whole female sex.

"Well, I hope you're satisfied," my mother said when I got home. I put Mrs. Brackett's shoe on the table.

"I've made some progress," I said.

My mother looked at the shoe for a long time. Now that I had got something out of Mrs. Brackett, Mother began to think a little less of her. "You'd think a woman with feet like that would dress better," she said.

But what annoyed me was that at some stage in the afternoon's chase Noisy had slipped in and got Mother to cash him a cheque for twenty pounds.

June is the busy time of the year for us. There are all the June weddings. Noisy and Mrs. Brackett must have settled down again somehow, because I saw them driving through the town once or twice. I said to myself, "You wait till the rush is over."

In July, I went up to the Bracketts' house a second time. Rosie, the dark girl who works in our café, came with me, because she wanted to meet her aunt at the main-line station, three or four miles over the hill beyond Heading Mount, and I was taking her on there after I had spoken to Mrs. Brackett. I drove up to the house. The rhododendrons had died, and there were pods on them already going brown. The sun struck warm in front of the house. It was wonderfully quiet.

I left the girl in the car, reading a book, and was working out a sentence to say, when I saw Mrs. Brackett kneeling by a gold-fish pond, at the far side of the great lawn. She turned and saw me. I did not know whether to go over the lawn to her or to wait where I was. I decided to go over, and she got up and walked to me. Mother was right about her clothes. This time she was wearing a gaudy tomato-coloured cotton dress that looked like someone else's, and nothing on underneath it. I do not know why it was—whether it was because I was standing on the grass as she was walking over, whether it was my anxiety about how to begin the conversation, or whether it was because of her bare white arms, the dawdling manner of her walk, and the inquisitiveness of her eyes—but I thought I was going to faint. When she was two yards away, my heart jumped, my throat closed, and my head was swimming. Although I had often seen her driving through the town, and though I remembered our last meeting all too well, I had never really looked at her before. She stopped, but I had the feeling that she had not stopped, but was invisibly walking on until she walked clean through me. My arms went weak. She was amused by the effect she had on me.

"I know who you are," she said. "You are Mr. Fraser's son. Do you want to speak to me?"

I did, but I couldn't. I forgot all the sentences I had prepared. "I've come about our cheque," I said at last. I shouted it. Mrs. Brackett was as startled by my shout as I was. She blushed at the loudness and shock of it—not a light blush but a dark, red, flooding blush on her face and her neck that confused her and made her lower her head like a child caught stealing. She put her hands behind her back like a child. I blushed, too. She walked up and down a yard or two, her head still down, thinking. Then she walked away to the house.

"You'd better come inside," she called back in an offhand way.

You could have put our house into the hall and sitting-room of Heading Mount. I had been in that room when I was a boy, helping the waitress when my father was there doing the catering for a party. I do not know what you'd have to pay for the furniture there—thousands, I suppose. She led me through the room to a smaller room beyond it, where there was a desk. I felt I was slowly walking miles. I have never seen such a mess of papers and letters. They were even spread on the carpet. She sat down at the desk.

"Can you see the bill?" she muttered, not looking at me and pointing to the floor.

"I've got it here," I said, taking the bill out of my pocket. She jerked her head. The flush had gone, and now she looked as keen as needles at me.

"Well, sit down," she said.

She took the bill from me and looked at it. Now I could see that her skin was not white but was really pale and clay-coloured, with scores of little cracks in it, and that she was certainly nearer forty than thirty, as Mother always said.

"I've paid this," she said, giving the bill a mannish slap. "I pay every quarter."

"It has been running for three and a half years," I said, more at ease now.

"What?" she said. "Oh, well, I paid something, anyway. This isn't a bill. It's a statement."

"Yes," I said. "We have sent you the bills."

"Where's the date? This hasn't got any date on it."

I got up and pointed to the date.

"It ought to be at the top," she said.

My giddiness had gone. Noisy came into the room. "Hullo, Bob," he said. "I've just been talking to that beautiful thing you have got in the car." He always spoke in an alert, exhausted way about women, like someone at a shoot waiting for the birds to come over. "Have you seen Bob's girl, darling?" he said to her. "I've just offered her the key to my heart." And he lifted the silk scarf he was wearing in the neck of his canary-coloured pullover, and there was a piece of string round his neck with a heavy old door key hanging from it. Noisy gave a twitch to one side of his face.

"Oh, God, that old gag," said Mrs. Brackett.

"Not appreciated, old boy," said Noisy to me.

"Irresistible," said Mrs. Brackett, with an ugly mouth. She turned and spoke to me again, but glanced shrewdly at Noisy as she did so. "Let me try this one on you," she said. "You've already got my husband's cheques for this bill. I send him down to pay you, and he just cashes them?"

"I'm afraid not, Mrs. Brackett," I said. "That wouldn't be possible."

"You can't get away with that one, my pet," said Noisy. "Are you ready to go out?" He looked at her dress, admiring her figure. "What a target, Bob," he said.

"I don't think we will ask Mr. Fraser's opinion," she said coldly, but very pleased. And she got up and started out of the room, with Noisy behind her.

"You had better send me the bills," she called back to me, turning round from the door.

I felt very, very tired. I left the house and slammed the car door when I got in. "Now she wants the damn bills," I said to Rosie as I drove her up to Tolton station. I did not speak to her the rest of the way. She irritated me, sitting there.

When I got home and told my mother, she was short with me. That was the way to lose customers, she said. I was ruining all the work she and Dad had put into the business. I said if Mrs. Brackett wanted her bills she could come and get them herself. Mother was very shocked.

She let it go for a day or two, but she had to bring it up again. "What are you sulking about?" she said to me one afternoon.

"You upset Rosie this morning. Have you done those bills for Mrs. Brackett yet?"

I made excuses, and got in the car and went over to the millers and to the people who make our boxes, to get away from the nagging. Once I was out of the town, in the open country, Mrs. Brackett seemed to be somewhere just ahead of me, round a corner, over a hill, beyond a wood. There she was, trying to make me forget she owed us two hundred and twenty-eight pounds fourteen and fourpence. The moment she was in my head, the money went out of it. When I got back, late in the evening, Mother was on to me again. Noisy had been in. She said he had been sent down by his wife to ask why I had not brought the bills.

"The poor Wing Commander," my mother said. "Another rumpus up there." (She always gave him his rank if there was a rumour of another quarrel at Heading.) "She never gives him any peace. He's just an errand boy. She does what she likes with him."

"He's been offering you the key to his heart, Mother," I said.

"I don't take any stock of him," Mother said. "Or that pansy sweetheart stuff. Dad was the one and only for me. I don't believe in second marriages. I've no time for jealous women; they're always up to something, like Mrs. Doubleday thinking I spoke to her husband in the bank and she was caught with the chemist, but you always think the Fairy Prince will turn up—it's natural."

It always took a little time getting at what was in Mother's mind, yet it was really simple. She was a good churchwoman, and she thought Noisy was not really married to Mrs. Brackett, because he had been divorced by his first wife. She did not blame Noisy for this—in fact, she admired it, in a romantic way—but she blamed Mrs. Brackett, because, by Mother's theories, Mrs. Brackett was still single. And Mother never knew whether to admire single women for holding out or to suspect them of being on the prowl. One thing she was certain of. "Money talks," she said. The thing that made Noisy respectable for her, and as good as being married in church, was that he had married Mrs. Brackett for her money.

She talked like this the night we sat up and did that month's bills, but the next day—and this was the trouble with Mother—it ended in a row. I sent the bills up to Mrs. Brackett by our delivery van.

"That is not the way to behave," Mother said. "You should have taken them yourself."

And before the day was out, Mother was in a temper again. Mrs. Brackett had spoken to her on the telephone and said she had been through the bills and that we had charged her for things she hadn't had, because she'd been in the South of France at the time.

"I told you to go," Mother said to me.

I was angry, too, at being called dishonest. I got out the van and said I was going up at once.

"Oh, that's how it is," said my mother, changing round again. "Her Ladyship snaps her fingers and you go up at once. She's got you running about for her like Noisy. If I ask you to do anything, you don't pay any attention to me. But Mrs. Brackett—she's the Queen of England. Two of you running after her."

Mother was just like that with Father when he was alive. He took no notice. Neither did I. I went up to Heading. A maid let me in, and I sat there waiting in the drawing-room. I waited a long time, listening to the bees coming down the chimney, circling lower and lower and then roaring out into the room, like Noisy's car. I could hear Mrs. Brackett talking on the telephone in her study. I could hear now and then what she was saying. She was a great racing woman, and from words she said here and there I would say she was speaking to a bookmaker. One sentence I remember, because I think it had the name of a horse in it, and when I got back home later I looked up the racing news to see if I could find it. "Tray Pays On," she said. She came out into the room with the laughter of her telephone call still on her face. I was standing up, with our account book in my hand, and when she saw me the laughter went.

I was not afraid of her any more. "I hear there is some trouble about the bills," I said. "If you've got them, you can check them with the book. I've brought it."

Mrs. Brackett was a woman who watched people's faces. She put on her dutiful, serious, and obedient look, and led me again to the little room where the papers were. She sat down and I stood over her while we compared the bills and the book. I watched the moving of her back as she breathed. I pointed to the items, one by one, and she nodded and ticked the bills with a pencil. We checked for nearly half an hour. The only thing she said was in the middle of it—"You've got a double jointed thumb. So have I"—but she went right on.

"I can see what it is," I said at the end. "You've mistaken 1953 for '54."

She pushed the book away, and leaned back in the chair against my arm, which was resting on it.

"No, I haven't," she said, her small, unsmiling face looking up into mine. "I just wanted you to come up."

She gazed at me a long time. I thought of all the work Mother and I had done, and then that Mother was right about Mrs. Brackett. I took my hand from the chair and stepped back.

"I wanted to ask you one or two things," she said, confidingly, "about that property next to the shop. I'll be fair with you. I'm interested in it. Are you? All right, don't answer. I see you are."

My heart jumped. Ever since I could remember, Father and Mother had talked of buying this property. It was their day-dream. They simply liked little bits of property everywhere, and now I wanted it so that we could join the shop and the café.

"I asked because . . ." She hesitated. "I'll be frank with you. The bank manager was talking about it to me today."

My fright died down. I didn't believe that the bank manager—he was Mr. Pickering's brother-in-law—would let my mother down and allow the property to go to Mrs. Brackett without giving us the offer first.

"We want it, of course," I said. And then I suspected this was one of her tricks. "That is why I have been getting our bills in," I said.

"Oh, I didn't think that was it," she said. "I thought you were getting married. My husband says you are engaged to the girl you brought up here. He said he thought you were. Has she any money?"

"Engaged!" I said. "I'm not. Who told him that?"

"Oh," she said, and then a thought must have struck her. I could read it at once. In our town, if you cough in the High Street the chemist up at the Town Hall has got a bottle of cough mixture wrapped up and waiting for you; news travels fast. She must have guessed that when Noisy came down dangling the key to his heart, he could have been round the corner all the time, seeing Rosie.

"I'm glad to hear you're not engaged," Mrs. Brackett said

tenderly. "I like a man who works. You work like your father did—God, what an attractive man! You're like him. I'm not flattering you. I saw it when you came up the first time."

She asked me a lot of questions about the shop and who did the baking now. I told her I didn't do it and that I wanted to enlarge the restaurant. "The machine bakeries are getting more and more out into the country," I said. "And you've got to look out."

"I don t see why you shouldn't do catering for schools," she said. "And there's the Works." (Her father's main factory.) "Why don't you get hold of the catering there?"

"You can only do that if you have capital. We're not big enough," I said, laughing.

"How much do you want?" she said. "Two thousand? Three? I don't see why we couldn't do something."

The moment she said "we" I came to my senses. Here's a funny turnout, I thought. She won't pay her bills, but first she's after these shops, and now she's waving two thousand pounds in my face. Everyone in our town knew she was artful. I suppose she thought I was green.

"Not as much as two thousand," I said. "Just the bill," I said, nodding at it.

Mrs. Brackett smiled. "I like you. You're interested in money. Good. I'll settle it." And, taking her cheque book from the top of the desk, she put it in her drawer. "I never pay these accounts by cheque. I pay in cash. I'll get it tomorrow at the bank. I'll tell you what I'll do. You've got a shoe of mine. Bring it up tomorrow evening at, say, half past eight. I'll be back by then and you can have it." She paused, and then, getting up, added quickly, "Half tomorrow, half in October."

It was like dealing with the gypsies that come to your door.

"No, Mrs. Brackett," I said. "I'd like all of it. Now." We stared at each other. It was like that moment months ago when she had driven at me in her car and I had reversed down the drive with one eye watching her and one on the road as I shot back. That was the time, I think, I first noticed her—when she opened her mouth to shout a word at me and then did not shout. I could have stayed like this, looking into her small, pretty, miser's blue eyes, at her determined head, her chopped-off fair hair, for half an hour. It was a struggle.

She was the first to speak, and that was a point gained to me. Her voice shook a little. "I don't keep that amount of money in the house," she said.

I knew that argument. Noisy said she always had two or three hundred pounds in the safe in the wall of her study, and whether this was so or not, I could not help glancing towards it.

"I don't like being dictated to," she said, catching my glance. "I have told you what I will do."

"I think you could manage it, Mrs. Brackett," I said.

I could see she was on the point of flying into one of her tempers, and as far as I was concerned (I don't know why), I hoped she would. Her rows with Noisy were so famous that I must have wanted to see one for myself. And I didn't see why she should get away with it. At the back of my mind, I thought of all the others down in the town and how they would look when I said I had got my money out of Mrs. Brackett.

Yet I wasn't really thinking about the money at all, at this moment. I was looking at her pretty shoulders.

But Mrs. Brackett did not fly into a temper. She considered me, and then she spoke in a quiet voice that took me off my guard. "Actually," she said, lowering her eyes, "you haven't been coming up here after money at all, have you?"

"Well—" I began.

"Sh-h-h!" she said, jumping up from her chair and putting her hand on my mouth. "Why didn't you ring me and tell me you were coming? I am often alone."

She stepped to the door and bawled out, "Jimmy!" as if he were a long way off. He was—to my surprise, and even more to hers—very near.

"Yes, ducky?" Noisy called back from the hall.

"Damn," she said to me. "You must go." And, squeezing my hand, she went through the drawing-room into the hall.

"What time do we get back tomorrow evening?" she said boldly to Noisy. "Half past eight? Come at half past eight," she said, turning to me, for I had followed her. "I'll bring back the cash."

The sight of Noisy was a relief to me, and the sound of the word "cash" made Noisy brighten.

"Not lovely little bits of money!" he exclaimed.

"Not you," said Mrs. Brackett, glaring at him.

"How did you work it, old boy?" said Noisy later, giving me one of his most quizzical twitches as he walked with me to my van. When I drove off, I could see him still standing there, watching me out of sight.

I drove away very slowly. My mind was in confusion. About half a mile off, I stopped the car and lit a cigarette. All the tales I had heard about Mrs. Brackett came back into my mind. It was one thing to look at her, another thing to know about her. The one person I wished I had with me was Noisy. He seemed like a guarantor of safety, a protection. To have had my thoughts read like that by her filled me with fear.

I finished my cigarette. I decided not to go straight home, and I drove slowly all along the lower sides of the oak woods, so slowly and carelessly that I had to swerve to avoid oncoming cars. I was making, almost without knowing it, for the Green Man, at Mill Cross. There was a girl there I had spoken to once or twice. No one you would know. I went in and asked for a glass of beer. I hardly said a word to her, except about the weather, and then she left the bar to look after a baby in the kitchen at the back. That calmed me. I think the way she gave me my change brought me back to earth and made me feel free of Mrs. Brackett's spell. At any rate, I put the threepence in my pocket and swallowed my beer. I laughed at myself. Mrs. Brackett had gypped me again.

When I got home, it was late, and my mother was morose. She was wearing a black dress she often wore when she was alone, dressed up and ready to go out, yet not intending to, as if now that my father was dead she was free if someone would invite her. Her best handbag was beside her. She was often waiting like this, sitting on the sofa, doing nothing but listening to the clock tick, and perhaps getting up to give a touch to some flowers on the table and then sitting down again. Her first words shook me.

"Mrs. Brackett was down here looking for you," she said sharply. "I thought you were with her. She wants you to be sure to go up tomorrow evening to collect some money when she comes back from Tolton. Where have you been?"

"Let the old bitch post it or bring it in," I said.

Mother was horrified at the idea of Mrs. Brackett soiling her hands with money.

"You'll do as I tell you," she said. "You'll go up and get it.

If you don't, Noisy will get his hands on it first. You'd think a woman with all that money would go to a decent hairdresser. It's meanness, I suppose."

And then, of course, I saw I was making a lot of fuss about nothing. Noisy would be there when I went up to Heading. Good old Noisy, I thought; thank God for that. And he'll see I get the money, because she said it in front of him.

So the next evening I went. I put my car near the garage, and the first person I saw was Noisy, standing beside his own car. He had a suitcase in his hand. I went over to him.

"Fairy Queen's been at work," he said. He nodded at his tyres. They were flat. "I'm doing some quick thinking."

At that moment, a top window of the house was opened and someone emptied a suitcase of clothes out of it, and then a shower of cigarettes came down.

"She's tidying," he said. "I've got a quarter of an hour to catch the London train. Be a sweetie-pie and run me over there."

I had arrived once more in the middle of one of the Brackett rows. Only this time Noisy was leaving it to me. That is how I felt about it. "Hop in," I said.

And when we were off and a mile from Heading, he sat up in the seat and looked round. "Nothing on our tail," he said.

"Have you ever heard of a horse called Tray?" I asked him. "Tray Pays something? Tray Pays On—that can't be it."

"Tray Pays On?" repeated Noisy. "Is it a French horse?"

"I don't know," I said.

"Bloody peasant? Could be," said Noisy. "Sounds a bit frog to me."

We got to Tolton station. Noisy was looking very white and set with hatred. Not until he was standing in the queue getting his ticket did it occur to me what Noisy was doing.

"The first time I've travelled by train for fifteen years," he called to me across from the queue. "Damned serious. You can tell her if you see her"—people stared—"the worm has turned. I'm packing it in for good."

And as he went off to the train, he called, "I suppose you are going back? No business of mine, but I'll give you a tip. If you do, you won't find anything in the kitty, Bob." He gave me his stare and his final twitch. It was like the crack of a shot. Bang on, as he would have said. A bull's-eye.

I walked slowly away as the London train puffed out. I took his advice. I did not go back to Heading.

There were rows and rows between the Bracketts, but there was none like this one. It was the last. The others were a chase. This was not. For only Mrs. Brackett was on the road that night. She was seen, we were told, in all the likely places. She had been a dozen times through the town. Soon after ten o'clock she was hooting outside our house. Mother peeped through the curtains, and I went out. Mrs. Brackett got out of her car and marched at me. "Where have you been?" she shouted. "Where is my husband?"

"I don't know," I said.

"Yes, you do," she said. "You took him to Tolton, they told me."

"I think he's gone to London," I said.

"Don't be a damn liar," she said. "How can he have? His car is up there."

"By train," I said.

"By train," she repeated. Her anger vanished. She looked at me with astonishment. The rich are very peculiar. Mrs. Brackett had forgotten people travel by train. I could see she was considering the startling fact. She was not a woman to waste time staying in one state of mind for long. Noisy used to say of her, "That little clock never stops ticking."

"I see," she said to me sarcastically, nodding out the words. "That's what you and Jimmy have been plotting." She gave a shake to her hair and held her chin up. "You've got your money and you don't care," she said.

"What money is that?" I said.

"What money!" she exclaimed sharply, going over each inch of my face. What she saw surprised her at first. Until then she had been fighting back, but now a sly look came to her; it grew into a smile; the smile got wider and wider, and then her eyes became two curved lines, like crow's wings in the sky, and she went into shouts of laughter. It sounded all down the empty street. She rocked with it.

"Oh, no!" she laughed. "Oh, no, that's too good! That's a winner. He didn't give you a penny! He swiped the lot!"

And she looked up at the sky in admiration of that flying man. She was still grinning at me when she taunted breathlessly. "I mean to say—I mean to say—"

I let her run on.

"It was all or nothing with you, wasn't it?" she said. "And you get nothing, don't you?"

I am not sure what I did. I may have started to laugh it off and I may have made a step towards her. Whatever I did, she went hard and prim, and if ever a woman ended anything, she did then. She went over to the car, got in, and slammed the door.

"You backed the wrong horse when you backed Jimmy," she called out to me.

That was the last of her. No more Mrs. Brackett at the shop. "You won't hear another word from her," my mother said.

"What am I supposed to do—get her husband back?" I said.

By the end of the week, everyone in the town was laughing and winking at me.

"You did the trick, boy," the grocer said.

"You're a good-looking fellow, Bob," the ironmonger said.

"Quite a way with the girls," the butcher said. "Bob's deep."

For when Mrs. Brackett went home that night, she sat down and paid every penny she owed to every shopkeeper in the town. Paid everyone, I say. Bar me.

EIGHT

Noisy Flushes the Birds

THINGS were quiet in the town; they'd been quiet for a year. "You put on your clothes," Mother said one evening, after we had closed the shop, "and it isn't worth it." That hat she bought in Ainsworth, she said, the blue one—she'd only worn it once.

But it was September now and, in our part of the country, if anything happens, September is the time for it. The harvest is in, people have nothing to do, except think of how they can annoy one another. I have heard holiday visitors put this down to the strong air, the variable warm Atlantic winds that send us half asleep so that we don't know whether we are alive or dreaming; Miss Croggan, the headmistress of the girls' school, says it's the Celtic blood taking time off to stir up old feuds. But nothing had happened, so far, this year. There was nothing to compare, for example, with the week Teddy Longfellow introduced two lunatics to the town and persuaded Major Dingle—Nigerian police, retired, and a stickler for the "right people"—that they were a pair of baronets looking for a large property in the neighbourhood. The year before that, there was Hoblin, the farmer, who used disguised voices on the telephone, pretending that he was the Chief Constable, an official from the Ministry of Agriculture, the County Medical Officer, and so on, inquiring into a report that Teddy Longfellow had been watering his milk; he kept the story up for days, until Teddy nearly pulled his red beard off with panic.

And to move from fiction to fact, we had had no scandal to match the break-up of the Brackett marriage. No Bentleys about at night, I mean. No Noisy Brackett roaring through the town, followed a few minutes later by his wife chasing him. Their married life had been, for us, like one of those air displays when suddenly a pair of jets scream the place down, vanish into a whistle and, then, silence; suddenly, five minutes later, they are back again, down your neck, like wasps. Mother and I closed the shop in the evening, as I say, and we sat down doing nothing.

"Can't you talk?" she said. "Your father used to."

"I've been on my legs all day," I said.

Like an enormous, simple-minded cheese the September moon came slowly over the houses opposite and we stared at it. The size of it, Mother said, upset her.

And then—as if the moon had started them off—things began to happen. One thing after another. I caught it first. I went out to a dance on the Saturday night and, driving back, I got engaged to a girl called Claudia Dingle. I knew before I went that it was ten to one I would get engaged to someone or other. Claudia was the daughter of Major Dingle up at the Old Rectory, the man Teddy Longfellow had made a fool of. She was a tall girl with a small cloudy head of golden hair that seemed to be blowing off her head like flame, yet with a voice as cool as a water ice. She was so slight that I thought she would snap in two when she laughed. She had just come back from a finishing school in Switzerland. You should have heard the band play up at the Old Rectory and at our house, too! Mother pretended not to hear first of all when I told her and then said "Every time you go to a dance you get engaged." When I said "Only twice," Mother said:

"They don't get their bread from us; they deal with Higgs." Up at Claudia's house the Major said:

"That hulking lad who comes round the back door with the bread and works in the café! Is the girl out of her mind?"

"Anyway," said Claudia on the second day, "it'll be divine to work in the shop. And you don't always have to be a baker."

"Actually, my sweet," I said, putting on a drawling voice like hers, "I do."

She said she didn't mean it that way. She said it wasn't her fault she was upper class and she'd adore to go out in the van with me.

Any time I got engaged it always upset me. It upset other people, too, and Mother got moody; and Claudia had no tact either, coming in and out of the shop and wanting to look at the bakehouse and saying how divine it was, when we were busy, and upsetting the girls. But the thing that set Mother against her was saying she was going to have the announcement put in *The Times*. Mother thought she meant the *County Times* and so did I, but Claudia meant the London *Times*.

"Everyone does," Claudia said.

"I never heard of it in this town yet," I said. "I'd look a damn fool."

Mother said it was daft; no one in the town would know. I argued this with Claudia.

"I meant *people*, not the town," said Claudia. She didn't mean any harm; her finishing school had finished her.

The announcement went into the London *Times*.

One evening when I had been out at her house I came back home early and Mother was sitting at the window.

"What are you sitting there for; you can't see to read," I said to her.

"Troubling about me—that is new," Mother said. "I've had my life." And then she said, changing her voice to something like Mrs. Dingle's refined accents, and mocking:

"We've had another of your old lady friends in this afternoon— Mrs. Brackett. It never rains but it pours."

My heart gave a jump like a fish.

"What did she want—credit?" I said.

"She's asked you and this girl—what is her name?—Claudia— to dinner," said my mother. "She asked me. No, I said, not me. I never go out, not since Dad died." Mother thought eating with anyone but our relations a wickedness and only went to their houses because it was painful; and she looked like the Ten Commandments at anyone else who invited her to go out.

"She read about it in that London paper," Mother said, accusing Claudia and me. And then we had the usual line about making your bed and lying on it.

"You can go and see the nobs if you like," she said. "And feast yourself on all this getting engaged and getting divorced. Dad was the one and only for me and we were true. You think you want the Fairy Prince, it's womanlike—but it's all soft pansy nonsense. I blame *her*; you don't know whether she's married or single; lady she may call herself, but I don't see she's even a woman, not a real woman." And Mother added: "She's got stout."

The women in our town got stout or thin from day to day, according to Mother's moods. Father used to say he never knew a town where the weight and measurements of women changed so often and where an ordinary dress or coat was ever of the right length.

I switched on the light and I saw Mother's face looking square and offended, suspicion puffing it out. I expected her to look sulky, but I was astonished to see it was worse than that. She looked insulted and miserable.

"She paid her bill," Mother said bitterly. She might have been looking at her grave in the churchyard. She was also suspicious.

"We had a long chat," Mother said. "She came inside." (Mother referred to the room at the back of the shop which was a mixture of sitting-room, store-room and office. When Mother came out of it with anyone who had been "asked inside" she always had a peculiar look on her face—pleased and unnatural. You could never get her to say what "they" had said.)

I was as surprised as Mother that Mrs. Brackett had paid. And I was suspicious, too.

"After five years, about time, too," I said. "I wonder what put that idea into her head?" I said.

"Why ask me?" said Mother. "I'm not getting engaged to all these girls; you were the one chasing after her, driving her husband out of the house."

"Chasing after Mrs. Brackett!" I said.

Mother was on to her old tale. You won't believe it, but she blamed me for Mrs. Brackett's divorce? Just because I ran into Noisy Brackett that evening a year before and he asked me to give him a lift to the station. How did I know he was leaving his wife?

We sat saying nothing.

"Well," said Mother, "you've come in. Haven't you any news?"

News! We had it next day in the lunch hour when the shop was closed. I was eating a chop when something went by with a roar. I mean something in the street. There was a screech at the sharp left bend at the Church and then a noise like someone tumbling dustbins over. I put my knife and fork down.

"Sit down," said Mother, getting up herself and going to the window. "That's Noisy Brackett. He's back."

Mother was holding the curtains. She was lit up with excitement. Even her brown hair shone.

"I knew he'd come back," she cried. And she touched her hair here and there and brushed the crumbs off her dress.

"If it's Noisy he's hit something," I said, getting up again.

"Sit down," she said. She turned on me in a temper.

"People leave cars all over this town, no wonder there are accidents. The police ought to stop it," she shouted.

Mother had always thought that all cars should be cleared out of the town so that Noisy Brackett could have a clear run through at ninety miles an hour. Mother smiled again. She was in heaven. If it had been anyone else but Noisy she would have screamed, pushed me to the door, pulled me back—but not for Noisy. He was a god; he could do anything.

I didn't believe it was Noisy; I think I know a Bentley when I hear one. But when I went up the street I found out Mother was right. People were still looking at the tyre marks on the street and the pavement. A couple of shopkeepers were looking at the back doors of their vans that had been cannoned down the hill. It was Noisy, they said. He had gone off now, nobody knew where. But the police, of course, had got him somewhere outside the town.

At first Mother was upset that Noisy had gone clean through the town without stopping for a word with us. But when Mother heard that he had been summoned for dangerous driving she was in Paradise. He would be back! He would be up before the Court. And if any of those stuffed animals on the Bench dared to do anything to her Noisy she would put arsenic in their bread, she would tell their wives all she knew, and so on. But, underneath and more powerful, her feeling was different. You have got to know Mother. Noisy was back. That meant, for her, that "they"—Mrs. Brackett and Noisy—were reconciled. The divorce was off. "*He* loved *Her*." He was back in Heading, that beautiful house, full of those things worth thousands, life was normal; love—"the one and only"—was triumphant after all. And, to crown it, that dear sweet girl Claudia and I were invited there to dinner at the very throne of matrimonial happiness, an object lesson to us all. In the week following my engagement and Noisy's summons to appear in court on a charge of "wanton driving to the public danger" I have not known Mother so suddenly turn to happiness since Father's death.

All the same, Mrs. Brackett did not turn up at the Court when Noisy's case came on. Mother was a bit put out by this when I told her, but she said that it never looks nice when women are mixed up in the law; her own father left it in his will that no woman should go to his funeral. But I'll tell you who did turn up—I mean aside from half the town, and someone from the Ainsworth Press—Teddy Longfellow. He was Noisy's witness. He had been in the car at the time. Teddy was a funny man. He had a loud reddish suit on, with yellow squares on it, but it was not that—people said he got himself up to look like Satan. It was the way his hair came to a point in front and stood up in a couple of horns at the sides; and his beard. It was his stammer that made people say he had been a German spy.

But we had come to look at Noisy, to see how he would get out of it. The police had got him thoroughly tied up. There he was, the same old Noisy. Small, thin—"his poor chest", Mother used to say—with a head of oily crinkly black hair, his gypsyish skin and still the dandy. He was all nerves and illness in an electric way and the women loved him for that. And there was that sudden twitch to one side of his face. It pulled the skin down from the eye, which seemed to stare out from the middle of calamity like the end of a pistol, before his face went back into dozens of soft smiling wrinkles. We knew he'd get off somehow, but how we could not imagine. He denied, of course, that he was doing fifty, because, as he said, he knew that corner by heart. And Teddy Longfellow denied it also.

"I was practically at a standstill, sir," Noisy said to the Bench, with a shocked, polite glance at the police. "But an extraordinary thing happened. I've never known it happen before in twenty-five years of driving; Le Mans, Monte Carlo Brooklands. I sneezed, sir, just on the turn. A blinding sneeze, sir, without warning, quite extraordinary, like an explosion, like a bomb flash. Visibility absolutely nil. I didn't know where I was. I lost control. Never done it before. It was a mercy I was only doing twenty-two at the time, as Teddy, I mean the witness has just said. Perhaps I ought to say I suffer from hay fever. I got it in India."

And when he said "sneeze" Noisy's face gave one of his twitches and sudden stares with his left eye, as if he were going to produce a sample sneeze in court, a final burst, to make sure. The Chairman even started to raise his hand to ward it off. Well, the Bench hummed and ha'ed, but, of course, Noisy got off. Afterwards, at the Red Lion, he did one or two of these sneezes to show us; one of his Squadron Leaders during the war, he said, could do it with a monocle in his eye, without dropping it.

"I must pop in and have a word with your mama, Bob," Noisy said to me. And when he came to the shop he gave Mother a kiss and said:

"What's happened? You look ten years younger, Mrs. Fraser. I wonder if you would add to all your kindnesses and cash me a teeny weeny little cheque. Yes? You're quite sure? Now, isn't that like old times?'

"Come inside," Mother said, blushing with happiness, leading him to the room at the back. "I'm ashamed of you." They stayed inside talking quite a while and when they came out Mother's face was blissful.

"Now remember your promise! Go and see," said my mother, and she walked with him to the doorstep of the shop.

"I will. You bet I will, Mrs. Fraser. Bang on." Noisy smiled and waved to her. I walked a few yards with him. His face changed, he gave a serious twitch and said, in a dead, quizzing voice:

"How is she? How's the Fairy Queen? Have you seen her?"

"Not to speak to," I said.

He looked as though he didn't quite believe me.

"I hear she paid her bill," he said.

"Yes," I said.

"Lovely money," he said. "I've got a spot of trouble there. Keep it under your hat—she's got her tiny little hands on my birds. She won't give them up. You don't know my birds! Yes, you do. That big case of birds that stands inside the door at Heading. Tropical birds. They're mine."

I didn't remember them. Heading was so full of things.

"She can have what she likes, but she's not going to have my birds," said Noisy. "I'm going to get them. I've got to: I've sold them. I need the cash." Noisy's face was now hard and serious; he lit a cigarette and wagged it up and down on his lips, studying my van. "Wonderful woman, the Fairy Queen, really one of the best. But there's going to be a burglary."

We got to his car and Teddy Longfellow was there.

"Take a look at this. T'that's what we w'want," Teddy said. He was nodding to our van, which was parked behind his car. "Take out the shelves and Bob's your uncle."

"Hear that?" said Noisy to me. "He's a natural car thief, that's how he made all his money. See you one of these days." They got into Noisy's car, Noisy turned to give a tremendous sneeze for my benefit, there was the lovely throb of his engine and he was off.

You pass Teddy Longfellow's house on the Ainsworth road. It stands on a hill, one of those modern houses of glass and steel with a spiral staircase enclosed in a glass tower in front and something like the top of a lighthouse on the roof. It was built just as the war broke out and people said Longfellow had built it so that he could signal to the Germans from it. Claudia and I drove past once or twice and I was telling her that Teddy had made a fortune out of cotton and was a damn good farmer, the only up-to-date farmer in the district. I started telling her about the two fake baronets he had introduced to the town. The place, I said, is full of snobs. Of course, there I put my foot in it. I'd clean forgotten that Claudia's father, the Major, had been Teddy's victim. Class is a funny thing. Claudia was a pretty girl, no brain as Mother said, I give you that; but sweet and she stood up to the old Major and her mother with a will of her own; but when it came to class and family—well, she was her mother all over again. I've seen it since. I got the lot. Teddy was not a gentleman; he was just a shot-up businessman—at the word "business' her face went sick—pretending to be a county gentleman and trying to buy his way in. He was loud. He was vulgar. He was rude. Of course, he wasn't a German, but loads of Germans came to visit him after the war. They came, Claudia said, to look at his pictures.

"They're worth a lot, aren't they?" I said.

"You're always talking about money," Claudia said.

"It's what I live on," I said.

"I don't know how much they're worth," said Claudia. "And I'm not interested. I only know my parents took Mrs. Brackett over there one day and she proved to him his big Cézanne was fake. He's never forgiven her."

"Cézanne—who's he?" I said.

"French, a painter," she said. "A very great painter."

"Oh," I said. "Must be, if he's a friend of Mrs. Brackett's. I'm ignorant."

As I say, she was a sweet girl; you couldn't blame her. We had a bit of a quarrel on the way home. She told me her father had tried to stop her from driving with me on the bread round. He told her she was breaking the law, because of the licence. Of course, Mrs. Dingle had put the Major up to that. I, like a fool, not thinking, said I'd often taken our girls out in it, the girls from the shop.

"And Mrs. Brackett, I suppose," said Claudia sulkily.

"Old Mrs. B., the Fairy Queen!" I said. "I'm not a bloody fool."

"She's not old," said Claudia.

"No, I suppose she isn't," I said. "She *looks* young. Very young sometimes."

"Young!" exclaimed Claudia. "Thirty-eight—I don't call that young."

That was another thing my father used to say about the women of our town. They changed their age faster than in any other place he had ever known. A woman might be thirty in the morning and fifty-five by six in the evening or vice versa.

"Like bread," he used to say. "You see it rise, then it goes flat."

The last thing I wanted to do was to go to have dinner with Mrs. Brackett. The idea that just because I was engaged to Claudia Dingle I had to be paraded before the friends of her family, and Mrs. Brackett above all, preyed on my mind. I had scarcely seen Mrs. Brackett for a year, not since the time she came down to our house shouting and asking what I'd done with her husband. I had kept out of her way. Claudia was dragging me into this and I couldn't help saying to Mother: "That's the last time I get engaged at a dance."

"It is," said Mother. "Who's in a mood now?"

But the day before the dinner I was walking up the town and just as I got to the garage petrol pumps I saw Mrs. Brackett. I was going to dodge into the paper shop, but I went on because I saw at once something was happening. Something that nearly made me laugh out loud. I had caught Mrs. Brackett on the point of cheating the garage hand. It was the prettiest sight in the world. She had just had a gallon of petrol put in her car and the garage hand— it was Johnny Gibbs—was standing there with her money in his open hand and telling her that the price was a penny more. She was cocking an eyebrow at him, which she well knew how to do, and gave a glance up and down the street. She was beginning to blush. Then she saw me. She turned her back on Johnny and came slowly towards me, like a cat. She was a small woman and

I felt the old empty feeling I always had when I saw her walk; that she was going to dawdle her way clean through me.

"Hullo, stranger," she said in a pleased, ringing, boyish voice. "I've been in twice to congratulate you, but you weren't there." Mother had not told me about the second time.

Mrs. Brackett held out her hand. It was a small, square hand and strong; Claudia's hands were long and limp and you could feel the bones in them.

I didn't say much. I didn't know what to say.

"I'm glad you've shaved off your moustache," she said, looking me over.

Even I noticed that Mrs. Brackett had altered. She still had something of the impudent twelve-year-old boy about her, but a boy who had tidied himself up. In Noisy's time she looked like what they call a "young varmint", with her hair chopped as if she had cut it herself, her red check shirt and her dusty old jeans and the lipstick always hit or miss. Now she was wearing a dress, terrible colours, of course—geranium with yellow flowers on it— but a dress and smart shoes and she had been to the hairdresser's. And she had got her figure down. I don't say she looked pretty, because the bones of her face were too strong, but she looked alive. And something else—I couldn't make it out. When I said this to Mother, later on, Mother said:

"It's the divorce. Mrs. Gordon was the same when she was divorced. She's trying to look respectable and sort of sad. A woman has to think."

That wasn't my idea of Mrs. Brackett. I thought she looked more like a woman, I mean one with a brain.

"Thanks for settling the bill," I said. I wanted to show her I had won in the end and that I was glad all that nonsense was over.

Mrs. Brackett didn't like that. She flushed. And she bent forward her head and studied her shoes for quite a while. Her dress was cut very low. Then she looked up quickly and caught me looking.

"Weddings are expensive," she said, very cool. I laughed.

"The bride's parents pay," I said.

Mrs. Brackett gave a shake to her head, as if a bullet had whizzed near her.

"I bet you've told Claudia that," she said, mocking me, but she was laughing. "You are a one, aren't you?" And her little eyes closed into slits of glee as she laughed.

"Tomorrow night," she said. She stepped into her car and she was off.

Johnny Gibbs stood there with his hand open. Both of us watched her go up the town and then stared at each other; he was damn nearly accusing me of plotting robbery.

Claudia was hanging about for me at home and when she had gone Mother said:

"Why are you so rude to that poor girl? What is the matter with you?"

"You heard her," I said. "She's trying to improve me," for I had told them about meeting Mrs. Brackett, and Claudia had been asking what I was going to wear. I had led her on and she was frightened I was just going to walk out of the bakehouse at seven o'clock in my overalls covered in flour and go up to Heading as I was.

"Why have I got to go up there anyway?" I said to Mother.

"The gardens are beautiful. Dad and I used to go up every spring when the rhododendrons were out. They'll take you round the gardens," said Mother, daydreaming.

"You keep on saying 'they'—I bet you anything you like Noisy won't be there," I said. "And it's September—the rhododendrons were over four months ago."

"You needn't be rude to me," Mother said. "He will be there. He promised me."

I told her about Johnny Gibbs and the penny.

"She's always up to something," I said.

"I bet she is," said Mother gaily. "You take up with the nobs and get yourself engaged. What d'you expect? Dad and I were content to be in business."

"Ah," I said, remembering. "That's a word Claudia doesn't like. Teddy Longfellow's in *business*. She doesn't like that."

"There's a lot of things girls don't like they have to get used to," said Mother.

But Mother was as agitated as I was, when the day for Mrs. Brackett's party came. One of her suspicious moods set in. It began with her suspecting the cash register and the bills for flour; she suspected one of the waitresses at our café; women who came into the shop began to put on weight—always a bad sign with Mother—and the colours of their clothes didn't suit them. The men looked shifty, she said; she didn't like a bank manager who drank and she was furious that the butcher opposite was having his shop painted—what a time of year! She was sharp with the girls at the shop—Rosie, the dark one, was almost in tears—and all three girls kept half-turning their heads and walked about round-shouldered because they knew Mother was watching them. If I came out of the bakery into the office or the shop, Mother stopped serving and watched me, too. The worst of all was that she suddenly did not trust Noisy.

"He's a man," she said.

"They're out for what they can get, both of them," she said. She suddenly remembered Mrs. Brackett had once talked of buying the property next door to us and she was glad anyway that we had stepped in and bought it a few months before.

"There is always a plot between those two," she said.

"You didn't tell me Mrs. Brackett had been in twice," I said.

"I did," said Mother. "Are you starting calling everyone a liar? Even your own Mother!"

I didn't think of it at the time—I never did think until after these moods were over—but I remember Dad used to say to her when she was like this:

"What's on your conscience, Mother?"

I'll come to that later.

Still she made an effort when I picked up Claudia at the Old Rectory and brought her back to show to Mother. Claudia was wearing a pale blue dress and her hair was cloudy and lovely. Mother wiped a tear at the sight of her and she was laughing when we waved goodbye; but when I turned back I saw Mother's face looking black with wretchedness as if she had seen us off to our execution or that we had left her to hers. I had the terrible feeling that we were off to the other side of the world and would never see her again and I blamed Claudia for this.

It was a light evening with a mackerel sky, the glimmer of the moon beginning on the stubble, and glinting on the heavy trees and the warm air smelled of the harvest. I was telling Claudia what the Government subsidy meant to the farmers who were complaining, though, for a fact, I could name three who had ten thousand in the bank . . .

"Look," said Claudia interrupting. A soft owl flew over the lane.

"And that's not counting Teddy Longfellow," I said. "He must be worth a quarter of a million."

"When you used to come up here to see the Bracketts was Rosie the one you took with you?" Claudia asked. "The poor girl has got spots."

"I took her to see her brother," I said. "I think it was her brother."

"Oh, look," said Claudia, "another owl. They're like ghosts." And took her hand from mine. She was a jealous girl.

But we were at Heading, driving through the deep walls of rhododendrons.

What a change: not in the house itself—it was a long L-shaped stone house with a wing making the angle—but in the garden. The lawn in front was rough; the mower had not been over it for months; one of the two climbing roses that had spread along the building had fallen off in a heap that entangled the flower-beds. They had not been weeded or touched—all so trim and well looked after in Noisy's time—but now let go. There was a stack of logs beside the wide front door, no one had bothered to move them in. Mrs. Brackett's car, in need of a wash, stood near, and there was a station wagon not far from it.

"Whose is that?" I asked.

Claudia didn't know.

We went into the house. The door was open and Claudia called out. We were in the wide hall room that went to the back of the house. Then a tall, fair-haired man with a broken nose and wearing plimsolls came out of the drawing-room.

"Hullo," he said. "My name's Fobham, not that it matters. They're upstairs having a jaw."

It was Lord Fobham. He lived at Abbey Moor. He took Claudia's coat and then said something to me that I didn't hear. I was standing there staring. For—against the wall, was Noisy's case of birds. It was about four feet high, mounted on a stand, and contained a strange collection of stuffed birds perched on branches—birds of paradise, a pair of parrots, a golden pheasant, an oriole, an Indian kingfisher—so Lord Fobham said later. I was gaping at them. I was thinking Noisy must be mad to suppose he could walk in and lift a case like that.

"Awfully pretty. Victorian," said Lord Fobham to me. He had a busy manner, never standing still, as if he were shaking his bones up.

"It must weigh a lot," I said.

"Take a couple of footmen to lift it," said Lord Fobham.

"I didn't mean weigh," I said, confused. "I mean they must be worth a bit." Claudia bit her lip.

"No, don't think so, twenty-five quid the lot, no more. You pick them up anyway," said Lord Fobham briskly. Claudia said, to put me in my place:

"They're beautiful. They're priceless."

"You mean collectors after them?" said Lord Fobham, getting interested in Claudia. "What would they give for a case like that?" Claudia studied them. She gave a severe glance at me and said:

"You'd better ask my father—but I'd say a hundred pounds."

"I'd give a hundred and fifty pounds," I said to annoy her.

"What!" said Lord Fobham, getting keen. "You mean that?" Lord Fobham was always selling off bits of family property, pictures and heirlooms. At this Mrs. Brackett and Lady Fobham came downstairs.

"What's this lot worth, Sally?" said Lord Fobham. "Mr. Fraser will give you a hundred for it."

"It was me," said Claudia.

"I wouldn't take three," said Mrs. Brackett.

"Well," said Lord Fobham to me, "if it's worth that to her I bet you'd easily find an American who'd give you twice that. What about your cousin?" he said to his wife.

"Don't be silly. He hasn't got a penny," said Lady Fobham. "It would smash if you moved it."

"Don't be a damn fool. Pack it properly, case it up. Like we did with all that china," said Lord Fobham to his wife. "Use your brain. Look. It's light." And he put his hands under the stand to tilt it.

"Come and have a drink and have a look at the other lots before you make up your mind," said Mrs. Brackett sarcastically.

"Damn funny. I never knew it, did you?" said Lord Fobham to me, looking back covetously at the case as we went into the drawing-room. "Probably worth eight hundred pounds."

"Where did you get it from?" he called to Mrs. Brackett.

"It was my father's," said Mrs. Brackett.

"Darling," said Lady Fobham. "He'd sell me."

"No offers," said Lord Fobham. "Are you in the business?" he said eagerly to me.

"No, Mr. Fraser's a baker," said Mrs. Brackett.

"Ah, you can tell me," said Lord Fobham, "something I've

always wanted to know. Why can't I get a decent crust on a loaf nowadays? Bread never has any crust."

"Go to Mr. Fraser and you'll get all the crust you want," said Mrs. Brackett, going over to Claudia. "Darling, what a pretty dress. What are you drinking?"

"Ha! Ha! Ha!" Lady Fobham laughed. "Are you a baker? What fun! I thought bakers were little men. You're as tall as my husband."

"Taller. Use your eyes," said Lord Fobham to his wife. "God, how much gin did you put in this, Sally?" Mrs. Brackett talked to me.

"Gosh, she's pretty. Gosh, she's young," she said. "You know how to pick them. Have you known each other long?"

"Why does your father stuff his birds?" Lord Fobham was saying to Claudia. "I always shoot 'em."

"He doesn't stuff birds," said Claudia.

"Oh," said Lord Fobham. "Where does he shoot? Not up at Teddy Longfellow's, I hope. He shot a fox." And to me he said: "I always ask Sally about the gin—she waters it."

"I do think Sally's wonderful about clothes," said Lady Fobham to me, when Mrs. Brackett poured out more drinks. "She's got the most marvellous lack of colour sense I ever saw—tomato red— it's her personality brings it off. How do you do it, Sally?"

"It's easy," said Mrs. Brackett. "I don't wear anything underneath."

"Really!" said Lady Fobham.

"No one to speak to Alice," Lord Fobham commanded, jerking a thumb at his wife. "A couple of martinis and she goes middle class."

I don't know how long we sat there. In spite of what Lord Fobham said the drinks were not watered this evening. They were strong. We went at last to dine in the large kitchen. Mrs. Brackett's maid had gone home. Lord Fobham poured the wine.

"Oh, how lovely. The '53," said Claudia, clapping her hands and nodding to me. "Look," she said to me.

"It was the '51 I poured over Noisy," said Mrs. Brackett.

"Sally," said Lord Fobham, who had drunk quite a lot. "I never liked him."

"You're wrong there," said Mrs. Brackett. "*I* liked him a lot. Mr. Fraser likes Noisy, don't you?"

She looked at me innocently. I started to tell them about the way Noisy sneezed in court, but a look from Claudia showed me I ought not to have begun it. I went on all the same. But they were all beginning to shout.

"He's trying to tell a story. Everyone keep quiet," said Lady Fobham kindly, flashing rings at me.

"I can't see it," said Lord Fobham to me when I had done. "You mean he sneezed his hands off the wheel. He was plastered."

"I sneeze very loudly," said Claudia, helping.

"You ask yourself," said Lord Fobham, picking out a large potato from a dish and adding, "Go on, pick one yourself," to his wife. "You ask yourself what makes a man attractive to a woman . . ."

"No one asked," said Lady Fobham.

"Claudia knows," said Mrs. Brackett.

Lord Fobham poured more wine. We were making a terrible noise.

"All I can say . . ." Lord Fobham said. "All I can say . . ." but he couldn't get a word in edgeways.

"All you can say—what?" said Lady Fobham.

"Why are your kitchen chairs so hard?" he said to Mrs. Brackett. "My bottom's got points on it. No," he went on. "All I can say is I'm not like Teddy Longfellow, an atheist, reads Darwin, thinks you can go to bed with any man's wife. I believe in humility."

"What!" cried Mrs. Brackett. "Humble—you!"

"I said humility," said Lord Fobham drunkenly. "Not humble. Don't be so damn middle class. There's a difference."

"There's no place like home," Lady Fobham began to sing, but stopped. "Why are you looking so surprised, all of you?"

Everyone became quiet. There was a silence broken only by the sound of the coffee-pot sizzling. There were candles on the table. The curtains were not drawn. Outside the night was dark. The mackerel sky had thickened.

Presently Mrs. Brackett said in a conversational voice:

"There's a man looking through the window." We had drunk so much that we all laughed together.

"A man," said Lady Fobham. "How nice."

"Through the end window," said Mrs. Brackett.

"I don't blame him," said Lord Fobham. "I went to dine with a fellow in Rio and half-way through dinner his wife said

'There's a man walking round the ceiling'. You're plastered, Sally."

"I'm tight, but I'm not plastered," said Mrs. Brackett. We all turned to look at the windows. There was nothing to see, but by her voice I knew Mrs. Brackett was not joking.

"I'll go and look," I said and left the room. I went out in the passage, through a large farm scullery to the back door and out into the garden. This part of the garden was sheltered by a high yew hedge and the light from the dining-room lit it fairly well. The night was dark. I was in the shadow, but I could see no one. I was just going inside again when I saw what looked like a large dog jump to the hedge. I went across to look. No sign of a dog. I went right up to the hedge: it was too dense for any dog to get through. And then, as I moved, I trod on something soft. I looked down and there was a man lying under the hedge with his hands hiding his head. I was treading on him. I stepped back.

"Get up," I said.

But before I knew what to do, the man jumped to his feet and paused to stare. That curly hair, that twitch to the face was unmistakable. It was Noisy. He gave a leap and ran to the gate and was out of the garden before I could do anything. I didn't know what to do. Then I shouted to him. My shout brought out Lord Fobham and Mrs. Brackett, too.

"Who was it?" she said.

"I don't know," I said. "He looked like a gypsy."

"Get after him," they cried. So I ran and I could see Noisy dodging along the shadows of the barns; he vaulted a five-barred gate and into the field beyond it. I let him, of course; anyway, though I've got long legs I've never been much of a runner. Noisy was small, he sprinted fast. I got to the last lot of outbuildings and Mrs. Brackett was coming up, shouting "Where is he?"

"He's over the gate and into the field," I said. In fact, I had not seen where he went.

Mrs. Brackett and I started for the field, when we heard a car starting up on the other side of the house. "That's Bertie Fobham," said Mrs. Brackett, climbing over the gate, but at that very moment Lord Fobham came walking up to us.

Mrs. Brackett had been grinning so far. She loved a hunt. But at this sound of a car driving off and with Lord Fobham beside us her grin went and a look of excited awakeness came to her boyish face.

"Quick," she said, pulling me by the coat. We started back. She rushed back through the yard and garden to the house and through it. And then we both stopped. The front door was wide open and where Mrs. Brackett's case of birds had stood there was now only the stand.

"It's Noisy. He's got them," said Mrs. Brackett.

"He can't have done it alone," I said.

We rushed out on to the drive. Lord Fobham's car was there and so was hers.

"Get in," she said. "Bertie's a dead loss. I bet he's in the water butt."

Far away, a good three-quarters of a mile across the flat fields, we could see the red tail-light of a car turn into the main road and its headlights fan northwards.

"There are two cars," I said, pointing to the splashes of light on the trees.

Mrs. Brackett was a fast driver. We were out of the long deep drive between the rhododendrons, past the estate cottages and in a little more than a minute were going northward on the winding road. Sometimes we saw the tail-light of the other car, sometimes we saw lights daubing the trees. There is a cross-roads not far off and when we were a quarter of a mile off we saw the car turn. As it turned it was picked out by the light of another car which turned in the opposite direction.

"There you are, two. That's our van," I said. Distinctly I saw our green van.

"What is our van doing up here?"

Mrs. Brackett did not answer. She had the racing instinct. Given a choice between chasing a van and a racing car, she chose the latter. At the cross-roads we let the van go. There is a high ridge of open common with a narrow, bumpy but straight road rising and falling for miles, running through scattered coppices of ghostly beeches, leaning and flattened, although we were far inland, by the Atlantic winds. The little dot of light in the distance led us on.

"That's Noisy," she said. I said nothing. I was sure it wasn't.

For Mrs. Brackett it must have been like the old days, the revival of those fierce pursuits of her married life. Her cheek bones were set, her eyes were happy. The wind blew her hair back and I saw her strong straight forehead; and all the time she drove, she was turning her head and talking to me, but in an inspired way, keeping an eye on the leaping road.

"Where did you meet Claudia?" she said as the needle rose steadily on the speedometer. "At a dance, I see. Which dance? When was that? And then you took her home? Is that when you got engaged? In the car? How old is she? Gosh, she's young."

I answered the questions. Suddenly Mrs. Brackett turned her head and came out with a blunt question.

"You're not in love with her, are you?" she said. "All right, you don't want to talk about it. I don't think you are in love with her. They've no money, you know."

"I'm not interested in money," I said violently.

"Keep your hair on," she said. Her voice changed and became nervous. "You don't like me, do you? All right, don't answer that one. When are you going to be married?"

"Not for a long time," I said to stop her talking.

"I think you're wise," she said. "It'd be unfair on her. We're gaining."

And we were. The other car was not more than half a mile ahead. I had been trying to get a real sight of it for a long time. I was trying to think whose car it was for I was convinced that Noisy was in our van, though how he had got it unless, of course, he had pitched some tale to Mother, I couldn't imagine.

"We've got him," said Mrs. Brackett and, in her excitement, squeezed my hand. I squeezed hers. Almost at once, the engine spluttered, our speed died. Within fifty yards we stopped and the other car was away over the brow of the next hill.

The silence of the country flowed in on us.

"Well?" said Mrs. Brackett.

"Sorry," I said and let Mrs. Brackett's hand go. I don't know why I had held it.

"Thank you," said Mrs. Brackett, taking her hand away. No petrol. It was the old story: Mrs. Brackett was too mean to fill up her car. It had happened over and over again in her pursuits of Noisy. We all knew it. I smiled. She looked small, indignant and surprised, like a child. We sat there staring on the dead road, in the night silence of the Common, listening to the engine cool and to the small movements of animals in the gorse.

"Bad luck," said Mrs. Brackett. "Damn." She pulled her dress down over her knees.

"Bertie Fobham will be along in a minute," she said.

"If he got out of the water butt," I said. "He's probably followed the van."

"Yes, the van. What's going on between you and Noisy?" she said.

"Nothing," I said.

She studied me. Then she gave that small shake to her head which either meant she was changing her mind about something or telling a whopper. She sat up straight.

"All right," she said. "Have it your own way. I'll tell you something. They're *his* bloody birds. Not mine. I kept them. I knew he'd come for them. I wanted him to, that's why I kept them. Now he's got them, he can keep them. That's funny—I don't want to see him any more. He's sweet, I was mad about him and I was damn pretty when I married him—but from a woman's point of view, he's no good. He wants a mother. Someone to pet him," she said slyly, "and cash his cheques."

"He told me he was going to get the birds. I thought it was one of his jokes," I said. I told her the story.

"Honour bright?" she said, like a schoolgirl. Then she added, "Typical Noisy to come and peep through the window. I expect he's fallen for your Claudia."

She glanced shrewdly to see how I would take that.

"All right," she said. "Another failure. Wash it out. That's the rotten attractive thing about him—he likes risk."

It was no good sitting there. Lord Fobham was obviously not coming to look for us. There were never any cars on that road at this time of night. It was unlikely there would even be a night lorry. It was four miles to Tolton, the nearest garage. I moved to get out.

"Where are you going?" she said, pulling my arm.

"I'm going to walk to Tolton to get some petrol," I said.

"I'm not going to stay here alone to be raped by some game-keeper and I'm not going to walk," she said, "not in these shoes." I sat back.

"So that's that," I said. "What are we going to do?"

"That's that," she said. "What are you worrying about?"

"Claudia," I said. "Who's going to take her home?" She considered this.

"The Major," she said. "I'm sure he clocks her in and out, doesn't he?"

"Yes, he does."

Mrs. Brackett moved towards me.

"Poor Mr. Fraser," she said putting her arm in mine and resting her head on my shoulder. "Always in car trouble."

Yes, I thought, the Major will fetch her. And with that, my conscience was set free. I moved Mrs. Brackett's arm away and she sat up with annoyance for a second, then I put my arm round her and she put her head on my shoulder again.

"Mr. Fraser," she said. "You're an old hand, aren't you? I bet you'll kiss me next."

I did kiss her.

"Well that took a long time," she said. "About a year by my reckoning. All right, don't speak." She suddenly laughed.

"Do you know, when Bertie Fobham offered me fifty pounds for those birds I nearly closed on it. We could have loaded them up ourselves."

I kissed her again. She drew away from me and said:

"I suppose you know what you're doing?"

"No, I don't," I said and I was speaking the truth. I tried to pull her to me, but adroitly she opened the door of the car and stepped out.

"Let us walk up and down," she said, "and listen to the owls." And so we walked up and down a hundred times, I should think, asking me questions about myself, the shop and about Mother; she talked about the first time I went up to Heading to ask her to pay her bill.

"Gosh!" she said.

"You're lucky," she went on. "You've got your head screwed on."

We must have walked up and down until two in the morning and then there were lights on the road. A lorry came along after all. We siphoned some petrol and then drove back.

"You drive," she said and I did, with my arm round her waist. I could feel the heat of her face through my jacket. There was no one at Heading, of course, when we got there. At a quarter to three Claudia rang up while Mrs. Brackett and I were having a drink. I explained to Claudia what had happened. She said simply:

"Oh! Why aren't you at home?"

And rang off.

I don't know what time I got home. Now and then through the breaking mackerel sky, the September moon dodged in and out as I drove back. No longer the big yellow moon of the night when I got myself engaged to Claudia, but white, half gone and tipped up. It seemed as it went in and out of the clouds to be turning towards me and turning away, like Mrs. Brackett's busy, chattering head when the chase was on. The next morning Claudia broke off her engagement. Mrs. Dingle and the Major sent the announcement to *The Times*.

Mother didn't say anything until the afternoon. She shut herself up in the office and went through the bills.

"Staying out all night round the lanes with a married woman ten years older than yourself," Mother said. "I don't blame the girl."

The word "lanes" meant only one thing to Mother.

"Two pounds three—what is this?" said Mother, reading from a bill. "I'm glad you're out of it. Now we'll get some work done."

"I'd still be in it," I said, "if you hadn't let Noisy wheedle the van out of you."

"He brought it back. It's in the garage, you can see it. He thanked me. I don't often get thanks."

She looked wistfully at another bill and then at me.

"I don't know what he is up to and I wouldn't believe him if he told me. I knew he'd break his promise and not go back to her." She sighed with pleasure. "A woman's a fool who believes a word that comes out of Noisy."

Then Mother took off her glasses and began a tirade.

"And another thing. I may be an old woman—but don't think I'm blind. Don't think I don't know what brought Mrs. Brackett down here, paying her bill, as large as life, asking you up there and all that la-di-da soft soap about how pleased I must be and that this Claudia was the most wonderful girl in the world. I said to her 'Well, Mrs. Brackett, it will work itself out one way or the other, won't it? I could put my oar in, but I won't. It never lasts with him and I'm not breaking my heart.'"

Mother paused. A memory distracted her.

"The second time she came, she bought three dozen meringues," she said. "Did she give you any last night? Well, they keep."

"But," said Mother getting up from Father's old desk and flushing up with temper. "If you think I talked Mrs. Brackett into breaking it up, you're a very wicked boy . . ."

"I didn't say anything of the sort," I said.

"Think, I said, not say," said Mother.

And after that, I did begin to think and the more I thought the more I remembered what Father used to say about Mother's conscience.

Mother put her hand on the desk.

"Oh, you've upset me, with all this love," she said. She had gone pale. She had frightened herself.

"And now I suppose it will be Mrs. Brackett down here day and night, forty-five if she's a day, buying meringues and congress tarts until she's sick and you'll be hiding, all innocent, in the bakehouse, leaving it to your Mother. I wouldn't be that woman's dressmaker."

Mother went to the mirror over the mantelpiece and fiddled with her hair. "Age is what you feel," she said, getting ready for the battle.

NINE

Noisy in the Doghouse

"Sorry to hear about you and Claudia, Bob," Noisy Brackett said, finishing a glass of beer and leaving me at the Crown one morning. "The Fairy Queen on the job again, I suppose? Take a tip from me. The next time you get engaged to a lovely thing like Claudia, steer clear of Fairy Queens. They turn funny when they see another girl get her man. Their little brains start working."

Noisy knew the whole story. Everyone in our town knew it. When I walked up the street, everyone from the dogs upwards was silently giving me advice: "Fall for a divorced woman, ten years older than yourself [and some said twenty]—don't be a fool, boy!" I despised them all, but not Noisy. He had been married to her, I was in love with her; he and I were the only normal men in the town, and that was a thought I clung to. For the more I loved her the more I wanted to be saved from her, and Noisy was a living example of that salvation.

One good thing—the weather broke. Gales blew over the countryside and tore down the telephone wires. We were cut off from Heading for a day or two. Mother had a fright when the chimney caught fire at the back of our bakery; she thought the shop had gone. This, and the sign blowing off at the café, kept me outside and out of her sight. She had got as nervy as the weather. When I got in, I would find her sitting beside Father's photograph, which stood on a table by the window. She would get up and move about the room, trying the brown leather chair of the three-piece first, but it disagreed with her in some way. She moved to the next chair and glared back at the other as if it had deceived her. But now her arms couldn't settle to this one either, and she lifted her elbow to see why. Then her knees got annoyed, and with a groan she got up and returned to the upright chair by the window and turned Father's photograph an inch or so to the light, as if she were trying to shake him into talking to her.

This happened night after night. While Mother was doing

this, I had one eye on her and one on the newspaper, but my mind was four miles away, up at Heading with Mrs. Brackett, trying to catch sight of her face as it floated by, but all I could see was the drawing-room there and its three white-painted doors— the door she and I had come in by that night, the open door leading to the room where her farming papers were scattered over the floor, and a third door at the end of the room, which was closed. I never knew a door so closed. It watched us like a conscience. It seemed even to watch me now when I was at home. I could hear Mrs. Brackett saying, "What are you doing here at this time of night, Mr. Fraser?" But the only thing I could remember was the parting in her hair, for she had kept her head lowered when she was sitting beside me. After that, I would try without any luck to see again that small movement in the pupils of her blue eyes, a movement as tiny as the click of a camera shutter, when she looked up to say goodbye. I was going to say, "Where does that door lead to?" but the sight of her eyes taking a cool snapshot of what was going on inside me stopped me, and like a fool, I left.

I used to look at Mother over my paper. She would be staring at me, afraid of me and herself. We could not go on like this. So one evening when I came in from the Crown, I dived into it. I thought I would make her laugh. "Major Dingley says I ought to be horsewhipped," I said.

No answer from Mother.

"He said it to Lord Fobham over at the Crown. Noisy told me," I said.

Mother was still silent, but when Noisy's name came up she reached for her handbag and looked for the mirror.

"Lord Fobham said—" I went on.

"I don't want to know what Lord Fobham or any of those pots said," Mother said.

And she didn't. Mother thought it was wrong to know what people like that talked about, just as she mistrusted foreigners. They were "daft", and she was sorry for them.

"He said, Lord Fobham said," I went on, " 'Can't do that. Can't horsewhip a man any more. No horses. Nothing but cars. The roads weren't made for them.' "

"Where's the cleverness in that?" Mother said. "We know who needs the tanning. The telephone's working again. She's been on the line three times this morning. I told her you were out."

Mrs. Brackett, of course! She was after me!

"What did she order?" I said, playing it light.

"Order!" said Mother. "She was a good customer till you and her husband went stark staring mad."

We were silent again. I thought of something else; I had heard a rumour going round.

"Teddy Longfellow says Noisy's got an Argentine girl now— an air hostess," I said. "They say he's going to marry her." I couldn't have said anything worse if I'd tried. I thought Mother was going to hit the ceiling, burst, have a heart attack, or die. I'd never seen her face go so purple, then almost black. It nearly doubled its size. Her voice was always loud, but now she shouted, "I won't have you going over to the Red Lion like this." (I don't know why she always called the Crown the Red Lion.) "You know what drink did to your father. Teddy Longfellow was a German spy in the war. He signalled. Don't ask me who he signalled to, but he signalled. Everyone knows he signalled."

And Mother jumped up, went to the window, and pulled the blind down three inches, as if she, too, were signalling, but for the Army or someone to come and help her defend the country. If she had seen Noisy, or if she had seen Teddy Longfellow scratching his beard—he always picked at his beard at one corner of his mouth when he talked—she would have called out, "Help! I'm signalling. Didn't you see it? I'm signalling. Come in. You've upset me, both of you."

"Chinese air hostess!" she turned, raging on me. "There aren't any Chinese here. Don't be a fool."

"Argentine," I said.

"You're always contradicting what I say," she said. She sat down and became fretful. "He can't," she said. "He's a married man."

"He's divorced," I said.

"You keep telling me that. I'm not deaf," she said. "The rat— why did he let her?"

There was a long silence; she was frightened by what she had said. At last she became calm. She took out her handkerchief, in case she was going to need it.

"I didn't mean that—not rat," she said. She put her handkerchief back in her bag. Then she scowled. "Argentine meat," she said mournfully. "Your Father would never touch it."

And then Mr. Pickering, the solicitor, came over to see us.

"Good evening, Mrs. Fraser," said Mr. Pickering. "The wind's still bad, but you've got the bloom of spring on you."

His nose, Mother said to me afterwards, had the bloom on it, too. We were waiting for him; in fact, that is why Mother had on her dark-blue dress and had her handbag beside her. A lucky thing had happened, and if it hadn't I think I might have gone mad with my mind fixed on Mrs. Brackett. The Mill House at Galeford Priors had come up for sale privately, and Mother and I jumped at the chance of it—Mother because she liked a bit of property, and I because I knew it was cheap and because, as Father used to say, "Nothing clears the mind like buying property. It sobers you up."

But buying the Mill House gave us only a small respite. Since the night Claudia had broken our engagement I had neither seen nor spoken to Mrs. Brackett. I did everything to stop myself. I'd go out in the car and make it go the other way. I'd walk up to the telephone and all round it, but I never lifted the receiver. I spent my time thinking of new things to do. I mended the sign on the café. I even whitewashed one wall of the garage, and though I thought I had painted her out with every brushstroke, she came up through the paint. But that evening, after Mr. Pickering left, I had almost come to the end of everything that could prevent me trying to see her. I tried the usual little actions. I went round to the bakehouse to talk to the men. I came back and washed and shaved. I changed out of my working clothes. I put on my grey suit, but nothing happened, so I changed out of it into my brown. I came downstairs. There was only one thing left for me. I said to Mother, "Let's go into Wetherington to the pictures."

"Get me my coat," Mother said, "I'm going out. Don't gape at me. I suppose your mother can go out, too?"

Mother's temper was the worst side of her; it is the same with me.

"Go on, get out!" she cried. "Go and chase your fancy woman. I'm not stopping you. I want to telephone."

Every family has its terrible sentences. Mother did not often answer the telephone, except in the shop, and when I was a child, if Mother announced she wanted to "use the telephone" she meant that everyone must get out of the house. Father used to say she would like the street cleared, too.

I left her, but you see the situation I was in; there was nothing
to stop me going up to see Mrs. Brackett. Nothing at all. I got
out my car, but I was too startled to know where to drive, and, in
fact, I just drove to the end of the town, then round it, and came
back again to the cross-roads near our house to see if the lights
were on. I drove out of the town again and then did the same
journey once more, because I couldn't remember *which* lights
were on. The second time they were all out.

All idea of going up to Mrs. Brackett's went. Mother's mysteriousness saved me. I found myself going south to Wetherington
at last and I was glad. Mrs. Brackett's house was in exactly the
opposite direction, and every mile I put between her and myself
made me gladder. It was one of those clear black evenings when
the sky has been cleaned up by the wind and the stars have been
brushed as bright as buttons, and if you had asked me after half
an hour where I was going, I would have said I didn't know, I
was just letting the car take me where it wanted.

Then I woke up. I had seen a signpost and I knew suddenly
where I had been going all the time, where I had been thinking of
going for a week or more without knowing it. I was going to
see Noisy. I was only two miles from his new house. I drove
faster. All the feelings that had weighed me down for a couple of
weeks fell off. Good old Noisy! Once I saw him I would be all
right. If there was one person who could save me from Mrs.
Brackett, it was her ex-husband.

There is a stony lane up to Noisy's cottage. I had never been
there in his time, but I knew where it was. I had once sheltered
there with Claudia in a storm when it was a ruin. I remember
she had been afraid there would be bats when we went upstairs,
but there weren't. This cottage was on Teddy Longfellow's estate
and stood under a row of beeches that sighed all the time—very
rare trees in our part of the country. The land around it used to
be grazing land, but Teddy had changed all that. Noisy had been
living there for the best part of a year, after the divorce, rebuilding
the place on his own. He was good with his hands and very
patient.

I drove up to the cottage. It lay back behind new high wooden
palings with a wide gate. The first thing I saw gave me a start;
it was Brewster's cab and Teddy Longfellow's car beyond it.

Beery Brewster was the taxi-driver in our town. I got out and went to open the gate, but I couldn't open it. I switched on my torch. I saw through a crack that there was a sort of lever and a bolt on it, and, on the gatepost, a bell. A bell in the country! And then I saw there was a wire running from the other side of the gate to an upper window of the cottage. I pressed the bell. A light came on over the front door and then another in the bedroom above, and the bedroom window opened and a grey-haired old woman with a shawl over her put her head out.

"Who is it?" she screeched in a nasal voice.

"Bob Fraser!" I called out. I put the light of my torch on her face. It gave a sudden twitch to the left eye that I would have recognized anywhere.

"Put that light out!" Noisy called out in his wartime voice. The wire squeaked, the gate opened. I went in, and Noisy was at the door with a wig in his hand and the shawl on his shoulders.

"Come in. We've quite a party in here. Welcome to the dog-house. Why didn't you bring your mother? Old Brewster's dead drunk in the kitchen. She had a terrible drive."

Sitting by the fire in Noisy's little sitting-room, comfortable and happy, was Mother, with a glass of whisky in her hand.

"Oh, put that silly wig away," Mother said, laughing at him. "You frightened me out of my life. I hate those things. No!" screamed Mother. For Noisy had put the wig on again.

"It keeps away the undesirables," Noisy said to me, under-lining the word, giving a twitch to his face. "Request permission to land. Permission refused." He took the wig off and admired it. "The old lady is like a mother to me. I'll get you a drink."

I sat down next to Mother, and she muttered, "What are you following me about for? Who looks a fool now?" And she nodded at the wig. "Argentine hostess—you'd believe anything."

And Mother laughed, united with herself and comfortable for the first time for weeks. "Teddy Longfellow's here," she whispered to me, anxious to make her call on Noisy at this hour respectable. And she straightened her dress. "What have you come here for? Haven't I got a life?"

Mother gave me a short, sharp rap on the knee to stop me replying, for Teddy Longfellow came in.

"Here, Teddy," said Noisy, handing him a drink.

"You haven't cut down those blasted f-fir trees yet, I see," said Teddy, fingering his beard at the end of his lower lip. His stammer, Noisy said, was worth ten thousand a year to him; it doubled his consonants and his income.

Teddy Longfellow scared everyone in our neighbourhood and enjoyed doing it. With his beard and the twist he gave to his hair and his eyebrows, he indeed looked like the devil. He used to alarm the parson during the war by praising Hitler, and annoy the hunting people by calling foxhounds "those ruddy useless dogs". Teddy liked causing trouble; it was he who had started this tale about Noisy's Argentine girl and—it turned out—had given him the wig. And, of course, he helped Noisy get his case of stuffed birds back from Heading, from under Mrs. Brackett's nose, and had pinched our van to do it. As he sat there he eyed Mother and me to see if he could see any more chances of annoying us.

"I said when are you going to c-c-cut down those firs?" Teddy said.

"No can do," said Noisy. "Useful for emergency landings in poor visibility. When I get them in line I know I'm bang on the runway."

"You won't get off the ground when the bomb drops anyway," said Teddy.

"You don't think there will really be a bomb, do you, Mr. Longfellow?" Mother said anxiously to Teddy.

"Bob," said Noisy. "Come out here. I'll show you the place. I can't bear to see that swine falling for the woman I love."

And Noisy gave me a peculiar look. I have often thought of it since. I got up and went out of the room with him.

"Now," said Noisy. "Here's the passage. All my own work. I did every bit myself. I put in those two doors. These stairs were rotten; I had to replace half the treads. Come up. Oak, my boy, solid oak. Yes, I did all the painting. Made a bathroom. The geyser was falling to bits. I got a nice lad down at the airport to fix it for me. See? Hot. Cold. I did all the plumbing."

He turned on the taps. All the pipes in the house jumped, whistled, and thundered.

"Beautiful sound, isn't it? Nothing like your own plumbing. Don't go away," he said. "Look at this. You sit in the bath, pull this ring—front gate closed, no one can get in. Pull this—open it. Front door, too. Wonderful what you can do if there are no

bicycle as I was going up. The curtains were not drawn, and I could see two lamps shining in the long sitting-room. The front door was open, and after I had rung the bell I walked in the wide hall where Noisy's case of birds had once stood—the marks of the stand were still on the carpet—and I called out, "Anyone at home?"

All the white doors in the hall were closed except one leading to the drawing-room. I listened. Then I heard talking: Mrs. Brackett was speaking on the telephone. I went farther in and I heard her say "There's someone here", but she still went on talking. More I couldn't catch until two or three words made me stop. She was saying the name of that horse again: "Tray [or something or other] Pays On." Exactly the words she had said two years or more ago, the second time I came up to ask her to pay our bill, and when she made all the trouble about it and I was afraid of her. I wasn't afraid of her now and I wasn't afraid of the house and all its things. The three or four big pictures in the room even looked smaller and the chairs rather shabby.

I heard her ring off and she came out fast from the room. When she saw me, the telephone look went dead on her face. She hesitated and then said, "Hullo! That was Kitty Fobham." Then she shook her head and said, "Actually, it wasn't."

Does that make two lies? I don't know: the moment she boldly said them she lowered her head and put out a foot as if she were sketching something in a hurry on the carpet, and then took a few steps aside before she looked at me again. She had a real liar's walk. It was her body that told the lies—I mean the way she walked, how her hips moved and her arms. Her tongue, I must say, usually told the truth. If it didn't, her head gave that shake to warn you she was going to try something on. That was why people who spread stories about her really liked her. And when I say her body told lies, I mean they were the kind of lies any man likes to hear.

"They told me you telephoned," I said.

"Why didn't you ring me back?" she said.

"I've come instead," I said.

"You don't say! Well, sit down. I've been washing my hair," she said. She pointed to the deep, green settee where we had sat the night that had ended my engagement with Claudia. It was too low for me; I'm tall.

Mrs. Brackett looked plain. There was a line across her forehead, and her hair was darker because it was wet. It ended in rat-tails, just like the hair of a maid we used to have years ago. Mrs. Brackett went to the far side of the fireplace and held her hair down to dry it by the fire. We both spoke at once.

She said, in her cattle dealer's voice, "I wanted to see you. I expect you think it was my fault Claudia broke up with you. I'm sorry."

I said, "What is this 'Pays On'? 'Say Pays On'? 'Tray Pays On'? You said it on the telephone."

"Pays on?" she said, throwing her hair back and looking at me. "What d'you mean? On the blower—I said that?"

"I don't know," I said. "You said it once before, when I came up here years ago, as well, about the bill."

She smiled. "Still on about the bill," she said. "What's the matter? Haven't you paid your water rates? I don't know what you're talking about. 'Pays on'? Never heard of it." And she lowered her head to the fire. "I'll never get this dry," she said.

"That's it. Pays On," I said. "Is it a horse? Noisy said it was a horse."

She sat up and again threw her hair back from her broad low forehead when she heard Noisy's name.

"When I came up here," I went on. "Noisy said it sounded like one of those French horses."

"A French horse? I never heard . . ." She stopped. She opened her mouth and put her tongue in her cheek, like a child caught stealing. She got up and walked over to a side table where the drinks stood. I watched the way she walked. She was wearing one of her terrible dresses of blue stuff with little yellow and red daisies on it. It looked like someone else's. And a tomato-coloured cardigan. I remember her saying, the night when Claudia and I had dinner there, that it puts a woman "one up in the conver" if you give a man a shock at the sight of your clothes and it "makes the other women look sick".

"A horse." She laughed. "What will you have to drink?" she said, turning round. "Noisy told you that?"

"Yes."

"Well," she said. "I will tell you." And she spoke like someone spelling out to a child. "It's not a horse, it's a man. A Frenchman who lives in the country. It's French."

"Nothing for me," I said. "Why talk in French. Is it smart or something?"

"You're a suspicious character, Bob," she said. "You sound sore. What's the matter? Has flour gone up? Can't you sell your cream puffs?"

I kept my temper, because her voice had changed and was soft.

"Let's see," I said. "He's a man. And he's French. And he lives in the country. He wouldn't be a peasant, would he?"

"Good!" she said, laughing. "That's it—a French peasant. A real peasant."

I nodded. " 'Bloody peasant,' Noisy said," I said, giving a scratch behind my ear.

She gave me a long look, which died away, and she said outright, "All right, you win. I was talking about you."

"That's funny," I said. "Noisy thought it was a horse."

"Noisy has better manners than me. Can we drop it?"

"What?" I said. "Is it something insulting? I didn't know that. What's wrong with it? It's no worse than silly bitch, is it?"

I thought Mrs. Brackett was going to fly at me, but she didn't. She stuck her chin out. She said quietly, seriously, "I apologize."

"That's all right," I said. "It's best to begin with a row."

"Damn, damn, damn," she said. "I really do apologize. Honour bright." And then her eye gave that little flick. "Begin what?" she said.

I got up to walk over to the table to her.

"No," she said. "Stay where you are. If you don't want a drink, I do." I sat down again, but when she brought her drink, she came over to my side of the fireplace and sat on the stool there. We were silent for quite a time.

"I've bought the Mill House," I said.

"That's nice of you," she said. "You've changed the subject. How did you hear about it?"

She was sharp where there was a question of a deal. I told her about it. I said I thought of turning it into an hotel, and we argued about that a long time—how you'd never get a manager in a place like that.

"How much did you give for it?" she said.

I didn't answer, but—it just came into my head, and I didn't mean it—I said, "How would *you* like to manage it?"

She was as surprised as I was. "I don't like being mocked," she said. "Is that what you came up to say? Of course I wouldn't manage your hotel. Anyway, it's a crime to do anything like that with that place. D'you always go about sitting in cars with women and then ask them to manage hotels. Did you ask Claudia? Why are you so mad about money?"

Jealous! I pricked up my ears. The room seemed to smile at me. There was a picture on one of the walls of a lot of cardinals drinking wine, and the central one had his smiling face turned towards us. Even the white door at the end of the room might have opened; I wouldn't have been surprised.

"She was only a girl of nineteen," I said. "Since Father died, I am responsible."

"Pooh. You're only twenty-two yourself."

"Thirty," I said.

"How old d'you think I am?" she said, putting her head back and moving to the sofa. In a way, she looked her worst, but I wasn't looking at her face. I remember Noisy once saying he was twenty-three hundred years old and that she was twelve.

"Twelve," I said.

"I'm thirty-three," she said, giving the short shake to her head. "Actually, thirty-six. And don't copy Noisy."

Thirty-six, I was thinking—that will be something to tell Mother the next time she starts on me about Mrs. Brackett's age. When I looked at her again, she was very friendly.

"I'm selling this house, if you're in the buying mood," she said. "I can't afford it."

I shook my head. "Why don't you sell it to Teddy Longfellow?" I said. "I saw him at Noisy's last night. He's rich."

She started. "The liar!" she said, blushing. "Noisy said you weren't there."

"I wasn't when you rang," I said.

She smiled and leaned towards me. "Did you see this girl of his, the Argentine girl everyone is talking about?"

I was the biggest fool in the world, I felt so confident of her.

"Yes," I said carelessly, and I laughed.

"What is she like—young? I'm glad he's got a girl."

I was in it; I had to go on. "Yes, young," I said.

"Is she tall?" Mrs. Brackett moved nearer to me. "Tell me what she's like."

"Dark," I said. "Yes, tall."

"Taller than me? Pretty? What is she like? What did she say?"
She started arranging her hair as she talked.

"Taller," I said. "A bit—kind of stiff. I've only seen her in
uniform. She didn't say much. No, I don't think she said anything.
Teddy Longfellow was there, and Mother. Something dead about
her."

"Is she working? I mean is she air-hostessing still?"

I was beginning to enjoy this.

"I think they've grounded her."

"Why?" Mrs. Brackett said anxiously.

"I don't know," I said.

"You must have some reason," she said.

"She just looked grounded."

"How can anyone look grounded? She sounds like a dummy
to me," said Mrs. Brackett, with an unnatural laugh. "Stiff as a
board, in uniform. Doesn't she speak? Poor Noisy—serves him
right. He likes a chat."

She put her hand on my arm and said excitedly, "I'll tell you
what we'll do. Let's go and see them. I'll ring him up."

"No," I said, alarmed by what I'd said.

"Yes," she said, moving away, but I caught her arm and held
her.

"My hair is wet," she said, shaking to get away, but I held her
arm and presently she stopped pulling.

"Please," she said. "You're hurting me." I slackened my hold
and she got up at once. She was a trickster.

"I'm going to see them," she said, looking at her watch and
going towards the door.

"It's ten o'clock," I said. "They'll be in bed."

Mrs. Brackett stopped at the door. She went very white. With
her hair plastered down and her mouth suddenly small and her
eyes startled as if I had hit her, she looked ugly.

"That," she said, coming back a step to me, "was a dirty
remark."

"Trays Pays On," I said.

She looked as if she would throw something, if there had been
anything near. Then her eyes almost closed and she laughed and
laughed and came and sat down near me. "You're not the same as
when you first came up here. What has happened to you?" she said
softly to me.

"Nor are you," I said, moving towards her.

She began pulling at the thread of the settee as she had done before. I can't remember what we said, but we did get on to the subject of the door at the end of the room and where it led to. To the second staircase, she said. And one thing led to another.

The next morning, when I had seen to the vans, I rang her. I was mad to hear her voice. There was no reply. Several times I rang, and there was no answer. Mother came into the room behind the shop to look at me, and every time the phone rang she and I moved to it. At last I had to go to Wetherington in the afternoon—it was early closing with us, and Mother wanted to come with me and go shopping. There was something secretive about Mother, because she wouldn't, as she usually did, tell me where to pick her up in the town. Usually, I found her outside the biggest draper's, but today she wouldn't say for a long time, and then she said, "In the station yard." This puzzled me. She had what we used to call her broody look, like a hen sitting heavily, and occasionally she'd break out into the first line of a song, but stop because she could never remember the others. In the end, I met her at the station, looking comfortable and sly, as though she had eaten something good, and when we drove away, she was soft-tempered and dreamy. She had got her week of anger off her mind. We had been driving for twenty minutes when she said, "They don't tell you anything. It's daft. Your Uncle Dan in Canada has been dead for years."

She had been to a fortune-teller.

"Well, who else could it be?" she said.

We got back to the shop, and I drove into the yard at the side and straight for the garage, which I had left open. It was dark now, and I had put the headlights full on. Just as the car was going into the garage, Mother clutched my arm and cried out "Stop, Bob! There's a woman there!"

She was right. There, standing against the whitewashed wall, stood a tall young girl, smiling. For a moment I thought it was Molly Gibson; she was dark. Then I looked again. It was not a girl—not a living girl. It was Noisy's cardboard girl from the Argentine Air Lines.

"Oh, it gave me a turn, I thought you'd kill her," Mother said. "What is it? Who put it there?"

We got out. Mother looked at me suspiciously. It was what the fortune-teller had said, she told me: there'd be a visitor from overseas.

I examined the figure. "It's Noisy's," I said. "It's got the key to his heart hanging on the back."

Mother came and looked. Her face darkened. "You've upset Noisy. You don't listen to me. You've upset him. I could see it the other night." And Mother marched out of the yard, down the street to our house.

I knew Noisy was always playing the fool, but there was always something behind his jokes. And then—it was natural—I felt a bit uneasy about Noisy ever since I had fallen in love with Mrs. Brackett. He was friendly, but he had changed. I had once or twice caught him giving me a strange look, his face not twitching, but still as stone; his eyes very sharp, sarcastic.

I went to the bakehouse, but the men didn't know anything about the dummy. I went along to the café and asked the two girls there. Had Noisy been in, I asked the first girl.

"No," she said.

"Are you sure?" I asked.

The other girl came out of the kitchen.

"Has Noisy been in today? Any time?"

"No," said the girls.

I told them there was a poster in the garage.

"Oh," said the eager girl from the kitchen. "That was Mrs. Brackett. She left it this afternoon." And she gave me a knowing smile; I did not like it.

"Did she leave a message?" I said, not letting on. "You're sure it was Mrs. Brackett?"

"Yes," they said. And there was no message.

They were grinning behind my back when I left. I saw them in the mirror. You can imagine what was going on in my head. I didn't mind the joke, but Mrs. Brackett and Noisy in it together!

I went back to our house.

"Mrs. Brackett brought it," I said to Mother.

Mother ignored this. Her temper was rising. "Trying to make a laughing-stock of your mother!" she said. "Telling me he had an Argentine girl up there! Do you think anyone in his senses would believe a twopenny tale like that?"

"I didn't make it up," I said.

"I'm sure you didn't," she said. "You haven't the brains. All this love has made you stupid. Going about with your mouth wide open, you'd swallow anything, and the business goes to ruin. Two customers complained the bread was burned yesterday —the whole lot. The whole town's laughing at you. Noisy's taken your measurements, my boy. Running after another man's wife! They've made fools of you. And I am glad. It will teach you a lesson. And don't ask me to be sorry. I told you this divorcing was all my eye. Oh, I wish your father was alive!"

"Why would they put it there?" I said. "Anyway, it was Mrs. Brackett."

I was going to say more; I was in a temper, too. I went round to the shop again and I sat at the desk staring at the telephone, and then I rang Mrs. Brackett.

"I have been trying to ring you," I said.

"That is a change," she said. "Is anything the matter?"

Her voice sounded cold.

I laughed. It was so lovely to hear her. "Well," I said. And I laughed again.

"What is the joke?" she said.

I was still laughing as I began. "I—"

"Are you ringing me up about that dummy?" she said sharply. "You are? You found it? Bad luck for you. Listen. I don't like being mocked. I had ten years of that kind of thing with Noisy."

God, I thought. Mother storming at me at home, and Mrs. Brackett shouting from up on the hill.

"I don't want any more stable boy jokes." Mrs. Brackett had a temper. We all had tempers, I suppose—Mother, me, Mrs. Brackett, and all of us.

She slammed down the telephone.

I would have let her temper go and waited for her to cool off and to come running down. What stopped me was not my own temper, but what was clearer every moment I thought of it: that she and Noisy had got together again, for how else could she have got hold of the dummy?

I ran into the yard, and that damn silly thing was still smiling away at me as I got into the car. I drove up to Heading. I was mad. The servant was coming down on her bicycle, just as I had seen her two days before. This time I could have gladly knocked her over.

But Mrs. Brackett was not at Heading. She had gone out. I came slowly back to the shop. I did not know what to do. Several times my hand went to the telephone. I was tempted to ring Noisy to tell him what I thought of him, but I couldn't. I went over to the Crown.

And there I heard something that changed my mind. Teddy Longfellow was in the bar talking to the landlord, who was polishing glasses and lifting each one to his eye to see if it was clean as he listened.

"They cut fifty pounds' worth of wire", Teddy was saying.

"He told me that on the phone," said the landlord.

"Hullo, Bob," said Teddy. "Did you hear this?"

"What was that? Have they cut your wire?" I said to Teddy. He often had trouble with hooligans who let his cattle out.

"Up at Mr. Brackett's," said the landlord.

"Noisy's had burglars," said Teddy.

I looked at the landlord, for I never believed any tale that Teddy came along with, but the landlord put a glass down and said: "This afternoon. When he was out."

"Well they wouldn't do it when he was in!" said Teddy scornfully.

Yes. Out (I thought). With Mrs. Brackett, delivering that poster to me, but Teddy's next words put another light on it.

"I told Noisy just now it sounds like the job of a sex maniac to me," said Teddy to the landlord, "cutting all that wire, smashing a kitchen window—all to get at a woman! I told Noisy months ago it was a mistake to keep a foreign woman up there."

"What woman?" said the landlord.

"Bob knows her, don't you, Bob?" said Teddy.

That was enough for me. Noisy had not been with Mrs. Brackett; in fact it was clear from the far-away tone of Teddy's voice that he was going to spread the rumour that *I* was with her. He was picking away at his beard fast, delighted with himself. It was clear he had had a peep into my garage.

What puzzles me now is why I didn't let it go at that. I suppose I was so relieved to see that Noisy and Mrs. Brackett were not in this together that I didn't stop to ask myself "Whose side are you on?" but went straight off eagerly to ring up Noisy. If only I hadn't rung him!

"This is going to cost you a pretty penny, Bob," Noisy said before I could get a word in. "A hundred feet of wire chopped up to bits, two locks gone, kitchen window smashed, geyser not working—add the men's time at union rates . . ."

"I don't know what you're talking about."

"And then," Noisy went on. "There's the emotional side. No one thinks of that nowadays. That's what I can't get over. Bob, you rotten free-lance, breaking up a happy home. Think of all those poor children crying, 'Where's Mummy? When's she coming back from the Argentine?' Tragedy of easy divorce, divided homes, one more little delinquent attacking women in parks, Father's sad evidence—"

"Listen, Noisy—"

"Bob, you bloody daylight burglar. Over."

"I've got her," I said. "She put her in our garage."

"Who did?"

"Your wife."

"My ex-wife, if you please," said Noisy.

"We found her when we got back from Wetherington this afternoon."

"Who's we?" said Noisy.

"Mother and I," I said.

"Mother in it, too," said Noisy. "My God! Radio silence, old boy. I'll be over in five minutes."

He came with his usual roar. "Let me see her," he said, and we went into the garage. He sniffed the air. "It's damp in here. Bad for the poor girl's chest." He looked at her proudly. "Isn't she a peach? Now, my sweetie," he said to her, "you stay where you are, do as you are told. It will be all right. We're going to lock you in, so you don't get up to tricks." And he closed the garage door.

"Aren't you going to take her back?" I said as he locked the door himself.

"Bob," he said very seriously, "when Teddy Longfellow and I broke into Heading that time and got my case of birds back, they were my birds, weren't they? We didn't steal anything, did we? We didn't touch a thing that wasn't our own—right? We didn't do any damage, did we? We didn't break a kitchen window and leave filthy footmarks on the floor, did we? One of the cleanest jobs you ever saw, I bet, wasn't it? And we didn't lift anything lying about, like a pair of service wire clippers, for example?" He was scowling. "Oh, yes," he said, "we're going to get them back. Jump in. I know her hideouts. We'll buzz up to Heading to see if the clippers are there, but if they're not they'll be in her car. And remember, Bob, for future reference"—he gave that twitch to his eye as he turned his head to me—"when the Fairy Queen takes off she's never got more than a gallon of gas in the tank. That cuts the target area down to eleven miles. She can't be at the Fobhams', for instance."

We were off. The roar of Noisy's car was unmistakable in our town, and of course it brought Mother to the door.

We tried Heading first—"the ancestral home", Noisy said— and drew nothing, then to the Duck outside Tolton, the Lamb at Forth Hill, then the Aylesbury Arms, the Green Man, and the Sailor's Return.

"Bob," said Noisy, getting whiter in the face after every pub, "the Fairy Queen is not one of those who, in the normal free-for-all, can dish it out but can't take it. Something must have got her on the raw."

I told him the story—well, three-quarters of it.

"Tall, dark girl, you said. Didn't talk much, you said? Very nice," he said, grinning. "Anything else?"

"I said I thought she was grounded," I said.

Noisy laughed loudly. "Wrong there, Bob," he said. "She's in uniform."

He became thoughtful. "Of course, I can see she was getting her own back on me, but why dump that lovely creature at *your* place? That's what foxes me."

We drove on, missing the Harrow at Denton Bridge, because the man there watered the gin. "There's only one more chance," Noisy said, driving now on the wrong side of the road. "Play the game or get out of the bed!" he shouted at a passing car.

We seemed to lose our way in by-lanes. Suddenly he pulled up at a pub called the Fox and stopped in the yard. We did not get out.

"The only thing I can think of, Bob, is you were making a pass at her. Yes, that's what it must have been," Noisy said as we sat there. "Never make a joke when you're making a pass at a woman. They don't like it. You're right down the drain if you do. And let me tell you, I don't care a damn if you *are* down the drain. But I want my wire clippers back. They've been with me in France, in Egypt, in India, and I've never seen the man who'd dare lay a finger on them."

We looked round the yard.

"What did I tell you?" said Noisy suddenly. "See that? She's here."

He pointed to Mrs. Brackett's car. We sat gazing at it.

"Keep your eyes skinned, Bob," said Noisy at last. He got out and went over to her car, opened the door, and looked around inside. He came back with the heavy pair of service wire clippers in his hand.

"Mission accomplished," he said. "Let's get drunker."

We considered the peaceful white walls of the inn, the bare trees, the lights shining behind the curtained windows.

"It brings back memories," said Noisy. "Many's the time we've finished up here, the Fairy Queen and I, after a row. Funny to think she's in there now, all on her own, knocking them back. Mind if I come in, too, for old time's sake?"

For I had begun to move for the door.

There was a loud noise coming from the bar, where the locals were, but we went into the small one. Sitting alone in a chair by the bar was Mrs. Brackett.

"Scotland Yard," said Noisy thickly, turning back the lapel of his coat.

Mrs. Brackett put her drink down and, looking at Noisy, she blushed. "I see you've brought the Sergeant," she said, glancing coldly at me.

"We didn't know whether this was going to be a strong-arm job, did we, Bob?" said Noisy. "It's all right. We're both drunk."

"Mr. Fraser's quite free with his arms, too," said Mrs. Brackett primly. "Why doesn't he sit down? Is he going?" For Noisy had sat down beside her.

"I'm mad about her, aren't you, Bob?" said Noisy. "A real bit of old Newgate, isn't she? No, Bob's not going."

"Well, why doesn't he join in the conversation?" said Mrs. Brackett. "Has flour gone up again? Or is he worried about his new girl?"

"Oh," cried Noisy, "has Bob got a new girl? He didn't tell me that. Bob, what's this, you rotten seducer? You never told me."

"A foreign girl—Argentine, I believe," said Mrs. Brackett. "Very dark, very tall. They'll make a handsome pair. She used to be an air hostess, isn't that so, Mr. Fraser? Grounded . . ."

"Much better grounded," said Noisy. "You know where they are."

"A bit stiff in her uniform," said Mrs. Brackett.

"That will wear off when they get married," said Noisy.

I laughed, but Noisy didn't and neither did Mrs. Brackett when she looked at me.

"With a fine fellow like Bob, of course it will," said Noisy. "Good-looking, too."

"Yes," said Mrs. Brackett. "And doing well. He's just bought the Mill House. He asked me to manage it. It's going to be an hotel."

"Go on!" said Noisy. "What? Eight ten a week and all found?"

"You won't know him in ten years' time. He'll have bought the town," said Mrs. Brackett.

"Well, all I can say," said Noisy, "I hope he's found the right woman."

"She sounds absolutely cut out for him," said Mrs. Brackett. "Has she got any money, Mr. Fraser?"

"*Mr.* Fraser, *Mr.* Fraser!" said Noisy in a shocked way. "You don't seem to know each other too well. Come and sit over here, Bob, and get acquainted. This is Mrs. Brackett. Will you excuse me a minute?"

And Noisy went out.

"I love you," I said to Mrs. Brackett. "Let us go. Now."

Mrs. Brackett's face softened.

"I've been in love with you since I first saw you," I said.

"I was mad about *you*, actually," said Mrs. Brackett. "But"—giving a shake to her head—"I don't like technique."

"It was just a joke."

"Really?" said Mrs. Brackett. "Well, I haven't got a sense of humour. Ask Noisy."

"But last night you loved me," I said.

"Hold it a minute," she said. "I'll tell you."

She got up and went to the street door. "Noisy's a long time," she said. "Has he gone? I didn't hear him."

Then Noisy came in and met her there.

"I thought you'd gone," said Mrs. Brackett.

"No, my sweet, just taking the air," said Noisy, taking her arm. "Nice to be missed."

Mrs. Brackett hesitated.

"I'm going home," she said and suddenly pushed violently past him out of the pub.

We stared at the closed door. The closed door in the sitting-room at Heading came into my mind. I don't know what was in Noisy's, but we both went after her. At once we heard a shout from her across the yard.

"Bloody funny!" she shouted and came marching in a fury across the yard, opened the door of Noisy's car, and got in and slammed it. Noisy sauntered up to her.

"You damn well drive me!" she shouted at him.

Noisy turned to me, shrugged, and beckoned, but I was staring at her car. Someone had let the air out of the two back tyres. Suddenly, I heard Noisy's car roar. He had taken off.

Mrs. Brackett's car stood in our garage at home for three weeks. It took me twenty minutes to pump its tyres, and where she and Noisy went that night I do not know. I went after them. They weren't at Heading. They weren't at his cottage. Nor in the days, even the weeks that followed. The Post Office said they had gone abroad. The damp got into the hostess of the Argentine Air Lines. She peeled and she buckled and fell over. I told one of the men to pitch her in the dustbin. He brought the key hanging on the back to me, and I told him to throw that away, too. On second thoughts, I broke up the dummy girl myself.

Mother said nothing, but once or twice she goes on about the future—the usual thing. "If you knew what was going to be you'd act differently," she says. "People ought to tell you, then you'd know," she says. And then she gets on to Teddy Longfellow saying there isn't any future, and I tell her I agree with him. A few weeks ago, Heading came up for sale. Mother says the class of trade is changing in our town.

TEN

The Marvellous Girl

THE official ceremony was coming to an end. Under the sugary chandeliers of what had once been the ballroom of the mansion to which the Institute had moved, the faces of the large audience yellowed and aged as they listened to the last speeches and made one more effort of chin and shoulder to live up to the gilt, the brocaded panels of the walls and the ceiling where cherubs, clouds and naked goddesses romped. Oh, to be up there among them, thought the young man sitting at the back, but on the platform the director was passing from the eternal values of art to the "gratifying presence of the Minister", to "Lady Brigson's untiring energies", the "labours of Professor Exeter and his panel" in the Exhibition on the floor below. When he was named the Professor looked with delight at the audience and played with a thin gold chain he had taken from his pocket. The three chandeliers gave a small united flicker as if covering the yawns of the crowd. The young man sitting at the back stared at the platform once more and then, with his hands on his knees, his elbows out and his eye turned to the nearest door got ready to push past the people sitting next to him and to be the first out—to get out before his wife who was on the platform with the speakers. By ill-luck he had run into her before the meeting and had been trapped into sitting for nearly two hours, a spectator of his marriage that had come to an end. His very presence there seemed to him an unsought return to one of those patient suicides he used to commit, day after day, out of drift and habit.

To live alone is to expose oneself to accident. He had been drawing on and off all day in his studio and not until the evening had he realized that he had forgotten to eat. Hunger excited him. He took a bus down to an Italian restaurant. It was one of those places where the proprietor came out from time to time to perform a private ballet. He tossed pancakes almost up to the ceiling and then dropped them into a blaze of brandy in the pan—a diversion that often helped the young man with the girls he now sometimes took there. The proprietor was just at the blazing point when two women came into the restaurant in their winter coats and stood still, looking as if they were on fire. The young man quickly gulped down the last of a few coils of spaghetti and stood up and wiped his mouth. The older, smaller of the two women was his wife and she was wearing a wide hat of black fur that made her look shorter than he remembered her. Free of him, she had become bizarre and smaller. Even her eyes had become smaller and, like mice, saw him at once and gave him an alert and busy smile. With her was the tall, calm girl with dark blue eyes from their office at the Institute, the one she excitedly called "the marvellous girl", the "only one I have ever been able to get on with".

More than two years had gone by since he and his wife had lived together. The marriage was one of those prickly friendships that never succeeded—to *his* astonishment, at any rate—in turning into love, but are kept going by curiosity. It had become at once something called "our situation"; a duet by a pair of annoyed hands. What kept them going was an exasperated interest in each other's love affairs, but even unhappiness loses its tenderness and fascination. They broke. At first they saw each other occasionally, but now rarely; except at the Institute where his drawings were shown. They were connected only by the telephone wire which ran under the London pavements and worried its way under the window ledge of his studio. She would ring up, usually late at night.

"I hope it's all right," she'd say wistfully. "Are you alone?"

But getting nothing out of him on that score, she would become brisk and ask for something out of the debris of their marriage, for if marriages come to an end, paraphernalia hangs on. There were two or three divans, a painted cupboard, some rugs rolled up, boxes of saucepans and frying pans, lamps—useful things stored in the garage under his studio. But, as if to revive an intimacy, she'd always asked for some damaged object; she had a child's fidelity to what was broken: a lampshade that was scorched, an antique coal bucket with one loose leg, or a rug that had been stained by her dog Leopold whose paws were always in trouble. Leopold's limp had come to seem to the young man, the animal's response to their hopeless marriage. The only sound object she had ever wanted—and got into a temper about it—was a screwdriver that had belonged to her father whom she detested.

Now, in the restaurant, she put up a friendly fight from under the wide-brimmed hat.

"I didn't know you still came here," she said.

"I come now and again."

"You must be going to the opening at the Institute."

"No," he said. "I haven't heard of it."

"But I sent you a card," she said. "You must go. Your drawings are in the Exhibition. It's important."

"Three drawings," said the girl warmly.

"Come with us," his wife said.

"No. I can't. I'm just going to pay my bill."

A lie, of course. She peered at his plate as if hoping to read his fortune, to guess at what he was up to. He turned to the girl and said with feeling:

"Are you better now?"

"I haven't been ill," said the girl.

"You said she'd been in hospital," he said to his wife.

"No I didn't," she said. "She went to Scotland for a wedding."

A quite dramatic look of disappointment on the young man's face made the girl laugh and look curiously at him. He had seen her only two or three times and knew nothing much about her, but she was indeed "marvellous". She was not in hospital, she was beautiful and alive. Astounding. Even, in a bewildering way, disappointing.

The waiter saved him and moved them away.

"Enjoy yourselves," said the young man. "I'm going home."

"Goodbye," the girl turned to wave to him as she followed his wife to the table.

It was that "goodbye" that did for him. It was a radiant "goodbye", half laughing, he had seen her tongue and her even teeth as she laughed. Simply seeing him go had brought life to her face. He went out of the restaurant and in the leathery damp of the street he could see the face following him from lamp to lamp. "Goodbye, goodbye," it was still saying. And that was when he changed his mind. An extraordinary force pulled his scattered mind together; he determined to go to the meeting and to send to her, if he could see her in the crowd, a blinding, laughing, absolute Goodbye for ever, as radiant as hers.

Now, as he sat there in the crowded hall there was no sign of her. He had worn his eyes out looking for her. She was not on the platform with his wife and the speakers of course. The director, whose voice suggested chocolate, was still thanking away when, suddenly, the young man did see her. For the light of the chandeliers quivered again, dimmed to a red cindery glow and then went out, and as people gasped "Oh", came on strongly again and one or two giggled. In that flash when everyone looked up and around, there was a gap between the ranks of heads and shoulders and he saw her brown hair and her broad pale face with its white rose look, its good-humoured chin and the laugh beginning on it. She turned round and she saw him as he saw her. There are glances that are collisions, scattering the air between like glass. Her expression was headlong in open conniving joy at the sight of things going wrong. She was sitting about ten rows in front of him but he was not quick enough to wave for now, "plonk", the lights went out for good. The audience dropped *en masse* into the blackness, the hall sank gurgling to the bottom of the sea and was swamped. Then outside a door banged, a telephone rang, feet shuffled and a slow animal grunting and chattering started everywhere and broke into irreverent squeals of laughter.

Men clicked on their lighters or struck matches and long anarchic shadows shot over the walls. There was the sudden heat of breath, wool, fur and flesh as if the audience had become one body.

"Keep your seats for a moment," the director said from the darkness, like God.

Now was the time to go. Darkness had wiped out the people on the platform. For the young man they had become too intimate. It seemed to him that his wife who sat next to her old lover, Duncan, was offering too lavish a sight of the new life she was proposing to live nowadays. Duncan was white-faced and bitter and they were at their old game of quarrelling publicly under their breath while she was tormenting him openly by making eyes at the Professor who was responding by making his gold chain spin round faster and faster. The wife of the director was studying all this and preparing to defend her husband in case the longing in those female eyes went beyond the Professor and settled on *him*.

How wrong I was about my wife's character, the young man thought. Who would have thought such wistful virginity could become so rampant. The young man said: "Pull yourself together,

Duncan. Tell her you won't stand any more of it. Threaten her with Irmgard . . ."

Darkness had abolished it all.

It was not the darkness of the night outside. This darkness had no flabby wet sky in it. It was dry. It extinguished everything. It stripped the eyes of sight; even the solid human rows were lumped together invisibly. One was suddenly naked in the dark from the boots upwards. One could feel the hair on one's body growing and in the chatter one could hear men's voices grunting, women's voices fast, breath going in and out, muscles changing, hearts beating. Many people stood up. Surrounded by animals like himself he too stood up, to hunt with the pack, to get out. Where was the girl? Inaccessible, known, near but invisible. Someone had brought a single candle to the desk at which the director stood like a spectre. He said:

"It would seem, ladies and gentlemen, that there has been a failure of the . . . I fear the . . . hope to procure the. . . ."

There was a rough animal laugh from the audience and, all standing up now, they began to shuffle slowly for the doors.

"Get out of my way. Please let me pass," the young man shouted in a stentorian voice which no one heard for he was shouting inside himself. "I have got to get to a girl over there. I haven't seen her for nearly a year. I've got to say 'Goodbye' to her for the last time."

And the crowd stuck out their bottoms and their elbows, broadened their backs and grew taller all around him, saying:

"Don't push."

A man, addressing the darkness in an educated voice, said: "It is remarkable how calm an English crowd is. One saw it in the Blitz."

The young man knocked over a chair in the next row and in the next, shoving his way into any gap he could find in the clotted mass of fur and wool, and muttering:

"I've only spoken to her three times in my life. She is wearing blue and has a broad nose. She lives somewhere in London—I don't know where—all I know is that I thought she was ill but it turns out that she went to a wedding in Scotland. I heard she is going to marry a young man in Canada. Think of a girl like that with a face as composed as a white rose, but a rose that can laugh —taking her low voice to Canada and lying at night among thou-

sands of fir trees and a continent of flies and snow. I have got to
get to the door and catch her there and say 'Goodbye'."

He broke through four rows of chairs, trod on feet and pushed,
but the crowd was slow and stacked up solid. Hundreds of feet
scraped. Useless to say to them:

"A fox is among you. I knew when I first saw this girl that
she was to be dreaded. I said just now in a poetic way that her
skin is the colour of a white rose, but it isn't. Her hair has the gloss
of a young creature's, her forehead is wide and her eyebrows are
soft and arching, her eyes are dark blue and her lips warm and
helpless. The skin is really like bread. A marvellous girl—everyone
says so—but the sure sign of it is that when I first saw her I was
terrified of her. She was standing by an office window watching
people in the street below and talking on the telephone and laughing and the laughter seemed to swim all over her dress and her
breasts seemed to join in and her waist, even her long young legs
that were continuing the dance she had been at—she was saying—
the night before. It was when she turned and saw me that my
sadness began.

"My wife was there—it was her office—and she said to me in a
whisper:

"'She is marvellous, isn't she? The child enjoys herself and she's
right. But what fools girls are. Sleep with all the boys you like,
don't get married yet, it's a trap, I keep telling her."

"I decided never to go to that office again."

The crowd shuffled on in the dark. He was choking in the smell
of fur coats, clamouring to get past, to get to the door, angrily
begging someone to light one more match—"What? Has the world
run out of matches and lighters?"—so that he could see her, but
they had stopped lighting matches now. He wanted to get his
teeth into the coat of a large broad woman in front of him. He
trod on her heels.

"I'm sorry," he wanted to say. "I'm just trying to say 'Goodbye'
to someone. I couldn't do it before—think of my situation. I didn't
care—it didn't matter to me—but there was trouble at the office.
My wife had broken with that wretched man Duncan who had
gone off with a girl called Irmgard and when my wife heard of it
she made him throw Irmgard over and took him back and once
she'd got him she took up with the Professor—you saw him

twiddling his gold chain. In my opinion it's a surprise that the
Exhibition ever got going, what with the Professor and Duncan
playing Cox and Box in the office. But I had to deliver my
drawings. And so I saw this girl a second time. I also took a rug
with me, a rug my wife had asked for from the debris. Oh yes,
I've got debris.

"The girl got up quickly from her desk when she saw me.
I say *quickly*. She was alone and my sadness went. She pointed
to the glass door at the end of the room.

" 'There's a Committee meeting. She's in there with her husband
and the others.'

"I said—and this will make you laugh Mrs. Whatever-your-
name-is, but please move on—I said:

" 'But *I* am her husband,' I said.

"With what went on in that office how could the girl have
known? I laughed when I said this, laughing at myself. The girl
did not blush; she studied me and then she laughed too. Then she
took three steps towards me, almost as if she was running—I
counted those steps—for she came near enough to touch me on
the sleeve of my raincoat. Soft as her face was she had a broad
strong nose. In those three steps she became a woman in my eyes,
not a vision, not a sight to fear, a friendly creature, well-shaped.

" 'I ought to have known by your voice—when you telephone,'
she said.

"Her mistake made her face shine.

" 'Is the parcel for the Exhibition?' she said.

"I had put it on a chair.

" 'No, it's a rug. It weighs a ton. It's Leopold's rug.'

" 'I've got to go,' I said. 'Just say it's Leopold's. Leopold is a
dog.'

" 'Oh,' she said. 'I thought you meant a friend.'

" 'No. Leopold wants it, apparently. I've got a lot of rugs. I
keep them in the garage at my studio. You don't want a rug,
do you? As fast as I get rid of them some girl comes along and
says, "How bare your floor is. It needs a rug," and brings me one.
I bet when I get back I'll find a new one. Or, I could let you have
a box of saucepans, a Hoover, a handsaw, a chest of drawers, fire-
tongs, a towel rail. . . .'

"I said this to see her laugh, to see her teeth and her tongue
again and to see her body move under its blue dress which was

light blue on that day. And to show her what a distance lay between her life and mine.

" 'I've got to go,' I said again but at the door I said,

" 'Beds too. When you get married. All in the garage.'

"She followed me to the door and I waved back to her."

To the back of the fur-coated woman he said, "I can be fascinating. It's a way of wiping oneself out. I wish you'd wipe yourself out and let me pass. I shall never see her again."

And until this night he had not seen her again. He started on a large design which he called *The Cornucopia*. It was, first of all, a small comic sketch of a dustbin which contained chunks of the rubbish in his garage—very clever and silly. He scrapped it and now he made a large design and the vessel was rather like the girl's head but when he came to drawing the fruits of the earth they were fruits of geometry—hexagons, octagons, cubes, with something like a hedgehog on top, so he made the vessel less like a girl's head; the thing drove him mad the more he worked on it.

September passed into October in the parks and once or twice cats on the glass roof of the studio lost their balance and came sliding down in a screech of claws in the hurly-burly of love.

One night his wife telephoned him.

"Oh God. Trouble," he said when he heard her plaintive voice. He had kept out of her way for months.

"Is it all right? Are you alone?" she said. "Something awful has happened. Duncan's going to get married again. Irmgard has got her claws into him. I rang Alex—he always said I could ring—but he won't come. Why am I rejected? And you remember that girl—she's gone. The work piles up."

"To Canada?" he said.

"What on earth makes you say that?" she said in her fighting voice.

"You said she was."

"You're always putting words into my mouth. She's in hospital."

"Ill," he said. "How awful. Where is she?"

"How do I know?" she said. "Leopold," and now she was giggling. "Leopold's making a mess again. I must ring off."

"I'm sorry," he said.

Ill! In hospital! The picture of the girl running towards him in the office came back to him and his eyes were smeared with tears. He felt on his arms and legs a lick of ice and a lick of fire.

His body filled with a fever that passed and then came back so violently that he lost his breath. His knees had gone as weak as string. He was in love with the girl. The love seemed to come up from events thousands of years old. The girl herself he thought was not young but ancient. Perhaps Egyptian. The skin of her face was not rose-like, nor like bread, but like stone roughened by centuries. "I am feeling love," he said, "for the whole of a woman for the first time. No other woman exists. I feel love not only for her face, her body, her voice, her hands and feet but for the street she lives in, the place she was born, her dresses and stockings, her bus journeys, her handbags, her parties, her dances. I don't know where she is. How can I find out? Why didn't I realize this before?"

Squeezed like a rag between the crowd he got to the doorway and there the crowd bulged and carried him through it backwards because he was turning to look for her. Outside the door was an ambitious landing. The crowd was cautiously taking the first steps down the long sweep of this staircase. There was a glimmer of light here from the marble of the walls and that educated man gripped his arm and said, "Mind the steps down," and barred the young man's way. He fought free of the grip and stood against the wall. "Don't be a damn fool," said the educated man, waving his arms about. "If anyone slips down there, the rest of you will pile on top of them." The man now sounded mad. "I saw it in the war. A few at a time. A few at a time," he screamed. And the young man felt the man's spit on his face. The crowd passed him like mourners, indecipherable, but a huge woman turned on him and held him by the sleeves with both hands. "Thornee! Thornee! Where are you? You're leaving me," she whimpered. "Dear girl," said a man behind her. "I am here." She let go, swung round and collided with her husband and grabbed him. "You had your arm round that woman," she said. They faded past. The young man looked for a face. Up the stairs, pushing against the procession going down, a man came up sidling against the wall. Every two or three steps he shouted, "Mr. Zagacheck?" Zagacheck, Zagacheck, Zagacheck came nearer and suddenly a mouth bawled into the young man's face with a blast of heavily spiced breath.

"Mr. Zagacheck?"

"I am not Mr. Zagacheck," said the young man in a cold clear voice and as he said it the man was knocked sideways. A woman took the young man's hand and said:

"Francis!" and she laughed. She had *named* him. It was the girl, of course. "Isn't this wild? Isn't it marvellous? I saw you. I've been looking for you," she said.

"I have been looking for you."

He interlaced his fingers with her warm fingers and held her arm against his body.

"Are you with your wife?" she said.

"No," he said.

She squeezed his hand, she lifted it and held it under her arm.

"Are you alone?" he said.

"Yes."

"Good," he said. "I thought you'd gone." Under her arm he could feel her breast. "I mean for good, left the country. I came to say 'Goodbye'."

"Oh yes!" she said with enthusiasm and rubbed herself against him. "Why didn't you come to the office?"

He let got of her hand and put his arm round her waist.

"I'll tell you later. We'll go somewhere."

"Yes!" she said again.

"There's another way out. We'll wait here and then slip out by the back way."

The crowd pressed against them. And then, he heard his wife's voice, only a foot away from him. She was saying: "I'm not making a scene. It's you. I wonder what has happened to the girl."

"I don't know and I don't care," the man said. "Stop trying to change the subject. Yes or no? Are you?"

The young man stiffened: "This is the test. If the girl speaks the miracle crashes."

She took his arm from her waist and gripped his hand fiercely. They clenched, sticking their nails into each other, as if trying to wound. He heard one of the large buttons on his wife's coat click against a button of his coat. She was there for a few seconds; it seemed to him as long as their marriage. He had not been so close to his wife for years. Then the crowd moved on, the buttons clicked again and he heard her say:

"There's only Leopold there."

In a puff of smoke from her cigarette she vanished. The hands of the girl and Francis softened and he pressed hard against her.

"Now," he whispered. "I know the way."

They sidled round the long wall of the landing, passing a glimmering bust—"Mr. Zagacheck," he said—and came to the corner of a corridor, long and empty, faintly lit by a tall window at the end. They almost ran down it, hand in hand. Twice he stopped to try the door of a room. A third door opened.

"In here," he said.

He pulled her into a large dark room where the curtains had not been drawn, a room that smelled of new carpet, new paint and new furniture. There was the gleam of a desk. They groped to the window. Below was a square with its winter trees and the headlights of cars playing upon them and the crowd scattering across the roads. He put his arms round her and kissed her on the mouth and she kissed him. Her hands were as wild as his.

"You're mad," she said. "This is the director's room," as he pushed her on to the sofa but when his hands were on the skin of her leg, she said, "Let's go."

"When did you start to love me?" he said.

"I don't know. Just now. When you didn't come. I don't know. Don't ask me. Just now, when you said you loved me."

"But before?"

"I don't know," she said.

And then the lights in the building came on and the lights on the desk and they got up, scared, hot-faced, hot-eyed, hating the light.

"Come on. We must get out," he said.

And they hurried from the lighted room to get into the darkness of the city.

ELEVEN

The Cage Birds

JUST as he was getting ready to go to his office, the post
came.

"A card from Elsie," Mrs. Phillips said. " 'Come on Wednesday.
All news when we meet. I've got Some Things. Augusta'." She
turned the card over. There was a Mediterranean bay like a loud
blue wide open mouth, a small white town stretching to a furry
headland of red rocks. A few villas were dabbed in and a large
hotel. The branch of a pine tree stretched across the foreground
of the picture splitting the sea in two. Her husband had been
brushing his jacket and stopped to look at the card: he started
brushing again. In ten years, it seemed to her, he had brushed half
the suit away, it was no longer dark grey but a parsimonious
gleam.

They looked at each other, disapproving of the foreign scene;
also of the name Elsie had given herself: Augusta. They had never
got used to it.

"Ah ha! The annual visit! You'd better go," he said. And then
he laughed in his unnatural way, for he laughed only when there
was no joke, a laugh that turned the pupils of his eyes into a pair
of pin-heads. "Before her maid gets hold of the things."

"I'll have to take the boy. It's a school holiday."

"Half fare on the bus," he said. "She always gives you something
for the fare."

And he laughed at this too.

"She forgot last year," she said.

He stopped laughing. He frowned and reflected.

"You shouldn't let her forget. Fares have gone up. All across
London! When I was a boy you could do it for sixpence. Get off
at Baker Street—that'll save fourpence."

He put the brush down. He was a youngish man whose sleeves
were too short, and he was restlessly rubbing his red hands together
now, glistering at the thought of the economy; but she stood still,
satisfied. When they were first married his miserliness had shocked
her, but now she had fallen into abetting it. It was almost their

romance; it was certainly their Cause. When she thought of the mess the rest of her family was in, she was glad to have years of girlhood anxiety allayed by a skinflint. She knew the sharp looks the shopkeepers and neighbours gave him when his eyes filled with tears as he haggled over a penny or two, and counted the change in his open martyred hand. But she stood by him, obstinately, raising her chin proudly when, giving his frugal laugh, he cringed at a counter or a ticket office. He had the habit of stroking his hands over the legs of his trousers and smiling slyly at her when he had saved a penny, and she, in ten years of marriage, had come to feel the same excited tingle in her own skin as he felt in his.

"Get out of my way. We're going to Auntie's tomorrow," she said to the boy when he came back from school in the afternoon. "Here"—and she gave him the postcard—"look at this."

She was in the kitchen, a room darkened by the dark blobs of the leaves of a fig tree hanging their tongues against the window. It was an old tree, and every year it was covered with fruit that looked fresh and hopeful for a few weeks, and then turned yellow and fell on to the grass, because of the failure of the London sun. The dirty-minded woman next door said those leaves put ideas into your head, but Mrs. Phillips couldn't see what she meant. Now she was ironing a petticoat to put on for the visit tomorrow and the boy was looking at the mole on her arm as it moved back and forth, her large grey eyes watching the iron like a cat. First the black petticoat, then her brassière, then her knickers; the boy watched restlessly.

"Mum. Where is Auntie's house?" the boy said looking at the card.

"There," she said, straightening up and dashing a finger at random on the card.

"Can I swim?"

"No, I told you. We're not going there. We haven't got the money for holidays. That's where Auntie Elsie lives in the summer."

"Where's Uncle Reg?"

That was the trouble; the kid asking questions.

"I told you. He's gone to China, Africa—somewhere. Stop kicking your shoes. They're your school shoes. I can't afford any more."

Then she put down the iron with a clump and said: "Don't

say anything about Uncle Reg tomorrow, d'you hear? It upset Auntie."

"When are we going to see her?"

"Tomorrow. I keep telling you."

"On a bus?"

"On a bus. Here," she said, "give me those shirts of yours."

The boy gave her the pile of shirts and she went on working. She was a woman who scarcely ever sat down. She was wearing a black petticoat like the one she had ironed, her arms were bare and when she lifted up a garment he could see the hair in her armpits; hair that was darker than the tawny hair that was loose over her sweating forehead. What disturbed the boy was the way she changed from untidy to tidy and especially when she put on her best blouse and skirt and got ready to go out. The hours he had to wait for her when, going to the cupboard and looking at the dresses hanging there, she changed herself into another woman!

She was this other woman the next day when they went off to the bus stop. She was carrying a worn, empty suitcase and walked fast so he had almost to run to keep up with her. She was wearing a navy blue dress. She had tied a grey and white scarf round her head so that the pale face looked harder, older and emptier than it was. The lips were long and thin. It was a face set in the past; for the moment it was urging her to where she was going but into the past it would eventually fall back. At the bus stop she simply did not see the other people standing there. The boy looked at her raised chin with anxiety and when the bus came, she came down out of the sky and pushed the boy on and put the case under the stairs.

"You sit there," she said. "And see no one takes it."

The annual visit! Her sister had come over from that island in June this year, early for her. It used to be Christmas in Reg's time and, for that matter, in the time of that other man she had never met. This new one had lasted three years; he was called Williams and he was buying the headland on the postcard, and he was a June man. He couldn't stand the mosquitoes. Her sister said: "They suck his blood. He's like beef to them." But who was the blood-sucker? You ask *him*! Those women have to get it while they can. At the Ritz one minute—and the next, where are they? She called herself Augusta now. But Grace stuck to calling her Elsie: it was virtuous.

London was cabbaged with greenery. It sprouted in bunches along the widening and narrowing of the streets, bulging at corners, at the awkward turnings that made the streets look rheumatic. There were wide pavements at empty corners, narrow ones where the streets were packed. Brilliant traffic was squeezing and bunching, shaking, spurting, suddenly whirling round bends and then dawdling in short disorderly processions like an assortment of funerals. On some windows the blinds of a night worker were drawn and the milk bottle stood untouched at the door; at the Tube, papers and cigarette litter blowing, in the churchyards women pushing prams. The place was a fate, a blunder of small hopes and admired defeats. By the river one or two tall new buildings stuck up, prison towers watching in the midst of it. The bus crossed the river and then gradually made north to the Park and the richer quarters.

"There's your dad's shop," she said to the boy. They passed a large store.

"There's his window, first floor," she pointed up. That was where he worked in the week.

Now the streets were quieter, the paint was fresher, the people better dressed. By a church with a golden statue of St. George and the Dragon outside it, she got the boy off the bus and walked to a new building where there was a man in blue uniform at the door.

In this instant the boy saw his mother change. She stopped, and her grey eyes glanced to right and then to left fearfully. Usually so bold, she cringed before the white building and its balconies that stuck out like sun decks. She lowered her head when the porter with the meaty despising nose opened the door into the wide hall. She was furtive and, in the lift, she tried to push the suitcase out of sight behind the boy; she felt ashamed. She also nervously trembled fearing to be suspected of a crime.

"Take your cap off in the lift when you're with a lady," she said to the boy, asserting to the porter that she was respectable. With both hands the startled boy clawed the cap off his head.

The porter was not going to let them out of his sight. On the eleventh floor the door slid open. Across the hall of carpet and mirrors which made her feel she was a crowd of women at many doors and not one, he led her to the door. They boy noticed it had no knocker. No bang, bang, bang, iron on iron, as on their door at home; a button was pressed and a buzz like hair spray at the barber's could be heard. There were he noticed white bars behind the figured glass on the door where ferns were frosted.

Presently a maid wearing a pretty apron opened the door and let them in, looking down at their shoes. A green carpet, mirrors framed in mirror again, hotel flowers, lilies chiefly, on a glass topped table of white metal: the flat was like the hall outside. It smelled of scent and the air stood warm and still. Then they were shown into a large room of creamy furniture, green and white satin chairs. There were four wide windows, also with white metal strips on them, beyond which the fat trees of the Park lolled. Did Auntie own them? At one end of the room was a small bar of polished bamboo. Then out of another room came Auntie herself taking funny short steps which made her bottom shake, calling in a little girl's voice "Grace!" She bent down low to kiss him with a powdery face, so that he could see the beginning of her breasts. Her brooch pricked his jersey, catching it. "Oh, we're caught." She disentangled it.

"It's torn my jersey," the boy whined.

"There you are. Look. I'll take it off and put it here." She put the brooch on the table.

"Umph. Umph," she said going back to him and kissing him again. Auntie had the tidiness of a yellow-haired doll. She was as pink as a sugared almond and her kiss tasted of scent and gin.

"You've lost a lot, Grace," she said to her sister. "Look at me. It's that French food. I've put on seven pounds. It shows when you're small. Mr. Williams is coming today. I flew in yesterday from Paris. I've got some lovely things. It's no good anyone thinking they can leave me in Paris on my own."

"Is Uncle Reg in Paris?" said the boy.

His mother blushed.

"Keep quiet. I told you," she said with a stamp.

Elsie's round blue eyes looked at the boy and her lips pouted with seductive amusement. She wriggled a shoulder and moved her hips. The boy grew up as she looked at him.

"What do you like for tea? I've got something for you. Come with me and see Mary. Sit down, Grace."

When the boy had gone the two sisters took up what they felt to be their positions in the room. Grace refused to take off her scarf and refused also out of dread of contamination from the expense of the satin, to sit back on the sofa; she kept to the edge from where she could get a good view of everything. Elsie sat with her beautiful silk legs drawn up on the seat of a chair and lit a cigarette and touched the hair that had been made into a golden crust of curls that morning.

Grace said: "The carpet's new."

"They never last more than a year," Elsie said with a cross look. She was pretty, therefore she could be cross. "People drop cigarettes. I had the whole place done." And with that she restlessly got up and shut the window.

"The curtains as well. Mr. Williams paid five hundred pounds for the curtains alone! I mean—you've got to be kind to yourself. No one else will be. We only live once. He spent nearly as much in the bedroom. I saw the bills. Come and look at it."

She got up and then sat down again. "We'll see it in a minute."

"You're all barred in," Grace said.

"We had burglars again. I just got in—Mr. Williams took me to Ascot. He likes a bit of racing—and I rushed back, well, to tell you the truth I must have eaten something that didn't agree with me, duck pâté I think that's what it was and I had to rush. He must have followed me in, this man, I mean, and when I came out my handbag was open and he had cleared one hundred and fifty pounds. Just like that." She lowered her voice. "I don't like the man on the lift. Then at Christmas when we were on the island they came in again. The staff here were off duty, but you'd have thought people would see. Or hear . . . That's what staff is like these days."

"What happened?"

"They took my mink coat and the stole, and a diamond clasp, a diamond necklace and Mr. Williams's coat, a beautiful fur lined coat—he carried on, I can tell you—and all my rings. Well, not all. We got the insurance but I don't keep anything here now except what I'm wearing. The brooch—did you see it? Mr. Williams gave it to me as a consolation, I was so upset. Pictures—that's where he puts his money usually. Everything's going up. You want to put your money into things. That's why we put those bars on the door and the windows. And—come here, I'll show you."

They walked into the bedroom and on the door that gave on to the balcony there was a steel grille that closed like a concertina.

"You're caged in," said Grace.

Elsie laughed.

"It's what Mr. Williams said. Funny you should say it. He likes a joke—Reg could never see one, d'you remember? 'Birdie—we'll keep you in a cage.' Ah now," she pointed to the white bed where dresses were laid out. "Here it all is. I've picked them all out."

But Grace was looking at a white cupboard with a carved and gilded top to it. The doors were open and thrown inside was a pile of summery hats, some had fallen out on to the violet carpet of the bedroom. Half of them were pink—"My colour."

"Oh," said Elsie in a bored voice, already tired of them. "That's what I got in Paris. I told you. On the way back."

Elsie led her sister out of the bedroom again.

The cringing had gone; Grace sat stiffly, obstinately, hardened, without curiosity, looking at the luxury of the room.

"I heard from Birmingham the day before yesterday," she said in a dead voice.

Elsie's pretty face hardened also.

"Mother's ill," said Grace.

"What is it?" said Elsie.

"Her legs."

"I hope you didn't tell her this address," Elsie accused.

"I haven't written yet."

"Grace," said Elsie in a temper, "Mother has her life. I have mine. And she never writes."

She went to the bar, saying in the middle of her temper, "This is new. I know its no good asking you," and she poured herself a glass of gin and vermouth and then resumed her temper, raising her small plump doll's chin so that Grace should know why her chin and throat and shoulders could, when her lips pouted and her eyes moistened, draw men's eyes to the hidden grave eyes of her breasts. Men would lower their heads as if they were going to charge and she kept her small feet nimble and ready to dodge. It was a dogma in the minds of both sisters that they were (in different but absolute ways) who they were, what they were, on their own and immovable in unwisdom.

This was their gift, the reward for a childhood that had punished them.

"Listen," said Elsie in her temper, "you haven't seen me. 'How is Elsie?' 'I don't know. I don't know where she is.' I've got my life. You've got yours. If Dad had been alive things would be different."

"I never say anything," said Grace grimly. "I mind my own business. I wouldn't want to say anything."

Suddenly Elsie became secretive.

"Mary," she nodded to the room where the maid and the boy were, "always has her eye on the clothes. I don't trust anybody. You know these girls. You have to watch them. 'Where's my red dress?' 'At the cleaner's, ma'am.' I wasn't born yesterday. But you can *use* them, Grace, I *know*. Let's go and look."

Gay and confiding she took Grace back to the bedroom and looked at the dresses spread out on the bed. She held up a blue one.

"It's funny, I used to be jealous of your clothes. When we went to church," Elsie said. "Do you remember your blue dress, the dark blue one with the collar? I could have killed you for it and the bank manager saying, 'Here comes the blue bird of happiness.' Aren't kids funny? When you grew out of it and it came down to to me, I hated it. I wouldn't put it on. It was too long. You were taller than me then, we're the same now. Do you remember?"

"And here is a black," she said holding up another. "Well, every picture tells a story. Mr. Williams threw it out of the window when we were in Nice. He has a temper. I was a bit naughty. This one's Italian. It would suit you. You never wear anything with flowers though, do you?"

She was pulling the dresses off the bed and throwing them back again.

"Reg was generous. He knew how to spend. But when his father died and he came into all that money, he got mean—that's where men are funny. He was married—well, I knew that. Family counted for Reg. Grace, how long have you been married?"

"Ten years," said Grace.

Elsie picked up a golden dress that had a paler metallic sheen to it, low in the neck and with sleeves that came an inch or two below the elbow. She held it up.

"This would suit you, Grace. You could wear this colour with your hair. It's just the thing for cocktails. With your eyes it would be lovely. Mr. Williams won't let me wear it, he hates it, it looks hard, sort of brassy on me—but you, look!"

She held it against her sister.

"Look in the mirror. Hold it against yourself."

Against her will Grace held it to her shoulders over her navy woollen dress. She saw her body transformed into a sunburst of light.

"Grace," said Elsie in a low voice. "Look what it does to you. It isn't too big."

She stepped behind and held the dress in at the waist. Grace stood behind the dress and her jaw set and her bones stiffened in contempt at first and then softened.

"There's nothing to be done to it. It's wonderful," said Elsie.

"I never go to cocktail parties," said Grace.

"Look. Slip it on. You'll see."

"No," said Grace and let go of a shoulder. Elsie pulled it back into place.

"With the right shoes," Elsie said, "that will lift it. Slip it on. Come on. I've never seen anything like it. You remember how things always looked better on you. Look."

She pulled the dress from Grace and held it against herself.

"You see what I look like."

"No," she went on, handing it back. She went to the bedroom door and shut it and whispered, "I paid two hundred and forty pounds for it in Paris—if you're not going to wear it yourself you can't have it. I'll give it to Mary. She's had her eye on it."

Grace looked shrewdly at Elsie. She was shocked by her sister's life. From her girlhood Elsie had wheedled. She had got money out of their aunt; she drew the boys after her but was soon the talk of the town for going after the older men, especially the married. She suddenly called herself Augusta. It baffled Grace that men did not see through her. She was not beautiful. The blue eyes were as hard as enamel and she talked of nothing but prices and clothes and jewellery. From this time her life was a procession through objects to places which were no more than objects, from cars to yachts, from suites to villas. The Mediterranean was something worn in the evening, a town was the setting for a ring, a café was a looking glass, a night-club was a price. To be in the sun on a beach was to have found a new man who had bought her more of the sun.

Once she giggled to Grace:

"When they're doing it—you know what I mean—that's when I do my planning. It gives you time to yourself."

Now, as Grace held the golden dress and Elsie said in her cold baby voice: "If you don't keep it to wear I'll give it to Mary," Grace felt their kinship. They had been brought up poor. They feared to lose. She felt the curious pleasure of being a girl again, walking with Elsie in the street and of being in the firm humouring position of the elder sister of a child who, at that time, simply amused them all by her calculations. Except for their father, they were a calculating family. Calculation was their form of romance. If I put it on, Grace thought, that doesn't mean I'll keep it for myself. I'll sell it with the rest.

"All right. I'll just try it," she said.

"I'll unzip you," said Elsie, but let Grace pull her dress over her head, for the navy wool disgusted her. And Grace in her black slip pouted shyly, thinking "Thank heavens I ironed it yesterday." To be untidy underneath in an expensive flat like this—she would have been ashamed.

She stepped into the golden dress and pulled it up and turned to the long mirror as she did this, and at once to her amazement, she felt the gold flowing up her legs and her waist, as if it were a fire, a fire which she could not escape and which, as Elsie fastened it, locked her in. The mirror she looked in seemed to blaze.

"It's too long."

"We're the same height. Stand on your toes. Do you see?"

Grace felt the silk with her fingers.

"Take off your scarf."

Grace pulled it off.

Her dead hair became darker and yet it, too, took on the yellow glint of the flame.

"It's too full," said Grace for her breasts were smaller than Elsie's.

"It was too tight on me. Look!" Elsie said. She touched the material here and there and said, "I told you. It's perfect."

Grace half smiled. Her face lost its empty look and she knew that she was more beautiful than her sister. She gazed, she fussed, she pretended, she complained, she turned this way and that. She stretched out an arm to look at the length of the sleeve. She glowed inside it. She saw herself in Elsie's villa. She saw herself at one of those parties she had never been to. She saw her whole life changed. The bus routes of London were abolished. Her own house vanished and inside herself she cried angrily, to her husband looking at the closed door of the bedroom, so that her breasts pushed forward and her eyes fired up with temper:

"Harry, where are you? Come here! Look at this."

At that very moment, the bedroom door was opened. The boy walked in and a yard behind him, keeping not quite out of sight, was a man.

"Mum," the child called with his hands in his pockets, "there's a man."

The boy looked with the terror of the abandoned at the new woman he saw and said:

"Where's Mum?" looking at her in unbelief.

She came laughing to him and kissed him. He scowled mistrustfully and stepped back.

"Don't you like it?"

As she bent up from the kiss she had a furtive look at the man in the room: was it Mr. Williams? He was gazing with admiration at her.

But Elsie was quick. She left Grace and went into the sitting-room and Grace saw her sister stop suddenly and heard her say, in a voice she had never heard before—a grand stagey voice spoken slowly and arrogantly as if she had a plum in her mouth, her society voice:

"Oh you! I didn't invite you to call this afternoon." The man was dark and young and tall, dandified and sunburned. He was wearing a white polo neck jersey and he was smiling over Elsie's golden head at Grace who turned away at once. Elsie shut the bedroom door. As she did so, Grace heard her sister say:

"I have got my dressmaker here. It's very inconvenient."

To hear herself being called "my dressmakers" and not "my sister," and in that artificial voice, just at the moment of her stupefying glory, to have the door shut in her face! She stared at the door that separated them, and then in anger went over to the door and listened. The boy spoke.

"Ssh," said Grace.

"I am annoyed with you. I told you to telephone," Elsie was saying. "Who let you in?"

Grace heard him say: "Get rid of her. Send her away."

But Elsie was saying nervously, "How *did* you get in?" And quite clearly the man said:

"The way I went out last night, through the kitchen." Grace heard a chair being pushed and Elsie say:

"Don't, I tell you. Mr. Williams will be here. Stop."

"Here, help me," said Grace to the boy. "Pick them up." She had the suitcase on the bed and quickly started to push the dresses into her case. "Come on."

She tried to unzip the yellow dress but she could not reach.

"Damn this thing," she said.

"Mum, you said a word," said the boy.

"Shut up," she said. And, giving up, she pushed the navy dress she had taken off into the case, just as Elsie came back into the room and said to the boy: "Go and talk to the gentleman." The boy walked backwards out of the room, gaping at his mother and his aunt until Elsie shut the door on him.

"Grace," she said in an excited, low voice, wheedling. "Don't pack up. What are you doing? You're not going? You mustn't go."

"I've got to get my husband his supper," said Grace sharply. Elsie opened her handbag and pulled out a five-pound note and pushed it into Grace's hand. "There's time. That's for a taxi. Something awkward's happened. Mr. Williams will be here in a minute and I can't get rid of this man. I don't know what to do. It is a business thing about the villa and he's pestering me and Mr. Williams loathes him. I met him on the 'plane. I was very very silly. If Mr. Williams comes, I'll say he's come with you from the dress shop. And you can leave with him."

"You *said* Mr. Williams knew him," said Grace with contempt.

"Did I? I was a bit silly," Elsie wheedled. "You know what a fool I am—I let this gentleman drive me from the airport—well, that's harmless, I mean . . . Grace, you look wonderful in that dress. I only mean go out of the flat *with* him." She looked slyly and firmly at Grace.

Into Grace's mind came that scene from their girlhood outside their school when Elsie made her stand with a young man and hold his arm to prevent him getting away while she fetched a new red coat. The young man had a marvellous new motor-bike. It was the first time Grace had held a young man's arm. She would never forget the sensation and the youth saying:

"She's a little bitch. Let's go."

And how, just as she was going to say wildly, "Oh yes" and

he squeezed her arm, Elsie came running back and pulled him to the motor-bike and shouted to Grace: "So long."

Grace hesitated now, but then she remembered Elsie's society voice: "My dressmaker." And with that she had a feeling that was half disgust and half fear of being mixed up in Elsie's affairs. For Grace the place was too grand. The lies themselves were too grand. And there was this revelation that for years in every annual visit, Elsie had concealed and denied that they were sisters, just as she denied the rest of the family.

"No, Elsie," Grace said. "I've got to get back to Harry."

She was tempted to leave the suitcase, but she thought, "She'd only think I'm a fool if I leave it."

"I'll take the case and I'd best go. Thanks, though, for the taxi."

"Good-bye ma'am," she said to Elsie in a loud, proud voice as they went into the sitting-room.

"Come on," she called to the child. "Where are you?"

He was sitting on a chair staring at the man, and particularly at his jacket, as if his eyes were microscopes. The man had walked over to the window.

Grace took the boy by the hand.

"Say Good-bye to the lady," Grace said, pulling the boy who, scared still by the strangeness of his mother in her glory, said:

"Good-bye, Auntie."

They sat in the taxi.

"Sit down," said Grace to the boy. He had never been in a taxi before. He took a timid look at her. She was overpowering.

"I haven't been in a taxi since your dad and I came back from our honeymoon," she said. London had changed. There were only doors to look at, doors at first of the rich houses in the park and herself arriving at them, begin taken into drawing-rooms. She wished her suitcase was not so shabby. She would go into the doorways of hotels; palaces seemed familiar; streets wider; she looked at the windows of shoe shops. She looked at the handbags women were carrying. The taxi came to the river and there she gleamed, as she passed over the sad, dirty, dividing water, but through the poorer streets, past the factories, the railway arches, the taxi went fast, passing the crowded buses. She was indignant with traffic lights that stopped them.

"Mum," said the boy.

She was day-dreaming about the effect she would have on her husband when she opened the gate of her house.

"Do you like it?" she said.

"Yes. But Mum . . ."

"Look," she said, excited. "We're nearly there. There's Woolworth's. There's Marks's. Look, there's Mrs. Sanders. Wave to Mrs. Sanders. I wonder if she saw us."

Then the taxi stopped at the house. How mean it looked!

"Your dad is home," she said as she paid the driver and then opened the gate and looked at the patch of flower-bed. "He's been watering the garden." But when she was paying the taxi driver the door of the house opened and her husband stood there with his eternal clothes-brush held in horror in the air. He gaped at her. His eyes became small.

"You took a cab!" he said, and looked as if he were going to run after it as it grunted off. "How much did you give him?"

"She paid," she said.

"Come in," he said. "Come in." And he went into the dark hall, put the brush down and rubbed his hands as she lifted the suitcase into the house. The boy crept past them.

"What did he charge?" her husband said.

Not until then did he see the dress.

"Couldn't you get it into the case?" he said when they were in the small room that was darkened by the drooping bodies of the leaves of the fig tree. "That colour marks easily."

"That's why I took the cab."

She watched her husband's eyes as she posed, her own eyes getting larger and larger, searching him for praise.

"It wants the right shoes," she said. "I saw some as we came back just now, in Walton's."

She looked at him and the ghost of her sister's wheedling attitude came into her head as she let it droop just a little to one side.

"And my hair done properly. It blew about in the taxi. Jim was at the window all the time."

Her husband's eyeballs glistered with what looked like tears.

"You're not thinking of keeping it for yourself?" he said, his face buckling into smiles that she knew were not smiles at all.

"Why not?" she said, understanding him. "There's eighty pounds worth in the case there."

"You're rich," he said.

She opened the case.

"Look," she said.

"You'd better get it off, you'll mark it cooking," he said, and went out of the room.

From her bedroom she saw him in the back garden spraying his roses and brushing the green fly off with his finger. He was shaking the syringe to see if there was a drop more in it and she heard him ask the boy if he had been playing with the thing and wasting the liquid.

She gave a last look at herself in the mirror. She despised her husband. She remembered the look of admiration on the face of the man in her sister's flat. She took off the dress and pulled her woollen one out of the case and put it on. The golden woman had gone.

That evening as they sat at their meal, her husband was silent. He grunted at her account of the visit. She did not tell him she had been called "the dressmaker". Her husband was sulking. He was sulking about the dress. She tried to placate him by criticising her sister.

"There was a man there, someone she picked up on the 'plane. She was trying to get rid of him because this man with all the property, Mr. Williams, was expected. I don't envy her. She lives in a cage. Two burglaries they've had."

"They're insured." His first words.

She could still feel some of the gold of the dress on her skin, but as she went on about her sister, the grey meanness which in some way was part of her life with her husband, which emanated from him and which, owing to the poverty of her life as a girl, seemed to her like a resource—this meanness crept over her and coated her once more.

"And you talk of wearing the dress of a woman like that," he said. And then the boy said, with his mouth full of potato:

"The man took Auntie's brooch off the table. I saw him. The pin was sticking out of his pocket. I saw it. It tore my best jersey."

"Tore your jersey!" said her husband.

"What's this?" they both said together, united. And they questioned the child again and again.

Husband and wife studied each other.

"That wasn't a pin," the father said to the boy.

"No," said his wife, in her false voice. "She'd got the brooch on." And she signalled to her husband, but her husband said to the boy:

"Did he come in the taxi with you?"

"No," said the boy and his mother together.

"I asked the boy."

"No," said the boy.

"Just as well," he said to his wife. "You see what they might say when they find out. I told you I don't like you going to that place. You lose your head."

The next day she packed the gold dress with the rest and sold the lot, as usual, to the dealers.

TWELVE

The Camberwell Beauty

August's? On the Bath Road? Twice-Five August—of course I knew August: ivory man. And the woman who lived with him—her name was Price. She's dead. He went out of business years ago. He's probably dead too. I was in the trade only three or four years but I soon knew every antique dealer in the South of England. I used to go to all the sales. Name another. Naseley of Close Place? Jades, Asiatics, never touched India; Alsop of Ramsey? Ephemera. Marbright, High Street, Boxley? Georgian silver. Fox? Are you referring to Fox of Denton or Fox of Camden—William Morris, art nouveau—or the Fox Brothers in the Portobello Road, the eldest stuttered? They had an uncle in Brighton who went mad looking for old Waterford. Hindmith? No, he was just a copier. Ah now, Pliny! He was a very different cup of tea: Caughley ware. (Coalport took it over in 1821.) I am speaking of specialities; furniture is the bread and butter of the trade. It keeps a man going while his mind is on his speciality and within that speciality there is one object he broods on from one year to the next, most of his life; the thing a man would commit murder to get his hands on if he had the nerve, but I have never heard of a dealer who had; theft perhaps. A stagnant lot. But if he does get hold of that thing he will never let it go or certainly not to a customer—dealers only really like dealing among themselves—but every other dealer in the trade knows he's got it. So they sit in their shops reading the catalogues and watching one another. Fox broods on something Alsop has. Alsop has his eye on Pliny and Pliny puts a hand to one of his big red ears when he hears the name of August. At the heart of the trade is lust but a lust that is a dream paralysed by itself. So paralysed that the only release, the only hope, as everyone knows, is disaster; a bankruptcy, a divorce, a court case, a burglary, trouble with the police, a death. Perhaps then the grip on some piece of treasure will weaken and fall into the watcher's hands and even if it goes elsewhere he will go on dreaming about it.

What was it that Pliny, Gentleman Pliny, wanted of a man like August who was not much better than a country junk dealer? When I opened up in London I thought it was a particular Staffordshire figure, but Pliny was far above that. These figures fetch very little though one or two are hard to find: The Burning of Cranmer, for example. Very few were made; it never sold and the firm dropped it. I was young and eager and one day when a collector, a scholarly man, as dry as a stick, came to my shop and told me he had a complete collection except for this piece, I said in my innocent way: "You've come to the right man. I'm fairly certain I can get it for you—at a price." This was a lie; but I was astonished to see the old man look at me with contempt, then light up like a fire and when he left, look back furtively at me; he had betrayed his lust.

You rarely see an antique shop standing on its own. There are usually three or four together watching one another: I asked the advice of the man next door who ran a small boatyard on the canal in his spare time and he said, "Try Pliny down the Green: he knows everyone." I went "over the water", to Pliny; he was closed but I did find him at last in a sale-room. Pliny was marking his catalogue and waiting for the next lot to come up and he said to me in a scornful way, slapping a young man down, "August's got it." I saw him wink at the man next to him as I left.

I had bought myself a fast red car that annoyed the older dealers and I drove down the other side of Newbury on the Bath Road. August's was one of four little shops opposite the Lion Hotel on the main road at the end of the town where the country begins and there I got my first lesson. The place was closed. I went across to the bar of the hotel and August was there, a fat man of sixty in wide trousers and a drip to his nose who was paying for drinks from a bunch of dirty notes in his jacket pocket and dropping them on the floor. He was drunk and very offended when I picked a couple up and gave them to him. He'd just come back from Newbury races. I humoured him but he kept rolling about and turning his back to me half the time and so I blurted out:

"I've just been over at the shop. You've got some Staffordshire I hear."

He stood still and looked me up and down and the beer swelled in him.

"Who may you be?" he said with all the pomposity of drink.

I told him. I said right out, "Staffordshire. Cranmer's Burning."
His face went dead and the colour of liver.

"So is London," he said and turned away to the bar.

"I'm told you might have it. I've got a collector," I said.

"Give this lad a glass of water," said August to the barmaid.
"He's on fire."

There is nothing more to say about the evening or the many
other visits I made to August except that it has a moral to it and
that I had to help August over to his shop where an enormous
woman much taller than he in a black dress and a little girl of
fourteen or so were at the door waiting for him. The girl looked
frightened and ran a few yards from the door as August and his
woman collided belly to belly.

"Come back," called the woman.

The child crept back. And to me the woman said, "We're
closed," and having got the two inside, shut the door in my face.

The moral is this: if The Burning of Cranmer was August's
treasure, it was hopeless to try and get it before he had time to
guess what mine was. It was clear to him I was too new to the
trade to have one. And, in fact, I don't think he had the piece.
Years later, I found my collector had left his collection complete
to a private museum in Leicester when he died. He had obtained
what he craved, a small immortality in being memorable for his
relation to a minor work of art.

I know what happened at August's that night. In time his
woman, Mrs. Price, bellowed it to me, for her confidences could
be heard down the street. August flopped on his bed and while
he was sleeping off the drink she got the bundles of notes out of
his pockets and counted them. She always did this after his racing
days. If he had lost she woke him up and shouted at him; if he had
made a profit she kept quiet and hid it under her clothes in a chest
of drawers. I went down from London again and again but August
was not there.

Most of the time these shops are closed. You rattle the door
handle; no reply. Look through the window and each object
inside stands gleaming with something like a smile of malice,
especially on plates and glass; the furniture states placidly that it
has been in better houses than you will ever have the silver speaks
of vanished servants. It speaks of the dead hands that have touched
it; even the dust is the dust of families that have gone. In the

shabby places—and August's was shabby—the dealer is like a
toadstool that has grown out of the debris. There was only one
attractive object in August's shop—as I say—he went in for ivories
and on a table at the back was a set of white and red chessmen
set out on a board partly concealed by a screen. I was tapping my
feet impatiently looking through the window when I was astonished
to see two of the chessmen had moved; then I saw a hand, a long
thin work-reddened hand appear from behind the screen and
move one of the pieces back. Life in the place! I rattled the door
handle again and the child came from behind the screen. She
had a head loaded with heavy black hair to her shoulders and a
white heart-shaped face and wore a skimpy dress with small
pink flowers on it. She was so thin that she looked as if she would
blow away in fright out of the place, but instead, pausing on tiptoe,
she swallowed with appetite; her sharp eyes had seen my red car
outside the place. She looked back cautiously at the inner door
of the shop and then ran to unlock the shop door. I went in.

"What are you up to?" I said. "Playing chess?"

"I'm teaching my children," she said, putting up her chin like a
child of five. "Do you want to buy something?"

At once Mrs. Price was there shouting:

"Isabel. I told you not to open the door. Go back into the
room."

Mrs. Price went to the chessboard and put the pieces back in
their places.

"She's a child," said Mrs. Price, accusing me.

And when she said this Mrs. Price blew herself out to a larger
size and then her sullen face went blank and babyish as if she had
travelled out of herself for a beautiful moment. Then her brows
levelled and she became sullen again.

"Mr. August's out," she said.

"It is about a piece of Staffordshire," I said. "He mentioned it
to me. When will he be in?"

"He's in and out. No good asking. He doesn't know himself."

"I'll try again."

"If you like."

There was nothing to be got out of Mrs. Price.

In my opinion, the antique trade is not one for a woman, unless
she is on her own. Give a woman a shop and she wants to sell
something; even that little girl at August's wanted to sell. It's

instinct. It's an excitement. Mrs. Price—August's woman—was living with a man exactly like the others in the trade: he hated customers and hated parting with anything. By middle age these women have dead blank faces, they look with resentment and indifference at what is choking their shops; their eyes go smaller and smaller as the chances of getting rid of it became rarer and rarer and they are defeated. Kept out of the deals their husbands have among themselves, they see even their natural love of intrigue frustrated. This was the case of Mrs. Price who must have been handsome in a big-boned way when she was young, but who had swollen into a drudge. What allured the men did not allure her at all. It is a trade that feeds illusions. If you go after Georgian silver you catch the illusion, while you are bidding, that you are related to the rich families who owned it. You acquire imaginary ancestors. Or, like Pliny with a piece of Meissen he was said to keep hidden somewhere—you drift into German history and become a secret curator of the Victoria and Albert museum—a place he often visited. August's lust for "the ivories" gave to his horse-racing mind a private oriental side; he dreamed of rajahs, sultans, harems and lavish gamblers which, in a man as vulgar as he was, came out, in sad reality, as a taste for country girls and the company of bookies. Illusions lead to furtiveness in every-day life and to sudden temptations; the trade is close to larceny, to situations where you don't ask where something has come from, especially for a man like August whose dreams had landed him in low company. He had started at the bottom and very early he "received" and got twelve months for it. This frightened him. He took up with Mrs. Price and though he resented it she had made a fairly honest man of him. August was to be *her* work of art.

But he did not make an honest woman of her. No one dis-approved of this except herself. Her very size, growing year by year, was an assertion of virtue. Everyone took her side in her public quarrels with him. And as if to make herself more respectable, she had taken in her sister's little girl when the sister died; the mother had been in Music Hall. Mrs. Price petted and prinked the little thing. When August became a failure as a work of art, Mrs. Price turned to the child. Even August was charmed by her when she jumped on his knee and danced about showing him her new clothes. A little actress, as everyone said, exquisite.

It took me a long time to give up the belief that August had the Cranmer piece—and as I know now, he hadn't got it; but at last I did see I was wasting my time and settled into the routine of the business. I sometimes saw August at country sales and at one outside Marlborough something ridiculous happened. It was a big sale and went on till late in the afternoon and he had been drinking. After lunch the auctioneer had put up a china cabinet and the bidding was strong. Some outsider was bidding against the dealers, a thing that made them close their faces with moral indignation; the instinctive hatred of customers united them. Drink always stirred August morally; he was a rather despised figure and he was, I suppose, determined to speak for all. He entered the bidding. Up went the price: 50,5,60,5,70,5,80,5,90. The outsiders were a young couple with a dog.

"Ninety, ninety," called the auctioneer.

August could not stand it. "Twice-Five," he shouted.

There is not much full-throated laughter at sales; it is usually shoppish and dusty. But the crowd in this room looked round at August and shouted with a laughter that burst the gloom of trade. He was put out for a second and then saw his excitement had made him famous. The laughter went on; the wonder had for a whole minute stopped the sale. "Twice-five!" He was slapped on the back. At sixty-four the man who had never had a nickname had been christened. He looked around him. I saw a smile cross his face and double the pomposity that beer had put into him and he redoubled it that evening at the nearest pub. I went off to my car and Alsop of Ramsey, the ephemera man who had picked up some Victorian programmes, followed me and said out of the side of his mouth:

"More trouble tonight at August's."

And then to change the subject and speaking for every dealer south of the Trent, he offered serious news.

"Pliny's mother's dead—Pliny of the Green."

The voice had all the shifty meaning of the trade. I was too simple to grasp the force of this confidence. It surprised me in the following weeks to hear people repeat the news: "Pliny's mother's dead" in so many voices, from the loving memory and deepest sympathy manner as much suited to old clothes, old furniture and human beings indiscriminately, to the flat statement that an event of business importance had occurred in my eventless

trade. I was in it for the money and so, I suppose, were all the rest—
how else could they live?—but I seemed to be surrounded by a
dreamy freemasonry, who thought of it in a different secretive
way.

On a wet morning the following spring I was passing through
Salisbury on market day and stopped in the square to see if there
was anything worth picking up at the stalls there. It was mostly
junk but I did find a pretty Victorian teapot—no mark, I agree—
with a chip in the spout for a few shillings because the fever of
the trade never quite leaves one even on dull days. (I sold the
pot five years later for £8 when the prices started to go mad.)
I went into one of the pubs in the square, I forget its name, and I
was surprised to see Marbright and Alsop there and, sitting near
the window, Mrs. Price. August was getting drinks at the bar.

Alsop said to me:

"Pliny's here. I passed him a minute ago."

Marbright said: "He was standing in Woolworth's doorway.
I asked him to come and have one, but he wouldn't."

"It's hit him hard his mother going," Marbright said. "What's
he doing here? Queen Mary's dead."

It was an old joke that Gentleman Pliny had never been the same
since the old Queen had come to his shop some time back—
everyone knew what she was for picking up things. He only
opened on Sundays now and a wealthy crowd came there in their
big cars—a new trend as Alsop said. August brought the drinks
and stood near, for Mrs. Price spread herself on the bench and never
left much room for anyone else to sit down. He looked restless and
glum.

"Where will Pliny be without his mother," Mrs. Price moaned
into her glass and, putting it down, glowered at August. She had
been drinking a good deal.

August ignored her and said, sneering:

"He kept her locked up."

There is always a lot of talking about "locking up" in the trade;
people's minds go to their keys.

"It was kindness," Mrs. Price said, "after the burglars got in at
Sampson's, three men in a van loading it up in broad daylight.
Any woman of her age would be frightened."

"It was nothing to do with the burglary," said August, always
sensitive when crime was mentioned. "She was getting soft in the

head. He caught her giving his stuff away when she was left on her own. She was past it."

Mrs. Price was a woman who didn't like to be contradicted.

"He's a gentleman," said Mrs. Price, accusing August. "He was good to his mother. He took her out every Sunday night of his life. She liked a glass of stout on Sundays."

This was true, though Mrs. Price had not been to London for years and had never seen this event; but all agreed. We live on myths.

"It was her kidneys," moaned Mrs. Price. One outsize woman was mourning another, seeing a fate.

"I suppose that's why he didn't get married, looking after her," said Marbright.

"Pliny! Get married! Don't make me laugh," said August with a defiant recklessness that seemed to surprise even himself. "The last Saturday in every month like a clock striking he was round the pubs in Brixton with old Lal Drake."

And now, as if frightened by what he said, he swanked his way out of the side door of the pub on his way to the Gents.

We lowered our eyes. There are myths, but there are facts. They all knew—even I had heard—that what August said was true, but it was not a thing a sensible man would say in front of Mrs. Price. And—mind you—Pliny standing a few doors down the street. But Mrs. Price stayed calm among the thoughts in her mind.

"That's a lie," she said peacefully as we thought, though she was eyeing the door waiting for August to come back.

"I knew his father," said Alsop.

We were soon laughing about the ancient Pliny, the Bermondsey boy who began with a barrow shouting "Old Iron" in the streets, a man who never drank, never had a bank account—didn't trust banks—who belted his son while his mother "educated him up"— she was a tall woman and the boy grew up like her, tall with a long arching nose and those big red ears that looked as though his parents had pulled him now this way now that in their fight over him. She had been a housekeeper in a big house and she had made a son who looked like an old family butler, Cockney to the bone, but almost a gentleman. Except, as Alsop said, his way of blowing his nose like a foghorn on the Thames, but sharp as his father. Marbright said you could see the father's life in the store at the back of the shop; it was piled high with what had made the father's money, every kind of old-fashioned stuff.

"Enough to furnish two or three hotels," Alsop said. Mrs. Price nodded.

"Wardrobes, tables . . ." she said.

"A museum," said Marbright. "Helmets, swords. Two four-posters the last time I was there."

"Ironwork. Brass," nodded Mrs. Price mournfully.

"Must date back to the Crimean War," said Marbright.

"And it was all left to Pliny."

There was a general sigh.

"And he doesn't touch it. Rubbish he calls it. He turned his back on it. Only goes in for the best. Hepplewhite, marquetries, his consoles. Regency."

There was a pause.

"And," I said, "his Meissen."

They looked at me as if I were a criminal. They glanced at one another as if asking whether they should call the police. I was either a thief or I had publicly stripped them of all their clothes. I had publicly announced Pliny's lust.

Although Mrs. Price had joined in the conversation, it was in the manner of someone talking in her sleep; for when this silence came, she woke up and said in a startled voice:

"Lal Drake."

And screwing up her fists she got up and, pausing to get ready for a rush, she heaved herself fast to the door by which August had left for the Gents, down the alley a quarter of an hour before.

"The other door, missis," someone shouted. But she was through it.

"Drink up," we said and went out by the front door. I was the last and had a look down the side alley and there I saw a sight. August with one hand doing up his fly buttons and the other arm protecting his face. Mrs. Price was hitting out at him and shouting. The language!

"You dirty sod. I knew it. The girl told me." She was shouting. She saw me, stopped hitting and rushed at me in tears and shouted back at him.

"The filthy old man."

August saw his chance and got out of the alley and made for the cars in the square. She let me go and shouted after him. We were all there and in Woolworth's doorway was Pliny. Rain was still falling and he looked wet and all the more alone for being wet. I walked off and, I suppose, seeing me go and herself alone and giddy in her rage she looked all round and turned her temper on me.

"The girl has got to go," she shouted.

Then she came to her senses.

"Where is August?"

August had got to his car and was driving out of the square. She could do nothing. Then she saw Pliny. She ran from me to Pliny, from Pliny to me.

"He's going after the girl," she screamed.

We calmed her down and it was I who drove her home. (This was when she told me, as the wipers went up and down on the windscreen, that she and August were not married.) We splashed through hissing water that was like her tears on the road. "I'm worried for the child. I told her, 'Keep your door locked.' I see it's locked every night. I'm afraid I'll forget and I won't hear him if I've had a couple. She's a kid. She doesn't know anything." I understood that the face I had always thought was empty was really filled with the one person she loved: Isabel.

August was not there when we got to their shop. Mrs. Price went in and big as she was, she did not knock anything over.

"Isabel?" she called.

The girl was in the scullery and came with a wet plate that dripped on the carpet. In two years she had changed. She was wearing an old dress and an apron, but also a pair of high-heeled silver evening shoes. She had become the slut of the house and her pale skin looked dirty.

"You're dripping that thing everywhere. What have you got those shoes on for? Where did you get them?"

"Uncle Harry, for Christmas," she said. She called August Uncle Harry. She tried to look jaunty as if she had put all her hope in life into those silly evening shoes.

"All right," said Mrs. Price weakly looking at me to keep quiet and say nothing.

Isabel took off her apron when she saw me. I don't know whether she remembered me. She was still pale, but had the shapeliness of a small young woman. Her eyes looked restlessly and uncertainly at both of us, her chin was firmer but it trembled.

She was smiling too and, because I was there and the girl might see an ally in me, Mrs. Price looked with half-kindness at Isabel; but when I got up to go the girl looked at me as if she would follow me out of the door. Mrs. Price got up fast to bar the way. She stood on the doorstep of the shop watching me get into the car, swollen with the inability to say "Thank you" or "Goodbye". If the child was a child, Mrs. Price was ten times a child and both of them standing on the doorstep were like children who don't want anyone to go away.

I drove off and for a few miles I thought about Mrs. Price and the girl, but once settled into the long drive to London, the thought of Pliny supplanted them. I had been caught up by the fever of the trade. Pliny's mother was dead. What was going to happen to Pliny and all that part of the business Pliny had inherited from his father, the stuff he despised and had not troubled himself with very much in his mother's time. I ought to go "over the water"—as we say in London—to have a look at it some time. In a few days I went there; I found the idea had occurred to many others. The shop was on one of the main bus routes in South London, a speckled early Victorian place with an ugly red brick store behind it. Pliny's father had had an eye for a cosy but useful bit of property. Its windows had square panes (1810) and to my surprise the place was open and I could see people inside. There was Pliny with his nose which looked servile rather than distinguished, wearing a long biscuit-coloured tweed jacket with leather pads at the elbows like a Cockney sportsman. There, too, were August with his wet eyes and drinker's shame, Mrs. Price swelling over him in her best clothes, and the girl. They had come up from the country and August had had his boots cleaned. The girl was in her best too and was standing apart touching things in the shop, on the point of merriment, looking with wonder at Pliny's ears. He often seemed to be talking at her when he was talking to Mrs. Price. I said:

"Hullo! Up from the country? What are you doing here?" Mrs. Price was so large that she had to turn her whole body and place her belly in front of everyone who spoke to her.

"Seeing to his teeth," she said nodding at August and, from years of habit, August turned too when his wife turned, in case it was just as well not to miss one of her pronouncements, whatever else he might dodge. One side of August's jaw was swollen.

Then Mrs. Price slowly turned her whole body to face Pliny again. They were talking about his mother's death. Mrs. Price was greedy, as one stout woman thinking of another, for a melancholy tour of the late mother's organs. The face of the girl looked prettily wise and holiday-fied because the heavy curls of her hair hung close to her face. She looked out of the window, restless and longing to get away while her elders went on talking, but she was too listless to do so. Then she would look again at Pliny's large ears with a childish pleasure in anything strange; they gave him a dog-like appearance and if the Augusts had not been there, I think she would have jumped at him mischievously to touch them, but remembered in time that she had lately grown into a young lady. When she saw him looking at her she turned her back and began writing in the dust on a little table which was standing next to a cabinet; it had a small jug on it. She was writing her name in the dust I S A B. . . . And then stopped. She turned round suddenly because she saw I had been watching.

"Is that old Meissen?" she called out, pointing to the jug.

They stopped talking. It was comic to see her pretending, for my benefit, that she knew all about porcelain.

"Cor! Old Meissen!" said August pulling his racing news-paper out of his jacket pocket with excitement, and Mrs. Price fondly swung her big handbag; all laughed loudly, a laugh of lust and knowledge. They knew, or thought they knew, that Pliny had a genuine Meissen piece somewhere, probably upstairs where he lived. The girl was pleased to have made them laugh at her; she had been noticed.

Pliny said decently: "No, dear. That's Caughley. Would you like to see it?"

He walked to the cabinet and took the jug down and put it on a table.

"Got the leopard?" said August, knowingly. Pliny showed the mark of the leopard on the base of the jug and put it down again. It was a pretty shapely jug with a spray of branches and in the branches a pair of pheasants were perching, done in transfer, The girl scared us all by picking it up in both hands, but it was charming to see her holding it up and studying it.

"Careful," said Mrs. Price.

"She's all right," said Pliny.

Then—it alarmed us—she wriggled with laughter.

"What a funny face," she said.

Under the lip of the jug was the small face of an old man with a long nose looking sly and wicked.

"They used to put a face under the lip," Pliny said.

"That's right," said August.

The girl held it out at arm's length and, looking from the jug to Pliny, she said: "It's like you, Mr. Pliny."

"Isabel!" said Mrs. Price. "That's rude."

"But it is," said Isabel. "Isn't it?" She was asking me. Pliny grinned. We were all relieved to see him take the jug from her and put it back in the cabinet.

"It belonged to my mother," he said. "I keep it there," Pliny said to me, despising me because I had said nothing and because I was a stranger.

"Go into the back and have a look round if you want to. The light's on."

I left the shop and went down the steps into the long white store-room where the white-washed walls were grey with dust. There was an alligator hanging by a nail near the steps, a couple of cavalry helmets and a dirty drum that must have been there since the Crimean War. I went down into streets of stacked up furniture. I felt I was walking into an inhuman crypt or worse still one of those charnel houses or ossuaries I had seen pictures of in one of my father's books when I was a boy. Large as the store was, it was lit by a single electric light bulb hanging from a girder in the roof and the yellow light was deathly. The notion of "picking up" anything at Pliny's depressed me, so that I was left with a horror of the trade I had joined. Yet feelings of this kind are never simple. After half an hour I left the shop. I understood before that day was over and I was back in the room over my own place that what had made me more wretched was the wound of a sharp joy. First, the sight of the girl leaving her name unfinished in the dust had made my heart jump, then when she held the vase in her hands I had felt the thrill of a revelation; until then I had never settled what I should go in for but now I saw it. Why not collect Caughley? That was it. Caughley; it was one of those inspirations that excite one so that every sight in the world changes; even houses, buses and streets and people are transfigured and become unreal as desire carries one away—and then, cruelly, it passes and one is left exhausted. The total impossibility of an impatient young man like myself collecting Caughley which hadn't been made since 1821 became brutally clear. Too late for Staffordshire, too late for Dresden, too late for Caughley and all the beautiful things. I was savage for lack of money. The following day I went to the Victoria and Albert and then I saw other far more beautiful things enshrined and inaccessible. I gazed with wonder. My longing for possession held me and then I was elevated to a state of worship as if they were idols, holy and never to be touched. Then I remembered the girl's hands and a violent day dream passed through my head; it lasted only a second or two but in that time I smashed the glass case, grabbed the treasure and bolted with it. It frightened me that such an idea could have occurred to me. I left the museum and I turned sourly against my occupation, against Marbright, Alsop and above all Pliny and August, and it broke my heart to think of that pretty girl living among such people and drifting into the shabbiness of the trade. I S A B—half a name, written by a living finger in dust.

One has these brief sensations when one is young. They pass and one does nothing about them. There is nothing remarkable about Caughley—except that you can't get it. I did not collect Caughley for a simple reason; I had to collect my wits. The plain truth is that I was incompetent. I had only to look at my bank account. I had bought too much. At the end of the year I looked like getting into the bankruptcy court unless I had a stroke of luck. Talk of trouble making the trade move; I was Trouble myself, dealers could smell it coming and came sniffing into my shop and at the end of the year I sold up for what I could get. It would have been better if I could have waited for a year or two when the boom began. For some reason I kept the teapot I had bought in Salisbury to remind me of wasted time. In its humble way it was pretty.

In the next six months I changed. I had to. I pocketed my pride and I got a dull job in an auctioneer's; at least it took me out of the office when I got out keys and showed people round. The firm dealt in house property and developments. The word "develop" took hold of me. The firm was a large one and sometimes "developed" far outside London. I was told to go and inspect some of the least important bits of property that were coming into the market. One day a row of shops in Steepleton came up for sale. I said I knew them. They were on the London

Road opposite the Lion Hotel at the end of the town. My boss was always impressed by topography and the names of hotels and sent me down there. The shops were in the row where August and one or two others had had their businesses, six of them.

What a change! The Lion had been re-painted; the little shops seemed to have got smaller. In my time the countryside had begun at the end of the row. Now builders' scaffolding was standing in the fields beyond. I looked for August's. A cheap café had taken over his place. He had gone. The mirror man who lived next door was still there but had gone into beads and fancy art jewellery. His window was full of hanging knick-knacks and mobiles.

"It's the tourist trade now," he said. He looked ill.

"What happened to August?"

He studied me for a moment and said, "Closed down", and I could get no more out of him. I crossed the street to The Lion. Little by little, a sentence at a time in a long slow suspicious evening I got news of August from the barmaid as she went back and forth serving customers, speaking in a low voice, her eye on the new proprietor in case the next sentence that came out of her might be bad for custom. The sentences were spoken like sentences from a judge summing up, bit by bit. August had got two years for receiving stolen goods; the woman—"She wasn't his wife"— had been knocked down by a car as she was coming out of the bar at night—"not that she drank, not really drank; her weight really"—and then came the final sentence that brought back to me the alerting heat and fever of its secrets: "There was always trouble over there. It started when the girl ran away."

"Isabel?" I said.

"I dunno—the girl."

I stood outside the hotel and looked to the east and then to the west. It was one of those quarters of an hour on a main road when, for some reason, there is no traffic coming either way. I looked at the now far-off fields where the February wind was scything over the grass, turning it into waves of silver as it passed over them. I thought of Isab . . . running with a case in her hand, three years ago. Which way? Where do girls run to? Sad.

I went back to London. There are girls in London too, you know. I grew a beard, reddish: it went with the red car which I had managed to keep. I could afford to take a girl down to the south coast now and then. Sometimes we came back by the Brixton road, sometimes through Camberwell and when we did this I often slowed down at Pliny's and told the girls, "That man's sitting on a gold mine." They never believed it or, at least, only one did. She said: "Does he sell rings? Let us have a look."

"They're closed," I said. "They're always closed."

"I want to look," she said, so we stopped and got out.

We looked into the dark window—it was Saturday night—and we could see nothing but as we stared we heard a loud noise coming, it seemed, from the place next door or from down the Drive-in at the side of Pliny's shop, a sound like someone beating boxes or bath tubs at first until I got what it was: drums. Someone blew a bugle, a terrible squeaky sound. There was heavy traffic on the street, but the bugle seemed to split it in half.

"Boys' Brigade, practising for Sunday," I said. We stood laughing with our hands to our ears as we stared into the dark. All I could make out was something white on a table at the back of the shop. Slowly I saw it was a set of chessmen. Chess, ivories, August—perhaps Pliny had got August's chessmen.

"What a din!" said the girl. I said no more to her for in my mind there was the long forgotten picture of Isabel's finger on the pieces, at Steepleton.

When I've got time, I thought, I will run over to Pliny's; perhaps he will know what happened to the girl.

And I did go there again, weeks later, on my own. Still closed. I rattled the door handle. There was no answer. I went to a baker's next door, then to a butcher's, then to a pub. The same story. "He only opens on Sundays," or, "He's at a sale." Then to a tobacconist's. I said it was funny to leave a shop empty like that, full of valuable stuff. The tobacconist became suspicious.

"There's someone there all right. His wife's there."

"No she's not," his wife said. "They've gone off to a sale. I saw them."

She took the hint.

"No one in charge to serve customers," she said.

I said I'd seen a chessboard that interested me and the tobacconist said: "It's dying out. I used to play."

"I didn't know he got married," I said.

"He's got beautiful things," said his wife. "Come on Sunday."

Pliny married! That made me grin. The only women in his

life I had ever heard of were his mother and the gossip about
Lal Drake. Perhaps he had made an honest woman of *her*. I went
back for one last look at the chessmen and, sure enough, as the
tobacconist's wife had hinted someone *had* been left in charge,
for I saw a figure pass through the inner door of the shop. The
watcher was watched. Almost at once I heard the tap and roll
of a kettle drum, I put my ear to the letter box and distinctly
heard a boy's voice shouting orders. Children! All the drumming I
had heard on Saturday had come from Pliny's—a whole family
drumming. Think of Pliny married to a widow with kids; he
had not had time to get his own. I took back what I had thought
of him and Lal Drake. I went off for an hour to inspect a house
that was being sold on Camberwell Green, and stopped once
more at Pliny's on the way back. On the chance of catching him.
I went to the window: standing in the middle of the shop was
Isabel.

Her shining black hair went to her shoulders. She was wearing
a red dress with a schoolgirlish white collar to it. If I had not
known her by her heart-shaped face and her full childish lips, I
would have known her by her tiptoe way of standing like an
actress just about to sing a song or give a dance when she comes
forward on the stage. She looked at me daringly. It was the way,
I remembered, she had looked at everyone. She did not know
me. I went to the door and tipped the handle. It did not open.
I saw her watching the handle move. I went on rattling. She
straightened and shook her head, pushing back her hair. She did
not go away. She was amused by my efforts. I went back to the
window of the shop and asked to come in. She could not hear,
of course. My mouth was opening and shutting foolishly. That
amused her even more. I pointed to something in the window,
signalling that I was interested in it. She shook her head again. I
tried pointing to other things; a cabinet, an embroidered fire-
screen, a jar three feet high. At each one she shook her head. It was
like a guessing game. I was smiling, even laughing, to persuade
her. I put my hands to my chest and pretended to beg like a dog.
She laughed at this and looked behind, as if calling to someone.
If Pliny wasn't there, his wife might be, or the children. I pointed
upwards and made a movement of my hands, imitating someone
turning a key in a lock. I was signalling. "Go and get the key
from Mrs. Pliny," and I stepped back and looked up at a window

above the shop. When I did this Isabel was frightened; she went
away shouting to someone. And that was the end of it; she did
not come back.

I went away thinking. Well, that is a strange thing!

What ideas people put into your head and you build fancies
yourself—that woman in the bar at Steepleton telling me Isabel
had run away and I imagining her running in those poor evening
shoes I'd once seen, in the rain down the Bath Road, when what
was more natural in a trade where they all live with their hands
in one another's pockets—Pliny had married, and they had taken
the girl on at the shop. It was a comfort to think of. I hadn't
realized how much I had worried about what would happen
to a naïve girl like Isabel when the break up came. Alone in the
world! How silly. I thought, one of these Sundays I'll go up there
and hear the whole story. And I did.

There was no one there except Pliny and his rich Sunday
customers. I even went into the store at the back, looked everywhere. No sign of Isabel. The only female was a woman in a
shabby black dress and not wearing a hat who was talking to a
man who was testing the door of a wardrobe, making its squeak,
while the woman looked on without interest, in the manner of
a dealer's wife; obviously the new Mrs. Pliny. She turned to make
way for another couple who were waiting to look at it. I nearly
knocked over a stack of cane chairs as I got past.

If there was no sign of Isabel, the sight of Pliny shocked me.
He had been a dead man, permanently dead as wood, even clumsy
in his big servile bones, though shrewd. Now he had come to
life in the strangest, excited way, much older to look at, thinner
and frantic as he looked about him this way and that. He seemed
to be possessed by a demon. He talked loudly to people in the
shop and was watchful when he was not talking. He was frightened,
abrupt, rude. Pliny married! Marriage had wrecked him or he
was making too much money; he looked like a man expecting
to be robbed. He recognized me at once. I had felt him watching
me from the steps going down to the store. As I came back to
the steps to speak to him he spoke to me first, distinctly in a loud
voice:

"I don't want any of August's men here, see?"

I went red in the face.

"What do you mean?" I said.

"You heard me," he said. "You know what he got."

Wells of Hungerford was standing near, pretending not to listen. Pliny was telling the trade that I was in with August—publicly accusing me of being a fence. I controlled my temper.

"August doesn't interest me," I said. "I'm in property. Marsh, Help and Hitchcock. I sold his place, the whole street."

And I walked past him looking at a few things as I left.

I was in a passion. The dirty swine—all right when his mother kept an eye on him, the poor old woman, but now—he'd gone mad. And that poor girl! I went to the tobacconist for the Sunday paper in a dream, put down my money and took it without a word and was almost out of the door when the wife called out:

"Did you find him? Did you get what you wanted?" A friendly London voice. I tapped the side of my head.

"You're telling me," the wife said.

"Well, he has to watch everything now. Marrying a young girl like that, it stands to reason," said the wife in a melancholy voice.

"Wears him out, at his age," suggested the tobacconist.

"Stop the dirty talk, Alfred," said the wife.

"You mean he married the *girl*?" I said. "Who's the big woman without a hat—in the store?"

"What big woman is that?" asked the tobacconist's wife. "He's married to the girl. Who else do you think—there's no one else."

The wife's face went as blank as a tombstone in the sly London way.

"She's done well for herself," said the tobacconist. "Keeps her locked up like his mother, wasn't I right?"

"He worships her," said the woman.

I went home to my flat. I was nauseated. The thought of Isabel in bed with that dressed up servant, with his wet eyes, his big raw ears and his breath smelling of onions! Innocent? No, as the woman said, "She has done well for herself." Happy with him too. I remembered her pretty face laughing in the shop. What else could you expect, after August and Mrs. Price.

The anger I felt with Pliny grew to a rage but by the time I was in my own flat Pliny vanished from the picture in my mind. I was filled with passion for the girl. The fever of the trade had come alive in me; Pliny had got something I wanted. I could think of nothing but her, just as I remember the look August gave Pliny when the girl asked if the jug was Meissen. I could see her holding the jug at arm's length, laughing at the old man's face under the lip. And I could see that Pliny was not mad; what was making him frantic was possessing the girl.

I kept away from Pliny's. I tried to drive the vision out of my mind, but I could not forget it. I became cunning. Whenever my job allowed it—and even when it didn't—I started passing the time of day with any dealer I had known, picked up news of the sales, studied catalogues, tried to find out which ones Pliny would go to. She might be with him. I actually went to Newbury but he was not there. Bath he couldn't miss and, sure enough, he was there and she wasn't. It was ten in the morning and the sale had just started. I ran off and got into my car. I drove as fast as I could the hundred miles back to London and cursed the lunch-time traffic. I got to Pliny's shop and rang the bell. Once, then several long rings. At once the drum started beating and went on as if troops were marching. People passing in the street paused to listen too. I stood back from the window and I saw a movement at a curtain upstairs. The drumming was still going on and when I bent to listen at the letter box I could hear the sound become deafening and often very near and then there was a blast from the bugle. It was a misty day south of the river and for some reason or other I was fingering the grey window and started writing her name, I S A B . . . hopelessly, but hoping that perhaps she might come near enough to see. The drumming stopped. I waited and waited and then I saw an extraordinary sight; Isabel herself in the dull red dress, but with a lancer's helmet on her head and a side drum on its straps hanging from her shoulders and the drum sticks in her hand. She was standing upright like a boy playing soldiers, her chin up and puzzling at the sight of the letters B A S I on the window. When she saw me she was confused. She immediately gave two or three taps to the drum and then bent almost double with laughter. Then she put on a straight face and played the game of pointing to one thing after another in the shop. Every time I shook my head, until at last I pointed to her. This pleased her. Then I shouted through the letter box: "I want to come in."

"Come in," she said. "It's open."

The door had been open all the time; I had not thought of trying it. I went inside.

"I thought you were locked in."

She did not answer but wagged her head from side to side.

"Sometimes I lock myself in," she said. "There are bad people about, August's men."

She said this with great importance, but her face became ugly as she said it. She took off the helmet and put down the drum.

"So I beat the drum when Mr. Pliny is away," she said. She called him Mr. Pliny.

"What good does that do?"

"It is so quiet when Mr. Pliny is away. I don't do it when he's here. It frightens August's men away."

"It's as good as telling them you are alone here," I said. "That's why I came. I heard the drum and the bugle."

"Did you?" she said eagerly. "Was it loud?"

"Very loud."

She gave a deep sigh of delight.

"You see!" she said, nodding her head complacently.

"Who taught you to blow the bugle?" I said.

"My mother did," she said. "She did it on the stage. Mr. Pliny —you know when Mr. Pliny fetched me in his motor-car—I forgot it. He had to go back and get it. I was too frightened."

"Isab . . ." I said.

She blushed. She remembered.

"I might be one of August's men," I said.

"No you're not. I know who you are," she said. "Mr. Pliny's away for the day but that doesn't matter. I am in charge. Is there something you were looking for?"

The child was gone when she put the drum aside. She became serious and practical: Mrs. Pliny! I was confused by my mistake in not knowing the door was open and she busied herself about the shop. She knew what she was doing and I felt very foolish.

"Is there something special?" she said. "Look around." She had become a confident woman. I no longer felt there was anything strange about her. I drifted to look at the chessmen and I could not pretend to myself that they interested me, but I did ask her the price. She said she would look it up and went to a desk where Pliny kept his papers and after going through some lists of figures which were all in code she named the sum. It was enormous —something like £275 and I said, "What!" in astonishment. She put the list back on the desk and said, firmly:

"My husband paid £260 for it last Sunday. It was carved by

Dubois. There are only two more like it. It was the last thing he did in 1785."

(I found out afterwards this was nonsense.)

She said this in Pliny's voice; it was exactly the sort of casual sentence he would have used. She looked expressionlessly and not at all surprised when I said, "Valuable," and moved away.

I meant, of course, that she was valuable and in fact her mystery having gone, she seemed conscious of being valuable and important herself, the queen and owner of everything in the shop, efficiently in charge of her husband's things. The cabinet in the corner, she said, in an offhand way, as I went to look at it, had been sold to an Australian. "We are waiting for the packers." We! Not to feel less knowing than she was, I looked around for some small thing to buy from her. There were several small things, like a cup and saucer, a little china tray, a christening mug. I picked things up and put them down listlessly and, from being indifferent, she became eager and watched me. The important, serious expression she had had vanished, she became childish suddenly and anxious: she was eager to sell something. I found a little china figure on a shelf.

"How much is this?" I said. It was Dresden; the real thing. She took it and looked at the label. I knew it was far beyond my purse and I asked her the price in the bored hopeless voice one puts on.

"I'll have to look it up," she said.

She went to the desk again and looked very calculating and thoughtful and then said, as if naming an enormous sum:

"Two pounds."

"It can't be," I said.

She looked sad as I put it back on the shelf and she went back to the desk. Then she said:

"I tell you what I'll do. It's got a defect. You can have it for thirty-five shillings."

I picked it up again. There was no defect in it. I could feel the huge wave of temptation that comes to one in the trade, the sense of the incredible chance, the lust that makes one shudder first and then breaks over one so that one is possessed, though even at that last moment, one plays at delay in a breathless pause, now one is certain of one's desire.

I said: "I'll give you thirty bob for it."

Young Mrs. Pliny raised her head and her brown eyes became brilliant with naïve joy.

"All right," she said.

The sight of her wrapping the figure, packing it in a box and taking the money so entranced me, that I didn't realize what she was doing or what I had done. I wasn't thinking of the figure at all. I was thinking of her. We shook hands. Hers were cold and she waved from the shop door when I left. And when I got to the end of the street and found myself holding the box I wondered why I had bought it. I didn't want it. I had felt the thrill of the thief and I was so ashamed that I once or twice thought of dropping it into a litter box. I even thought of going back and returning it to her and saying to her: "I didn't want it. It was a joke. I wanted you. Why did you marry an awful old man like Pliny?" And those stories of Pliny going off once a month in the old days, in his mother's time, to Lal Drake that old whore in Brixton, came back to me. I didn't even unpack the figure but put it on the mantelpiece in my room, then on the top shelf of a cupboard which I rarely used. I didn't want to see it. And when in the next months—or even years—I happened to see it, I remembered her talking about the bad people, August's men.

But, though I kept away from Pliny's on Sundays, I could not resist going back to the street and eventually to the shop— just for the sight of her.

And after several misses I did see her in the shop. It was locked. When I saw her she stared at me with fear and made no signals and quickly disappeared—I suppose into the room at the back. I crossed the main road and looked at the upper part of the house. She was upstairs, standing at a window. So I went back across the street and tried to signal, but of course she could only see my mouth moving. I was obsessed by the way I had cheated her. My visits were a siege for the door was never opened now. I did see her once through the window and this time I had taken the box and offered it to her in dumb show. That did have an effect. I saw she was looking very pale, her eyes ringed and tired and whether she saw I was remorseful or not I couldn't tell, but she made a rebuking yet defiant face. Another day I went and she looked terrified. She pointed and pointed to the door but as I eagerly stepped towards it she shook her head and raised a hand to forbid me. I did not understand until, soon, I saw Pliny walking about the shop. I moved off. People in the neighbourhood must often have seen me standing there and the tobacconist I went to gave me a look that suggested he knew what was going on.

Then, on one of my vigils, I saw a doctor go to the side door down the Goods Entrance and feared she was ill—but the butcher told me it was Pliny. His wife, they said, had been nursing him. "He ought to convalesce somewhere. A nice place by the sea. But he won't. It would do his wife good. The young girl has worn herself out looking after him. Shut up all day with him." And the tobacconist said what his wife had said a long time back. "Like his poor mother. He kept *her* locked in too. Sunday evening's the only time she's out. It's all wrong."

I got sick of myself. I didn't notice the time I was wasting for one day passed like a smear of grey into another and I wished I could drag myself away from the district, especially now Pliny was always there. At last one Saturday I fought hard against a habit so useless and I had the courage to drive past the place for once and did not park my car up the street. I drove on, taking side streets (which I knew, nevertheless, would lead me back), but I made a mistake with the one-ways and got on the main Brixton road and was heading north to freedom from myself.

It was astonishing to be free. It was seven o'clock in the evening and to celebrate I went into a big pub where they had singers on Saturday nights; it was already filling up with people. How normal, how cheerful they were, a crowd of them, drinking, shouting and talking; the human race! I got a drink and chose a quiet place in a corner and I was taking my first mouthful of the beer, saying to myself: "Here's to yourself, my boy," as though I had just met myself as I used to be. And then, with the glass still at my lips, I saw in a crowd at the other end of the bar Pliny, with his back half-turned. I recognized him by his jug-handle ears, his white hair and the stoop of a tall man. He was not in his dressy clothes but in a shabby suit that made him seem disguised. He was listening to a woman who had a large handbag and had bright blonde hair and a big red mouth who was telling him a joke and she banged him in the stomach with her bag and laughed. Someone near me said: "Lal's on the job early this evening." Lal Drake. All the old stories about Pliny and his woman came back to me and how old Castle of Westbury said that Pliny's mother had told him, when she was saying what a good son he was to her, that the one and only time he had been with a woman he had come home and told her and put his head in her lap and cried "like a child" and promised on the Bible he'd never do such a thing again. Castle swore this was true.

I put down my glass and got out of the pub fast without finishing it. Not because I was afraid of Pliny. Oh no! I drove straight back to Pliny's shop. I rang the bell. The drum started beating a few taps and then a window upstairs opened.

"What do you want?" said Isabel in a whisper.

"I want to see you. Open the door."

"It's locked."

"Get the key."

She considered me for a long time.

"I haven't got one," she said, still in a low voice, so hard to hear that she had to say it twice.

"Where have you been?" she said.

We stared at each other's white faces in the dark. She had missed me!

"You've got a key. You must have," I said. "Somewhere. What about the back door?"

She leaned on the window, her arms on the sill. She was studying my clothes.

"I have something for you," I said. This changed her. She leaned forward trying to see more of me in the dark. She was curious. Today I understand what I did not understand then; she was looking me over minutely, inch by inch—what she could see of me in the sodium light of the street lamp—not because I was strange or unusual—but because I was not. She had been shut up either alone or with Pliny without seeing another soul for so long. He was treating her like one of his collector's pieces, like the Meissen August had said he kept hidden upstairs. She closed the window. I stood there wretched and impatient. I went down the Goods Entrance ready to kick the side door down, break a window, climb in somehow. The side door had no letter box or glass panes, no handle even. I stood in front of it and suddenly it was opened. She was standing there.

"You're *not* locked in," I said.

She was holding a key.

"I found it," she said.

I saw she was telling a lie.

"Just now?"

"No. I know where he hides it," she said lowering her frank eyes.

It was a heavy key with an old piece of frayed used-up string on it.

"Mr. Pliny does not like me to show people things," she said. "He has gone to see his sister in Brixton. She is very ill. I can't show you anything."

She recited these words as if she had learned them by heart. It was wonderful to stand so near to her in the dark.

"Can I come in?" I said.

"What do you want?" she said cautiously.

"You," I said.

She raised her chin.

"Are you one of August's men?" she said.

"You know I'm not. I haven't seen August for years."

"Mr. Pliny says you are. He said I was never to speak to you again. August was horrible."

"The last I heard he was in prison."

"Yes," she said. "He steals."

This seemed to please her; she forgave him that easily. Then she put her head out of the doorway as if to see if August were waiting behind me.

"He does something else, too," she said.

I remembered the violent quarrel between August and poor Mrs. Price when she was drunk in Salisbury—the quarrel about Isabel.

"You ran away," I said.

She shook her head.

"I didn't run away. Mr. Pliny fetched me," she said and nodded primly, "in his car. I told you."

Then she said: "Where is the present you were bringing me?"

"It isn't a present," I said. "It's the little figure I bought from you. You didn't charge me enough. Let me in. I want to explain."

I couldn't bring myself to tell her that I had taken advantage of her ignorance, so I said:

"I found out afterwards that it was worth much more than I paid you. I want to give it back to you."

She gave a small jump towards me. "Oh please, please," she said and took me by the hand. "Where is it?"

"Let me come in," I said, "and I will tell you. I haven't got it with me. I'll bring it tomorrow, no not tomorrow, Monday."

"Oh. Please," she pleaded. "Mr. Pliny was so angry with me for selling it. He'd never been angry with me before. It was terrible. It was awful."

It had never occurred to me that Pliny would even know she had sold the piece; but now, I remembered the passions of the trade and the stored up lust that seems to pass between things and men like Pliny. He wouldn't forgive. He would be savage.

"Did he do something to you? He didn't hit you, did he?"

Isabel did not answer.

"What did he do?"

I remembered how frantic Pliny had been and how violent he had sounded, when he told me to get out of his shop.

"He cried," she said. "He cried and he cried. He went down on his knees and he would not stop crying. I was wicked to sell it. I am the most precious thing he has. Please bring it. It will make him better."

"Is he still angry?"

"It has made him ill," she said.

"Let me come in," I said.

"Will you promise?" ·

"I swear I'll bring it," I said.

"For a minute," she said, "but not in the shop."

I followed her down a dark passage into the store and was so close that I could smell her hair.

Pliny crying! At first I took this to be one of Isabel's fancies. Then I thought of tall, clumsy, servant-like Pliny, expert at sales with his long-nosed face pouring our water like a pump, repentant, remorseful, agonized like an animal, to a pretty girl. Why? Just because she had sold something? Isabel loved to sell things. He must have had some other reason. I remembered Castle of Westbury's story. What had he done to the girl? Only a cruel man could have gone in for such an orgy of self-love. He had the long face on which tears would be a blackmail. He would be like a horse crying because it had lost a race.

Yet those tears were memorable to Isabel and she so firmly called him "Mr. Pliny". In bed, did she still call him "Mr. Pliny"? I have often thought since that she did; it would have given her a power—perhaps cowed him.

At night the cold white-washed store-room was silent under the light of its single bulb and the place was mostly in shadow, only the tops of stacked furniture stood out in the yellow light, some of them like buildings. The foundations of the stacks were tables or chests, desks on which chairs or small cabinets were piled. We walked down alleys between the stacks. It was like walking through a dead, silent city, abandoned by everyone who once lived there. There was the sour smell of upholstery; in one part there was a sort of plaza where two large dining tables stood with their chairs set around and a pile of dessert plates on them. Isabel was walking confidently. She stopped by a dressing-table with a mirror on it next to a group of wardrobes and turning round to face it, she said proudly:

"Mr. Pliny gave it all to me. And the shop."

"All of this?"

"When he stopped crying," she said.

And then she turned about and we faced the wardrobes. There were six or seven, one in rosewood and an ugly yellow one and they were so arranged here that they made a sort of alcove or room. The wardrobe at the corner of the alley was very heavy and leaned so that its doors were open in a manner of such empty hopelessness, showing its empty shelves, that it made me uneasy. Someone might have just taken his clothes from it in a hurry, perhaps that very minute, and gone off. He might be watching us. It was the wardrobe with the squeaking door which I had seen the customer open while the woman whom I had thought to be Mrs. Pliny stood by. Each piece of furniture seemed to watch—even the small things, like an umbrella stand or a tray left on a table. Isabel walked into the alcove and there was a greeny-grey sofa with a screwed up paper bag of toffees on it and on the floor beside it I saw, of all things, the lancer's helmet and the side drum and the bugle. The yellow light scarcely lit this corner.

"There's your drum," I said.

"This is my house," she said, gaily now. "Do you like it? When Mr. Pliny is away I come here in case August's men come . . ."

She looked at me doubtfully when she mentioned that name again.

"And you beat the drum to drive them away?" I said.

"Yes," she said stoutly.

I could not make out whether she was playing the artless child or not, yet she was a woman of twenty-five at least. I was bewildered.

"You are frightened here on your own, aren't you?"

"No I am not. It's nice."

Then she said very firmly:

"You will come here on Monday and give me the box back?"

I said: "I will if you'll let me kiss you. I love you, Isabel."

"Mr. Pliny loves me too," she said.

"Isab . . ." I said. That did move her.

I put my arm round her waist and she let me draw her to me. It was strange to hold her because I could feel her ribs, but her body was so limp and feeble that, loving her as I did, I was shocked and pulled her tightly against me. She turned her head weakly so that I could only kiss her cheek and see only one of her eyes and I could not make out whether she was enticing me, simply curious about my embrace or drooping in it without heart.

"You *are* one of August's men," she said getting away from me. "He used to try and get into my bed. After that I locked my door."

"Isabel," I said. "I am in love with you. I think you love me. Why did you marry a horrible old man like Pliny?"

"Mr. Pliny is not horrible," she said. "I love him. He never comes to my room."

"Then he doesn't love you," I said. "Leaving you locked up here. And you don't love him."

She listened in the manner of someone wanting to please, waiting for me to stop.

"He is not a real husband, a real lover," I said.

"Yes, he is," she said proudly. "He takes my clothes off before I go to bed. He likes to look at me. I am the most precious thing he has."

"That isn't love, Isabel," I said.

"It is," she said with warmth. "You don't love me. You cheated me. Mr. Pliny said so. And you don't want to look at me. You don't think I'm precious."

I went to take her in my arms again and held her.

"I love you. I want you. You are beautiful. I didn't cheat you. Pliny is cheating you, not me," I said. "He is not with his sister. He's in bed with a woman in Brixton. I saw them in a pub. Everyone knows it."

"No he is not. I *know* he is not. He doesn't like it. He promised his mother," she said.

The voice in which she said this was not her playful voice; the girl vanished and a woman had taken her place and not a distressed woman, not a contemptuous or a disappointed one.

"He worships me," she said and in the squalid store of dead junk she seemed to be illumined by the simple knowledge of her own value and looked at my love as if it were nothing at all.

I looked at the sofa and was so mad that I thought of grabbing her and pulling her down there. What made me hesitate was the crumpled bag of toffees on it. I was as nonplussed and, perhaps, as impotent as Pliny must have been. In that moment of hesitation she picked up her bugle and standing in the aisle, she blew it hard, her cheeks going out full and the noise and echoes seemed to make the shadows jump. I have never heard a bugle call that scared me so much. It killed my desire.

"I told you not to come in," she said. "Go away."

And she walked into the aisle between the furniture, swinging her key to the door.

"Come back," I said as I followed her.

I saw her face in the dressing-table mirror we had passed before, then I saw my own face, red and sweating on the upper lip and my mouth helplessly open. And then in the mirror I saw another face following mine—Pliny's. Pliny must have seen me in the pub.

In that oblong frame of mahogany with its line of yellow inlay, Pliny's head looked winged by his ears and he was coming at me, his head down, his mouth with its yellowing teeth open under the moustache and his eyes stained in the bad light. He looked like an animal. The mirror concentrated him and before I could do more than half turn he had jumped in a clumsy way at me and jammed one of my shoulders against a tall-boy.

"What are you doing here?" he shouted.

The shouts echoed over the store.

"I warned you. I'll get the police on you. You leave my wife alone. Get out. You thought you'd get her on her own and swindle her again."

I hated to touch a white-haired man but, in pain, I shoved him back hard. We were, as I have said, close to the wardrobe and he staggered back so far that he hit the shelves and the door swung

towards him so that he was half out of my sight for a second.
I kicked the door hard with my left foot and it swung to and hit
him in the face. He jumped out with blood on his nose. But I
had had time to topple the pile of little cane chairs into the alleyway
between us. Isabel saw this and ran round the block of furniture
and reached him and when I saw her she was standing with the
bugle raised like a weapon in her hand to defend the old man
from me. He was wiping his face. She looked triumphant.

"Don't you touch Mr. Pliny," she shouted at me. "He's ill."

He *was* ill. He staggered. I pushed my way through the fallen
chairs and I picked up one and said: "Pliny, sit down on this."
Pliny with the bleeding face glared and she forced him to sit
down. He was panting. And then a new voice joined us; the
tobacconist came down the alley.

"I heard the bugle," he said. "Anything wrong? Oh Gawd,
look at his face. What happened, Pliny? Mrs. Pliny, you all right?"
And then he saw me. All the native shadiness of the London streets,
all the gossip of the neighbourhood came into his face.

"I said to my wife," he said, "something's wrong at Pliny's."

"I came to offer Mr. Pliny a piece of Dresden," I said, "but he
was out at Brixton seeing his sister, his wife said. He came back
and thought I'd broken in and hit himself on the wardrobe."

"You oughtn't to leave Mrs. Pliny alone with all this valuable
stock, Mr. Pliny. Saturday night too," the tobacconist said.

Tears had started rolling down Pliny's cheeks very suddenly
when I mentioned Brixton and he looked at me and the tobacconist
in panic.

"I'm not interested in Dresden," he managed to say.

Isabel dabbed his face and sent the tobacconist for a glass of
water.

"No, dear, you're not," said Isabel.

And to me she said: "We're not interested."

That was the end. I found myself walking in the street. How
unreal people looked in the sodium light.

THIRTEEN

The Spree

THE old man—but when does old age begin?—the old man
turned over in bed and putting out his hand to the crest of
his wife's beautiful white rising hip and comforting bottom, hit
the wall with his knuckles and woke up. More than once during the
two years since she had died he had done this and knew that if old
age vanished in the morning it came on at night, filling the bedroom
with people until, switching on the light, he saw it staring at
him; then it shuffled off and left him looking at the face of the
clock. Three hours until breakfast; the hunger of loss yawned
under his ribs. Trying to make out the figures of the clock he
dropped off to sleep again and was walking up Regent Street
seeing, on the other side of it, a very high-bred white dog, long
in the legs and distinguished in its step, hurrying up to Oxford
Circus, pausing at each street corner in doubt, looking up at each
person as he passed and whimpering politely to them: "Me? Me?
Me?" and going on when they did not answer. A valuable dog
like that, lost! Someone will pick it up, lead it off, sell it to the
hospital and doctors will cut it up! The old man woke up with
a shout to stop the crime and then he saw daylight in the room
and heard bare feet running past his room and the shouts of his
three grandchildren and his daughter-in-law calling, "Ssh! Don't
wake Grandpa."

The old man got out of bed and stood looking indignantly at
the mirror over the washbasin and at his empty gums. It was
awful to think, as he put his teeth in to cover the horror of his
mouth, that twelve or fourteen hours of London daylight were
stacked up meaninglessly waiting for him. He pulled himself
together. As he washed, listening to the noises of the house, he
made up a speech to say to his son who must be downstairs by
now.

"I am not saying I am ungrateful. But old and young are not
meant to be together. You've got your life. I've got mine. The
children are sweet—you're too sharp with them—but I can't

stand the noise. I don't want to live at your expense. I want a place of my own. Where I can breathe. Like Frenchy." And as he said this, speaking into the towel and listening to the tap running, he could see and hear Frenchy who was his dentist but who looked like a rascally prophet in his white coat and was seventy if he was a day, saying to him as he looked down into his mouth and as if he was really tinkering with a property there:

"You ought to do what I've done. Get a house by the sea. It keeps you young."

Frenchy vanished, leaving him ten years younger. The old man got into his shirt and trousers and was carefully spreading and puffing up the sparse black and grey hair across his head when in came his daughter-in-law, accusing him—why did she accuse?

"Grandpa! You're up!"

She was like a soft Jersey cow with eyes too big and reproachful. She was bringing him tea, the dear sweet tiresome woman.

"Of course I'm up," he said.

One glance at the tea showed him it was not like the tea he used to make for his wife when she was alive, but had too much milk in it, tepid stuff, left standing somewhere. He held his hair-brush up and he suddenly said, asserting his right to live, to get out of the house, in the air he could breathe:

"I'm going in to London to get my hair cut."

"Are you sure you'll be all right?"

"Why do you say that?" he said severely. "I've got several things I want to do."

And, when she had gone, he heard her say on the stairs:

"He's going to get his hair cut!"

And his son saying, "Not again!"

This business, this defiance of the haircut! It was not a mere scissoring and clipping of the hair, for the old man. It was a cere-monial of freedom; it had the whiff of orgy; the incitement of a ritual. As the years went by leaving him in such a financial mess that he was now down to not much more than a pension, it signified desire—but what desire? To be memorable in some streets of London, or at least, as evocative as an incense. The desire would come to him, on summer days like this, when he walked in his son's suburban garden, to sniff and to pick a rose for his button-hole; and then, already intoxicated, he marched out of the garden gate on to the street and to the bus stop, upright and vigorous, carrying his weight well and pink in the face. The scents of the barbers had been creeping into his nostrils, his chest, even went down to his legs. To be clipped, oiled and perfumed was to be free.

So, on this decent July morning in the sun-shot and acid suburban mist, he stood in a queue for the bus, and if anyone had spoken to him, he would have gladly said, to put them in their place:

"Times have changed. Before I retired, when Kate was alive—though I must honestly say we often had words about it—I always took a cab."

The bus came and whooshed him down to Knightsbridge, to his temple—the most expensive of the big shops. There, reborn on miles of carpet he paused and sauntered, sauntered and paused. He was inflamed by hall after hall of women's dresses and hats, by cosmetics and jewellery. Scores of women were there. Glad to be cooled off, he passed into the echoing hall of provisions. He saw the game, the salmon and the cheese. He ate them and moved on to lose twenty years in the men's clothing department where, among ties and brilliant shirts and jackets, his stern yet bashful pink face woke up to the loot and his ears heard the voices of the rich, the grave chorus of male self-approval. He went to the end where the oak stairs led down to the barbers; there, cool as clergy they stood gossiping in their white coats. One came forward, seated him and dressed him up like a baby. And then—nothing happened. He was the only customer and the barber took a few steps back towards the group saying:

"He wasn't at the staff meeting."

The old man tapped his finger irritably under his sheet. Barbers did not cut hair, it seemed. They went to staff meetings. One called back:

"Mr. Holderness seconded it."

Who was Holderness?

"Where is Charles?" said the old man to call the barbers to order. Obsequiously, the man began that pretty music with his scissors.

"Charles?" said the barber.

"Yes. Charles. He shaved me for twenty years."

"He retired."

Another emptiness, another cavern, opened inside the old man.

"Retired? He was a child!"

"All the old ones have retired."

The barber had lost his priestly look. He looked sinful, even criminal, certainly hypocritical.

And although the old man's head was being washed by lotions and oils and there was a tickling freshness about the ears and his nostrils quickened, there was something uneasy about the experience. In days gone by the place had been baronial, now it seemed not quite to gleam. One could not be a sultan among a miserable remnant of men who held staff meetings. When the old man left, the woman at the desk went on talking as she took his money and did not know his name. When he went upstairs, he paused to look back—no, the place was a palace of pleasure no longer. It was the place where—except for the staff—no one was known.

And that was what struck him as he stepped out of the glancing swing doors of the shop, glad to be out in the July sun, that he was a sultan, cool, scented and light-headed, extraordinary in a way, sacred almost, ready for anything—but cut off from expectancy, unknown nowadays to anybody, free for nothing, liberty evaporating out of the tips of his shoes. He stepped out on the pavement dissembling leisure. His walk became slower and gliding. For an hour shop windows distracted him, new shops where old had been, shocked him. But, he said, pulling himself together, I must not fall into *that* trap. Old people live in the past. And I am not old! Old I am not! So he stopped gliding and stepped out wilfully, looking so stern and with mouth turned down, so corrupt and purposeful with success, that he was unnoticeable. Who notices success?

It was always—he didn't like to admit it—like this on these days when he made the great stand for his haircut and the exquisite smell. He would set out with a vision, it crumbled into a rambling dream. He fell back, like a country hare, on his habitual run, to the shops which had bought his goods years ago, to see what they were selling and where he knew no one now: to a café which had changed its decor, where he ate a sandwich and drank a cup of coffee; but as the dream consoled, it dissolved into final melancholy. He with his appetite for everything, who could not pass a shop window, or an estate agent's, or a fine house, without greed watering in his mouth, could buy nothing. He hadn't the cash.

There was always this moment when the bottom began to fall out of his haircut days. He denied that his legs were tired, but he did slow down. It would occur to him suddenly in Piccadilly that he knew no one now in the city. He had been a buyer and seller, not a man for friends; he knew buildings, lifts, offices, but not people. There would be nothing for it but to return home. He would drag his way to the inevitable bus-stop of defeat and stand, as so many Londoners did, with surrender on their faces. He delayed it as long as he could, stopping at a street corner or gazing at a passing girl and looking around with that dishonest look a dog has when it is pretending not to hear its master's whistle. There was only one straw to clutch at. There was nothing wrong with his teeth, but he could ring up his dentist. He could ring up Frenchy. He could ring him and say: "Frenchy? How's tricks?" Sportily. And (a man for smells) he could almost smell the starch in Frenchy's white coat, the keen, chemical, hygienic smell of his room. The old gentleman considered this and then went down a couple of disheartened side streets. In a short *cul de sac*, standing outside a urinal and a few doors from a dead-looking pub, there was a telephone box. An oldish, brown motor coach was parked empty at the kerb by it, its doors closed, a small crowd waiting beside it. There was a man in the telephone box, but he came out in a temper, shouting something to the crowd. The old man went into the box. He had thought of something to say:

"Hullo, Frenchy! Where is that house you were going to find me, you old rascal?"

For Frenchy came up from the sea every day. It was true that Frenchy was a rascal, especially with the women, one after the other, but looking down into the old man's mouth and chipping at a tooth he seemed to be looking into your soul.

The old man got out his coins. He was tired but eagerness revived him as he dialled.

"Hullo, Frenchy," he said. But the voice that replied was not Frenchy's. It was a child's. The child was calling out: "Mum. Mum." The old man banged down the telephone and stared at the dial. His heart thumped. He had, he realized, not dialled Frenchy's number, but the number of his old house, the one he had sold after Kate had died.

The old gentleman backed out of the box and stared, tottering with horror, at it. His legs went weak, his breath had gone and sweat bubbled on his face. He steadied himself by the brick wall. He edged away from the bus and the crowd, not to be seen. He thought he was going to faint. He moved to a doorway. There was a loud laugh from the crowd as a young man with long black hair gave the back of the bus a kick. And then, suddenly, he and a few others rushed towards the old man, shouting and laughing.

"Excuse us," someone said and pushed him aside. He saw he was standing in the doorway of the pub.

"That's true," the old man murmured to himself. "Brandy is what I need," and, at that, the rest of the little crowd pushed into him or past him. One of them was a young girl with fair hair who paused as her young man pulled her by the hand and said kindly to the old man:

"After you."

There he was, being elbowed, travelling backwards into the little bar. It was the small Private Bar of the pub and the old man found himself against the counter. The young people were stretching their arms across him and calling out orders for drinks and shouting. He was wedged among them. The wild young man with the piratical look was on one side of him, the girl and her young man on the other. The wild young man called to the others: "Wait a minute. What's yours, Dad?"

The old man was bewildered. "Brandy."

"Brandy," shouted the young man across the bar.

"That's right," said the girl to the old man, studying his face. "You have one. You ought to have got on the first coach."

"You'd have been half-way to bloody Brighton by now," said the wild young man. "The first bloody outing this firm's had in its whole bloody history and they bloody forgot the driver. Are you the driver?"

Someone called out: "No, he's not the driver."

"I had a shock," the old man began, but crowded against the bar no one heard him.

"Drink it up then," the girl said to him and, startled by her kindness, he drank. The brandy burned and in a minute fire went up into his head and his face lost its hard bewildered look and it loosened into a smile. He heard their young voices flying about him. They were going to Brighton. No, the other side of Brighton. No, this side—well to bloody Hampton's mansion, estate, something. The new chairman—he'd thrown the place open. Bloody thrown it, laughed the wild man, to the Works and the Office and, as usual, "the Works get the first coach". The young girl leaned down to smell the rose in the old man's buttonhole and said to her young man, "It's lovely. Smell it." His arm was round her waist and there were the two of them bowing to the rose.

"From your garden?" said the girl.

The old man heard himself, to his astonishment, tell a lie.

"I grew it," he said bashfully.

"We shan't bloody start for hours," someone said. "Drink up."

The old man looked at his watch; a tragic look. Soon they'd be gone. Someone said: "Which department are you in?" "He's in the Works," someone said. "No, I've retired," said the old man, not to cause a fuss. "Have another, Dad," said the young man. "My turn."

Three of them bent their heads to hear him say again, "I have retired," and one of them said: "It was passed at the meeting. Anyone retired entitled to come."

"You've made a mistake," the old man began to explain to them. "I was just telephoning to my dentist . . ."

"No," said one of the bending young men, turning to someone in the crowd. "That bastard Fowkes talked a lot of bull but it passed."

"You're all right," the girl said to the old man.

"He's all right," said another and handed the old man another drink. If only they would stop shouting, the old man thought, I could explain.

"A mistake . . ." he began again.

"It won't do you any harm," someone said. "Drink up."

Then someone shouted from the door. "He's here. The driver."

The girl pulled the old man by the arm and he found himself being hustled to the door.

"My glass," he said.

He was pushed, holding his half empty glass, into the street. They rushed past him and he stood there, glass in hand, trying to say, "Goodbye" and then he followed them, still holding his glass, to explain. They shouted to him "Come on" and he politely followed to the door of the bus where they were pushing to get in.

But at the door of the bus everything changed. A woman wearing a flowered dress with a red belt, a woman as stout as himself, had a foot on the step of the bus and was trying to heave herself up, while people ahead of her blocked the door. She nearly fell.

The old man, all smiles and sadness, put on a dignified anger. He pushed his way towards her. He turned forbiddingly on the youngsters.

"Allow me, madam," he said and took the woman's cool fat elbow and helped her up the step, putting his own foot on the lower one. Fatal. He was shoved up and himself pushed inside, the brandy spilling down his suit. He could not turn round. He was in, driven in deeply, to wait till the procession stopped. "I'm getting out," he said.

He flopped into the seat behind the woman.

"Young people are always in a rush," she turned to say to him.

The last to get in were the young couple.

"Break it up," said the driver.

They were slow for they were enlaced and wanted to squeeze in united.

The old man waited for them to be seated and then stood up, glass in hand, as if offering a toast, as he moved forward to get out.

"Would you mind sitting down," said the driver. He was counting the passengers and one, seeing him with the glass in his hand, said, "Cheers."

For the first time in his adult life, the old man indignantly obeyed an order. He sat down, was about to explain his glass, heard himself counted, got up. He was too late. The driver pulled a bar, slammed the door, spread his arms over the wheel and off they went, to a noise that bashed people's eyeballs.

At every change of the gears, as the coach gulped out of the narrow streets, a change took place in the old man. Shaken in the kidneys, he looked around in protest, put his glass out of sight on the floor and blushed. He was glad no one was sitting beside him for his first idea was to scramble to the window and jump through it at the first traffic lights. The girl who had her arm round her young man looked round and smiled. Then, he too looked around at all these unknown people, belonging to a firm he had never heard of, going to a destination unknown to him, and he had the inflated sensations of an enormous illegality. He had been kidnapped. He tipped back his hat and looked bounderish.

The bus was hot and seemed to be frying in the packed traffic when it stopped at the lights. People had to shout to be heard. Under cover of the general shouting, he too shouted to a couple of women across the gangway:

"Do we pass the Oval?"

The woman asked her friend, who asked the man in front, who asked the young couple. Blocks of offices went by in lumps. No one knew except someone who said: "Must do." The old man nodded. The moment the Oval cricket ground came into sight, he planned to go to the driver and tell him to let him off. So he kept his eyes open, thinking:

What a lark. What a thing to tell them at home. "Guess what? Had a free ride. Cheek, my boy," he'd say to his son, "that's what you need. Let me give you a bit of advice. You'll get nowhere without cheek."

His pink face beamed with shrewd frivolity as the coach groaned over the Thames that had never looked so wide and sly. Distantly a power station swerved to the west, then to the east, then rocked like a cradle as the young girl—restless like Kate she was—got out of her young man's arms and got him back into hers, in a tighter embrace. Three containers passed, the coach slackened, then choked forward so suddenly that the old man's head nearly hit the back of the head of the fat lady in front. He studied it and noticed the way the woman's thick hair, gold with grey in it, was darker as it came out of her neck like a growing plant and he thought, as he had often done, how much better a woman's head looks from behind, the face interferes with it in front. And then his own chin went slack and he began a voluptuous journey down corridors. One more look at the power station which had become several jumping power stations, giving higher and higher leaps in the air, and he was asleep.

A snore came from him. The talking woman across the gangway was annoyed by this soliloquizing noise which seemed to offer a rival narrative; but others admired it for its steadiness which peacefully mocked the unsteady recovery and spitting and fading energy of the coach and the desperation of the driver. Between their shouts at the driver many glanced admiringly at the sleeper. He was swinging in some private barber's shop that swerved through space, sometimes in some airy corridor, at other times circling beneficently round a cricket match in which Frenchy, the umpire, in his white linen coat, was offering him a plate of cold salmon which his daughter-in-law was trying to stop him from eating; so that he was off the coach, striking his way home on foot at the tail of the longest funeral procession he had ever seen, going uphill for miles into fields that were getting greener and colder and emptier as snow came on and he sat down plonk, out of breath, waking to hear the weeping of the crowds, all weeping for him, and then, still walking, he saw himself outside the tall glass walls of a hospital. It must be a hospital for inside two men in white could be clearly seen in a glass-enclosed room, one of them the driver, getting ready to carry him in on a stretcher. He gasped, now fully awake. There was absolute silence. The coach had stopped; it was empty: he was alone in it, except for the woman who, thank God, was still sitting in front of him, the hair still growing from the back of her neck.

"Where . . ." he began. Then he saw the hospital was, in fact, a garage. The passengers had got out, garagemen were looking under the bonnet of the bus. The woman turned round. He saw a mild face, without make-up.

"We've broken down," she said.

How grateful he was for her mild face. He had thought he was dead.

"I've been asleep," he said. "Where are we?"

He nearly said: "Have we passed the Oval?" but swallowed that silly question.

"Quarter past three," he said. Meaning thirty miles out, stuck fast in derelict country at a cross roads, with a few villas sticking out in fields, eating into the grass among a few trees, with a hoarding on the far side of the highway saying, blatantly, "Mortgages" and the cars dashing by in flights like birds, twenty at a time, still weeping away westwards into space.

The woman had turned to study him and when he got up, flustered, she said in a strict but lofty voice:

"Sit down."

He sat down.

"Don't you move," she said. "I'm not going to move. They've made a mess of it. Let them put it right."

She had twisted round and he saw her face, wide and full now, as meaty as an obstinate country girl's, and with a smile that made her look as though she were evaporating.

"This is Hampton's doing," she said. "Anything to save money. I am going to tell him what I think of him when I see him. No one in charge. Not even the driver—listen to him. Treat staff like cattle. They've got to send another coach. Don't you move until it comes."

Having said this she was happy.

"When my husband was on the Board nothing like this happened. Do you know anyone here—I don't. Everything's changed."

She studied his grey hair.

The old man clung for the moment to the fact that they were united in not knowing anybody. His secretiveness was coming back.

"I've retired," he said.

The woman leaned further over the back of the seat and looked around the empty bus and then back at him as if she had captured him. Her full lips were the resting lips of a stout woman between meals.

"I must have seen you at the Works with John," she said. "It was always a family in those days. Or were you in the office?"

"I must get out of this," the old man was thinking and he sat forward nearer to her, getting ready to get out once more. "I must find out the name of this place, get a train or a bus or something, get back home." The place looked nameless.

But, since his wife had died, he had never been as near to a strange woman's face. It was a wide, ordinary, baby-like face damp in the skin, with big blue eyes under fair, skimpy eyebrows, and she studied him as a soft, plump child would study—for no reason, beyond an assumption that he and she were together in this; they weren't such fools, at their ages, to get off the coach. It was less the nearness of the face than her voice that kept him there.

It was a soft, high voice that seemed to blow away like a child's and was far too young for her, even sounded so purely truthful as to be false. It came out in deep breaths drawn up from soft but heavy breasts that could, he imagined, kick up a hullabaloo, a voice which suggested that by some silly inconsequent right she would say whatever came into her head. It was the kind of voice that made the old man swell with a polite, immensely intimate desire to knock the nonsense out of her.

"I can smell your rose from here," she said. "There are not many left who knew the firm in John's time. It was John's life work."

He smiled complacently. He had his secret.

She paused and then the childish voice went suddenly higher. She was not simply addressing him. She was addressing a meeting.

"I told him that when he let Hampton flatter him he'd be out in a year. I said to John, 'He's jealous. He's been jealous all the time'."

The woman paused. Then her chin and her lips stuck out and her eyes that had looked so vague, began to bulge and her voice went suddenly deep, rumbling with prophecy.

"'He wants to kill you,' I said. You," said the woman to the old man, "must have seen it. And he did kill him. We went on a trip round the world, America, Japan, India," her voice sailed across countries. "That's where he died. And if he thinks he can wipe out that by throwing his place open to the staff and getting me down there, on show, he's wrong.'

My God, she's as mad as Kate's sister used to get after her husband died, thought the old man. I'm sitting behind a mad woman.

"Dawson," she said and abruptly stood up as the old man rose too. "Oh," she said in her high regal style gazing away out of the window of the bus. "I remember your name now. You had that row, that terrible row—oh yes," she said eagerly, the conspirator. "You ring up Hampton. He's afraid of you. He'll listen. I've got the number here. You tell him there are twenty-seven of his employees stranded on the Brighton road."

The old man sighed. He gave up all idea of slipping out. When a woman orders you about, what do you do? He thought she looked rather fine standing there prophetically. The one thing to do in such cases was to be memorable. When is a man most memorable? When he says "No".

"No, I wouldn't think of it," he said curtly. "Mr. Hampton and I are not on speaking terms."

"Why?" said the woman, distracted by curiosity.

"Mr. Hampton and I," he began and he looked very gravely at her for a long time. "I have never heard of him. Who is he? I'm not on the staff. I've never heard of the firm." And then like a conjuror waving a handkerchief, he spread his face into a smile that had often got him an order in the old days.

"I just got on the coach for the ride. Someone said 'Brighton'. 'Day at the sea,' I said. 'Suits me.' "

The woman's face went the colour of liver with rage and unbelief. One for the law, all the rage she had just been feeling about Hampton now switched to the old man. She was unbelieving.

"No one checked?" she said, her voice throbbing. She was boiling up like the police.

The old gentleman just shook his head gently. "No one checked" —it was a definition of paradise. If he had wings he would have spread them, taken to the air and flown round her three times, saying, "Not a soul! Not a soul!"

She was looking him up and down. He stood with a plump man's dignity, but what saved him in her eyes were his smart, well-cut clothes, his trim hair and the jaunty rose; he looked like an old rip, a racing man, probably a crook; at any rate, a bit of a rogue on the spree, yet innocent too. She studied his shoes and he moved a foot and kicked the brandy glass. It rolled into the gangway and he smiled slightly.

"You've got a nerve," she said, her smile spreading.

"Sick of sitting at home," he said. Weighing her up—not so much her character but her body—he said: "I've been living with my daughter-in-law since my wife died."

He burst out with confidence, for he saw he had almost conquered her.

"Young and old don't mix. Brighton would suit me. I thought I would have a look around for a house."

Her eyes were still busily going over him.

"You're a spark," she said, still staring. Then she saw the glass and bent down to pick it up. As she straightened she leaned on the back of the seat and laughed out loud.

"You just got on. Oh dear," she laughed loudly, helplessly. "Serves Hampton right."

"Sit down," she said. He sat down. She sat down on the seat opposite. He was astonished and even shy to see his peculiar case appreciated and his peculiarity grew in his mind from a joke to a poem, from a poem to a dogma.

"I meant to get off at the Oval, but I dropped off to sleep," he laughed.

"Going to see the cricket?" she said.

"No," he said. "Home—I mean my son's place."

The whole thing began to appear lovely to him. He felt as she laughed at him, as she still held the glass, twiddling it by the stem, that he was remarkable.

"Years ago I did it once before," he said, multiplying his marvels. "When my wife was alive. I got a late train from London, went to sleep and woke up in Bath. I did. I really did. Stayed at the Royal. Saw a customer next day. He was so surprised to see me he gave me an order worth £300. My wife didn't believe me."

"Well, can you blame her?" the woman said.

The driver walked from the office to the garage and put his head into the coach and called out:

"They're sending a new bus. Be here four o'clock."

The old man turned: "By the way, I'm getting off," he shouted to the driver.

"Aren't you going on?" said the woman. "I thought you said you were having a trip to the sea."

She wanted him to stay.

"To be frank," said the old man. "These youngsters—we'd been having a drink—they meant no harm—pushed me on when I was giving you a hand. I was in the pub. I had had a bit of a shock. I did something foolish. Painful really."

"What was that?" she said.

"Well," said the old man swanking in his embarrassment, and going very red. "I went to this telephone box, you know, where the coach started from, to ring up my dentist—Frenchy. I sometimes ring him up, but I got through to the wrong number. You know what I did? I rang the number of my old house, when Kate—when my wife—was alive. Some girl answered, maybe a boy, I don't know. It gave me a turn, doing a thing like that. I thought my mind had gone."

"Well, the number would have changed."

"I thought, I really did think, for a second, it was my wife."

The traffic on the main road sobbed or whistled as they talked. Containers, private cars, police cars, breakdown vans, cars with boats on their roofs—all sobbing their hearts out in a panic to get somewhere else.

"When did your wife die?" said the woman. "Just recently?"

"Two years ago," he said.

"It was grief. That is what it was—grief," she said gravely and looked away from him into the sky outside and to the derelict bit of country.

That voice of hers, by turns childish, silly, passing to the higher notes of the exalted and belligerent widow—all that talk of partners killing each other!—had become, as his wife's used to do after some tantrum, simply plain.

Grief. Yes it was. He blinked away the threat of tears before her understanding. In these two years he seemed, because of his loneliness, to be dragging an increasing load of unsaid things behind him, things he had no one to tell. With his son and his daughter-in-law and their young friends he sat with his mouth open ready to speak, but he could never get a word out. The words simply fell back down his throat. He had a load of what people called boring things which he could not say; he had loved his wife; she had bored him; it had become a bond. What he needed was not friends, for since so many friends had died he had become a stranger: he needed another stranger. Perhaps like this woman whose face was as blank as his was, time having worn all expression from it. Because of that she looked now, if not as old as he was, full of life you could see; but she had joined his lonely race and had the lost look of going nowhere. He lowered his eyes and became shy. Grief—what was it? A craving. Yet not for a face or even a voice or even for love, but for a body. But dressed. Say, in a flowered dress.

To get his mind off a thought so bold he uttered one of his boring things, a sort of sample of what he would have said to his wife.

"Last night I had a dream about a dog," he began to test her out as a stranger to whom you could say any damn silly thing. A friend would never listen to damn silly things.

The woman repeated, going back to what she had already said, as women do:

"Remembering the telephone number—it was grief."

And then went off at a tangent, roughly. "Don't mention dreams to me. Last week at the bungalow I saw my husband walk across the sitting-room clean through the electric fire and the mirror over the mantelpiece and stand on the other side of it, not looking at me, but saying something to me that I couldn't hear—asking for a box of matches I expect."

"Imagination," said the old man, sternly correcting her. He

had no desire to hear of her dead husband's antics, but he did feel
that warm, already possessive desire, to knock sense into her. It was
a pleasant feeling.

"It wasn't imagination," she said, squaring up to him. "I packed
my things and went to London at once. I couldn't stand it. I drove
in to Brighton, left the car at the station and came up to London
for a few days. That is why when I heard about Hampton's party
at the office I took this coach."

"Saved the train fare. Why shouldn't Hampton pay?" she
grinned. "I told him I'd come to the party, but I'm not going.
I'm picking up the car at Brighton and going home to the
bungalow. It's only seven miles away."

She waited to see if he would laugh at their being so cunningly
in the same boat. He did not laugh and that impressed her, but she
sulked. Her husband would not have laughed either.

"I dread going back," she said sulkily.

"I sold my place," he said. "I know the feeling."

"You were right," said the woman. "That's what I ought to
do. Sell the place. I'd get a good price for it, too. I'm not exactly
looking forward to going back there this evening. It's very isolated
—but the cat's there."

He said nothing. Earnestly she said:

"You've got your son and daughter-in-law waiting for you,"
she said, giving him a pat on the knee. "Someone to talk to.
You're lucky."

The driver put his head into the door and said:

"All out. The other coach is here."

"That's us," said the woman.

The crowd outside were indeed getting into the new coach.
The old man followed her out and looked back at the empty
seats with regret. At the door he stepped past her and handed her
out. She was stout but landed light as a feather. The wild young
man and his friends were shouting, full of new beer, bottles in
their pockets. The others trooped in.

"Goodbye," said the old man, doing his memorable turn.

"You're not coming with us?" said the woman. And then
she said, quietly, looking around secretively. "I won't say anything. You can't give up now. You're worried about your
daughter-in-law. I know," she said.

The old man resented that.

"That doesn't worry me," he said.

"You ought to think of them," she said. "You ought to."

There was a shout of vulgar laughter from the wild young man and his friends. They had seen the two young lovers a long way off walking slowly, with all the time in the world, towards the coach. They had been off on their own.

"Worn yourselves out up in the fields?" bawled the wild young man and he got the driver to sound the horn on the wheel insistently at them.

"You can ring from my place," said the woman.

The old man put on his air of being offended.

"You might buy my house," she tempted.

The two lovers arrived and everyone laughed. The girl—so like his wife when she was young—smiled at him.

"No. I can get the train back from Brighton," the old man said.

"Get in," called the driver.

The old man assembled seventy years of dignity. He did this because dignity seemed to make him invisible. He gave a lift to the woman's elbow, he followed her, he looked for a seat and when she made room for him beside her, invisibly he sat there. She laughed hungrily, showing all her teeth. He gave a very wide sudden smile. The coach load chattered and some began to sing and shout and the young couple getting into a clinch again, slept. The coach started and shook off the last of the towny places, whipped through short villages, passed pubs with animal names, The Fox, The Red Lion, The Dog and Duck, The Greyhound and one with a new sign, The Dragon. It tunnelled under miles of trees, breathed afresh in scampering fields and thirty miles of greenery, public and private; until, slowly, in an hour or so, the bald hills near the sea came up and, under them, distant slabs of chalk. Further and further the coach went and the bald hills grew taller and nearer.

The woman gazed disapprovingly at the young couple and was about to say something to the old man when, suddenly, at the sight of his spry profile, she began to think—in exquisite panic—of criminals. A man like this was just the kind, outwardly respectable, who would go down to Hampton's Garden Party to case the place—as she had read—pass as a member of the staff, steal jewellery, or plan a huge burglary. Or come to her house and bash her. The people who lived only a mile and a half from where she lived had had burglars when they were away; someone had been watching the house. They believed it was someone who had heard the house was for sale. Beside her own front door, behind a bush, she kept an iron bar. She always picked it up before she got her key out—in case. She saw herself now suddenly hitting out with it passionately, so that her heart raced, then having bashed the old man, she calmed down; or rather she sailed into one of her exalted moods. She was wearing a heavy silver ring with a large brown stone in it, a stone which looked violet in some lights and she said in her most genteel, far-away voice:

"When I was in India, an Indian prince gave this ring to me when my husband died. It is very rare. It is one of those rings they wear for protection. He loved my husband. He gave it to me. They believe in magic."

She took it off and gave it to the old man.

"I always wear it. The people down the road were burgled."

The old man looked at the ring. It was very ugly and he gave it back to her.

"What fools women are," he thought and felt a huge access of strength. But aloud he said:

"Very nice." And not to be outdone, he said: "My wife died in the Azores."

She took a deep breath. The coach had broken through the hills and now cliffs of red houses had built up on either side and the city trees and gardens grew thicker and richer. The sunlight seemed to splash down in waves between them and over them. She grasped his arm.

"I can smell the sea already!" she said. "What are you going to tell your daughter-in-law when you ring up? I told the driver to stop at the station."

"Tell them?" said the old man. A brilliant idea occurred to him. "I'll tell them I just dropped in on the Canary Islands," he said.

The woman let go of his arm and, after one glance, choked with laughter.

"Why not?" he said grinning. "They ask too many questions. Where have you been? What are you doing? Or I might say Boulogne. Why not?"

"Well, it's nearer," she said. "But you must explain."

The wild young man suddenly shouted:

"Where's he taking us now?" as the coach turned off the main road.

"He's dropping us at the station," the woman called out boldly. And indeed, speeding no more, grunting down side streets, the coach made for the station and stopped at the entrance to the station yard.

"Here we are," she said. "I'll get my car."

She pulled him by the sleeve to the door and he helped her out.

They stood on the pavement, surprised to see the houses and shops of the city stand still, every window looking at them. Brusquely cutting them off, the coach bumped away at once downhill and left them to watch it pass out of sight. The old man blinked, staring at the last of the coach and the woman's face aged.

It was the moment to be memorable, but he was so taken aback by her heavy look that he said:

"You ought to have stayed on, gone to the party."

"No", she said, shaking brightness on to her face. "I'll get my car. It was just seeing your life drive off—don't you feel that sometimes?"

"No," he said. "Not mine. Theirs." And he straightened up, looked at his watch and then down the long hill. He put out his hand.

"I'm going to have a look at the sea."

And indeed, in a pale blue wall on this July day, the sea showed between the houses. Or perhaps it was the sky. Hard to tell which.

She said, "Wait for me. I'll drive you down. I tell you what— I'll get my car. We'll drive to my house and have a cup of tea or a drink and then you can telephone from there and I'll bring you back in for your train."

He still hesitated.

"I dreaded that journey. You made me laugh," she said.

And that is what they did. He admired her managing arms and knees as she drove out of the city into the confusing lanes.

"It's nice of you to come. I get nervous going back," she said as they turned into the drive of one of the ugliest bungalows he had ever seen, on top of the Downs, close to a couple of ragged firs torn and bent by the wind. A cat raced them to the door.

Close to it, she showed him the iron bar she kept behind the bush. A few miles away between a dip in the Downs was the pale blue sea again, shaped like her lower lip.

There were her brass Indian objects on the wall of the sitting-room; on the mantelpiece and, leaning against the mirror he had walked through, was the photograph of her husband. Pull down a few walls, reface the front, move out the furniture, he thought, that's what you'd have to do, when she went off to another room and came back with the tea tray, wearing a white dress with red poppies on it.

"Now telephone," she said. "I'll get the number." But she did not give him the instrument until she heard a child answer it. That killed her last suspicion. She heard him speak to his daughter-in-law and when he put the telephone down:

"I want £21,000 for the house," she said grandly.

The sum was so preposterous that it seemed to explode in his head and made him spill his tea in his saucer.

"If I decide to sell," she said, noticing his shock.

"If anyone offers you that," he said drily, "I advise you to jump at it."

They regarded each other with disappointment.

"I'll show you the garden. My husband worked hard in it," she said. "Are you a gardener?"

"Not any longer," he said as he followed her sulking across the lawn. She was sulking too. A thin film of cloud came over the late afternoon sky.

"Well, if you're ever interested let me know," she said. "I'll drive you to the station."

And she did, taking him the long way round the coast road and there indeed was the sea, the real sea, all of it, spread out like the skirt of some lazy old landlady with children playing all along the fringes on the beaches. He liked being with the woman in the car, but he was sad his day was ending.

"I feel better," she said. "I think I'll go to Hampton's after all," she said watching him. "I feel like a spree."

But he did not rise. Twenty-one thousand! The ideas women have! At the station he shook hands and she said:

"Next time you come to Brighton . . ." and she touched his rose with her finger. The rose was drooping. He got on the train.

"Who is this lady-friend who keeps ringing you up from Brighton?" his daughter-in-law asked in her lowing voice several times in the following weeks. Always questions.

"A couple I met at Frenchy's," he said on the spur of the moment.

"You didn't say you'd seen Frenchy. How is he?" his son said.

"Didn't I?" said the old man. "I might go down to see them next week. But I don't know. Frenchy's heard of a house."

But the old man knew that what he needed was not a house.

FOURTEEN

The Chain-Smoker

THE important thing was to stop Magnolia going to Venice.
"That I won't have," Karvo said. "Where is Chatty? Never
here when he is wanted. Drunk, I suppose. Or in bed. I bet he's
at his aunt's. Get him."

At that very moment Chatterton came into the office, opening
the door only about a foot and sliding in.

"Chatty!" Karvo made a sound like a wounded bull, indeed
almost wept. "You've heard the news?" Karvo waved the others
out of the office and Chatty sat down on the sofa opposite Karvo's
enormous desk; or, rather, he folded up there like a small piece
of human trellis that smoked, squeaked and coughed. He was an
illness in itself.

"Yes," Chatty said. "She has heard the doctor has stopped you
flying. She's heard you and Maureen are picking up the train in
Paris. She rang me half an hour ago."

"Chatty, you've got to stop her. I won't have that woman in
Venice," Karvo said. "You've got to keep her in London. I tried
to get you last night. Where were you?"

"I was with her," said Chatty. "At the Spangle."

"I'm very grateful to you," said Karvo, calming down.

Chatty swallowed a couple of pills off the palm of his hand.
"The fog got into my chest," he said. "She's still going to court.
But she doesn't know whether she will shoot you or commit
suicide. What she wants to do is to commit suicide first, then
shoot you and then sue the company for breach of contract.
Somewhere along the line she has got to fit in a scene at some
place like the Caprice in which she tears Maureen's dress off her
back. She would like to see blood—not pools of it, but visible
nail-stripes on Maureen's face, anywhere it will show—say on the
upper part of the back. She doesn't know whether it would be
better to do this in the restaurant—I told her it had been done too
often in restaurants—or in court, but I pointed out that Maureen
was not a material witness and would not be there."

Karvo paid no attention. He was looking at the script on his desk, but glancing up said, considerately:

"Chatty, are you all right? I can hear your chest from here. You're not going to crack up again?"

"I've been up half the night three nights running. She never wants to go to bed."

"I didn't have *that* trouble with her," Karvo grunted boastfully, looking at the script again.

"I made a mistake about Magnolia," Karvo went on. "I thought she would lift the whole story. She has the finest pair of arms I've ever seen in pictures, but she can't move them except up and down slowly like a cop holding up traffic. She can't move anything. You saw her. I thought she was Life. She's as dead as the Venus de Milo."

"It has no arms," said Chatty. "Magnolia *is* Life. I told her so last night. I said 'Magnolia, you're Life . . .'"

"*You* said that to her?" said Karvo suspiciously.

"Yes. She said you said she was Life. I said 'He was right. You're Life itself.' Actually, larger."

"It's no good in pictures," Karvo said.

"It's terrible out of pictures," Chatty said. "Awful in the evenings."

"You've got to stop her. I don't care how," Karbo said, shouting again.

"I know," said Chatty. "I'm having lunch with her." And he got up and used one of the telephones on Karvo's desk. "No. I know the time of the train, sweetie," he said in the murdered voice of the sick. "Bring me the Continental time-table in your own little loving hands."

"Why do you want that?" said Karvo, suspicious again.

"I was brought up on it; it's the only book I can read now without having a heart attack," said Chatty. The girl brought the book into the office and Chatty's face broke into dozens of small smiling lines, like a cracked plate and he did two or three more coughs. The girl looked protectively at him.

"What I dream of is a beautiful sanatorium with you looking after me," he said to the girl who said: "Oh Mr. Chatterton, no."

Karvo shook his head.

"You ought to stop smoking, Chatty."

"I appeal to the mother in them," said Chatterton. "If I stopped coughing I'd be useless to the firm. I'll try and get Magnolia down to the farm, Tony."

"That's a good idea," said Karvo generously. "It will do you good. You need pure air."

"I'm working on the idea that her ancestors travelled in cattle trucks. I doubt if it will work."

Karvo went very red. The innuendo reflected on his tastes. He was going to make a speech, but Chatty looked at his watch, said "I'll be late," and went.

Magnolia was not Karvo's first mistake. Art is the residue of innumerable rejections; so, in fact, is love. So is everything. Some rejections are more difficult than others. Karvo was the godhead of the organization; Chatty had had to give up years ago, after his first breakdown, but Karvo clung to him. He had drifted into becoming the oilcan of the machine, the worn-out doctor. Sooner or later, everyone from the doorman upwards was bound to turn to Chatty: the shrunk face, the one-lung chest, the shaky hand, the sad busy eyes, the weak, grating voice that seemed to contain the dregs of all the rumours in the world, concealed a dedication to all the things the machine had forgotten to do. The very weakness of the voice contained a final assuring sense that the situation, whatever it was, had hit bottom and that he had fallen back on forces only he was in touch with. What his official job was, neither he nor anyone knew. Except that he had to put everything right.

In black moments, he would say, "I'm the company's hangman." A shrewd actress would know she was losing her part if she found herself dining at Claridges alone with Chatty, with champagne on the table. One or two of Karvo's wives had had the disturbing experience of seeing Chatty arrive at the house with flowers and were alarmed by his tête-à-têtes. In the middle of an evening's drinking, actors would suddenly wonder why Chatty was telling them, again and again, that they were very great artists. Diners at the Spangle or the Hundred and Five would notice how a neat, sick man, darkened by sun lamp, so often seemed to be at a certain table with a girl who was leaning close to him and pouring out what was, momentarily, her heart, while he nodded and filled up her glass. They had seen some girls with elbows on the table, with tears running down their cheeks, and next to them, elbows on table too, not in tears, but wearing his wrecked expression, Chatty stroking a hand, listening, nodding, squeezing and—when a waiter passed—giving an efficient nod at the bottle. It would be replaced. Some held his arm. Others, once every half hour, he lightly kissed on the bare shoulder. He might ask to look at a ring. Or, gazing at their palms, tell their fortunes. To others he whispered a scandal: they leaned back open-mouthed and when he had finished they leaned towards him and went back satisfied to their own tale. In certain cases, the difficult ones, he might be driven almost to the edge (but never further) of his own secret. Very rarely, they laughed; occasionally simple ones would put an arm round his neck and rest a head on his shoulders, not thinking about him at all, their soft hunting eyes gazing round the restaurant and he would sit back happily, giving only an occasional glance at them. His job was done.

So now he was with Magnolia. She was a woman who easily changed size. She could inflate or contract. At the moment, not touching her smoked salmon, she was contracting. The large mouth had become no more than a slot, her large eyes a collection of flints, her flowing brows had stiffened and had the boding look of moustaches, her noble breasts were like a pair of grenades with the pins out; and those arms, usually so still and statuesque, now swiped about like Indian clubs as she talked. And Karvo said she could not move! Chatty, sitting beside her, came only up to her shoulder, and when she looked down at him, she looked as though she was planning eventually to get up and tread on him, affecting not to see he was there.

"These things never last with Karvo," he persisted, worn out, tasting the wine and pouring her a glass. She looked at it with hatred. "A girl like that can't hold him."

"A television starlet from Walsall," she sneered. "She can't act. And she smells. Ask the camera men. Something's happened to Karvo—what it is? You know him. His wife is at the back of this. Well, he's not going to get away with it. I'll kill her. Chatty, I'm going on that train. Why doesn't he fly?"

"The doctor stopped him."

"We always flew. He needs more than a doctor. I shall be on that train.

Her mouth widened and she started to eat. It looked as though she were eating what she had just killed.

"You know, Nolly," said Chatty, "you're a superb girl. Shall I tell you something? I found you, didn't I? Oh yes, I did. I saw you in *Potter's Clay* years before Karvo. It's all my fault. I made Karvo take you. I showed him what you were. I said 'She will lift the whole show, get it right off the ground.' You'll sit there like a goddess. When you move, just as you as doing now . . ."

She was putting a piece of smoked salmon towards her mouth but stopped and put her fork back to look at him.

"There," he exclaimed, "that movement! What you did that very minute! A small thing like that: you're a lady. There's breeding in it. I'll tell you something I never told you. When you and he went off that first evening I knew something was on; I came in here and I got plastered." She was bored.

"Why?"

Chatty turned his head away.

"Stop bitching. You know why."

And he turned his head back again and gazed at her and blinked. He had sunk lower on the banquette so that she now swelled enormously over him, and as she swelled, so he sank lower, reached for his glass and drained it recklessly and stared up at her through the glass he drank. She studied him with the slow astonishment of a cat that is not quite sure whether she has a mouse beside her; then with horror; then with the look of a mother who says to her baby "I could eat you," but a mother who is going to do it, and not eat, but gnaw. He put out his small brown hand and rested it on her leg and controlled his surprise at the monumental size of it.

Chatty rarely had to go as far as this; most girls—and Magnolia was one—could recognize the difference between the pass direct and a pinch that was the retraction of a careless preceding remark. With Magnolia his normal methods had failed: expressing unbelief, then sympathy, then fierce indignation at the man—he was cracking up, had lost his reason, it was "his age" etc. etc.—Chatty would then attack the other woman, mentioning false or disorganized teeth, affected voice and adding minutiae of his own: rubbing calves, perhaps, or inturned toes. He would throw in the name of some interesting man ("not in the theatre, darling") and drop into a word or two of French. *Tout passe, tout casse, tout lasse*—wasted, by the way, on Magnolia who did not speak French. He would then, if they were still difficult, move on towards his own secret.

He was a waif: they were both lonely waifs. Chatty's secret: that was what everyone wanted to know and they became alert at this stage. Why wasn't he married? Was he queer? Was he nothing? Mother's boy? Auntie's boy? He evaded thise insinuations by talking about his farm. Ah, but what went on at that farm? Who was this woman he called Aunt Laura down at the farm? There were times when it seemed that only the desperate pass, what he called the final solution, would do.

"Darling I want to bite that lovely shoulder. Come down to the farm with me."

They were almost agog. What orgies went on there? They would discover the secret. Discreetly he moved to enthusiastic anti-climax.

"We shall be on our own. There's only Aunt Laura there. She's deaf. Looking after her bed-ridden sister. Very religious. I'll show you my Hereford herd. We can cut down nettles. Aunt Laura's woman who used to come up from the village to cook is in hospital, but we'll manage. It's the simple life. Just ourselves. What d'you say?"

He had never known them not to say "No". Very apologetically too. Apologizing calmed them. Then he would pay the bill, drop them in the firm's car, saying "In the old days I used to slip away to Paris." Just the idea! But not with him, oh dear God no! They could do better than that—and sometimes did, and when he dropped them at their flat, he had dissolved an illusion and given them a new one.

But Chatty did not offer Aunt Laura to Magnolia. He had seen that this case was too desperate: also, what would any sane woman sooner do—go to Venice or to Wiltshire? No Press in Wiltshire. So when he said "Stop bitching" and there was no answering twitch of her leg to his hand, he took a long and conquering breath.

"I know how you feel," he said. "I feel as you do. I said to Karvo 'You don't understand Magnolia. She's virginal. There's an inner chastity, something single-hearted, when she loves she loves once and for all. I feel it, you feel it, the audience feels it. She's a one-man woman. Bucky and the Bronsinki boy—oh yes, I know about *them*, but that doesn't alter the inner truth'."

Magnolia looked strangely at him. The idea that she had an inner nature was new to her, that it was virginal, amazed. Her mouth started to become its normal size, her brows began to curve—at the recollection, of course, of Bucky and the Bronsinki boy—and she looked with the beginning of curiosity at Chatty: she had the sensation that he was revealing an unsuspected vacancy in her life. Chatty, always sensitive to hopeful change, took his hand off her leg—a good move: Magnolia tried out a feeling of austerity. It made her feel important. Still, her refrain did not change, except in tone. There was a just detectable new note of self-sacrifice.

"I'm going on that train. I hate trains. Why doesn't he fly? Well, I'm going on it. I've got my reservation."

Was a moral nature being born? Chatty put his hand back quickly.

"We'll go together," he said. "I've got a reservation too."

"You? You have? Here," she said coarsely, "what's the bloody idea? Is this one of Karvo's bloody tricks?" A dangerous moment! Moral natures are not born suddenly. Chatty gave a violent grip of righteousness to her leg. He spoke in a righteous voice, not forgetting to put some of the ginger of the underhand in it.

"My job's at stake, too," he said out of the corner of his mouth. "I don't know about you, but I know what I'm doing. We're going together to rescue him. We've got to save that man, between us. It's worth ten thousand a year to me. But money's nothing. I don't know why I should save him—well, I do know. It's for you."

"I'm going to raise hell at the Gare de Lyon," she stuck to it. "I've got their seat numbers. I'll turn the dining-car upside down. I'll . . ."

"No, darling. Listen to me. Wait till we get to Venice. The Paris Press is no good to you. They'll be in Venice, anyway."

Chatty made one of his body-wrecking efforts and sent up a hard stare into Magnolia's eyes. He noted, with satisfaction, as the stare continued, that when she removed his hand from her leg, she did so with a primness which must have been a new thing for her.

Months afterwards Chatty told Karvo that until the Magnolia episode, and in spite of all his experience, he had never realized what genius owes to lucky insights. The plan was clumsy and full of risks. You had to choose between evils. Better a scene at

the Gare de Lyon—without the Press—than a scene at Venice;
the thing to avoid was something, thank God, that had not got
into Magnolia's stupid head. She could easily have flown to Venice
on her own and waited to trap him at the Gritti as he arrived.
Why didn't she think of that?

"I tumbled on the obvious," Chatty said. "My task was to
encourage this new growth of virtue in Magnolia. There is a
detective in every virtuous woman—you know, 'I'm having my
husband followed.' It was the idea of *following* you that had
narrowed her mind."

He clinched with Magnolia quickly.

"Show me that ticket," he snapped at her. Half-bewildered she
got it out of her bag. He took it and said:

"We'll scrap this part. Let me have it. We'll fly to Paris while
Maureen is being sick in the Channel and pick up the train
there."

Magnolia got up from the table and had a look of dawning
righteousness on her face. ("She looked ready to sing *Fight the
good fight*," Chatty said.)

"I admit," she said to Chatty, "I was wrong about you."

Chatty went back to Karvo.

"Well?" said Karvo vehemently.

"We're going *with* you. I can't stop her."

"Chatty," shouted Karvo.

"Listen. The first principle in dealing with problems is to break
them into their parts. First of all, I am restoring her virginity. I
am doing that for self-protection."

"Stop being so clever. I have to think of the Press. She can't
come with me. That's the whole point."

Chatty began a long fit of coughing. He coughed up and down
the sofa.

"There's nothing to be done about that. I've gone the whole
hog with her."

Karvo looked cynically and despisingly at Chatty. Chatty understood the look.

"No, I agree, not that. Loyalty to the company does not go
as far as that," said Chatty, wiping his eyes.

Karvo growled at him.

"We shall travel in the back part of the train," said Chatty.

"That won't do, I tell you," shouted Karvo. "This is serious."

"Tony, pictures have destroyed your intelligence. You're going to Venice, aren't you? You leave Paris on the *Adriatique* at 15.30. Right? So Magnolia and I have to be on it. I have got our reservations, but by some mistake, in the office—I don't know who the girl is who looks after your reservations, but you ought to sack her—Magnolia and I are leaving Paris at 7.36 in the morning, on the Geneva non-stop."

"You're not going to Venice?"

"We *think* we are going to Venice. Spiritually Magnolia is travelling in the last coach on your train. Physically we shall be in Geneva."

"Why Geneva, for God's sake," said Karvo.

"The lake, the mountains, William Tell."

"She can fly from Geneva!" said Karvo.

"I am going to be very ill," said Chatty.

"Ill?" said Karvo. "Your mind's ill. Your brain has gone soft. You've made a mess of this. I shall fly. I shall have to fly and you know what the doctor said. Come to my funeral."

"I'll be laid out in Geneva," said Chatty, "a good half-day before you and Maureen get to Venice. Come to mine."

Chatty (Karvo used to say) would never have been one of the great directors; he always preferred the trees to the wood. An obscurantist. His plots were always entangled. He never thought things out. But he had two great gifts: a talent for confusing issues and above all for illness. This gave him the invalid's mastery of detail. When Chatty sickened he was inspired.

Before the flight to Paris he did not go to bed at all; he was on the telephone to Magnolia and drinking hard. It made him sound sincere. Take the calls to Magnolia first:

"Magnolia. Something terrible has happened. That Miss What's-her-name in the office must have spilled the beans. Karvo's heard something. The swine's catching the *morning* train to Venice."

He waited and prayed. No. Thank God! Magnolia did not say "There's no morning train to Venice."

"The 7.36. We've got to be there. We're flying tonight. I'm changing the tickets now."

"Call it off," said Magnolia suspiciously.

"No," shouted Chatty. "I'm getting on that train and so are

you. I've got the tickets in my pocket. You're not going to let them get away with it. They're committing *adultery*, Magnolia!"

"You're drinking, Chatty."

"Of course I'm drinking," said Chatty. "I'll have the car for the airport at 1.15. They must be in Paris already. No. I don't know where."

This decided Magnolia: that woman, in Paris!

As for illness, indispensable to the refinements of strategy: Chatty was a wreck when he got Magnolia into the 'plane. Only his fevered eyes seemed to be alive: they seemed to drag his body after them.

In the 'plane he muttered on and off during the flight. Half-way across the Channel he began fidgeting in his seat, going through his pockets and wearing Magnolia down with the words "I've forgotten my pills. I can't move without them." Magnolia was frightened by his state: the dawn gave him an awful yellow look. He collapsed into a chair at the Café at the Invalides and sent a waiter to see if there was a pharmacy open and told Magnolia the man could easily make a fatal mistake. She must go with him. No pharmacies were open. Magnolia's ignorance of French brought out her aggression.

"My friend is very ill," she said in English to the waiter. He did not understand.

"My husband is dying," she shouted. This episode made the arrival of Chatty and Magnolia at the Gare de Lyon seem like an ambulance party rushing to hospital with three minutes to spare before the train left or the patient died. Chatty was not going to have Magnolia running loose on the platform for half an hour scrutinizing every coach or finding out they were on the Geneva train.

They sat breathless in the compartment. Chatty had a wide range of coughs, from the short, dry hack to the display that came up from the ankles and seemed to split his eyes.

"A little more air." He got up to open the window.

"Sit down," said Magnolia. She was frightened. Her strong arms drew down the heavy window of the French train herself.

Then she watched. When he stopped coughing at last he told a terrible story about an injection for tetanus he had been given when he was a schoolboy, as the train moved off and laughed.

"Stop laughing," she said. "You'll bring it on again."

Her face, he was pleased to see, had grown severe. A firm, almost chaste look of moral reprimand was growing on it. He got out a cigarette.

"Don't smoke," she said, and repeated with appeal:

"Chatty, *please* don't smoke." He put his cigarettes away.

"You're right," he said.

"Try and sleep."

"I wish I could. People keep passing in the corridor. Do you mind if we pull down the blind."

"*I'll* do it," she said, commanding.

"Magnolia," he said. "You're being extraordinarily good to me. You're a saint. I'm sorry, I seem to be making a mess of this."

"It's not your fault," she said.

"It is."

"No, it's mine," she said on a note of noble confession. But she gave a grind to her teeth. "I ought to have flown." Oh God, thought Chatty, she's off again.

"If you had I would have gone with you," he said. "I'm going to see you through this thing. When I think of that bastard twelve coaches up the train . . ."

"Twelve?" she said, uncrossing her legs and frowning.

"You can imagine how I feel," he said. "I look at you and I see a woman he has never seen."

"Sleep," she said sternly.

"I can't," he said.

"You must."

"I've made a mess of my life. I'm sorry for a lot of things I've done. Why did I let him take you?"

Chatty closed his eyes but not completely. He had to keep an eye on her. He was not going to have her slipping out into the corridor, searching the coaches or talking to informative strangers. He was surprised to discern, though mistily through his lashes, that she was looking neither restless nor relaxed, but sat there rigidly gazing at him with apprehension. A novel combination of feelings was growing in her. As virtue was increased by her mission and by looking after him, so a new fear was born too; the fear that is native to virtue. She was travelling alone in a railway compartment with a man in a chaotically disturbed state—a man who, so he said, had repressed certain feelings for years. She was in his hands. And in a foreign country too. As she watched the French meadows and the licentious woodlands go by, she wondered if he would go mad and attack her. These were pleasant sensations; they made her feel prim. What did she, what did anyone know about Chatty? In sleep he looked very ugly.

At Dijon he opened his eyes and sneezed.

"When the sun rises the moon sneezes," he said. "Old Chinese proverb."

He laughed. She did not like that. He *was* mad! She sat back and squeezed her legs together tightly.

The ticket inspector came in.

"What did he say? He was looking at me," asked Magnolia, afterwards.

"He said he had seen you in a picture. 'Disarmed'."

Magnolia looked happy for the first time.

"I wish I spoke French like you do," she said. "Teach me some words." And taking out her mirror made up her face.

"And," said Chatty, leering, as the train clattered through the long sidings and went out of Dijon, "he was looking at the drawn blinds. The frogs never miss anything. They have imagination."

Magnolia closed her bag and was on guard.

"I can't eat," said Chatty when he heard the luncheon bell tinkle. "But I'll take you along. You must eat something."

"No," she said. "I don't want anything."

She was either not being distracted from her revenge or she was becoming increasingly the nurse. Chatty wished he knew which it was.

Hours passed sleepily and then, seeing her restive, he told her about his Aunt Laura. She used to go to Aix where the waters are good for the kidneys. The doctors could not decide whether she had two or two and a half kidneys. Many people, he said, have extra rudimentary organs. Magnolia saw herself approaching his secret.

"Two and a half! Is she really your Aunt?" she said.

"I will tell you the honest truth," said Chatty.

"Yes?"

"I don't really know. We were brought up to call her Auntie. She has been like a mother to us. And yet more like a nun than a mother. Something must have happened to her; some disappointment—she gave up everything for us."

Magnolia found herself wondering how she would look as a nun.

Chatty said, "Say what you like, there is *something* about nuns. I can see it in you," he was saying. "All women have a nun inside them." It was pleasant to hear and made her idly double her watch on Chatty.

"Those poor nuns in Africa," she said, ready to put up a fight if he sprang at her.

Chatty was, of course, thinking of the approaching crisis. It would come when they got to Geneva. The question was whether she would see what had happened, at the station; or whether he might hold out until they saw Lake Léman. He was occupied with the fantasy that he might palm off the lake as the Mediterranean. He rejected it. He plumped for terrible scene at the station. He would stagger off the train and simply collapse on the platform. "Get a doctor. Get an ambulance," he would shout.

He suddenly heard Magnolia say irritably:

"When do we get to Venice?"

"An hour and a half, I should say."

"Don't you *know*?" said Magnolia getting crosser. And ruining everything, two inspectors slid back the door of the compartment, a young one and an old one. The old one had spread the news that Magnolia was on the train.

"When do we get to Venice?" she called out in English to the older one.

"Venice?" said the older inspector in English, too. "We are going to Geneva."

"Chatty!" shouted Magnolia.

"This is the Geneva train," said the younger inspector in French.

"Good lord," said Chatty, "they've put us on the wrong train."

"Give me those tickets," Magnolia shouted again.

The speed at which Magnolia left her religious order was something Chatty always remembered. Her face became crimson, then violet, marked by changing dabs of green; she swelled up, she rose up. She pushed Chatty aside and started on the inspectors. The older one stepped back and pushed the young one forward: the young one made a speech. She flew at Chatty:

"What is he saying?"

And not waiting for an answer, she declaimed that she was due at Venice that very moment, to receive the Festival prize that the train must be put into reverse; that a 'plane be brought instantly into the compartment; that the train itself must, if necessary, fly. The young inspector gazed at the fling of Magnolia's white arms from armpit to wrist, the terrifying spread of her fingers, the rise and fall of her volcanic bosom, the blue eyes that ripped him, the throat that boiled, the nostrils that went in and out like bellows, until tears of admiration formed in his young eyes. Chatty raised his eyebrows at the older inspector, who raised his eyes in profound understanding at Chatty. The lips of the young one did not speak, but they moved with unconscious, unavailing kisses.

"Can't act?" thought Chatty. "There ought to have been a train sequence in the film. Lift? She's lifting the train off the rails."

Of course, he reflected, Magnolia was life not art: that is what had got Karvo and what horrified Chatty. In his quick croak he made several speeches in French, conveying that, in the present misunderstanding, the French railways were not to blame. Exchanging glances the two inspectors conveyed that the next hour and a half would be hell. They showed eagerness to share this opportunity with Chatty, even to exchange places. The desire to experience hell with Magnolia shone in the eyes of the younger man. The older one's face indicated that, in the well-known relations between men and women, it is the nuance that is always interesting. They congratulated Chatty silently on his fortune. Think—they signalled to each other—of the reconciliation! Sadly, looking restlessly at each other, they went away to the end of the coach and glanced up the corridor to see if anything was happening yet and if their moment might come. Once, the older man went up to the compartment and then hurried back to report: the blinds which had shot up in the dispute were down again. The young man sighed sadly. The reconciliation already?

No, not the reconciliation. Magnolia was crying, letting tears bowl down her cheeks—if only she could have done that on the set!—she had tried to hit Chatty twice but, in the swaying of the train she had missed. He said nothing but, lighting a cigarette, fell into a run of quiet coughing. He had pulled down the blinds so that she could have a good cry undisturbed. After about fifty coughs the irritating sound made her forget to sob and reach for her handbag.

"You are a dirty swine. Karvo put you up to this," she said.

"There was no other way of getting you away from that man," he said. "I wanted you to myself."

"Don't you dare touch me," she said as he moved to the seat beside her. The fear she had amused herself with in the early part of the journey, now became real. He was abducting her. This was a rape. Chatty innocent? Chatty ill? Chatty, the orphan bachelor shedding a tear about his Aunt Laura? Aunt Laura my eye. He was nothing more than a dirty rapist. A new layer of virginity formed over her, icing her completely.

"Have you ever been to Geneva?" Chatty said.

"Don't insult me," said Magnolia.

"Beautiful lake," said Chatty.

No answer.

"Mont Blanc, not far," said Chatty.

No answer.

"I haven't been there for fifteen years," Chatty said. "Not since I was up at Appols in the sanatorium."

No comment.

"I left a lung up there."

"I'm getting a 'plane," said Magnolia. Chatty lit another cigarette.

"That's five you've smoked in the last half-hour. Look at the floor," said Magnolia. There was, Chatty noted, just a tiny bit of the nurse left in her. He tactfully picked up the cigarette stubs and put them in the ash tray and sat down again. There was nothing like a little tidying for getting a woman through a crisis.

"I've never told anyone this," he said. 'I've got to tell you. Well, no, you won't be interested?"

"What?" she snapped.

Chatty sighed.

"It's too painful," he said. "Some things one never gets over. Just a German girl I knew there—I mean there, Geneva."

"What German girl?" Magnolia sneered.

"Up at Appols, in the sanatorium where I was. We both were. She was very ill. It went on for months. We used to go for walks— not very far. We had one pair of lungs between us—it wasn't too bad. It was in May—flowers, you know, lambs—spring: we couldn't stand it. One morning we got into the funicular and said: 'Let's go off,' just like that, no luggage, just as we were. We were laughing all the way down. I got a car to drive us to Geneva. We went to an hotel, an old-fashioned one. Our room had two marble-encased wash-basins side by side, very handsome ones. Two people could stand there and wash together. You could wash each other—Swiss idea of marriage I suppose."

"Don't be disgusting," said Magnolia.

"We laughed so much at those basins," Chatty said, "that the first thing we did was to stand there splashing water at each other. We soaked the place. We couldn't stop laughing. I was drying myself with a big towel: I'd got my head in it. Suddenly I noticed she'd stopped laughing and I pulled the towel away from my face. She was leaning over the basin. It was splashed all over with blood. It was coming out of her mouth. A haemorrhage."

Magnolia leaned back to get farther away from him.

"I'd killed her," he said. "She died up at Appol two months later. I've never told anyone."

How often she had heard: "No one knows anything about Chatty".

"It wasn't your fault," she said at last.

"We were sex mad," he said. "I never slept with her."

"Oh," said Magnolia.

"You can live without it," said Chatty.

"What was her name?"

"Greta."

A shot of jealousy hit Magnolia. The hills were turning into mountains, the fields were steeper, she strained to see if there were yet a sight of the Alps. She wanted to be high up in them.

"Where's Appol?" she said.

"High up," he said. "There's an enormous lake at Geneva. We used to walk there. I shot a picture there once before I cracked up. I've always had the idea of doing *William Tell*."

Magnolia's business sense woke up.

"I've never told anyone this. I never told Karvo—he's not the kind of man who would understand. You're the only person who knows. You have sympathy. You know what it is to lose someone. Now you know why I cheated about the tickets. I wanted you to see the place and walk by the lake."

Magnolia's mind was still in Appol. How wonderful to be like Greta and die slowly, untouched, by the lake: Chatty attending her and telling Karvo the news.

Brusquely Chatty said:

"Forget it. I've got us rooms at the Splendide. We'll be there in twenty minutes. We'll have a drink. The Press will be there. I lined that up in London."

Mangolia came down from the high snows.

It *was* an abduction. She saw herself defending a virtue made absolute. It was a sensation she had not had since she was a girl of fifteen when she had knocked a man off his bicycle who had chased her across a common: a superb feeling.

In the taxi that took them from the railway station in Geneva to the hotel, she said to Chatty:

"The first thing to do is to find out about the 'plane to Venice."

"Wait," said Chatty, "till you see the view. I want to show you Greta's grave."

An hour later she was standing at the window of her hotel room looking out at that view. There was no 'plane until the morning. She would have to hold out all night. She could hear Chatty moving in the room next door. Presently there was a knock at her door: Chatty advancing already upon her?

She called out: "You can't come in."

But the door was open and the chambermaid was there. The gentleman in number sixty-seven next door, the maid said, had been taken very ill; would she come at once? Chatty was lying on his bed with his shoes off and a hole in the toe of one of his socks. He had a handkerchief to his mouth. He reached for her hand.

"Greta," he said. "A doctor."

Chatty is up at Appol. He reports to Karvo on the telephone.

"Just the rest I needed. I was coming here anyway. Magnolia was an angel. She still is. What she needs is a part as a nurse. When she visits me she comes into the room on tiptoe. She's bought a dress that looks like a uniform. She's got exactly the face that goes with high necks and starch. And she is full of suffering—no Karvo, suffering for *me*. Did I say nurse. A nun, that's her part."

And two or three weeks later:

"I'm getting out soon. She wants to move me down to Geneva to an old hotel—that place with double wash-basins, do you know? Remind me to tell you. It's a very morbid idea actually, but she is in that mood at the moment. It does her good to be morbid for a bit."

And later again.

"Yes. I've moved. No, *she's* got the wash-basin room. I'm on the same floor though. She comes along with a nice man called Ronzini or Bronzoni or something: she met him, yes, of course, in the bar. The uniform has gone—I miss it. Well, what did I tell you? It's all right now. She's just been in to say do I mind if Bronzoni drives her to Garda for a couple of days. Well, I don't mind, but I wonder what she has been telling that Italian. He said to me 'She needs rest Mr. Chatterton. You have caused her a lot of anxiety.' I have an idea she has told him she doesn't feel safe with me. No need for you to make funny remarks. I had a very trying job restoring her virginity: the sort of job that's beyond you, Karvo. You wouldn't recognize the girl who is going off to Garda for a couple of days. Exalted. I'll be back in London at the end of the month. For God's sake send me some money. Prices are very high here."

About the Author

V. S. PRITCHETT was born in England in 1900. He is a short-story writer, novelist, critic and traveler. His short stories have appeared in collections in the United States under the titles *The Sailor and the Saint, When My Girl Comes Home, Blind Love, The Camberwell Beauty,* and as individual contributions in *The New Yorker* and *Holiday.* Among his novels are *Mr. Beluncle, Dead Man Leading* and *The Key to My Heart.* Random House has also published *The Living Novel and Later Appreciations,* a collection of critical essays, most of which appeared originally in *The New Statesman,* and his Clark Lectures, *Meredith and English Comedy.* He has been a lifelong contributor to this paper and is now a director. His memoirs, *A Cab at the Door* and *Midnight Oil,* were published by Random House in 1968 and 1972. In 1973 he published a life of Balzac, and his most recent book, *The Gentle Barbarian,* is a study of the life and work of Turgenev.

Mr. Pritchett's extensive sojourns in Europe, the Middle East, and South America have led to the writing of several books on travel, among them *The Offensive Traveller.* With photographs by Evelyn Hofer, Mr. Pritchett has written *London Perceived, Dublin: A Portrait* and *New York Proclaimed.*

Mr. Pritchett has visited the United States, where he gave the Christian Gauss Lectures at Princeton, was Beckman Professor at the University of California in Berkeley, and has been writer in residence at Smith College, and Zisskind Professor at Brandeis University. He is a foreign Honorary Member of the American Academy of Arts and Letters and the American Academy of Arts and Sciences.

In 1975 he received a knighthood.